One of the things tumbled, legs seared off at the knees. It skidded into Bueller, knocked him to the side against the wall.

Bueller slammed into the surface, his head protected by the helmet but his shoulder hit hard. The force of the impact twisted him so as he fell away he saw what happened to Chin, as if watching it on a holoviewer in slow motion.
—The legless alien spun, scrabbled with its taloned hands, and slid in at Chin under his line of fire. Chin tried to lower his aim, but too late. The alien opened massive jaws and bit, latching onto Chin's thigh—
—Chin screamed. Blake yelled, 'Don't move!' and slid over a step to shoot the alien that had Chin in its teeth—
—The alien's legs were gone, but it still had its tail. It speared Chin's belly, jammed the pointed tail through him so it emerged between two ribs on his back. The ribs broke through the skin, showing splintered bones—
—Blake fired, hit the alien behind the hinge of its jaws. The thing convulsed and the teeth sheared through Chin's leg completely. For a second he stood there on one leg, the monster's tail helping him stay up. Then he fell . . .

Also available in the same series

Aliens™: The Female War
Aliens™: Genocide
Aliens™ v Predator:™ Prey
Aliens™ v Predator™: Hunters Planet

A L I E N S ™

EARTH HIVE

OMNIBUS EDITION

NIGHTMARE ASYLUM

Steve Perry

(Based on the Twentieth Century Fox motion pictures, the designs of H.R. Giger, and the graphic novels by Mark Verheiden and Mark A. Nelson)

A DARK HORSE SCIENCE FICTION NOVEL

MILLENNIUM

This edition first published in 1995 by Millennium
The Orion Publishing Group
5 Upper St Martin's Lane
London WC2H 9EA

ISBN: 1 85798 413 7

ALIENS™

BOOK ONE

EARTH HIVE

For Dianne, one more time;
And for Pat Dupre, former harpist
with the Denver Symphony, who saved
my soul in Baton Rouge during
the hippie autumn of 1970

"Fancy thinking the Beast was something you could hunt and kill…"
—William Golding,
Lord of the Flies

1

Even inside her bulky E-suit, Billie could feel the cold night bite at her. Sure, the land crawler blocked most of the icy wind, and they had pulled one of the crawler's portable heaters and turned it up full, pretending it was a campfire, but it was still cold. It was the best they could do—there wasn't any wood on the planet Ferro, and if there had been they sure as shit wouldn't be *burning* it. Wood was worth more per gram than platinum on this world. How the guys in the vids could chop it up and waste it was unreal.

The frozen wind howled like some kind of unhappy beast as it blew past the squat form of the crawler; the song changed to a whistle where it flowed over the tractor's sharp treads. The sounds were eerie. Every now and then through a patchy break in the roiling and thick clouds, the stars gleamed briefly, hard pinpricks against a dead-black curtain, glittering like diamonds caught in a laser beam. Even without the clouds it would have been dim; Ferro had no moons.

Well, right, so it wasn't comfortable out here, but at least the three of them weren't stuck inside the colony with the do-nothing dweebs, bored half stupid.

"Okay," Mag said, "what else we s'posed to do here? We ate the RTE rations and sang that fool song about logs and holes in the bottom of the sea. This is terminal droll, Carly."

At twelve, Mag was a year younger than Billie and Carly, and she always had a smart crack about everything.

Billie shivered inside her E-suit. "Yeah, juice brain, what else was on that old disc about camping?"

"If you two dweebs will shut up, I'll tell you."

Mag slapped herself over the heart. "Oh, killer clever," Mag said. "Got me."

"They used to tell stories," Carly said, pretending to ignore her. "Like ghosts and monsters and shit."

"Fine," Mag said. "So, tell us one."

Carly went off on a ramble about vampires and ghosts and Billie knew she'd pulled it from an old entcom file. Even so, it was one thing to see the vid in your cube, all warm and well lit, another thing to hear the story out here a klick away from the Main Building in the dark and cold and all. Spooky.

Windblown hail spattered briefly, like a handful of gravel tossed at them, but stopped just as Carly hit the climax of her story.

"—and every year, one of the survivors of that horrible night goes crazy—and now it's *my* turn!"

Mag and Billie both jumped as Carly lunged at them.

Then all three began to giggle.

"Okay, Mag, you're up."

"Yeah, okay. There was this old witch, see . . . ?"

Halfway through Mag's tale some ice pellets fell and bounced around. One must have gotten into the heater's circuits. The unit flashed brightly, blew its fuse, and died. As the glow faded, the only light they had left was from the stars and the crawler's LEDs. The night moved in on them, and the cold and the dark both thickened. All of a sudden, the Main Building seemed a lot farther than a klick away. More hail showered on them. Billie shivered, and it wasn't just from the cold.

"Aw, shit. Look at that. My dad is gonna be pissed we shorted out the aux heater. I'm getting into the crawler," Mag said.

"Come on, finish your story."

"Forget it. My ears are about to freeze off."

"Well, we have to at least let Billie tell one."

Carly nodded at Billie. "Your turn."

"I think Mag is right, let's get in the crawler."

"Come on, Billie, don't do a guppy-up on us."

Billie took a deep breath and blew out a cloud of cold fog. She remembered her dreams. They wanted something scary? Fine. "Okay. I got one for you.

"There are these . . . things. Nobody knows what planet they come from, but they showed up one day on Rim. They're the color of black glass, they're three meters long and have fangs as big as your fingers. They have acid for blood—you cut one and if it bleeds on you, it burns right through to the bone. Only you can't really cut them, 'cause they have skin as hard as a deep spacer's hull. All they do is eat and reproduce, they're like giant bugs, and they can bite through tool alloy, their teeth are diamond hard. . . ."

"Oh, wow," Carly said.

"If they catch you, you're *lucky* if they kill you," Billie continued. "Because if they *don't* kill you right off, it's worse than death. They put a baby monster inside of you, they ram it down your throat, and it grows in your body, grows until its teeth get sharp enough, and then it chews its way out, through meat and bone, it digs a hole in your guts—"

"Creesto, yuk!" Carly said.

Mag slapped herself over the chest.

Billie paused, waiting for the wisecrack.

But Mag said, "I—I don't . . . feel too good. . . ."

"Come on, Mag," Carly said. "This is moron-ville—"

"N-n-no, I—my stomach—ow!"

Billie swallowed, her throat dry. "Mag?"

"Ahh, it hurts!"

Mag slapped at her chest, as if she were trying to smash a rock beetle with her hand.

Suddenly the E-suit bulged over Mag's solar plexus, like a fist trying to punch through a sheet of rubber. The suit stretched impossibly.

"Aaahhh!" Mag's scream washed over Billie.

"Mag! No!" Billie stood, backed away.

Carly reached for Mag. "What is it?"

Mag's suit stretched again. Tore open. Blood fountained outward, bits of flesh sprayed, and a snakelike thing the size of Billie's arm flashed needle-pointed teeth in the dim starlight as it emerged from the dying girl.

Carly yelled, her voice breaking. She tried to back away, but the monster shot from Mag to Carly like a rocket. It fastened those terrible fangs on to her throat. It bit. Her blood looked black under the starlight as it spewed into the night. Her scream turned into a gurgle.

"No!" Billie screamed. "No! It was a dream! It wasn't real! It *wasn't*! No—!"

Billie struggled up from sleep screaming.

The medic leaned over her. She was on a pressor bed, and the fields held her firmly to the cushion like a giant hand. She struggled, but the harder she tried, the stronger the field became.

"No!"

"Easy, Billie, easy! It's only a dream! You're fine, everything is okay!"

Billie's breath came in gasps. Her heart pounded, she could feel her pulse in her temples as she stared up at Dr. Jerrin. The indirect light gleamed on the sterile white walls and ceiling of the medical center room. Only a dream. Just like the others.

"I'll get you a soporific patch," Jerrin began.

She shook her head, the pressor field would allow that much. "No. No, I'm okay now."

"You sure?"

He had a kindly face; he was old enough to be

Billie's grandfather. He had treated her for years, ever since she'd come to Earth. For the dreams. They weren't all the same, usually she dreamed about Rim, the world on which she'd been born. It had been thirteen years since the nuclear accident that had destroyed the colony on Rim, almost a decade since she left Ferro. And still the nightmares came, carrying her on wild and uncontrollable gallops through her nights. The drugs didn't help. Counseling, hypnosis, biofeedback, brainwave synthesization, nothing helped.

Nothing could stop the dreams.

He let her up and she moved to the sink to wash her face. The mirror frowned back at her. Her reflection was medium height, slim and tight from all the compulsive time she spent in the exercise chair. Her hair, usually cut short, had grown almost to her shoulders, the pale brown of it straight and nearly ash-colored. Pale blue eyes over a straight nose, a mouth just a hair too big. Not an ugly face, but nothing to cross the room to get a better look at. Not ugly, but cursed, sure enough. Some god somewhere must have her in his sights. Billie wished she knew why.

"Buddha, they're all around us!" Quinn yelled.

Wilks felt the sweat rolling down his spine under the spidersilk armor. The light was too dim, the helmet lamp didn't do shit, it was hard to see what was happening around them. The infrared wasn't working worth a crap, either. "Shut the fuck up, Quinn! Maintain your field of fire, we're gonna be fine!"

"Oh, fuck, Corp, they got the sarge!" That from Jasper, one of the other remaining marines. There had been twelve of them in the squad. Now there were four. "What are we gonna do?"

Wilks had the little girl in one arm, his carbine in the other hand. The little girl was crying. "Easy, honey," he said. "We're gonna be fine. We're going back to the ship, everything is gonna be okay."

Ellis, bringing up the rear, swore in Swahili. "Oh, man, oh, man, what the hell *are* these things?" he said.

It was a rhetorical question. Nobody fucking knew.

The heat pounded at Wilks, the air was cloying, it smelled like something dead left too long in the sunshine. Where the things had gotten to the walls of the place the flat everlast plastic had been overlaid with a thick and convoluted blackish-gray substance. It looked like some mad sculptor had covered the walls with loops of intestine. The twisted coils were as hard as plastecrete, but they put out warmth, some kind of organic decay, maybe. It was like an oven in here, but wetter.

Behind him, Quinn's caseless carbine came alive again, the sound of the shots battering Wilks's ears with muted echoes.

"Quinn!"

"There's a shitload of 'em behind us, Corp!"

"Shoot for targets," Wilks ordered. "Triplets only! We don't have enough ammo to waste on full auto suppressive fire!"

Ahead the corridor branched, but the pressure doors had come down and sealed both exits. A flashing light and Klaxon blinked and hooted, and a computer-chip voice kept repeating a warning that the reactor was approaching meltdown.

They were going to have to cut their way out, fast, or get slaughtered by those things. Or else fried into radioactive ash. Great fucking choice.

"Jasper, hold the kid."

"No!" the little girl yelled.

"I gotta open the door," Wilks said. "Jasper will take care of you."

The black marine moved in, grabbed the girl. She clutched at him like a baby monkey does its mother.

Wilks turned to the door. Pulled his plasma cutter from his belt, triggered it. The white-hot jet of plasma flashed out in a line as long as his forearm. He shoved the cutter against the fail-safe lock, waved it back and forth. The lock was made of tripolystacked carbon, but it wasn't designed to withstand the heat of a star. The carbon annealed, bubbled, and ran like water under the plasma jet.

The door slid up.

One of the monsters stood there. It lunged at Wilks, a long, toothed rod shooting from its open mouth like a spear at his face. Saliva dripped from its jaws in jellylike strings.

"Fuck!" Wilks dodged to his right and swung the plasma cutter up reflexively. The line caught the thing's neck, a neck that looked much too thin to support the impossibly large head. How could something like this even stand up? It didn't make any sense—

The alien creatures were tough, but the plasma was hot enough to melt industrial diamond. The

head fell off, bounced on the floor. It kept on trying
to bite Wilks, jaws oozing slime as it snapped at
him. Didn't even know it was dead.

"Move it, people! And watch it, the damned thing
is still dangerous!"

Jasper screamed.

"Jasper!"

One of the things had him, and it crunched his
head like a cat biting a mouse. The little girl—!

"Wilks! Help! Help!"

Another one of the monsters had the girl, it was
moving away with her. Wilks twisted, pointed his
weapon at it. Realized that if he shot it, the blood
would be an acid shower that would kill the child.
He'd seen that blood eat through armor that would
stop a 10mm caseless cold. He dropped his aim
lower, pointed the carbine at its legs. It couldn't run
if it didn't have any feet—

The corridor was full of the things, Quinn opened
up, his carbine on full auto, blasting. Armor-
piercing and explosive rounds tore through the
monsters, spanged from the walls, the stink of
propellant filled the air—

Ellis opened up with his flamer, and a stream of
fire painted the corridor, splashing from the aliens
and running in molten gobs down the intestined
wall—

"Help!" the little girl cried. "Oh, please, help!"

Oh, God!

"No!"

Wilks came awake, sweat drenching his hair and

face, running into his eyes. His issue coverall was wet. Oh, man.

He sat up. He was still in the cell, on the thin bunk, the dark plastic walls securely in place.

The door slid open. A guard robot was there, two and a half meters tall on its tractor treads, gleaming under the jail corridor's lights. The robot's electronic voice said, "Corporal Wilks! Front and center!"

Wilks rubbed at his eyes. Even a military brig with all its security couldn't keep the dreams out.

Nothing could stop the dreams.

"Wilks!"

"Yeah, what?"

"You are to report to MILCOM HQ, OTD."

"Fuck you, tinhead. I got two more days to serve on the S&D."

"You wish, pal," the bot said. "Your high-rank friends say otherwise. Up-levels wants you, OTD."

"What high-rank friends?" Wilks asked.

One of the other prisoners in the multi-unit cell, a fat man from Benares, said, "What friends, period?"

Wilks stared at the line bot. Now, why would the glitter want to see him on the double? Anytime rank started rumbling, it usually meant trouble for the grunts. He felt his gut churn, and it wasn't just the dregs of the chem-binge he'd gone on, either. Whatever this was, it wasn't good.

"Let's go, marine," the bot said. "I am to escort you to MILCOM HQ soonest."

"Lemme shower and clean up first."

"Negative, mister. They said, 'Soonest.' "

The burn scar that mostly covered the left half of his face began to itch suddenly. Oh, shit. Not just bad, but *real* bad.

Now what did they think he'd done?

2

There was a lot of trash orbiting Earth.

In the hundred years since the first satellites had lifted, careless astronauts or construction crews had lost bolts, tools, and other chunks of hardware. The small stuff, some of it whipping around at fifteen klicks a second relative, could punch a nasty hole in anything less dense than full-sheath armor, and that included people inside a ship coming or going. Even a chip of paint could dig a crater when it hit. While this was a danger to ships, most of the little stuff burned up on reentry; what didn't was collected by special robot rigs everybody called dust mops.

For a time there was a real risk that the big stuff would get to the ground—part of a construction ship flamed down and killed a hundred thousand people on the Big Island once, and also made Kona coffee exceedingly rare. Because of that and similar incidents, somebody finally realized there was a problem with all the orbiting junk. Laws were passed, and now anything bigger than a man got tagged and swept. And rather than create a new agency, the work was passed on to an organization that already existed.

This was why the Coast Guard cutter *Dutton* hung in high orbit over North Africa, starlight glistening on its armored boron-carbon hull, its crew of two yawning as they moved in to tag a derelict ship. Garbage Control's flight computer said this heap was about to start its fall, and before that happened, the thing had to be probed, checked for anybody who might be camping on it, then blasted into pieces small enough for the dust mops to collect. SOP.

"Probe ready to launch," Ensign Lyle said.

Next to him, the cutter's captain, Commander Barton, nodded. "Stand by and . . . launch probe."

Lyle touched the control. "Probe away. Telemetry is green. Visuals on, sensors on, one-second burn."

The tiny robot ship rocketed toward the battered freight hauler, feeding electronic information to the cutter behind it.

"Maybe this one is full of platinum ingots," Lyle said.

"Yeah, right. And maybe it's raining on the moon."

"What's the matter, Bar? You don't want to be rich?"

"Sure. And I want to spend ten years in the CG

pen fighting off the yard monsters, too. Unless you figured out a way to shut down the blue box?"

Lyle laughed. The blue box recorded everything that went on in the cutter, plus all the probe input. Even if the ship *was* full of platinum, there was no way to hide it from Command. And military officers didn't get salvage rights. "Well, not exactly," Lyle said. "But if we had a few million credits, we could *hire* somebody who might."

"Yeah, your mother," Barton said.

Lyle glanced at the computer flat screen. It was cheap hardware; the Navy had full holographics but the Guard still had to make do with the bottom-of-the-line Sumatran Guild electronics. The probe's retros flamed as it reached the hulk. "Here we are. Is that good flying, or what?"

Barton grunted. "Look at the hatch. It's bulged outward."

"Explosion, you think?" Lyle said.

"Dunno. Let's open this can up."

Lyle tapped at his keyboard. The probe extruded a universal hatch key and inserted it into the lock.

"No luck. Lock's shot," Lyle said.

"I'm not blind, I can see that. Pop it."

"Hope the inner hatch is closed."

"Come on, this piece of crap has been up here for at least sixty years. Anybody on it would be dead of old age. There ain't no air in there and if by some miracle somebody *is* home, they're in a suspension tank. And aside from *that*, this thing has about thirty minutes before it hits enough atmosphere to boil lead. Pop it."

Lyle shrugged. Touched controls.

The probe attached a small charge to the hatch and retroed back a hundred meters. The charge flared silently in the vacuum and the hatch shattered.

"Knock, knock. Anybody home?"

"Go see. And try not to bang the probe up too bad this time."

"That wasn't my fault," Lyle said. "One of the retros was plugged."

"So you say."

The tiny robot ship moved in through the opening in the derelict ship.

"Inner hatch is open."

"Good. Saves time. Move it in."

The probe's halogens lit as it moved into the ship.

The radiation alarm chimed on the computer's screen. "Kinda hot in there," Lyle said.

"Yep, hope you like your soypro well done."

"Mmm. I guess anybody in this baby would be toast by now. We'll have to give the probe a bath when it gets back."

"Chreesto, look at that!" Barton said.

What had been a man floated just ahead of the probe. The hard radiation had killed the bacteria that would have rotted him, and the cold had preserved what the vacuum hadn't sucked out of him. He looked like a leather prune. He was naked.

"Lordy, lordy," Lyle said. "Hey, check the wall behind him." He touched a control and the visuals enhanced and enlarged. Something was written on the bulkhead in smeary brown letters: KILL US ALL, it said.

"Damn, is that written in blood? Looks like blood to me."

"You want an analysis?"

"Never mind. We got us a flip ship."

Lyle nodded. They'd heard about them, though he himself had never opened one. Somebody went nuts and wasted everybody else. Opened a port and let the air out, or maybe flooded the ship with radiation, like this one. A quick death or a slow one, but death, sure enough. Lyle shivered.

"Find a terminal and see if you can download the ship's memory. The meter is running here."

"If the batteries are still good. Oops. Got motion on the detector."

"I see it. I don't believe it, but I see it. Nobody can possibly be alive, even somebody in a full rad suit would cook in this tub—"

"There it is. It's just a cargo carrier."

A short, squat robot crawled along a line of Velcro against the ceiling.

"We must have jolted it awake when we blew the hatch."

"Yeah, right. Get the memory."

The probe floated toward a control panel.

"Damn, look at those holes in the deck. Looks like something dissolved the plastic. Radiation wouldn't do that, would it?"

"Who knows? Who cares? Just dump the memory and pull the probe so we can blow this sucker. I have a date tonight and I don't want any overtime."

"You're the commander."

The probe connected to the control board. The

ship's power was almost gone, but sufficient to download the memory.

"Coming in," Lyle said. "Here's the ID scan, onscreen."

"No surprises here," Barton said. "Type five nuke drive, lotta deep-space time, bad shields, dead core. No wonder they junked this bucket. That's it. Shove it sunward, set the 10-CA and let's go home."

Lyle touched more controls. The probe placed the small clean atomic against a wall where it adhered. "Okay, three minutes to—aw, shit!"

The screen went blank.

"What did you do?"

"I didn't do *any*thing! The camera's gone out."

"Switch to memory drive. We lose another probe and the Old Man'll chew our asses to pulp."

Lyle touched a button. The computer took over the probe. Since it had memorized every centimeter of the flight in, it could retrace the flight and bring the probe back.

"It's clear," Lyle said a moment later. "Burning more fuel than it should, though."

"Maybe it snagged on something coming out. Doesn't matter."

"Probe docking. Outer hatch open. Let me see if I can get an eye on the sucker and see why it's wallowing so bad." Lyle ran his practiced hands over the controls.

"Holy fuck!" Barton said.

Lyle just stared. What the hell was that? Some kind of *thing* sat on the probe as it approached the ship. It looked like a reptile, no, a giant bug. Wait, it had to be some kind of suit, no way it could live in vac without a suit—

"Close the hatch!" Barton yelled.

"Too late! It's inside."

"Flood the bay with antirad! Pump the air out! Blow it back through the fucking door!"

A clang vibrated through the ship. Like a hammer smashing metal.

"It's trying to open the inner hatch!"

Frantically Lyle tapped controls. "Antirad spray on full! Evacuation pumps on!"

The banging continued.

"Okay, okay, don't worry, it can't get in. The hatch is locked. Nobody can break through a sealed boron-carbon hatch with his bare hands!"

Something crashed, ringing loudly. Then came the sound spacers fear more than anything: air rushing out.

"Close the outer hatch, goddammit!"

But the dropping air pressure tugged at Lyle. The cabin was filled with loose items being sucked toward the rear of the cutter. Light pens, coffee cups, a hard-copy magazine fluttering madly. He lunged at the controls, missed the emergency button, lunged again.

Barton, also half out of his chair, stabbed at the red button, but hit the computer override instead. The ship went to manual drive.

The cabin pressure raced toward zero. A hatch-sized hole blew air into space real damned fast. Lyle's eyes bulged, began to bleed. One eardrum popped. He screamed, but found the control for the external hatch.

"I got it! I got it!"

The outer hatch cycled shut. Emergency air tanks kicked on. The faux gravity pulled the two men back toward their seats. "Goddammit! Goddammit!" Barton said.

"It's okay, it's okay, it's closed!"

"Coast Guard Control, this is the cutter *Dutton!*" Barton began. "We have a situation here!"

"Oh, *man!*" Lyle said.

Barton twisted.

The thing stood right fucking there!

It had *teeth*! It came toward them. It looked hungry.

Barton tried to get up, fell, and hit the drive control. The ship was still on manual. The drive kicked on. The acceleration threw the monster backward, drove Lyle and Barton into their seats. Even though they couldn't move, the thing somehow managed to drag itself onward.

It was a nightmare. It couldn't be real.

The thing ripped chunks out of Lyle's seat as it pulled him from the chair. Blood sprayed as its clawed hands punctured his shoulders. It opened its mouth and a rod shot out, so fast Barton could hardly see it. The rod buried itself in Lyle's head like his skull was putty. Blood and brain tissue splashed. Lyle screamed in total terror.

The cutter, still under acceleration, headed directly toward the radioactive hulk in front of it.

The monster jerked that hellish thing from Lyle's skull. It made a sucking sound, like a foot pulled out of mud. The creature turned toward Barton.

Barton drew breath to scream, but the sound never came out—

At that instant the cutter smashed into the scuttled freighter—

—and the bomb the probe had set went off.

Both ships were destroyed in the explosion. Virtually everything was shattered into tiny bits that spiraled in a long loop toward Sol.

Everything except the blue box.

Wilks stared at the screen as it washed white.

Amazing how well the blue boxes were armored, to survive even a close atomic blast like that.

He looked at the guard bot. "Okay, I've seen it."

"Let's go," the bot said.

They were alone in a conference room in MIL-COM HQ. Wilks stood, and the bot led the way. If he'd had a gun, he would have shot the bot and tried to run. Yeah. Right.

As they walked along the corridor, Wilks put it together. So this was why they'd never kicked him out of the Corps. It was only a matter of time before humans stumbled across the aliens again. They hadn't wanted to believe him about what had happened on Rim, but the truth machines wouldn't let them off the hook that easy. The brain strainers had pulled it out of him, and the Corps never threw anything away that might be useful someday.

His belly clenched around a cold knot, like somebody had jammed a blade of liquid nitrogen into his guts. The bomb on Rim hadn't gotten them all. The military found itself in need of an expert on these things and Corporal Wilks was what it had. Probably didn't make them very happy, but they would make do.

He wasn't looking forward to this meeting. It certainly wasn't going to do him any good. Not at all.

3

Salvaje's place was almost directly under the huge reactor shield for the Southern Hemisphere Power Grid Switching Station. The PGSS field was big enough so it sometimes created its own weather. Mostly that was rain. Day and night, steady, unrelieved, dreary-as-shit rain. The building was eon-plas prefab, proof against the more or less constant downpour, a dull gray material that blended in against a sky the color of melted lead. It was a good place to hide. Nobody came here unless they had a reason, even the ground police avoided the rain when they could.

Pindar the holotech splashed through puddles, ankle deep despite the drainage pumps' attempts to clear the water. If Salvaje didn't have so much spare money he was willing to part with, Pindar would have avoided this scum hole. The building walls were thick with mold, even the retardant paint couldn't stop it, and there were rumors that you could catch a mutant strain of flu here that would kill you before you could get to a medic—which wouldn't help anyhow because even recombinant antivirals couldn't touch the stuff. Nice.

The door slid open on creaky runners as Pindar walked up the incline to Salvaje's place.

"You're late," came the ghostly voice from within.

Pindar stepped inside, stripped off the osmotic rainfilm that kept him dry, dropped the torn bits of spiderweb-thin plastic onto the floor. "Yeah, well, between my day job and this shit, it's lucky I can find time to sleep."

"I care nothing for your sleep. I pay well."

Pindar looked at Salvaje. He was ordinary enough. Medium height, hair slicked straight back in some kind of electrostatic hold, a little beard and mustache. He could have been thirty or fifty; he had one of those faces that don't seem to age much. He wore a plain black coverall and flexboots. Pindar wasn't sure what a holy man ought to look like, but Salvaje sure wasn't it.

"There," Salvaje said, pointing.

Pindar saw the cam on a table. "Damn, where'd you get that antique? It looks like an old ship's monitor—"

"Where I got it is not important. Can you use it to tie us into the Nets?"

"Señor, I can tie you into the Nets with a toaster and a couple of microwave cooker circuit boards. I am a very good technician."

Salvaje said nothing, only stared at Pindar with

those cold gray eyes of his. Pindar repressed a
shudder. Gave him the crawlies when he did that.
"Sí, I can put you on the air. But visual and auditory
only. No sublims, no subsonics, no olfactories. Be
pretty tame compared to what your competition is
throwing at the GU."

"The Great Unwashed will hear the truth of my
message without trickery. And they will see the
image of the True Messiah. Such things will be
enough. Behold!"

Salvaje touched a control on an old projector on
the table next to him and a hologram shimmered to
life behind him.

"*Madre de Dios!*" Pindar said softly.

The image was perhaps three meters from the tip
of its pointed, spiky tail to the top of its banana-
shaped and grotesque head. If it had eyes, they
seemed recessed just behind twin rows of needle-
tipped teeth. Pindar stepped to one side and saw
what appeared to be thick external ribs jutting from
the thing's back, and overall, it looked as if some
god playing a joke had created a manlike thing born
of giant insects. The monster was a dull black or
dark gray, and Pindar would not wish to meet such
a thing under any circumstances. He didn't know
what the Messiah was supposed to look like, either,
but he would bet all the iron in the Asteroid Belt
that this wasn't it.

"I can put you on the air in five minutes," Pindar
said, bending to pick up the antique camera. "Along
with your . . . messiah. It is your money. But I
wonder that anyone will look upon this thing and

think it might deliver them, señor. I myself would expect to see it in Hades."

"Do not blaspheme about that which you do not understand, technician."

Pindar shrugged. He accessed the camera's computer, tied it into a shunt, and rigged a relay transmitter. He moved quickly to the power unit and control console, tapping stolen codes into an orbiting broadcast satellite. He held off on the last digit, then turned to Salvaje. "When I input the final number, you will have three minutes before the WCC locks its trace of our signal. Two more minutes and they will find the dish I hid in Madras, and two minutes after that they will find this place. Best you hold your transmission to five minutes. I have an automatic cut off thirty seconds after that. I will have to find another bounce dish if you wish to broadcast again."

"Esta no importa," Salvaje said.

Pindar shrugged. "Your money."

Salvaje reached up, as if to stroke the dreadful image of the hologram floating in the air behind him. His fingers passed through the image. "Others will have heard the call. I must speak to them."

Crazy as a shithouse rat, Pindar thought. But of this he did not speak aloud. "All right. In four seconds. Three. Two. One." He input the final number.

Salvaje smiled into the camera's lens. "Good day, fellow seekers. I have come to you with the Great Truth. The coming of the True Messiah . . ."

Pindar shook his head. He would sooner worship his dog than this hideous image, which had to be a computer simulation. Nothing could really look like that.

The patient cafeteria was nearly empty, a dozen or so of the inmates shuffling their drug-calmed ways through the line with soft plastic trays. Billie moved in her own chemical fog, feeling tired, but unable to rest.

Sasha sat at a table next to the holoprojection chair, using a fork made of linear plastic to stir some ugly noodles around on her plate. The tableware was strong enough to lift the food but would curl up like cardboard if you tried to stick somebody with it. Somebody like yourself.

"Hey, Billie," Sasha said. "Check out Deedee, she's switching channels on the 'jector every three seconds. Why, I think that girl is mentally disturbed!"

Sasha laughed. Billie knew Sasha's history. She had pushed her father into a vat of jewelry cleaning acid when she was nine. She'd been here for eleven years because every time they asked her whether she'd do it again if she had the chance, she grinned and told them sure. Every day of the week and twice on Sunday.

Billie glanced at Deedee. The girl was gazing at the 'jector as if hypnotized. The tiny holograms blinked as she changed the channels. With four or five hundred choices, it would take even Deedee a while to see them all.

"C'mon, have a seat. Try some of this worm puke, it's real good."

Billie sat, almost collapsing.

"You on blues again?"

Billie sighed. "Greens."

"Crap, what'd you do, strangle a nurse?"

"The dreams."

Billie glanced at the tiny viewer in front of Deedee. A deep-space ship flew across the void. Blink. A car chase on a multilane surface road. Blink. A documentary on feral elves. Blink.

"C'mon, Billie," Sasha said, "you only have what, a month left until your hearing?"

"I won't skate this time either, Sash. They can't figure it out. They say my folks died in an explosion. I know better. I was *there*!"

"Ease up, kid. The monitors—"

"Hey, *fuck* the monitors!" Billie shoved her plate across the table, scattering the safety tableware and the noodles. The rubbery plate fell to the cushioned floor, bounced, but made hardly any sound. "They can send a ship a hundred light-years away to another system, they can make an android from amino soup and plastic, but they can't cure me of nightmares!"

Attendants appeared as if by magic, but Billie's rage couldn't stand any longer against the sedatives in her system. She slumped.

Behind her, Deedee said quietly, "Hold channel."

The image of a man with slicked-back hair and a smallish beard shined in the air before her. And behind him, behind him was—was—

"—join us, my friends," the man's voice spoke into the speaker implanted behind Deedee's mastoid bone. "Join the Church of Immaculate Incuba-

tion. Receive the ultimate communion. Become one
with the True Messiah. . . ."

Deedee smiled as the attendants came and
helped Billie to her feet. Billie didn't see the True
Messiah as she left.

"Dammit, let go!"

Then somebody pressed a green patch to her
carotid and Billie stopped even that much of strug-
gle.

Wilks and the robot reached the security door
leading into MILCOM HQ Intel One. A scanning
laser tapped a red dot against his eye and by the
time he had finished blinking, the door's comp had
IDed him and begun to roll open. The bot said, "Go
on in. I'll wait here."

Wilks did as he was told. He felt the pressure of
stares against him, knowing he was being watched
by computers and probably live guards, that his
every move was recorded. Fuck it.

There was only one other door in the corridor, so
he couldn't miss it. It opened as he approached. He
stepped into the office. Nothing but an oval table,
big enough to seat a dozen people, three chairs.
Two of the chairs were occupied. In one was a full
bird colonel, wearing interior regulations. No combat medals, a desk pilot. He'd be the MI officer in
charge. There was an oxymoron, "military intelligence."

The other man was in civilian garb, and he had
the look. Wilks would bet a month's pay this guy
was a t-bag—Terran Intelligency Agency. Any odds
anybody wanted.

"At ease, marine," the colonel said. Wilks wasn't aware that he'd been at attention. Old habits die hard.

Wilks noticed that the colonel, his name tag said "Stephens," kept his hands behind his back. Like maybe he was afraid to touch him.

Not so the civilian. He extended one hand. "Corporal Wilks."

Wilks kept his own hand down. Shake with one of these guys and you might need finger grafts.

The civilian nodded, withdrawing his offer of a handshake.

"You saw the recording," Stephens said.

"I saw it."

"What did you think?"

"I thought the guardsmen were lucky they got blown to atoms when they did."

The colonel and the civilian exchanged quick glances. "This is, ah, Mr. . . . Orona," Stephens said.

Yeah, right, and I'm King George the Second, Wilks thought.

"You ran into these things before, didn't you?" the one they called Orona said.

"Yeah."

"Tell me about it."

"What can I tell you that you don't already know? You've seen the recordings of my 'examination,' haven't you?"

"I want to hear it from you."

"Maybe I don't want to tell it to you."

Stephens glared at him. "Give the man the story, marine. That's an order."

Wilks almost laughed. Or what? You'll toss me in the brig? That's exactly where I'd rather be than here. But if they wanted him to talk, they could pry it out of him, the military had dope that could make a crowbar sing opera. He shrugged.

"All right. I was part of a unit sent to check on a colony on Rim. We'd lost contact with them. We found one survivor, a little girl named Billie. Everybody else had been slaughtered by some kind of alien. Same thing that got the guardsmen.

"One of them got onto the lander when it dusted off. Killed the pilot, crashed it. There were twelve of us in the squad, stuck on the ground. I was the only one who got out, me and the little girl. They shipped her off to live with relatives on Ferro, after they wiped her memory. She was a good kid, considering all the shit she saw. We spent some time awake on the ship before we climbed into the deep freezers. I liked her. She was tough.

"Later I heard there was another nest of the things somewhere, killed another colony. Supposedly a marine and a couple civilians got away from that one, too.

"When I got back, the medics patched me up, then took my brain apart. Only thing was, all of a sudden nobody wanted to know from aliens eating colonists and laying eggs in them. It got buried. Top secret, total wipe like the kid if I opened my mouth. That was more than a dozen years ago.

"That's it. End of story."

"You got a bad attitude, Wilks," Stephens said.

Orona smiled. "Colonel, do you suppose I might have a word with the corporal alone?"

After a moment Stephens nodded. "All right. I'll talk to you later."

He left the room.

Orona smiled. "Now we can talk freely."

Wilks laughed. "What? Do I have 'stupid' tattooed on my forehead? If there isn't a battery of recording gear going full blast right now I'll eat that fucking table. Probably the colonel is in the next room watching in full holographic surround. Give me a break, Orona, or whatever your name really is."

"All right," Orona said. "We'll play it your way. Stop me if I get any of it wrong.

"After you managed to escape from Rim, you spend six months in quarantine, to make sure you weren't infected with some kind of alien virus or bacteria. Nobody even tried to see you, no personal visits, nada. You wouldn't let them reconstruct your face."

"Women love scars," Wilks said. "Makes 'em sympathetic."

Orona continued. "When you were put back on active duty, you turned into a chemhound. Nine arrests and subsequent terms in the brig for Stoned and Disorderly. Three for assault, two for damage to property, one for attempted homicide."

"Guy had a big mouth," Wilks offered.

"I specialize in genetics, Corporal, but anybody who's ever taken a psych course can see you're on a one-way trip down the reaction tubes."

"So? It's my life. What do you care?"

"Before those two Coast Guard clowns blew themselves up, they downloaded the derelict's data banks. We have a trajectory of that old ship. We know where it came from before it came home to die."

"Ask me if I care."

"Oh, you should, Corporal. You're going there. Whatever your problems are don't matter. I need a specimen of the thing the Coast Guard found. You're going to bring me one."

"I won't volunteer for it."

"Oh, but you will." Orona grinned.

Wilks blinked. Something unhappy roiled around in Wilks's belly, like a trapped beast wanting to get out. While he was still wondering if he were about to vomit whatever was left from his most recent meal, Orona hit him with another one.

"You know that little girl you rescued? She's here. On Earth. In a mental center. They keep her sedated and run a lot of tests on her. She has these nightmares, you see. Apparently the brainwipe didn't completely take. She remembers things, in her dreams.

"You could wind up in a place like that, if you don't do the right thing."

Billie was here? He hadn't thought he'd ever see her again. He had been curious about her more than once. She was the only person who'd seen those things the way he had, least the only one he knew about. He stared at Orona. Then he nodded. If they wanted you, they would get you, he'd been in the Corps long enough to know that. He would go or damn sure wish he had. There were worse things than dying.

He took a deep breath. "Okay," he said. "I'll go."

Orona smiled, and when he did, it reminded Wilks of the aliens.

Damn.

Billie slept. She could hear voices in her dream, a distant overlay of ghostly sound wound among the shimmering and frightful images.

"—dreaming again. What'd you give her?"

A door loomed in front of Billie, partially open. Behind the door, blackness. Eyes gleamed in the dark there, and light flashed briefly on rows of serrated teeth.

"—thirty of Trinomine—"

The undulating door swung wide, creaking loudly. A kind of . . . presence oozed through. Billie couldn't see it clearly. . . .

"—thirty? That's twice the usual dosage. Aren't you worried about brain damage?"

The presence coalesced, forming a quavery image. Black, tall, toothed. The monster. It grinned at Billie. Gnashed those teeth. Moved toward her.

Billie was frozen. Couldn't even turn away as it came for her. She opened her mouth to scream—

"—well, that's a risk, isn't it? She's already halfway insane and none of the conventional therapies work. Besides, medical-grade androids have taken up to forty milligrams without significant damage—"

The monster reached for her. Opened its mouth. Slowly a toothed rod extruded itself from that hellish mouth. Came toward her, slow, oh, so slow, but she . . . couldn't . . . move. . . .

"—she's not an android, though—"

"—might as well be—"

A hand touched Billie's shoulder.

Billie awoke, her heart thudding rapidly. She was sweating hard.

It was Sasha.

"Oh, Sash. What are you doing here?"

"You have a visitor, Doc sent me to tell you."

"A visitor? I don't know anybody on Earth except the medics and the inmates here."

Sasha shrugged. "Doc says somebody is in V4 for you. You want me to go along?"

"No. I can handle it."

The truth was, she didn't feel particularly adept at the moment; the drugs coursed through her system and the latest nightmare still vibrated in her memory. But if she was ever going to get out of this place, she had to look as if she were in control.

Billie found her way down the hall, was admitted

into the visitor area. The door to V4 scanned her and admitted her into the "private" room. Inside was a monitor inset into the right wall and a single form-chair facing a fully polarized wall that shined like a black mirror.

Billie sat.

Who could it be?

The monitor came to life. Onscreen was a computerized image of a kindly, white-haired grandmother. Her chip-voice when she spoke was also kindly, but full of quiet authority. Billie also knew the voice was full of subsonics and sublims designed to calm and soothe a listener, as well as engender obedience.

"You are being monitored," Grandma said. "And any discussion of hospital therapy will result in termination of this visitation." Grandma smiled, forming lines at the corners of her eyes. "Visitation is a privilege and not a right. You are allowed ten minutes. Is this understood?"

"Yeah, right."

"Very good. Enjoy your visit."

Grandma smiled again and faded from the screen. A small red dot pulsed in her place, reminding Billie that the conversation was being recorded and observed.

The polarized wall faded from black to clear.

A man, one side of his face scarred, sat in the chair two meters away from her. He wore a military uniform.

Who . . . ?

"Hello, Billie."

It was as if somebody suddenly slammed a fist

into the side of her head. The jolt rocked her physically. Billie jerked and stared as a memory they'd tried to take away from her swam to the surface like a whale needing air.

It was him! The man who'd always saved her in her dreams.

"Wilks!"

"Yeah. How they treating you in here?"

"You—you're *real*!"

"Last time I looked, yeah."

"Oh, God, Wilks!"

"I wasn't sure you'd remember me."

"You—you look . . . different."

He touched the scars on his face. "Colonial Marine surgeons. Buncha butchers."

"Wh-what are you doing here?"

"They told me you were in this place. I figured I had to see you, once I found out you were having the dreams, too."

"About the monsters."

"Yeah. I don't sleep that well myself. Haven't since Rim."

"It was real, wasn't it?"

"Oh, yeah. It was real. They had me, I'm in as long as they keep reactivating my secrecy clause, but you were a civilian. They decided to wipe you, but it didn't work, least not all the way."

Billie slumped, but at the same time felt a sense of relief like none she'd ever known. It was *real*! She wasn't crazy! The dreams were memories, trying to get out!

* * *

Wilks stared at the kid. Well, she wasn't really a kid anymore, was she? Turned out to be a nice-looking woman, even in the hospital whites and obviously stoned on whatever they gave her.

He wasn't sure why he'd come, except that maybe she was the only other person who would understand the dreams he kept having. He'd tried to track her down a long time ago, along with the other marine and the civilians who'd escaped from the second bug nest, but they'd all been carefully hidden away. Probably in some medical center like this one, or on some outpost a dozen light-years from anywhere. Or maybe they were dead.

"Why did you come?" she asked.

He pulled his thoughts back to the young woman on the other side of the thick, clear plastic wall. "They found what they think is the homeworld for those . . . things," he said. "They're sending me there with some troops."

A few seconds went past. "To destroy it?"

Wilks smiled, but it was a sour expression. "To collect a 'specimen.' I think MI wants to use the things as some kind of weapon."

"No! You can't let them!"

"Kid, I can't stop them. I'm a corporal." And a drunk and chemhead brawler, he added mentally.

"Get me out of here," she said.

"Huh?"

"I'm not crazy. The memories are real. You can tell them. They're trying to convince me everything I remember is an illusion but you know the truth. Tell them. You saved me before, Wilks, do it again!

They're killing me in here with the drugs, the therapy! I have to get out!"

The monitor screen next to her flowered, and a white-haired old lady appeared there, smiling. "Discussion of therapy is not allowed," she said. "This visit is terminated. Please leave the visiting area immediately."

"Wilks, *please*!"

Wilks found himself standing, his fists clenched.

"Please leave the visiting area immediately," the old lady said.

Billie stood and leapt at the clear wall. She slammed her fists into the hard plastic. "Let me go!"

The door behind her opened and two large men entered. They grabbed Billie. The young woman struggled, but it was no use. The wall began to polarize and darken.

"Hey, fuckheads, let her go!" Wilks yelled. He lunged at the wall, slammed into it. He backed off, threw his shoulder into the wall again. The wall was unmoved.

The monitor on his side of the darkening plastic came to life. The same old woman. "This visit has been terminated. Please exit now. Thank you for coming. Have a nice day."

"Wilks! Help me!" Billie screamed.

Then the sound faded and the wall went totally dark, and she was gone.

Wilks leaned away from the wall. He stared at his hands. "Sorry, kid," he whispered. "I'm sorry."

5

Excerpts from the script of the top-secret audiovisual presentation "Theory of Alien Propagation," by Waidslaw Orona, Ph.D.

Note: This script/compgen AV recording is/are classified military document(s) and require a clearance of __A-1/a__ for reading/viewing. Penalties for illegal uses of this/these document(s) may include Full Brain Reconstruction and/or a fine of up to Cr. 100,000, and/or imprisonment in a Federated Penal Colony for up to twenty-five years.

FADE IN:

COMPUTER GEN PIX: Deep space, a b.g. of stars. Centered is AN ALIEN, sideview, curled into a fetallike ball. MUSIC PLAYS: Wagner's "Ride of the Valkyries."

V.O.

Humans suffer from self-centered notions as to the nature of life.

The Alien slowly uncurls. MUSICAL STING.

V.O. (CONT.)

Humans assume that alien life forms should conform to standards that match our own, including logic and morality.

The Alien is uncurled in its full glory now. Slowly it rotates to face the camera. MUSIC CONTINUES OVER.

V.O. (CONT.)

Even among humans, morality is ignored when expedient. Why should we expect more from an alien life form than we demand from ourselves?

The Alien stretches out its arms and legs and tail so that it becomes a parody of the man's-reach-should-equal-his-height illustration by Da Vinci. PUSH IN SLOWLY. The Alien expands to fill the screen.

V.O. (CONT.)

If we know nothing else, we must know this about aliens: First, they will not be like us. Second, truly understanding them will be almost impossible.

THE ALIEN

fills the screen; DIAL DOWN MUSIC and PUSH THROUGH TO BLACK.

                                          CUT TO:

EXT. ALIEN WORLD—DAY—ESTABLISHING

Here is a bleak, rocky planet. Very little greenery,
vast stretches of nothing.

                    V.O.
      Judging from the dense exoskeleton of the alien and
      its demonstrated adaptability, we must assume that
      its home planet is a harsh, desolate place.

                                          CUT TO:

EXT. HIVE

This is a ridged, antlike mound rearing up from the
cleared area around it, a thing composed of alien
spittle, laced with local plants and the exoskeletons
of alien prey.

                    V.O.
      We know from our previous encounters that the
      aliens have a queen-based hierarchy and that they
      form hives to protect their eggs and young hatch-
      lings.

INT. HIVE—EGG CHAMBER

The giant QUEEN, monstrous egg sac attached to
her rear, deposits eggs on the floor of the chamber.

V.O.

At the proper time, drone workers provide host bodies for the newborns.

TIME CUT TO:

INT. EGG ROOM

A GROUP OF PREY BEASTS held in place by WORKER ALIENS are attacked by HATCHLINGS IN THEIR LARVAL FORM. (These are hand-shaped lumps with fingers and tails, the latter of which wrap around the prey beasts' necks to secure them as the ovipositors are extruded and inserted down the prey's throats. See comp-image #3 for stock footage.)

V.O.

The parasitical breeding process is offensive to some in the scientific community, but completely natural for aliens living in a harsh environment.

CUT TO:

PREY BEAST

Its belly bulges from within. It screams, but silently, (MOS).

V.O.

Birth of the next stage is violent and fatal for the host.

C.U.—PREY'S BELLY

The skin bursts, tissue spews, and A BABY ALIEN, looking like a fat snake with sharp teeth, emerges.

> V.O. (CONT.)
> The young alien chews its way forth, where there may be a battle for dominance with other newly born aliens. We can only speculate at this point.

A GROUP OF BABY ALIENS

rip and tear at each other.

CUT TO:

EXT. HIVE—DAY

Overhead a spaceship ROARS by; below on the ground, A GROUP OF WORKER ALIENS watch the ship.

> V.O.
> How the aliens escape their world is, of course, complete speculation.

THE SHIP

lands and a SUITED FIGURE emerges, carrying assorted collecting gear and a wicked-looking hand weapon.

V.O. (CONT.)
However, it seems likely that some . . . outside force, perhaps a spacefaring species, interacted with the aliens.

THE SUITED FIGURE

returns to the ship, an alien egg inside a clear specimen bottle. From the size of the egg compared to the Collector, it is apparent that the Collector is much larger than a man, perhaps three times so.

CUT TO:

INT. COLLECTOR'S SPACESHIP

The Collector approaches the alien egg. Leans over it. The egg's portal flaps splay open. The Collector peers into the egg's interior.

V.O.
A small mistake in dealing with such predatory creatures would, of course, prove to be dangerous in the extreme. Probably fatal.

CUT TO:

EXT. COLLECTOR'S SPACESHIP

The ship lies crashed upon some world, fog swirling about it. PUSH IN AND THROUGH TO:

INT. COLLECTOR'S SHIP

The skeleton of the Collector, its chest burst open from within, sits in the control seat of the ship. In the b.g. are THREE HUMANS IN SPACESUITS. Light beams play over the dead giant as the humans examine it.

                    V.O.
Humans rely on technology to the point where they believe it has made them invincible. When dealing with creatures who have adapted to extremely hostile environments, such a belief can also prove dangerous.

EXT. CORPORATION LANDER

The lander lifts from the planet's surface.

CLOSER—ON THE LANDER

Clutching a strut on the lander's underside is AN ALIEN.

                    V.O. (CONT.)
Because an unsuited human cannot survive in the vacuum of space does not mean that some other complex life form cannot.

INT. CORPORATION STAR SHIP—CARGO BAY— HIGH ANGLE

Across the bay walk TWO MEN.

PULL BACK TO OTS (OVER-THE-SHOULDER)—ALIEN

It watches the men. Drool drips from its lethal jaws.

ALIEN'S POV—THE MEN

It moves in. They react in horror as it attacks. BLOOD SPLASHES, blanking the VP.

CUT TO:

INT. AIRLOCK

The hatch opens and the Alien is ejected by the outward blast of atmosphere. TRACK WITH IT as it flies into space, turning slowly.

V.O.
Ultimately, our limited contact with these creatures indicate that they have simple imperatives that control their lives. They kill, they breed, and they survive.

THE ALIEN

floats in the vacuum. It should be dead by human standards, but it slowly curls itself into a fetal ball, tail wrapped around the massive claw-hammer head and spiky body.

V.O.

Properly utilized, such aliens would make excellent warriors. Research into their composition could yield advances in armor, chemical and biological weapons, and perhaps even new ways to induce suspended animation for stellar travel.

PULL BACK—THE ALIEN

Dwindles into a tiny dot, then vanishes altogether in the cold blackness.

End of script/AV extract. Readers/viewers are once again warned that unauthorized use of this material may result in severe penalties, per MILCOM stat. reg. 342544-A, Revision II.

6

Billie sleeps, but it is not rest. In her dreams she is back on Rim. She sees her parents, sees the inside of the colony that plans to terraform the planet and turn it into paradise. Sees and is happy.

Things blur. Then she sees monsters.

Her life becomes a jumble of hiding, of fear, of waiting for them to find and kill her. She joins the rats under the floor, her mind and actions turn feral. Survival is all, and it is nothing, likely to stop at any moment.

She sees Wilks and the others, guns spraying. She hears the noise, feels the terror.

She feels Wilks's arms around her, feels the vibrations of his weapon as it fires. Watches the monsters shatter and fall, but knows there are too many of them.

There comes the worst moment, when the hard claws of a monster dig into her, lift her, and it carries her away to die. Then it falls, chopped off at the knees. Its blood eats smoking, stinking holes in the floor and it releases her. She doesn't wait, she scrabbles away before it can catch her again. The air is full of acrid fumes, the sound of Wilks's yelling, his gun shooting over and over until it is a continuous roar. The wounded monster's claws click on the floor as it drags itself toward Billie.

She screams. The only name that matters now.

"Wilks!"

The only one who can save her.

7

In the canned-air depths of MILCOM HQ, in the long hall with invisible doors two men walked: Orona and Stephens.

"He's as nuts as an orchard full of filbert trees," Stephens said. "If we hadn't needed to keep him on a leash, we'd have psych-DCed him years ago."

"True," Orona said. "But he's what we've got and GENstaff wants him along. You know how politics works."

"Yeah, GENstaff thinks he's some kind of monster killer, but I think he's a goddamn *crew* killer."

"You wanted a field command. I got you one."

"Right, carrying Jonah the Jinx into a potentially lethal force combatsit."

"Let me put it to you like this, Bill," Orona said. "GENstaff *will* have an experienced person onboard this project. The only other marine we know about

51

who has met these things face-to-face and survived the initial encounter disappeared. The woman and kid he saved also vanished and we don't know where they are. The girl Wilks saved is in the bughouse, doped to the gills. There was also a badly damaged android, but we don't have a clue as to what happened to it. We're full of mystery here. That leaves Wilks."

"I don't like it. He's unstable."

"I'm not asking you to *like* it, or like him. I am *telling* you that GENstaff says this is how it's going to be. If you're tired of being a marine, then *you* call up GENstaff and tell them you don't like it."

Stephens shook his head.

"He's been bumped to sergeant and put in charge of loading supplies," Orona continued. "How much damage can he do there?"

Colonel Stephens stood in the loading dock of the carrier watching the robots haul gear into the ship. He stopped a private heading for the hydraulic walkers. "What's in those crates, marine?"

The man snapped to attention. "Sir, plasma rifles and chargers."

Stephens stared at the hard black plastic boxes.

"Who in the hell authorized plasma weapons?"

"Sir, I don't know, sir. Sergeant Wilks ordered us to load them, sir. That's all I know, sir."

"As you were."

Stephens took the lift to CARG-OP. He saw Wilks directing a trio of cargo bots.

"Wilks!"

"Sir."

"Where did you get authorization to requisition plasma weapons?"

"I was ordered to supply the ground troops with appropriate weaponry, sir."

"And you thought blasters were appropriate? We aren't going to war here, Sergeant. We are supposed to collect specimens, not pieces."

"My experience—" Wilks began.

"—has distorted your mind," Stephens finished. "You've taken it upon yourself to provide grossly destructive weaponry when standard-issue carbines will do. That's what you used, wasn't it? And according to your own testimony a 10mm AP would stop one of these things just fine."

Rage flared in Wilks. "First time you face off with these 'things' you'll wish you had something better. Sir."

"GENstaff wants you along, Wilks, so you're along. But I won't jeopardize my mission by splattering potential specimens all over the countryside with weaponry designed to stop tanks. Have those blasters removed from the ship, mister. Is that clear?"

Wilks's voice was ice and steel. "Perfectly clear, Colonel."

The two electroball players darted back and forth inside the hexagonal, walled court, smashing the ball with charged paddles. The fist-sized orb rocketed into multicushioned patterns—three walls were the minimum allowed for a valid point—and came back at the players at over 120 kilometers an hour.

The player on the left executed a perfect six-wall attack. The player on the right was a half second slow in his response and the electroball smashed into his chest hard enough to knock him from his feet.

"Gotcha!"

The hit player came to his feet. "Your point."

"Ready?"

"Go ahead. Serve."

The player on the right smiled. "In a moment. Any news of the merger proposal with Climate Systems?"

Lefty shrugged. "I thought I told you. Our op Massey convinced them to go for it."

The player on the right laughed. "Made them an offer they couldn't refuse, eh?"

"Well. You don't know Massey, but yeah, something like that. Serve."

The two men sat hunched over a holographic table, fingers on the glove pad controls of the electroball game. Inside a clear hexagonal field the miniature players sweated as they darted back and forth, while their operators wore custom and expensive silk business suits and looked considerably fresher. They were well groomed, with ninety-credit hairstyles and precious gem collar studs. They looked very much like corporation vice presidents, which they were.

The tiny ball rocketed off four walls and went past the receiving player.

"Good shot," the man in the vivid green silks said. He wore a ruby the size of his thumb tip at his throat, the red contrasting nicely with the green.

"Yep, almost gave me a decent match," the one in the red silks said. His ornamental throat stud was of diamond, twice the size of his companion's ruby, and it glittered against the red. He was the senior VP of the two.

The hologram shimmered and vanished.

Green Silks said, "Listen, we need to talk about the biowarfare project."

Red nodded. "Anything from the government?"

The two of them stood and moved away from the table. Green said, "Nah, you know how these guys get when they want to keep things secret."

"We need to be in on this," Red said. "We are talking about major credits here. We've had offers from every milsupply corporation in the system if we can come up with the right product. We can't let the military get the jump on us here."

Green smiled. "Don't worry. I'm going to put Massey on it."

They reached a door. It *thwiped* open to admit them into an office the size of a small home. One wall was airglas, giving a view of the megapolis. On a clear day like today, the view was spectacular from eighty stories high. Rank certainly had its privileges.

"Okay, I've been hearing about this guy Massey, but I don't know him. Tell me."

Red moved to a desk big enough to seat five people without crowding.

Green went to a dispenser set into the wall across

from the desk. "Devil dust," he said to the dispenser. "Half a gram. You want anything."

"Yeah, get me an orgy-inhaler."

Green added Red's order to his own. After a second a small tray extruded itself from the machine. On the tray were a small mound of pink powder inside a hemispherical cup set next to a one-shot nasal tube. Green tossed the tube to Red and picked up the cup. He pressed the dust against his left eye as Red fired the compressed gas charge of the inhaler into his right nostril. Both men grinned as the chemicals took hold.

"You were saying about Massey?"

"Oh. Yeah. Him. Well, this guy is something else. MBA from New Harvard, doctorate in corp law from Cornell, post-doc work at Mitsubishi U. Could have had his pick of any company in the system but he *enlisted* in the Colonial Marines. Got a Silver Star in the Oil Wars, four Purple Hearts. Commanded a recon unit in the Tansu Rebellion on Wakahashi's World, picked up a few decorations there."

"Real patriot, huh?" Red said. He squirmed in his chair as another chemically powered orgasm rippled through him.

"Nah. He liked killing. Probably would have gone pretty high up but they court-martialed him. Tried to kill his CO."

"No shit?"

"Yeah. Thought the CO was a coward when he wouldn't order an attack on a bunch of civilians Massey thought might be hiding enemy sympathizers. *Might* be. Knocked the officer senseless and led the attack himself. Killed eighty-five men,

women, and children. Word is more than half of
them got dispatched by Massey personally."

"Man loved his job, hey?"

"Oh, yeah. We bought the tribunal off and put
him to work for us. Good help is so hard to find, you
know?"

Green laughed. Red joined him.

Massey sat at the table in his kitchen, his six-
year-old son on his lap. Behind him, Marla punched
the controls on the coffee maker.

"Be ready in a sec, hon," Marla said. She moved
up behind Massey and kissed his neck.

Massey smiled. "Thanks, babe." To his son he
said, "So, what's my boy up to today?"

"We're gonna go on a field trip to the zoo," the
boy said. "See a Denebian slime spider and maybe
the Bartlett snakes, if they'll come out."

"Sounds great," Massey said. He lifted the boy,
put him on the floor. "But Daddy's got to go to work
now. Say hello to the slime spider for me."

"Oh, Daddy, slime spiders can't talk!"

Massey grinned. "No? What about your uncle
Chad?"

Marla swatted at him with one hand. "My brother
is not a slime spider!" she said. But she laughed.

"No, that's true," her husband said. "He's only
got four limbs, not eight."

"Go, you'll be late for work. Here's your coffee."

Still smiling, Massey left. Yes. Work.

Nothing was more important than work.

Nothing.

Her teeth glittered like stars. They were so beautiful.

Closer she came, magnificent in her huge glory, black and deadly and purposeful. Her exoskeleton gleamed darkly as she leaned down toward Billie. Her mouth opened, and the smaller set of teeth on the inner lips also opened. She was the queen.

I love you, her thoughts came unspoken to Billie. *I need you*.

Yes, Billie thought.

She was the queen, and she reached for Billie, her clawed hands glistening.

Come and . . . join with me, the queen said.

Yes, Billie thought. Yes, I will.

Closer the queen came.

Easley and Bueller squatted behind the remains of the shattered building, a waist-level row of bricks and twisted rebar the only protection against the bunker's R-O-M gun. It couldn't see them but the stupecomp running the gun could probably pick up some heat leakage from their combat suits, and every now and then it would pop off a couple dozen 30mm AP rounds in their direction.

"Shit," Bueller said. "Fucker's got us pinned down!"

"Maybe not," Easley offered. "The thing's got service portals aft. I can launch a grenade in the right spot, it'll blow the power. Then we got his ass."

Three rounds of 30mm clipped a couple of centimeters of brick off the top of the wall over Bueller's head. He squatted lower. "Damn!"

"Okay, look," Easley said, "here's the play. You scoot down about twenty meters, put your weapon over the wall, and spray that sucker. I'll circle around behind it and blow it off line while it's potting at you."

Under the kleersteel faceplate of his helmet cover, Bueller frowned. The expression wrinkled the skintite that reached to his eyes, and the skull of the elite Colonial Marine whack-team embossed on the tite.

"Unless you got a better idea?" Easley said.

Bueller shook his head. "What the hell. Let's do it. Gimme a signal when you're ready to dance."

"Copy," Easley said. His voice was crisp in the helmet's bonephones. The com was standard military tightbeam and scrambled, so the geezer in the bunker couldn't hear them, or even if he could, he wouldn't be able to understand what they were saying.

Bueller moved off, keeping low. Every so often the range-of-motion gun would cap off a few more shots.

Easley lit a low-heat flare and dropped it. With any luck, the gun would think it was a suit leak and zero in on it. While it was doing that, he would blow that sucker. He moved off. He was good, one of the Corps' best, and damned if he was gonna get drilled by some geezer in a lock box.

When he got into position, Easley said, "Do it!"

Thirty meters away, crouched behind a big chunk of rubble that was probably once a house, Bueller whipped his carbine over the top and triggered it full auto. He waved it back and forth, so the motion sensors would get it. The sonics would have found it pretty quick anyhow, but he didn't want to take any chances.

Softsteel slugs spanged off the wall, chopping it away. It knew he was here, all right. Bueller pulled his weapon back so it wouldn't get hit.

Five seconds later, two things happened: a grenade went off and the robotic gun stopped shooting.

Bueller grinned. "Yeah! Way to go, buddy!" Easley must have rammed one right up the thing's drainpipe. Hell of an enema.

Ten seconds went past. "Easley?"

"You're buying the beer tonight, pal," came the reply.

Bueller stood. Oh, man, was *this* sweet! That old fart thought he could play with the best—

A round splashed against Bueller's chest.

"Oh, *shit!*"

He looked down, saw the spatter of phosphorescent green over his heart. If it had been armor-piercing, he'd be history. "Shit, shit, *shit!*"

"You got that right," Wilks said. "How do you do, Mr. Shit." He walked toward Bueller, a training sniper rifle dangling in one hand. Behind Wilks, Easley stood, helmet cover already off, a similar splash of green running down the formerly clear faceplate.

Backing Easley was a squad of marines in field underdress, watching. Wilks wore a synlin coverall and formplast boots.

"You guys stink," he said. "Sure, you sidestepped a few mines and avoided a couple of triplines and you managed to take out a robot gun, but you're still dead meat because you moved stupid."

Behind Wilks, Easley leaned over to the trooper next to him. "You getting this, Blake?"

The second marine, a short blond woman with her hair in the standard combat buzz, nodded. "Yup. Real learning experience. He made you guys look like dung birds."

Easley frowned. "Hey—"

Bueller cut in. "Wait a sec, Sarge. I heard Easley on the tightbeam!"

"No, you didn't. You heard me."

"But—but—that's—that's—"

"Cheating," Wilks finished. "Life is hard. You think these things we're going up against are going to play by some kind of rules?"

Bueller stared at the splotch on his suit.

"So, boys and girls, in honor of this stirring work by Easley and Bueller, we're going to spend the day on the shooting course. Full battle gear, combat scenarios until you can get across without being splashed." Wilks smiled at Bueller, then Easley. "If a wasted old geezer like me can fan two of the CMC's supposedly best whack-teams as easy as I did, the colonies are in a shitload of trouble if they ever need anything worse than a cut skinbonded. Saddle up, marines."

The squad moved off, grumbling.

"—Bueller, you asshole—"

"—damn, Easley, now look what you got us into—"

"—Buddha, you two guys looked like crap—"

Wilks watched them go, pleased. Of course, he

had to rag their asses, that was a TO's job, and since Stephens had busted him out of loading the ship, this was what he could do. But despite his criticism, these guys were good. They'd been together a year, they were all rated high in small arms, explosives, standard strategy and tactics. If he hadn't cheated, he wouldn't have gotten the two hot rods coming at him. They were a lot better than he'd expected. He'd go into enemy fire with this team anytime.

As they pulled armor from the carryall and began to suit up, Wilks remembered his squad on Rim. Were these guys as good as that unit had been? Probably. It was hard to say for sure until things went sour—drill wasn't the same as real, no matter how you tried to make it so. This squad had better scores in training and they moved real well when the return fire was nothing more than splashers. *If* they moved as well in the real world when the bad guys started coming, then, yeah, they would do better than the squad had on Rim.

He hoped to all the gods that they moved better. It was one thing to come up against a nest of the aliens, another thing to be on a planet full of the damned things. And who knew but that their homeworld might have worse living on it? Maybe the aliens he'd fought were like mice compared to the worst on their planet. That was a sobering thought. If this team was going to go down and come back, they needed to be good. They needed to be the best. If he could teach them everything he remembered, if he could drill them until they could pointshoot a demicredit out of the air, if he could teach them what they'd be up against . . .

"If" was a big word, even though it didn't look it. There wasn't going to be any room for error in this mission. Screwups would get somebody dead.

And not just dead. The old saying was wrong here: they could kill you and then they *could* eat you. And they would do worse if they took you alive.

The team began to amble back. Wilks brought his thoughts away from what might be to what was. "All right, children, let's see if we can't cross the street without getting run down by a hovercab, shall we? Blake, you take point, Easley, you're TC, Bueller, HW-tactical, Ramirez—"

He finished ordering the squad, then started to give them the scenario. No, he decided. Let them figure it out on the fly. Instead of telling them what they would face, he said, "It'll take forty-five seconds for the holocomp to program the new playing field. That's what you got, people. See if you can't look like marines and not a bunch of turds on legs this time!"

Wilks spoke into his comp-control mike.

Around them the crumbled walls and bunker began to shimmer and dissolve as the computer pulled the plug on the last scenario. Wilks turned and walked away as the obstacle course began to rebuild itself. It would look real and within limits even feel real, but it was an illusion.

What they would be facing when the time came was no illusion. You could spit on that, marine, and damn well make it shine.

8

The conference-room door loomed in front of Billie like the mouth of doom. The conference room in which the review team waited, as it had so many times before.

She took a deep breath and went inside.

Dr. Jerrin stood there, and he wasn't smiling.

Not a good sign.

"Have a seat, Billie," he said.

She looked at the other six faces. Three were doctors she knew, one a medical center administrator, one a legal rep for the government, one her legal rep, the last one here to make sure the usual lynching was all nice and legal.

Billie sat.

Jerrin looked at the other members of the team. He cleared his throat, fiddled with a flat screen on the table. "Ah, Billie, we seem to have come to an . . . impasse in your treatment."

"Really?" Billie said. She couldn't keep the irony out of her voice, but it didn't make any difference. This was only a matter of form. They weren't going to let her out. Not now. Probably not ever. She was going to spend her life in this place.

"Dr. Hannah has suggested a new treatment which, while fairly, ah, dramatic, offers a chance for us to stop these nocturnal episodes of yours."

Billie perked up, but only a little. "Really?" Less sarcasm now.

Jerrin looked at Hannah, a fat blonde from some cold climate, at least to judge by how frigid her words always seemed. Hannah said, "Yes, we've had some success in penal colony treatments with it. It is a fairly simple procedure, an operation using a fine surgical laser that eliminates predefined areas of certain cerebral complexes—"

"What?! You're talking about burning out my brain!"

"Now, Billie," Jerrin began.

"Fuck that! I won't!"

Hannah smiled, a sour expression. "It's not really up to you, dear. The state has certain prerogatives here. You are a danger to yourself and others with your fantasies—"

"They aren't fantasies! Wilks was here, Wilks, the marine who saved me on Rim! Ask him! Find him and ask him!"

She was on her feet now, yelling at Hannah.

The door opened and two orderlies came in, shockers in hand.

"What's she on?" Hannah asked, as if Billie were deaf or not in the room.

Jerrin said, "Triazolam, Haliperidol, Chlorpromazine, double maintenance dose."

"See?" Hannah said. "Habituation. We've rotated her through everything we have and she's used to them all. She shouldn't be able to do much more than walk—and look at her."

Billie struggled in the grip of the two orderlies, able to move them slightly despite their size.

Jerrin sighed. "I suppose you're right."

"Dr. Jerrin! No! Please!"

"It's for the best, Billie. You'll be a lot happier without the dreams."

"But what else will it cost me? Will that be all you take, the dreams?"

Jerrin stared at the table.

"Will it?"

"There may be some slight collateral damage. Minor loss of memory in some areas."

"You fuckers are going to burn who I am away, aren't you? Turn me into a zombie!"

"Now, Billie—"

With a strength born of terror, Billie jerked free of the orderlies and turned to run. She made it to the door before a third orderly slapped her side with his shocker. She fell, unable to control her voluntary muscles.

Oh, God! They were going to wipe her brain. She might as well be dead, because when they were done, there wasn't going to be anybody home.

9

Wilks stared at the computer image as the numbers and words swirled into oblivion. Damn. Had to look, didn't you, Wilks? Had to satisfy your fucking curiosity. Well, now you know.

And now that you do, what are you going to do about it?

Wilks slid out of the form-chair in front of the military terminal. The room was in the MILCOM library complex, normally reserved for officers, but he was a special case, wasn't he? And even if he hadn't been given an emergency clearance to use the system, he could have gotten into the files. You didn't do nineteen years in the Corps without learning a few things.

A few groundpounders sat in booths, working in the stale air as Wilks walked out of the library. It was hard to make rank without combat or offworld duty at least, and these guys were all cracking the files, studying, hoping tape-learning education would give them some kind of edge. He didn't think it would.

He'd have offered them his spot on the mission in a San Francisco second, if they wanted to trade, but that wasn't gonna happen. He was going, unless he ran, and he couldn't do that. He'd been running from it too long already.

Okay, pal. You got a look at what you wanted. Now, what *are* you gonna do about it? Walk away? You're probably gonna get chewed to soypro a few hours after you get to the aliens' world. The ship leaves in eight hours, and you are due to log in in six. What else can they do to you?

He nodded to himself as he passed a fat major leaving his studies. The major looked at the chevron rocker on Wilks's sleeve and frowned. He started to say something, probably going to rag Wilks about being in a restricted officers-only area, but Wilks turned slightly so the man could see the acid burn scars on his face.

The fat major paled, his hand going involuntarily to his own blubbery jowls. Wilks could almost see his mind working. Here was a noncom who wasn't supposed to be in here and a ranking officer should check to be sure he had reason and permission. On the other hand, the noncom in question had a face like a bad holovee monster program and maybe it was better just to let him pass. Surely he hadn't wandered in here by accident, somebody must have sent him.

Good thinking, fatso, Wilks thought. He smiled, stretching the scar tissue into a grimace.

Okay, fuck it. He was up to here with all this vermin scat. He knew a guy in Programming owed him a big favor. Time to call it in; wasn't like he was going to get to collect old debts much longer anyhow. Might as well go out in style.

Wilks headed to find the man who owed him.

The medical complex loomed like a gleaming and ugly beast of stressed plastecrete and ferrofoam and glass as Wilks left the cab and walked toward it. He had the section, the room number, and a theoretical schedule, courtesy of the programmer in MI-7. Getting off the base hadn't been a problem either, even though he was restricted. For every system they made to do something, there was a way around it. Rank might have its privileges, but the guys on the line knew a few tricks of their own.

The admit pad on the complex door was an old-style keypad, an antique, but that was why he had chosen this entrance, no eye reader. Wilks punched in the code he'd gotten.

The lock chimed and the door slid open. Hell, this was easier than swatting flies. He walked in.

A human guard leaned back in a chair at a desk, looking at porno projection from his handheld vid viewer. He saw Wilks and the naked bodies vanished as he shut the unit down and glanced at his admission roster.

"Can I help you?"

"Yeah, I'm supposed to see Dr. Jerrin."

The guard glanced down. Must have seen Jerrin's

name. He waved his hands over the console, brought up the appointment list. "And you are . . . ?"

"Emile Antoon Khadaji," he said, giving the man a name from an old book he'd once read.

The guard glanced down. "I don't see your name here, Monsieur Khadaji."

Wilks hadn't been able to find and get into the patient file, he hadn't had time, though he had gotten the doctor's name right. "I'm a last-minute deal," he said. "Somebody canceled."

The guard frowned. "I'll have to check with the doctor," he said.

"Fine. Check." He gave the guard a good view of his face. Guy with a face like his surely had psychological problems, right? The guard wasn't suspicious, just following the drill. Probably didn't have a lot to do, he had time to watch porno holos.

As the guard reached for the com unit to call the doctor, Wilks moved his right hand slowly toward his right hip. He had a multicharge pistol, a synapse scrambler, nestled in a flexskin holster on his belt just over his right buttock. He'd gotten the weapon on the black market; it was illegally boosted so it could deliver a stun charge at twice the ten-meter distance for approved civilian hardware.

Wilks looked up and down the hallway. Nobody around.

He pulled the stunner, brought it up, held it in both hands. The heavy plastic felt cool in his grip. It threw a fairly narrow beam, you had to aim it, but he'd had a target laser installed under the stubby barrel. The bright red dot danced over the guard and stopped on his forehead.

The guard looked up. "Hey!"

Wilks shot him.

The guard collapsed in his chair. Wilks moved to arrange him so he looked like he had dozed off. The man would wake up in half an hour with one bitch of a headache, but otherwise should be fine.

He pulled the guard's bar code ID off and clipped it to his shirt pocket. It wouldn't fool a scanner if the thing tried to match his retinal patterns to it, but a human passerby would see that Wilks had a tag and probably think nothing of it. By the time the guard came to, things would be all over, one way or another. But just in case, Wilks bent and fed in the security system lock code virus he'd gotten. The computer terminal digested the code. If it did what it was supposed to do, it would infect the main system in this building. Nobody was going to be calling for outside help from here for a long time, not unless they went to a window and hollered for it. That didn't do anything for internal security, but Wilks figured he could deal with that. He was a Colonial Marine, by all the gods, and the day he couldn't handle some sloppy rent-a-cops, he'd shoot himself. He tucked the stunner back into its holder under his civilian jacket and smiled.

Time to go pick up his date for the prom.

The door to Billie's room slid open. Locked to the bed by the pressor field as she was, she couldn't do more than turn her head slightly.

"Wilks!"

"Yep. Pack your socks, kid. We're going for a ride." He moved to shut the pressor field off.

"How did you—? Why—?"

"We'll talk later," he said. "Right now we need to hustle along. I might have made a couple of enemies on the way in here and I don't think we have time to discuss it."

Billie rolled from the bed. She grabbed a robe and put it on. "I'm ready."

"What, you don't want to fix your hair or spray makeup on or something?" He grinned.

"I'd crawl over broken glass to get out of here. Go."

He turned, stuck his head out into the hall. "Okay. Clear."

She followed him into the hall.

They were doing pretty well until they got to the elevator's atrium. The tube's doors opened and two orderlies and two guards came out, moving fast. The guards had their stunners out and the orderlies both waved shockers.

Wilks never hesitated. He pulled a pistol from under his jacket and fired. Billie watched the little red dot his weapon projected bounce across the heads of the guards and orderlies. Three of them went down, their own weapons clattering quietly on the softfloor. The last orderly, a new one that Billie didn't know, rolled and came up in some kind of martial arts stance, facing Wilks.

Wilks tucked his weapon away. "Stay behind me, kid."

The orderly moved in and swung the shocker like it was a sword.

Wilks dodged to his left, slapped the man's outstretched arm to one side, and punched him low on the ribs.

The orderly grunted, made as if to turn and swing the shocker again, and Wilks kicked the man, hitting the side of his knee with the edge of his boot.

Billie heard the orderly's knee crack as something gave in it.

The orderly's leg folded and he dropped, but Wilks pulled his foot back and thrust it out again, smashing his heel into the man's head. The orderly flew sideways and slammed into the corridor wall.

"The stairs?"

"That way!"

Billie followed Wilks down the hall to the end. She glanced at the guards and orderlies as she went past. He'd taken them out almost instantly, without even working up a sweat.

"Why didn't you shoot the last one?" she asked as they reached the stairwell.

"Pistol's charge was depleted," he said. "Didn't have time to reload."

They went down two flights—her room was on four—then Wilks led her into the second floor.

"This isn't the ground—" she began.

"I know. They'll have the doors covered by now. We have to find another exit."

She followed him. Two was quiet, and they moved briskly, but not at a run. A tech glanced at them as they passed his station. Wilks smiled and nodded. "How's it going?"

The tech nodded back. Then his control board lit up, pulling his attention away from them.

"Move," Wilks said to Billie. "That'll be the alarm."

Billie ran. There was an emergency escape window at the end of the corridor, but it required a staffer to open it. "That's a coded lock," Billie said.

"Yeah, and I didn't have time to get all the exit numbers," Wilks said. "But I have a nifty little master key, courtesy of the Colonial Marine Corps armory."

Billie found out what he meant as Wilks slapped a wad of what looked like hair gel onto the lock mechanism, squeezed it three times, and waved her back.

Behind them, the tech started yelling. "Hey, you two! Get away from that window! I've called Security!"

The gel flashed bright blue and started to sizzle as if it were a piece of soypro on a too hot grill. The lock's stacked plastic casing bubbled and ran like water.

"Don't look at it," Wilks said. "It'll burn your eyes."

Billie turned to see the tech coming toward them. "Wilks!"

"No problem." He pulled his pistol from under his jacket and pointed it at the tech.

The tech stopped. He held his hands out in front of him defensively. "Hey, hey, take it easy!"

"Get the hell out of here," Wilks said.

The tech turned and ran.

Wilks smiled. "Amazing what even an empty gun can do, ain't it?" He put the weapon away.

The lock dripped into a puddle on the floor, plastic slag. Wilks kicked the window and the unbreakable clearflex swung outward on its side hinges. He leaned out, looked down.

"Too high to jump, we'd break an ankle."

He pulled a small device from under his jacket. Billie watched as he unfolded a pair of handles that jutted at right angles from the thing, a rounded square of black plastic the size of a big man's hand.

Wilks pointed the device at the windowsill and touched a control on it. It popped loudly. A thin line of white sprayed out from a nozzle on the end and hit the sill. He touched another control and loops of the line paid out. "One, two, three, four," he said. "Okay, it's set. Climb onto my back," he said.

Billie obeyed.

With that, he stepped up onto the sill, turned to face the hallway, and began to climb down the outside wall. The line coming out of the thing in his hands looked awful thin to support them. He said, "Hang on, I'm going to lean back."

She clutched him tightly with her arms and legs. Holding them with his arms outstretched, he began to walk backward down the wall.

"Spider gear," he said. "Don't worry, this line'll support ten men without breaking."

It took no more than a few seconds for them to reach the ground.

As she slid from his back, Billie said, "Where are we going?"

"Does it matter?"

She shook her head. No. It didn't matter. Anywhere was better than having her brain diced and scrambled.

The pair of them hurried away.

10

"This is Salvaje, bringing you word of the True Messiah. Listen to me, my fellow seekers.

"I know that which you lack.

"I know of your incompleteness.

"I have the answer.

"The True Messiah can make you into a Holy Receptacle. For it is in bearing the sons and daughters of the Messiah that you will find your salvation. Listen, and know that I speak only the truth! False prophets and false gods have brought our world to the brink of ruination! False gods ask that you worship them from afar, but they remain cold and aloof and sterile. The True Messiah will join with you! You can feel the True Messiah, touch the True Messiah, become one with the True Messiah! Do not allow yourselves to be misled any longer, my brothers and sisters! Throw off the chains and shackles of your oppression, get rid of the old and make room in yourself for the new!

"The True Messiah is coming, brothers and sisters. Soon the communion will be possible, and only those who open themselves to the ultimate experience will survive the coming devastation that man has brought upon himself! Prepare, prepare yourselves for the Coming! Listen for the call in your dreams! Listen and heed!"

"That's it, doc," Pindar said. "We're off the air."

Salvaje shrugged. "Install a new dish. My message must continue to go forth."

It was Pindar's turn to shrug. "It's your money."

"Money means nothing, fool. My parents left me millions, the faithful send me millions more. Soon it will be worthless, as all the works of man will become worthless on this fouled planet. The True Messiah is coming. Soon."

Yeah, right, Pindar thought. Maybe he should take some of Salvaje's about-to-be-worthless credits and spend a couple of days in Madam Lu's Pleasure House. Long as the Messiah was coming, no reason why Pindar couldn't come a little himself.

"Anything you say," Pindar said. What a shamoo this guy was. Crazy as a stepped-on roach. But as long as he paid, what the hell. He could dance naked in peanut butter for all Pindar cared. Two more like him and he could retire.

True Messiah. Yeah. Right.

11

Green and Red came out of the theater where their limo idled, fanning up grit from the street-level plastecrete road. The driver touched a control and the rear door slid up. Green and Red entered the limo and sank into form-cushions whose machineries adjusted to fit them perfectly. "To the tower," Red ordered the driver.

The limo lifted slightly and slid away on its cushion of air.

"What did you think?" Green asked.

"Did people really used to go out to gather and listen to noise like that?"

Green laughed. "So the history books say. Rock concerts, they called them. Actually attending them instead of sitting comfortably in their own living rooms and watching it on the holovee."

"What was the point?"

"It was for the totality of it—sight, sound, smells, feelings—a shared experience."

Red shook his head. "A wonder we ever got civilized. Risking death on the unregulated roadways to listen to that jarring shit. Also a wonder they all weren't deaf."

"Hey, times change. We don't wear animal skins and hit each other over the head with clubs anymore, either."

"Speaking of clubs . . . how is the intercept going?"

"As well as could be expected."

"That business with whatshisname? Massey? No problems there?"

Green nodded. "No. It's been resolved."

"What exactly happened? I didn't get the full details."

Green reached over to the limo's bar and punched in a code. After a moment, the dispenser delivered two bulbs of some frothy blue liquid. Green took one, handed the second to Red. "Ah. Not bad for a robot bar."

"You were saying . . . ?"

"Ah, yes. Well, one of the communications people slipped up. Sent an uncoded file to Massey's residence. Computer didn't catch it. Real snafu. That would have been bad enough, but unfortunately, Massey's son accessed the material."

"Stupid," Red said, sipping at his drink.

"Extremely so. The boy showed it to his mother. Neither of them understood the full implications, of course, but they got enough of it to possibly compromise the mission. Massey was in the shower when the message came through. When he got out, his wife started babbling about what they'd seen." Green squirted more of the froth into his mouth. "Massey really had no choice, not if he wanted to maintain security."

The boy smiled at his father. Massey returned the smile. Reached out and took his son's head gently in his hands. The move was so fast the boy didn't have time to be surprised. A hard twist. The snap of bone, the instant limpness.

His wife's eyes widened in horror, but before she could even begin to digest the impact of what she had seen, Massey reached her. A single, practiced move, fast, no suffering. It had to be done, but he had grown fond of them, after all. It was the best he could do. They deserved that much.

"God. That's cold," Red said.

"Yes. It was SOP, of course, but they had been married for six years. Even as cover, you'd think he'd want somebody else to do the wetwork on this one. But he did it himself. The company made sure the investigative team from the local police were friendlies and Massey's story about coming home to find them dead was accepted. The local law figures it as a robbery gone bad or a wilding by somebody clever enough to bypass building security."

"What about the communications tech, wasn't there something about that?"

Green finished his bulb, punched up another one. Looked at Red with one eybrow raised.

"No, I'm fine."

Green said, "Massey took him out. Fed the body into an industrial disposal unit that makes fertilizer. Guy is probably helping flowers and vegetables grow in half a dozen countries by now."

"Pissed Massey off, I imagine."

"Well, that's the strange thing. Not personally. Massey killed him cleanly, no torture or anything, if what I heard is correct. It was just another job to him."

"Buddha, that *is* cold. Guy was responsible for the death of my spouse and kid, I'd want him to twist a little in the breeze before I finished him."

"Yeah, but you aren't a sociopath. With Massey, the job is what comes first, last, and always. He doesn't care what he has to do to get it done."

Red pretended to shiver. "We got some kind of failsafe on this guy?"

"Of course. You don't think we'd let a man like that run around without a control, do you? He's got a cap of C9 circset into his hypothalmus, along with a beeper. He ever turns on us, somebody in Security only has to get within a klick of him and send a coded pulse—and blammo! Massey's head turns into a big bowl full of mushy brain salad."

"Good," Red said. "Guys like him are necessary, but I'll sleep better knowing we can take him out if need be."

"Not to worry," Green said. "It's our job to think of these things. We've got it covered."

Massey left the funeral of his wife and son, looking somber but playing a role. He didn't feel anything in particular about the loss. One less woman and child didn't mean anything, and while it was true he'd gotten used to them, he'd get used to them being gone, too. That's how it was.

Behind him, his control dogged his heels, blending skillfully into the passersby outside the crematorium. The man was good, but Massey had spotted him months ago. He hadn't let on, of course, because it was better to have the devil you knew tailing you than the one you didn't know.

Massey wanted to grin, but he kept his face neutral as he caught a walk moving down from the crematorium level toward the elevated p-mover that would take him home. The company thought it was real clever, injecting a bioexplosive into his system during a routine physical. Massey had more money than he knew what to do with, and with enough credits, you could get a very good doctor. The C9 had been easy enough to remove. The pinhead-sized capsule had also been easy to load into a high-pressure injector gun. When Massey had taken his "vacation" to the Amazon Preserve a few weeks ago, they'd followed him, of course. The Preserve was almost twenty square kilometers of "authentic" rain forest, bounded by high containment fields that kept the animals in and civilization out. Local wildlife included such pests as insects, some of which liked to bite. Massey's control had lost his insect repellent, or so he'd thought, and when the mosquitoes began eating at him, one of them had bitten him particularly hard. He'd slapped his hand over the wound but missed the flying bug. Because that particular bite wasn't from an insect at all.

And now, that deadly C9 capsule was lodged in

the control's brain. The day he sent a coded pulse to kill Massey would be most surprising. And, Massey thought, particularly fitting. He'd kept the locator they'd put in, slightly altered. He didn't give a damn if they knew where he was for now. When he decided he didn't want them to know anymore, the beeper would stop sending its signal as quickly as he could touch a button on his belt.

The doctor who'd performed the surgery was now part of a batch of steel forming a bridge suspension on Mars, if Massey's information was correct. No loose ends to tangle things.

As long as they let him do his job, Massey wouldn't have any problems with the company. But if they somehow lost faith, well, there was no point in being unprepared. Mistakes happened, even though he didn't make them. Always better to be ready than not.

The job this time was a big one, worth a lot of credits. For him the money was just a way to keep score. So far, Massey was winning big. There wasn't anybody else close. The company thought it was clever, but they didn't belong in the same class with him. He was the best. He intended to keep on being the best for a long, long time.

While Wilks was only a sergeant and theoretically subject to command by any officer of line rank, the truth of it was that on this mission, only Stephens was going to be giving him orders. They wanted him on this ship and so they'd bent over and handed him the soap. Wilks figured he might as well use it.

The first thing he did was program the ship's

computer with a personal override, using the last bit of the favor he was owed. He could come and go pretty much as he wanted. Getting Billie on the ship was easier than getting her out of the medical center. When Wilks accompanied two of the spare hypersleep chambers into the loading bay, Billie was inside one of them, the lid opaqued. Nobody even bothered to question him; he waltzed past the trooper leaning against the door with nothing more than a few words.

"Hey, Sarge," the man said. "You cuttin' it kinda thin, ain'tcha? It's only five minutes to log-on deadline."

"Live fast, die young—" he began.

"—and leave a good-looking corpse," the trooper finished. He laughed.

Wilks shook his head. A lot of civilians believed that Colonial Marines were all steely-eyed, boot-tough, deadly as a box full of Acturian wasps and as sharp as a room full of needles. The entertainment vids made it out that little, if anything, got past a trained marine. That they could chew up nails and pee thumbtacks. The truth was that a basic trooper was usually a kid, barely old enough to be depilating his peach-fuzz whiskers, and as big a sucker as any teenager. It didn't take a genius to pass basic military entrance exams. If you could find your way to the test site and spell your name for the computer, you were probably bright enough to get in. How long you stayed alive after that depended on how well the training took and how stupid your officers were, but the myth of the take-charge marines was just that, a myth.

Wilks walked the chambers past the trooper, floating them easily on their humming repulsors. Nobody expected anybody to smuggle a person onto a military ship *leaving* Earth. Coming back, maybe, a lot of folks wanted to get home out in the frontier worlds, but few people wanted to go bad enough to sneak into an outbound ship.

Stephens would shit a square brick when he found out, but by then it would be too late. You weren't gonna turn a star hopper around and make a fifty-light-year run back to Earth to drop off a stowaway. And on this mission, you weren't going to take any side trips along the way, either. Hell, they were going to be gone more than a year in realtime, exactly how long was classified, time they got back all kinds of things could have changed.

Wilks shrugged. Stephens was an idiot. A desk rider, no field experience at all, much less in combat. He must have pulled in some chits to get this assignment, and he didn't have the least idea of how dangerous it was. Jerking the plasma weapons was his first stupid mistake. He just wanted to show Wilks who was in command. Well. He'd live to regret it. Probably they'd all live to regret it.

Wilks jockied the chambers into the sleep compartment. He touched a button and the lid on Billie's fanned up.

"Okay, kid, here's what's happening. We're going to go to the monsters' planet. You and I, we know how these things are, but nobody believes us. Probably we won't be coming back."

Her face went white.

"I can still off-load you, you want."

A long moment hung suspended between them. Finally, she shook her head. "I've lived with them most of my life," she said. "Might as well face them and get it over with, one way or the other."

He nodded. "That's about how I see it. All right. I'm going to run the lines into this unit and put you to sleep. See you on the other end."

"Yeah."

He started to close the lid.

"Hey, Wilks?"

"Yeah?"

"Thanks for coming to get me."

He shrugged. "We got something in common, kid. We both should have died on Rim."

She nodded. "Yes. I know."

"Maybe we can kick some bug-ass before we go."

She nodded again. "I'll keep that thought."

"I hope you don't dream, kid."

"You, too."

He shut the unit and moved it into place. It only took a few seconds to attach the cryo lines and power supply. He triggered the unit and set the timer.

"Sleep well, kid."

With that, Wilks turned and walked away.

12

DATA SCAN—SINGLE READING ONLY

:. :: ..: ..: ...:: ...:... ::.. . ....: . . . ..:::.::

Authorized Personnel, REQUIRED CLEARANCE TS-1. Bionational Internal Memorandum 385769.1/ A, rev. II

Operation Outreach

Progress Report:

Government vessel *Benedict* lifted as scheduled April 5, 2092 0900, Toowoomba Military Launch Pad. Standard ship crew, plus Squads 1–4, Fox Platoon, Company Able, 1st. Extee Division, Second Colonial Marines. Colonel H. S. Stephens, Commanding. (See attached, personnel appendix, A.)

Bionational ship K-014 launched in pursuit, echo-lock, 4/5/92, 0900.5, full robotics & expendable EXP-series android crew under the command of Executive Assistant, Security, P. Massey.

(Joel—You know the general layout of this, but I'll recap some of the particulars you might have missed while you were on vacation. The alien life form the guv guys want is the big nasty, and naturally they'd like to score it for their own weapons program. Needless to say this would compromise our own profit structure were it to happen. With the recent Supreme Court decision on patentable life forms, vis-à-vis created versus discovered, we might spend ten years in the fucking legal system trying to unsnarl this mess. So up-levels decided that we should tail the feds to the homeworld [the location of which is so damned secret we couldn't pry it out of anybody for blackmail or money] and get as much info as we could.

And, of course, we don't want the feds to get their own specimen. This guy Massey has his orders and he's the best there is—he will do *what*ever it takes to stop them.

You probably have heard that Research got its hands on a guy salvaged from a cargo express, one of ours, fortunately, with one of the big nasty embryos wrapped around his face. The ship was cold, systems dead, but somehow this thing had kept him in stasis, almost as if he'd been in a sleep tank. Hell, that alone is worth a fortune if we can figure out how the hell it did it.

Anyway, both the crewman and the bug on his face were still alive, so they've been brought to the Houston labs for analysis. We're still way ahead of the feds on this, and already geared up for full-scale

testing. Start figuring out ways to spend your bonus, Joel, we're all going to get rich off this one.
That's it on the main deal. There's some other stuff
in this memo the psycho boys are concerned about,
so I'll let you get to it. See you for lunch Tuesday—
Ben.)

    FILE EXCERPT—MEDICAL—Case #23325
—Maria Gonzales
    Patient is a 24 y/o unmarried WD, WN female
Caucasian Hispanic, gravida 0, complaining of
nightmares. Physical examination unremarkable,
no known allergies, PH of illness limited to minor
URIs, occasional general malaise, broken L. fibula,
age 09. Laboratory workups, including SMA-60,
CBC, urinalysis, CAT scan, all within normal limits.
Patient has ten-year BC implant, no other medica-
tions.
    DR. RANIER: Maria, tell me about the dream.
    GONZALES: Okay, okay, I'm ridin' on the sub-
way in L.A. with my mother—
    RANIER: Your mother died several years ago?
    GONZALES: *Sí*, cancer. (pause) We're on the
Wilshire tube going into downtown and the tube
is empty except for us. (pause—laugh) That's the
really scary part, you know? I never seen an
empty subway car.
    RANIER: Go on.
    GONZALES: So all of a sudden there is this loud
noise, like something hits the roof of the subway.
Then a scraping sound.
    RANIER: Scraping?
    GONZALES: (agitated) Yeah, like something dig-

ging, you know? But it's also like fingernails on
metal. (pause) [Examiner's Note: Patient exhibits
increasing nervousness, marked diaphoresis, pal-
lor.]

Anyway, then the train stops and I realize that
something is trying to get in. Something bad. So
I say to my mother, Mama, come on, we have to
get out of here! But Mama, she just sits there and
smiles at me, you know? (pause)

Then all of a sudden the roof tears open like it's
paper and these *things* claw right into the car.
Like nothing I've ever seen, they are *bestia, como
se dice*? monsters, with teeth and big heads like
bananas. I reach for Mama to pull her with me,
only she turns into one of the things, her face
stretches! It is too horrible! And it feels so . . .
real.

Case #232337—Thomas Culp
DR. MORGAN: What happened after the holovee
came on?
CULP: Well, the room looked distorted, twisted,
somehow. (pause) Then something like, came
out of the set, but it stretched the usual stopping
place of the holograms. Like a fist shoving
through a sheet of flexiplast. And then the
thing—some kind of monster—it grabbed me. I
couldn't move a fucking muscle! It opened its
mouth, had teeth as long as my fingers, and
inside was like another mouth, smaller, and it
opened, and, oh, Buddha! It *got* me and I couldn't
fucking move!

Case #232558—T. M. Duncan

DUNCAN: So I was standing next to the flight attendant, hitting on her a little, and then I noticed she looked familiar, like somebody I knew.

DR. FRANKEL: Familiar? Did you recognize her?

DUNCAN: Yeah, it took a second. She looked like my mother. So I figure, well, I shouldn't be trying to come on to my mother, then all of a sudden, her chest tore open and this thing looked like a snake or a big eel with a lot of teeth comes out, spewing blood and all and flew, fucking *flew* out of her right at my face! (pause) That's when I woke up, and man, I was never so glad in my life to be awake. I stayed up for two days.

Case #232745—C. Lockwood

LOCKWOOD: It was wet, slick with blood, shiny, hard, like some kind of giant dick with teeth and it wanted to jam itself into me!

In his office, Orona waved his computer to hold and turned to his assistant. "Interesting. All from within a fifty-klick area, you said?"

"Yessir. And the medicomp has collected a dozen other similar reports."

"What have the patients in common?"

"High ratings on the Cryer Scale and at least double digits on the Emerson Empathic."

"Ah. And the descriptions are identical?"

"Virtually identical."

"Etiology?"

"Unknown. Best guess the medicomp can come

up with is some kind of telepathic or empathic projection. Perhaps it is how the things communicate among themselves and perhaps they are trying to communicate with us."

"Hmm," Orona said. He frowned. "Our data so far do not indicate that the aliens are particularly intelligent, per se. And we've kept a pretty tight lid on this thing. And yet here we are having a wave of spontaneous . . . connections of some kind. Why now? And why here on Earth? There aren't any aliens here."

The computer readout over the bed carried a full-ride telemetry chart. The patient, Likowski, James T., lay in the pressor grip of a state-of-the-art Hyperdyne Systems Model 244-2 Diagnoster. His EEG, ECG, myotonous level, basal metabolic rate, systems mitosis rates, and full blood counts flowed in continuous waves, words, and patterns across the monitor. Blood pressure, respiration, and pulse rate were noted and logged. The diagnoster checked and corrected the temperature so the patient was not too cold nor too hot. The IV shunt in his left femoral vein fed him the perfect liquid mix of nutrients for optimum health. An indwelling Foley catheter and rectal drain carried away wastes. The company had spared no expense when it came to taking care of this particular patient. The clean room was under Full Isolation Technique, and all visitors, medical or corporate, wore full osmotic surgical suits with their own air supply. The south wall was mirrored one-way, and observers could see the patient directly through the triple-paned glass should they choose. Seven doctors formed the main care team, with six medical technicians working in shifts as monitors, plus eighteen guards and a Full Alert status for the entire wing of the mediplex. Likowski, James T., was not going anywhere, nor was anybody not cleared coming to see him.

Two men stood in the observation room, watching the patient. One was tall, fair, almost bald, and brilliant. He was Tobias Dryner, M.D., T.A.S., Ph.D., and the team leader. The other man was shorter, darker, hairier, and not quite so smart, but hardly stupid. He was Louis Reine, also M.D., T.A.S., but without the extra doctorate in biosystems. Still, he was a company man and a vice president in the Biomed Division, which counted for a lot. Dryner was in charge of the patient, but Reine was in charge of the project.

"How is he?" Reine asked.

Dryner waved his hand over a motion-sensitive control. "Listen for yourself."

The audio came on: "—somebody tell me what the hell is going on? What happened? I want to talk to my wife. Goddammit, why am I here? I feel fine! Just a little stomachache is all, I don't need all this crap!"

Dryner waved his hand again and the sound faded. He moved to a Magnetoencephalo axial holographic viewer away from the glass wall and stroked a control. The screens lit with the MAH scan, showing a man at quarter-scale. The image blurred, shifted, and the skin and overlying muscles faded to show the internal organs. The image began to rotate slowly on its axis. Dryner touched another control. Under the man's ribs, inside the stomach, the alien fetus glowed a computer-enhanced green.

"Give me a full size on the CE image," Dryner ordered.

The alien grew fourfold.

"Interesting," Reine said, watching as the image turned. "No wonder he has a stomachache."

"It is drawing small amounts of blood from a minor artery, here," Dryner said, pointing at the image with one finger. "Otherwise, it's not damaging him. The rate of growth is phenomenal. If this were a human baby, it would come to term in a matter of days, not months. The physiology is impossible; it can't be getting enough nourishment from him. Must be consuming stores of some kind, either that or one devil of a miraculous metabolic system."

"Looks something like a kidney bean with teeth," Reine observed. "Ugly bastard." A pause. "Does the pilot know it's in there?"

"As such, no. He feels a certain amount of discomfort. We have done a neural stimulation to up his own endorphin and enkephalin levels so he isn't feeling pain, merely pressure. We didn't want to risk drugging the parasite with something that might harm its system."

"Good idea."

"Of course, there are some ethical questions as to whether we should inform the patient, given the ultimate prognosis."

"Your opinion?"

"Well, we are studying a new life form. Behavior of the host organism could be important. Perhaps certain hormonal secretions would be altered if the patient knew. The effect of such changes on the parasite could be detrimental or beneficial—it is hard to say. Offhand, the Chemistry boys guess that an increase in epinephrine would probably accelerate the thing's growth."

"You mean that if he knows the thing is going to chew its way out and kill him when it comes to term he'd probably be scared shitless and the bug would like that?"

"It is possible."

Reine sighed. "This thing could be worth *billions*, you know that? And the pilot is living on borrowed time. He has family?"

"A wife and two children."

"They'll get the company policy?"

"Of course."

"Then tell him."

Red wadded up the hard-copy security fax and tossed it in a hook shot at the disposal unit. The thin sheet of plastic hit the field as it fell toward the mouth of the unit and vaporized with a yellow flash and a thin *pop*!

The door to the office opened and Green entered. The two men smiled at each other. Green said, "Read the fax from Houston?"

"Oh, yeah."

"I put out a few rumors, very hush-hush. Quan Chu Lin's people practically came all over themselves to make offers. He's willing to give us top credit for an exclusive if this pans out even half as good as I painted it."

Red snickered. "His ass. We can bootstrap this sucker up so high that Quan Chu's money will look like pocket lint."

"That's what I figured. But it doesn't hurt to bait the waters a little. Get the sharks all roiled up and ready to bite each other for a taste of what we can feed 'em."

"Right about that, pal. I'm already shopping for a house on Maui. Maybe I'll buy myself a ship and do the Belt next summer, what do you think?"

Green laughed. "Why not? You'll be able to afford it. Me, I'm thinking about getting one of the new Hyperdyne 129-4s—the love slave model."

"A pleasure droid? Nice. If your wife will let you."

"What the hell, maybe I'll get her one, too. That way she'll be so busy, she won't even notice I'm gone."

Both men laughed. If this went the way it should, it would be as good as winning the lottery. At least.

13

Salvaje lay on the whore's bed, watching the naked woman hang panties on the line strung across the end of the room. The apartment was a basic-dole unit in a high rise and the hot wind from the open window rose from the floors below, carrying with it the stench of too many people crammed into too small a space. Cooked vegetables and sweat and broken toilets added their odors to the stink.

The naked whore was pregnant, seven months along, at least, and carrying a hefty fetus from her look. Her implant had failed and she'd decided to have the baby. There was a nice market for healthy ones; people came down from the north who wanted a newborn without having to bear it themselves. She could get six months pay, easy. Besides, she knew there were some men who found something appealing about pregnant women. Not what he found appealing, but something.

Salvaje stared at her, an eagle watching a tasty mouse.

The whore finished hanging her underwear up. She turned toward him. He was also naked.

"*Dios*, is that all you gonna do, is watch me? You don' wan' to, you know, let me *do* something for you?" She formed a circle with her hand and moved it as a man would if masturbating. Then she touched her lips with a fingertip, her pubic hair with the other hand.

"No," he said. "I want to watch you. And I want you to tell me about how it feels to have a life inside of you."

The whore shrugged. "It's your money."

"Yes, it is. Come here."

She moved toward him on the bed, sat. He put one hand on her belly, under a pendulous breast. "You know the miracle of carrying life," he said. "It must be wonderful."

She laughed. "Oh, yeah, it's won'erful, okay. My back hurts, my feet swell all up, I got to go pee twelve, fifteen times a day and night. The baby kicks me so hard it almost knocks my pants off sometimes. Won'erful."

"Tell me more," he said. He felt himself stirring. Yes. She carried nothing more than a bastard whose father was a paying customer—he doubted the whore even knew or cared who had put it into her— but even so, she was closer to *knowing* than he was. He envied her, and until the Messiah arrived, this was as close as he could come to finding out how it felt.

She grinned at his erection. "Ah," she said, misunderstanding. "You want to know what it's like, okay, I tell you. I make it good for you. The best."

Later, as Salvaje reached the door to his own apartment, Pindar the technician slogged through the rain toward him.

"Where have you been, I've been waiting here almost a fucking hour!"

"I'll pay you for your time, don't worry."

"My time is exactly what I *am* worried about," Pindar said. "Like, where I am going to be spending it if I get caught doing this? You are getting kind of famous, you know. The G-boys have a monitoring team working to find you. Something is going on, something more than the usual sweep for somebody doing pirate 'casts. What are you into, here, Salvaje?"

Salvaje opened the door and the two of them moved in out of the rain. "They fear me," he said. "Because of my message."

"Ratshit," Pindar said. "There are a hundred like you breaking into the nets every day. They preach about everything from pure water to group sex being the way to God. The TCC doesn't work up a sweat trying to run them down, but somehow *you* rate a full-scale investigation. They want you bad. I have been questioned."

"And you told them . . . ?"

"Nothing, you think I'm stupid? They can bury a man so deep nobody can find him again. But I want

to know what I'm into here. Why are you so important?"

"I told you, my message."

"Listen—"

"No, *you* listen! You are nothing, you are an
insect! The Messiah is coming! I am a tool of the
incarnate god and I will not be slowed by such as
you. If you need something to fear, then fear me,
technician. I have eyes and ears everywhere, and if
you fail to serve me, there will be no hole deep
enough to hide you from my retribution, do you
understand?"

Pindar shook his head and started to turn away.

Salvaje grabbed him by the shoulders, spun him
around, and shoved him so hard the man fairly flew
backward to slam into the wall.

"Fuck!"

"If you do anything to thwart my broadcasts I will
see to it that you die in a way more horrible than
anything you can possibly imagine! Do you understand?"

The technician's eyes went wide with sudden
fear. "Yeah, yeah, okay, okay! It's just getting dangerous, that's all I wanted to say. It'll cost—"

"I care not what it costs! The time is almost upon
us. The message must continue. My organization is
formed, I have hundreds, thousands, who do my
bidding without knowing who I am, but I need the
message to go forth!"

Pindar stared at Salvaje. Salvaje felt nothing but
contempt for the technician. He was weak, cow-
ardly, fearing of things that had no meaning. The

Messiah would have no use for such as this. None at all.

Onboard the Bionational ship K-014 somewhere in the nowhen and nowhere of hypershift, Massey spoke to his crew of androids. They were experimental models with short lifespans and were definitely expendable. The company had made up just this one batch with their particular modifications, and if word got out how they'd been altered, the company would have to do some fast singing and dancing to explain it. The androids could have been programmed with the mission before leaving Earth, but Massey was not one to take chances. By keeping it to himself, risk was minimized. You couldn't pry an answer from somebody who didn't have it, and Massey could snuff his own life if he were ever captured, leaving only questions.

Massey stood in front of the holographic wall, images of the government transport ship *Benedict* floating just behind him. "All right," he said, "here is our target. There are five main entrances, three emergency hatches, nine service portals, counting the main bay. Our primary entrance will be the number one aft hatch, here." He pointed at the shimmering image. "Secondary entrance, in the event of blockage, will be the number two forward hatch here. Tertiary entrance will be the number one emergency hatch, here."

The androids watched, not speaking.

"You will be armed with splatterguns for soft targets only. While these are trained marines, we will have surprise on our side—they are not expecting us. Plus we have other ammunition in our arsenal.

"The crew and marine survivors will be kept alive until we reach our destination, where we will likely have further use for them. Access the tactical computer for your individual assignments, full data base assimilation by 0400 tomorrow. That's all."

The android crew sat, still unspeaking. They were, Massey knew, up to the task. There was some risk of failure, a tang of spice, as it were, but Massey did not doubt that he could overcome the slight chance. He had worked out the plan in the finest details, he had covered everything. He was the best there was at this kind of thing, and he would succeed. That was the point, really. Not the money he was paid, not the fortunes the company would make, not the deaths of the androids or the other crew. The thing was, as always, the challenge.

This was perhaps the trickiest job he had ever taken on, and he intended that it come out as smooth as machine lube on polished crystal. Massey had but one goal, the same as it had always been: to win. Anything less would not do. Better to die than to lose.

He grinned. He wasn't ready to die yet. So he wouldn't.

Onboard the transport ship *Benedict* when the marines came out of hypersleep, the surprise took a while to filter through to Stephens. Wilks wondered if the man would have noticed at all had not the head count come out one too many.

The squads picked it up right away—they all

knew each other—so Billie stood out for them. But Stephens was a chair jockey; he had a list of his troops somewhere and couldn't yet identify them by names or faces.

Wilks watched the colonel frown at the numbers on his flat screen.

"Sergeant Wilks," Stephens said.

"Sir."

"I've got a plus-one on my roster."

Wilks thought about letting it slide, just to see, but he'd find out sooner or later. No point in putting it off forever. "Yes, sir. I brought an extra person, sir."

Stephens blinked as if still groggy from the chamber. "What?"

"Sir. A civilian expert on the aliens."

"What?! Are you crazy? This is a top-secret military mission, Sergeant! I'll have your butt court-martialed! They'll put you in a pit so deep it'll take the ceiling light a year to get to you!"

Wilks could feel some of the marines smiling, but he didn't look to see which ones. He said, "Yes, sir."

Stephens looked at the troopers, and Wilks knew he was trying to figure out which one he didn't know. Trying and failing. He stalled. "I told them you were unreliable. You could have screwed up this entire mission, mister! G-ship balances are critical at light-year jumps! An extra person could have thrown us a parsec off while in hypershift!"

"I balanced the weight, sir. I dumped fifty kilos of that raspberry-flavored shit from stores just prior to lift off."

Behind Wilks, Bueller whispered to Easley: "Too bad. I liked that raspberry-flavored shit myself—"

"Shut up," Easley whispered back.

"I am going to throw you in the brig and scramble the code," Stephens said, still looking for who didn't belong. Since they were all still in robes over their sleeptites, there was nothing to give Billie away; a robe also covered her hospital clothes. As stupid as it was, Wilks was amused that Stephens couldn't make her. Confirmed his opinion of the colonel.

Time to flex a little muscle. "Sir, you could do that. But perhaps GENstaff might be interested in knowing why the CO didn't discover the stowaway before lift-off, given that a final inspection is part of the CO's duties. Sir."

Wilks knew this was Stephens's first field command and that he did not want anything to mar it, make him look bad. Now was the time for his pitch. "Sir, if I might have a more private word?"

Stephens was pissed, no doubt about it, but he had to be working the angles, trying to see how this was going to look once he got home. Since Wilks wouldn't bet a bent demicred that he was going to get home, that didn't much matter to him, but Stephens wouldn't be thinking like that.

Stephens turned and moved toward the aft wall.

Wilks followed him. Behind them, the squads stood at parade rest, watching and trying to hear.

When they were far enough away, Stephens turned. His fury was unabated. "This better be goddamned good, Wilks."

"Sir, if you could show that *you* were responsible for taking on a civilian expert, then there wouldn't be any problem. You buried a CMA code in your log, didn't you?"

Stephens glared at Wilks. If eyes were lasers, Wilks would have been a crisp brown spot sizzling on the deck by now. Wilks hadn't been able to check Stephens's CO log, the access commands for that were beyond his abilities as a computer break-in artist, but he was fairly certain that the colonel had installed a CMA—cover my ass—code so that it was dated near the start of the mission. This was SOP among nervous officers, a simple piece of insurance that could sit there unused, unless something wonky came up. It was easy enough. Log entries were all automatically timed and dated; a CMA code was some innocuous piece of input, usually a phrase that was related to whatever data were going in, but stilted in such a way that it didn't quite fit. If a situation arose that was unforeseen, the officer could use the code to cover himself by entering new data and then referring back to the phrase, as if it had been put there in anticipation of such happenings. Any lengthy phrase could be made to say almost anything a bright computer wanted later, and the officer could swear he or she had known about it in advance and covered it, but in code, so as to keep it secret from prying eyes.

Suppose your cook was stealing supplies and selling them on the black market. You came up a couple hundred kilos short when you did inventory. This would make a CO look bad. But if there was a code that said something like "Suspect that cook is stealing supplies, will allow him to continue to build case," then you knew you were on top of it, and what you did was justified in the interests of being certain. It was an old trick, one that shouldn't fool anybody who'd been in the service more than ten minutes, but one bad officers still used. Wilks was certain Stephens would have done it.

"Why should I help you?"

"Because, sir, you'd be helping yourself. I'll put the rumor out that our . . . discussion here is part of a clever subterfuge you worked up, for reasons of your own having to do with some kind of secret military business about which they don't want to know. When we get back to Earth, you're covered and I'll go quietly wherever you want me to go."

Stephens considered it. He didn't like it, Wilks could see that, but he was thinking about his future and that was the most important thing on his agenda. "All right," he said. "Trot him out and let me see him."

"See her," Wilks said.

"Where did you get her?"

"I broke her out of a mental hospital. Sir."

14

Wilks sat next to Billie in the mess hall as they picked at the reconstituted eggs and hard biscuits of the microwaved Ship Meal Packet. Billie had eaten worse, but not recently.

"You okay, kid?"

She nodded. "Yeah. A few aches and stiffness, but otherwise all right."

Wilks ate a bite of his too yellow scrambled eggs. As he did, Billie glanced around the room. First squad sat bunched in twos or threes at tables nearby. There were eight of them, and Billie had made a point of matching the names and faces within a few hours of awakening. Five men and three women. The women were Blake, Jones, and Mbutu. The men were Easley, Ramirez, Smith, Chin, and the tall blond one, Bueller. There were three other squads of Colonial Marines, thirty-two troopers in all, plus a skeleton ship's crew of nine. Counting herself, Wilks and the officer in charge, Stephens, that meant a total of forty-four people going to challenge an entire planet of the aliens.

There had been five times that many people on Rim, and only a single nest of the things there. And she and Wilks had been the only survivors. Not very encouraging.

She couldn't say how long she'd sat there blanked out, remembering, but Wilks pulled her back to the present. "I'm going to go shower," he said. "You going to be okay here?"

"Yes. I'm fine."

After Wilks left, Billie sat and stared at her cold food. The mess hall was not a large room. The other conversations were audible from time to time.

"Man, Stephens had a bug up his nose, hey?" Easley said.

"He's a groundpounder, what do you expect?" Chin said.

"Me, I think our sergeant is more than a little bit off the beam," Ramirez put in. "A few minutes short of an hour, if you know what I mean."

Blake pulled out a deck of cards. "Anybody for a little poker? Chin? Easley? Bueller?"

"Not me," Easley said. "I got walk-through duty. Keep a seat warm for me, though. Back in an hour." He stood and moved toward the door. There was a headset with throat pickup mike set into a recess there, and Easley took the com unit and slipped it on, nestling the earpiece into his left ear. "Watch Bueller, he deals from the bottom."

"Your ass, needledick," Bueller said.

"Big enough so your mother loves it," Easley said. He laughed and left.

Billie stared at her food. These guys did not know what they were up against, no matter what Wilks had told them. It was one thing to hear somebody tell it, another to face the things, to *feel* them.

Not something Billie wanted to do again, even though she knew she had to do it. Amazing how the memories came back. She felt as if she were a kid again. A scared kid.

Easley strolled down the corridor, the faux gravity making it feel almost like a walk through a building on Earth, maybe a bit lighter. He passed the first check station, flashed his lume into a couple of recesses the overheads didn't show, then spoke into the com, directly to the computer's recorder. "This is Easley, T. J., on walk-through duty, 1230 hours." He rattled off his serial number, the ship coordinates, and his findings: "Inspection so far reveals patent hull, no stress cracks, no animal or insect manifestations."

Yeah, and no runs, no hits, no errors.

This sucked, having to walk inspection. What did they make robots for? The things could see better, move faster, and they didn't care if they were missing a good poker game while they did it, either. This was make-work, Stephens was a by-the-tape commander, and next thing you knew he'd have them shining their boots and practicing close-order drill. Stupid.

Easley moved along, shining his light into dark

spots along the corridor, finding what he expected
to find: nothing.

As he reached the aft quarter of his intended
loop, he heard something. A faint, voicelike sound.
He stopped. Sounded like it was coming from the
number four cargo hold.

Easley hesitated. All walk-through was supposed
to do was check the hull sandwich, not go poking
into closed compartments. Whatever it was, it
wasn't his business.

The sound came again. Almost like somebody
talking very quietly.

Could be some kind of transfer echo, Easley
thought. That happened sometimes. An air-condi-
tioning vent picked up a voice on one part of the
ship and transferred it somewhere else. The dense
plastics and metals used on a no-frills military vessel did some strange things with vibrations. Easley
remembered once being able to hear guys singing
in the shower halfway around a T-2 troop ship.

Yeah, that's probably what it was. Besides, he was
only supposed to do the hull, that was the drill,
nothing else. He started to walk on.

There it was again.

Well, what the hell, he was curious. Might as well
check it out, it wasn't like he had an appointment
anywhere or anything.

He moved to the sliding door to the cargo area,
thumbed the open pad.

"—*Benedict* to K-014, telemetry data upload-
ing—"

Somebody was talking, no doubt about that, Easley heard. He moved through the cargo area,

rounded one of the stack-boxes. Well, would you look at this. It wasn't an echo transfer, there the guy was, right in front of him. He had his back turned, Easley couldn't ID him.

"Hey," Easley began, "what are you—?"

That was as far as he got. The figure spun and then Easley felt a tremendous pain lance his throat, as if somebody had stabbed him there.

"Uhhh!" Easley sucked air, felt it impeded, reached for his neck. Felt his hands touch something wet and hot extending from his throat. As big around as his thumb, all the way through!

He tried to yell, found his voice wouldn't work. All he could manage was a wordless groan. The sound turned to a gurgle as warm liquid ran down his damaged windpipe. "Mmmm! Aaughh!"

He recognized the man who had done it, but he couldn't say the name.

Something slammed into his solar plexus, and what air Easley had was stolen. He . . . couldn't . . . breathe!

He bent forward, pulling at the spike through his neck. It started to move, despite the slippery fluid coating it.

Then something smashed his head and it all went gray.

On the *Benedict*'s bridge the tech monitoring ship's systems cursed. The pilot, busy feeding corrected stellar coordinates into his console, glanced over. "What?"

"I show the aft number two interior lock open."

The pilot glanced at his own board. "Yeah, I see it."

The tech said, "Is there a drill scheduled? Nobody told me."

"That's a negative. Nothing on the board. Call the lock and find out what the hell is going on."

"Copy." The tech spoke into his throat mike. "This is Systems Control. Who opened the inner door there?"

The tech waited. Nobody responded.

"I say again, this is Systems Control. Respond, whoever is in lock A-2."

Nothing.

"Where is the camera?" the pilot asked.

The tech's hands danced over the controls. "I'm not getting a signal from the monitor in the lock."

"Dammit! Call the jarhead commander and find out what's going on!"

"Colonel Stephens, this is Systems Control, do you read?"

The pilot looked at his own board. "Buddha. Where the hell is he?"

"Maybe he's taking a shower, got his unit off," the tech said. "Hello?"

"What?"

"The hatch is cycling closed."

"Well, that's something. Stupid marines ought not to be playing with the hardware—"

"Uh-oh."

The pilot looked at his board, saw the source of the tech's new worry. The outer hatch cycling open.

"I don't know what's going on, but I'm going to stop it right now," the pilot said. "We've got a corrective burn coming up and I sure as hell don't need a hole in the barn wall when it happens. I'm going to override and close that sucker."

"Affirmative that," the tech said.

The pilot worked a control.

"Uh-oh," the tech said.

Both their screens showed that the hatch cover was still open.

"Somebody is going to be in real deep shit," the pilot said.

"Got an EVA," the tech said. "Hull pickup is still working." The tech switched on the exterior lamps. "Look."

The image of a spacesuited figure tumbled slowly in their field of view, brightly lit by the outside floods.

"Who the hell is that? What is he doing out there?"

Easley awoke.

What?

His throat!

He reached for it, found the ribbing of the suit with the gauntlet. He was in vac, zero gee, in a suit. Fluid from his wound floated up and clouded the suit's visor. Frantically, Easley tried to speak. To call for help.

"Ungh! Gaugghh!"

He couldn't make words.

He twisted his head, trying to see where he was.

There, there was the ship, but it was moving away!

He reached for his tool belt, looking for a squirt can, to push himself back to safety.

The tool belt was empty.

Panic gripped him in cold fingers. He coughed, choking from the wound in his throat. He was going to die!

No, no, wait, wait! They'd spot him. You couldn't go EVA without the proximity detectors seeing you. The lights were on, they knew he was here. They'd send somebody out for him, it would only be a couple of minutes at the most. He'd be okay. They could patch him up—

Something drifted in front of his face. At first his obscured vision wouldn't let him see just what it was. He pulled his head back as far as it would go, blinked several times. A small cylinder, about the size of a roll of quarter-credit coins, floated up against the plate. He slowly turned and the ship's lights angled across his faceplate, giving him a better view. The cylinder had a digital counter on it—

The coldness stabbed Easley all the way to his bones.

The cylinder was an AP grenade. And the flashing numbers on it were going down.

Five . . . Four . . . Three . . .

"Nnnooo!" Finally, he managed a word.

It didn't help. He was going to—

The hull pickups polarized as the blast of light washed over them and the spacesuited figure shattered soundlessly into fragments. Body fluids crystallized almost instantly in the cold vacuum, spraying into frozen, colorless, gauzy clouds against pinpoints of distant stars in the blackness. Pieces of suit and flesh tumbled away, some hit the ship's armor harmlessly.

On the bridge, the tech said, "Oh, man."

The pilot merely nodded. What a way to die. He wondered if the guy knew what hit him. He hoped not.

15

In Houston, Likowski, James T., had been given the news.

There was a *thing* growing inside of him. Sooner or later, it was going to pop out of him like a birthday surprise, eating its way free, and when it was born, he would die. So long, Jim. Nice knowing you.

Simple.

He had been numb with the shock, and when that had worn off, the fear had claimed him. He was going to die.

Dr. Dryner and Dr. Reine were sorry, but there was nothing they could do.

"Can't you kill it? Cut it out?"

"Not without killing you," Dryner said. "It's a very tenacious life form." He was calm, as if he

117

were discussing the weather. Easy for him. He didn't have a monster growing in his belly.

"Oh, God."

The two doctors stood next to where Jim sat on the bed, both of them safely wrapped in cleansuits. An armed guard stood just behind them, also suited. He had a handgun holstered on his right hip.

"So I'm like an incubation chamber for this thing." It was not a question.

"Yes. Listen, if it is any consolation, your wife will get the full insurance. She'll be taken care of."

"Oh, right, *that* makes me feel a whole lot better." The sarcasm made the words bitter. Now that he knew what it was, he was sure he could feel the thing moving inside him.

Getting ready to rip his guts out.

No!

"Hey!" he said, putting his hands over his belly. He suddenly stood up next to the bed, made himself sway a little.

The doctors showed concern.

"Likowski? Are you all right? James?"

"Telemetry, what's going on?"

They weren't worried about him, he realized, but about their pet creature inside him. Damn them.

"I—something's happening!" He began to jerk, as if losing muscular control. Yeah, something was happening, all right, but not what they thought. He snatched his arm away from Reine, slapping the man's face in the process. He danced in a little half circle, shivering.

Reine backed away. "Dammit!"

Come on, come on, get the guard over here!

"Give us a hand!" Reine ordered.

Good.

The guard, a burly man, wore his sidearm in a snatchproof rig, an old-style Delrin thumb-break strap keeping it safe in the holster. Jim knew about them, he'd done a tour in the Street Guard, they'd used the same kind of gear. If it had been a military hand ID unit, he wouldn't have a chance, but it wasn't, the guard was wearing gloves and the more sophisticated rig needed a bare hand for a print to register.

The guard grabbed him by the shoulders and Jim let himself be pushed toward the bed, where they could trigger the pressor field to hold him in place. "I'm—it's okay, it's gone now." He pretended to relax. "Thanks for the help," he said to the guard. He smiled.

When the guard smiled back from behind his clear faceplate, Jim reached down, rotated the thumb-break safety, popped the crow-tab, and pulled the gun from the holster. The weapon was a 4:4mm softslugger with a hundred-round magazine. The safety was in the trigger, it only had to be pulled. Jim twirled the pistol in his hand, pointed it at the guard, and fired.

Five rounds of hypervelocity softslugs tore into the man. The bullets were designed to mushroom on impact, to expend all of their energy on a human target without passing through the body. The entrance holes were small—the bullets would punch through class III body armor—but the missiles then expanded and dug craters the size of a baby's fist through vital organs.

The guard fell. He wasn't going to be getting up on his own.

Dryner and Reine turned to run, but Jim gave them two rounds each between the shoulder blades and they tumbled.

A siren hooted, over and over.

Jim turned to the mirrored wall and let go a dozen shots. The plastic chipped and shattered and he threw himself at it, falling through into a room with techs and more guards digging for weapons.

Jim came up, spraying the room. Men screamed and fell.

He paused long enough to dig out a spare magazine from the belt of a fallen guard, jamming it into the waistband of his hospital shorts. He ran.

Guards spilled into the hall. Jim shot them.

He found a keycard on a dead one next to the exit, waved the card at the scanner, and flattened himself against the wall as the door slid open.

Two guards came through, guns out. Jim emptied the last twenty shots in his softslugger into them. They fell like their legs had disappeared.

He ejected the empty magazine, snapped in the fresh one. Ran.

He made it to a building exit. Shot three unarmed people who tried to stop him. They didn't matter.

Outside it was hot, damp, the air had an oily stink, but that didn't matter, either. He was free.

He ran into the street. Behind him somebody yelled. He spun, fired a couple of shots, missed.

The softslugs spattered on the synstone walls like drops of dark paint dropped from a great height.

A hovercar fanned to a dragstop, almost hitting him.

Jim ran to the car, pointed the weapon at the woman driving. "Out!" he screamed.

The woman obeyed, terror in her eyes. He waved her away. She was a civilian, no reason to shoot her. He leapt into the car. Pulled the dragstop up, shoved the leaners on full. The car blew dust up, fanned away.

A round of hardball spanged against the car's body. A second tore through the canopy, but missed him by half a meter. Air whistled through the exit hole.

The car picked up speed. He had time to notice that the seats were vat-grown leather, a rich brown color, with the right smell. The control panel was real wood, burled and polished smooth.

They wouldn't catch him now.

At the complex's gate, a guard stepped out in front of the onrushing car, waving frantically for it to stop. She didn't have her gun out.

Jim ran the woman down. The car's front collision plate dented from the impact, the car slowed a little, but kept going. The gate was open.

The expressway entrance was ahead. It led through the city, to the suburbs. Where he and Mary had lived, before this happened. Where Mary was.

A police fanner rumbled into view behind him as he merged with the expressway traffic. The fanner flashed its lights. Vehicles moved aside to allow it room.

Jim put his car into full-speed mode. The whistling from the hole in the canopy went up in pitch, grew louder. The car was a hot machine, expensive, built for speed as well as looks, and quickly passed the speed limit.

The fanner was built to chase such cars, however. It gained on him.

The fanner would be armored. The softslugs wouldn't stop it.

They cranked up their hailer: "Stop your vehicle immediately! Houston Traffic Police!"

Jim laughed. What were they going to do? Give him a ticket? Take away his license?

The fanner pulled up level with him on his right. They were alone on the expressway now, the other traffic having dropped back or moved off to surface streets.

Jim looked at the two cops. In a second they would pull ahead of him and try to block him.

He had nothing to lose.

He shoved the control stick to the right. The car turned, slammed into the fanner. The traffic unit was larger, but he had inertia on his side. They veered toward the guardrail.

The fanner's driver tried to compensate, but too late. His engine screamed with power as he unleashed it, but the fanner dug into the rail, hit a support post, spun.

The impact slammed the fanner back into Jim's stolen car. Now both vehicles spun. Jim shoved his control forward, opened the drive fans to full again.

Slewed. Almost lost it and flipped, but powered out of the spin. Wobbled, then the gyros caught and held the car steady.

Not so lucky the cops. The fanner caught a rear blade on the rail, shattered the tough black plastic fan. Shards of jet sprayed. The loss of lift dropped the rear of the fanner. The friction flipped the vehicle like a man spins a coin on a table. The fanner smacked into the rail again, bounced, tumbled, and went over the side. It fell twenty meters and went through the roof of a fast-food shop.

Jim kept going.

He reached the resiplex where Mary was. Killed the fans. Got out, went to the building. Shot the guard who rose to stop him at the elevators.

The door to their unit opened. Mary's eyes went wide.

"Jim! I—they said—you were dead!"

"Not yet."

She reached out and they embraced. Hugged.

Down the hall, somebody yelled. "There he is!"

Of course. They would know where he lived.

"Good-bye, Mary. I just wanted to say that."

He twisted away from her, sprayed the hall. The slugs flattened on the walls as he waved the gun back and forth, ricocheted away, screaming almost like some tortured animal might.

"Aahh!" somebody said as they caught one.

"I have to go now, Mary. I love you."

It all felt unreal to him. Mary stood there, hands pressed to her face, as he turned and sprinted away.

He headed for the roof. Somebody would have a flier there he could steal.

Feet pounded behind him as he reached the roof. He found a flier with a card in the drive control. Smashed the door open. Got in. Lifted.

Bullets chewed at the flier, but he was off.

Where would he go? It didn't matter. He pointed the nose at the sun, shoved the power lever full on. Flew away. They'd never catch him. He was free. Free. Free.

But there was something large and ugly suddenly sitting in the seat next to him, something dark and monstrous. And his stomach started to hurt—

Likowski, James T. Lying on the pressor bed. His stomach hurt. Tears flowed from the outer corners of his eyes, ran down his face, pooled in his ears. The two doctors stood over him in their cleansuits, peering through protective faceplates, eyebrows raised. There was a guard behind them, but he wore no weapon. There was no need, and they would never have let anyone with a gun in here. Never.

All in his mind, Jim knew. A fantasy of escape that could not be.

The pain in his stomach increased, a sharp burning, as if a hot knife were being driven into him.

"Aahh!"

An amplified voice said, "Vital signs in flux, doctors! Heart rate up, blood pressure rising, myotonus pushing the limit."

Jim glanced at his own body. His bare flesh *bulged* suddenly, just under his sternum. The pain was incredible.

It was time!

Dryner reached out and touched the bulge on the patient's solar plexus. The skin immediately flattened. "Amazing," he said.

Reine said, "Get in here with the catch net!"

The man on the table screamed, a primal noise that set Reine's teeth on edge. Lord, what a sound! "Hurry up with that damned net!" Reine turned back toward the man on the table.

"Won't the pressor field hold it?" Dryner asked.

"I doubt it. Insufficient mass. Where the hell is the net?"

The amplified voice said, "Nobody is suited up out here, it'll take a minute—"

"This shouldn't be happening yet," Dryner said. "Our term estimates—"

"—were obviously wrong," Reine finished. "If somebody doesn't come through the lock in thirty seconds with that catch net I will fire the entire fucking staff!" he yelled. "None of you will ever work in this field again!"

To Dryner, Reine said, "This specimen is invaluable. Nothing can be allowed to happen to it, nothing!"

He leaned over the struggling man.

The patient screamed again. His flesh erupted, burst outward, and the alien's blind, toothed head came forth.

"Good God!" Dryner said, leaning away from it.

Reine, fascinated, leaned closer. "Why, look at it! Fascinating—"

"Here's the net!" somebody said.

Reine turned to look.

"Fuck!" Dryner said. "Look out!"

Reine twisted back toward the patient. Too slowly.

The thing shot out of the dying man. Impossibly fast, like a thick, armored, blood-slick arrow. It hit Reine's cleansuit, bit the osmotic material, and chewed through the heavy substance as if it were tissue paper.

Reine, horrified, stared at the thing.

"Bring the net!" Dryner yelled. "Hurry!"

Now Reine sought to bat at the thing, but its head was already inside the protective suit. He felt it reach his skin.

"Ahh! It's biting me! Get it off!"

Dryner reached for the thing's tail, but his gloved hands slipped on the gore that coated it. It moved away from his touch, pulling more of itself into Reine's suit.

"Help! Help me! Aahh! Oww!"

The tech with the catch net grabbed Reine, but the doctor twisted away from him in panic. In his fear, he tried to run from what was attacking him.

The inner hatch had not cycled closed. Reine ran for it.

"Louis, no! You'll breach isolation!"

Reine was beyond hearing, beyond caring. The only thing that mattered was that this *thing* was eating into him, burning like molten metal!

"Stop him!" Dryner yelled.

The tech reached for Reine, missed. Got in Dryner's way. They tangled, fell.

Dryner scrambled up, in time to see Reine clear the inner lock, lunge for the outer lock's control.

"Freeze the door controls!" Dryner yelled.

Too late. Reine pounded on the emergency override. The outer door slid wide. He staggered out into the hall.

Isolation was blown.

Dryner ran after his boss, yelling for him to stop.

"Kill it, kill it!" Reine screamed.

The security guards pulled their guns.

"No!" Dryner yelled. "Don't shoot it!"

The guard looked confused.

"Shoot him in the head!" Dryner commanded.

Now the guards really looked puzzled.

"Do it!"

The guards didn't move. Reine started to run. He might damage the specimen!

Dryner moved. He grabbed a gun from the nearest guard, who didn't try to stop him. Raised the weapon. Dryner had been a champion pistol shot while in college. Could have gone to the Olympics if he'd worked at it harder. He hadn't fired a gun in years, but the old reflexes were still there. Reine was only ten meters away. Dryner put the red dot square on the middle of the fleeing man's cleansuit helmet, took a deep breath, let part of it out, held it, and squeezed the trigger carefully, so as not to pull his aim off. At twelve meters now, it was an easy shot.

Reine's head shattered. He fell.

Dryner lowered the weapon. "Sorry, Louis," he said. "But you were the one who said how valuable the alien was. We can't chance hurting it."

The guards and techs stared at him.

"Now," he said, "bring the catch net."

He still had the gun. They all moved very fast.
And in the end, they didn't even need the net.
Apparently the thing liked where it was. Good. That
made it even easier.

16

Pindar the holotech lay on a table with a pressor field holding him down. He could turn his head, but that was about it. Since he was a tech, he knew how a pressor field worked, knew also it was impossible for an unaugmented man to break free of one. Even an expendable android built for short-term bursts of strength would have trouble with a functional pressor field, maybe it could escape, maybe not. That was an academic question, in any event. *He* wasn't going anywhere.

Two men in pearl-gray uniforms stood near the table, looking down at Pindar. The uniforms identified them as TIA, members of the Terran Intelligence Agency, and that was bad. Very bad. T-bags didn't stir themselves for menial crimes, only those that might threaten the security of the planet itself.

Pindar was in trouble, *aprieto mucho*, and he knew exactly why. Salvaje. After the last time with the man, Pindar had done some investigating on his own. He had stumbled across something he shouldn't know, something so terrifying he wanted to block it from his memory. And now, TIA had stumbled across him. He had known it was coming and he knew there was no way out.

One of the agents, a kindly looking man who could be somebody's grandfather, smiled at Pindar. He said, "Son, we have some questions we need answers to, if you don't mind."

The other agent, a lean, hatchet-faced young man with chocolate-colored skin, said, "You understand that we have full authority to question you in any manner in which we choose?"

Pindar licked dry lips. "*Sí*. Yes, I understand." Here it was. The beginning of the end. *Adios*, Pindar. Any way you look at it, you lose.

"Good," Grandfather said. He put a small plastic case upon the table next to the platform upon which Pindar lay. Opened the case. Removed from it a pressure syringe and a small vial of reddish fluid. Loaded the vial into the injector.

"I—I—there is no need for that," Pindar said. He hurried to get the words out. "I will answer your questions! I will tell you everything!"

Hatchet-face grinned, showing teeth that were too perfect to be natural. Vat-grown implants, had to be. "Oh, we know that, *Señor* Pindar. But this will save us all a lot of worry about how truthful your answers will be."

Grandfather leaned over Pindar, pressed the injector against the big artery in the tech's neck. Touched the firing stud. There was a small *pop!* and Pindar felt an icy rush begin in his throat, swelling to fill his head with coldness. *Dios!*

Hatchet-face looked at his chronometer. "Three. Four. Five. That's it."

Pindar felt the cold in his head change into a pleasant, muzzy warmth. It was okay. In fact, it was better than okay. He couldn't recall when he had felt so wonderful. His earlier worries evaporated like dew in the hot sunshine. Why, if he wanted to, he could get up off this table and leap into the air and fly like a bird! He didn't want to do that, though, he just wanted to lie here and visit with these nice men, Grandfather and Hatchet-face. After all, it was easy to see that they were his friends, and they cared deeply for him, and that anything he could do for them he should do, immediately.

"Feel good?" Grandfather asked.

"Yeah!"

"That's great. Mind if we ask you a few questions?"

"Why no, Grandfather, not at all!"

Orona leaned back in his chair. The TIA agent across from him wasn't wearing the pearl-gray uniform as regulations said he must while on duty, but there was no doubt about his identity. "Shall I run it?" he asked.

Orona nodded. "I hope you're wrong about this."

"They don't pay us to be wrong, Doctor. Sorry."

The agent touched a control on the holographic projector on Orona's desk. The air shimmered and the picture flowered. A close view of a man on a pressor table, smiling as if drugged.

"Tell us again," a voice off camera said. "Just like before."

"Sure," the man on the table said.

"After the last time, when Salvaje threatened me, I decided I had to find out more about what he was into.

"So I did some checking and discovered that he had hired other technicians to help him. I knew one of them slightly, Gerard, a contract worker for the Bionational Lab in Lima. I took the shuttle to Lima, made it a point to 'accidentally' bump into him. Bought him a few drinks. I learned that Salvaje had worked for Bionational before he started his crusade. Some kind of low-level administrator. He didn't need the money, he came from a rich family, but obviously he needed something from Bionat. Up and quit one day, but kept in touch with some of the techs. Gerard didn't know why Salvaje quit, and he only did some hardwiring for him, set up a small computer system. Salvaje paid well, that was all that was important.

"Gerard didn't know anything else about it, but that was enough. I knew that Salvaje had his own system.

"So I went to his place when he was visiting the pregnant whore and broke in."

The man on the table laughed. "His security was not so good as he thought. I got inside. Ran a download program and copied all his files. Took them home; he would never know I had been there.

"I found out where his messiah came from when

I ran an AV he had buried in a mathematical program."

The agent waved his hand and the image froze, floating silently in the air. "You'll want to see this while Pindar talks," he said. "We found it in his computer."

The agent touched some controls. The man on the table vanished and was replaced by a somewhat grainy picture of Bionational's logo. The logo was overstamped by a flaming red sign that said: Authorized Personnel, REQUIRED CLEARANCE TS-1, Bionational Internal AV 42255-1, composite.

Pindar's voice continued.

"It was a bad induction copy of a Bionational top-secret AV, for internal view only. Salvaje must have stolen it or had somebody steal it for him. Whoever had done it screwed it up, they lost part of the visual and all of the audio track, so there's no sound."

The image blurred, then resolved into a view of a clean room. A man lay on a table, bucking against a field. A spot on his solar plexus tore open and what appeared to be an eel's head the size of a man's fist emerged, flashing bloody needle-sharp teeth. Three men in cleansuits stood over the thing. The eellike creature shot out of the man on the table like a dart and latched on to one of the cleansuited men. It ripped a hole in his suit.

"The first part of the recording showed the birth of one of the things. Showed it attacking another man."

The camera's view switched to another pickup, zoomed in on the eel as it disappeared into the cleansuit. The pickup pulled back to show the

terrified face of the man in the suit. He was screaming, but there was no sound. The image blurred,
lost a couple of seconds, then re-formed.

Orona stared, fascinated.

The suited man ran. The camera lost him.

Two men fell as they tried to follow the fleeing
one.

The image changed again. Armed guards stood
in a corridor. A door opened and the cleansuited
figure ran into view, slapping at a hole in his suit
front. He lost control, shambled away.

The image jiggered. Another camera. The running man.

"They couldn't let it get away," the voice said.

The running man's head exploded, the cleansuit's helmet ballooned out, split, sprayed gore.

The image held, an angle on the body on the
floor.

"Now," the agent said. "We switch to . . ."

A huge room. Armored walls. Looked like a containment vessel for controlled fusion experiments.
Suspended from cables was a naked man's body.
No doubt that he was dead; most of his head was
gone.

A telemetry crawl ran across the image, but the
figures and words were not those of a human.

"I didn't see it at first," came the voice. "But I
figured it out fast enough when I saw the recording.
They left the thing inside the guy they'd shot. He
was a doctor, by the way, I saw that on the screen.
Had been head of a division of Bionational before
he became baby food.

"They put it in a place where it couldn't get out and they watched it."

The picture of the dead man froze.

"This is edited," the agent said. "Apparently this Salvaje couldn't get the other recordings, so this only hits the high points. Though he seems to have a hell of an organization, coded names and payouts, we're still working on those." He touched his control pad.

The image faded into another.

"Here's what it looks like about halfway grown," the agent said.

Orona stared. The thing appeared pretty much like the reconstruction on his own informational AV. But wait—*half* grown?

"Here is Salvaje's messiah," Pindar said. "It isn't a computer image as I thought, it is real."

The image faded again, went blank.

"Apparently neither Salvaje nor the technician were able to get past this point in the recording," the agent said. "But there is more. Our people have state-of-the-art recovery gear. We were able to pull another set of visuals from it."

The blank image faded in again.

This time the monster was larger, shaped slightly differently, with a massive cranial plate that branched antlerlike. It had an extra set of smaller arms coming from its chest area. The creature was huge, there was a scale built into the edge of the holo. The walls of the room were now covered with convoluted loops of shining black material, and the floor was dotted with garbage-can-sized eggs.

"My God," Orona said. "It's a queen!"

"One that doesn't need to be fertilized, apparently," the agent said.

Orona shook his head. "This could confirm my theory that a queen can develop from a drone as needed to continue the species. Some kind of hormonal change, perhaps."

The monster showed teeth, looking directly at the observation camera. The image faded and went blank again.

Orona waited.

"That's all there is of the stolen recording, I'm afraid," the agent said.

"Sweet baby Buddha's left nut," Orona said. "We've got to get it and those eggs. I'll make some calls, we'll seize the Lima laboratory in the interests of Terran Security."

The agent shook his head. "Too late for that."

Orona blinked. "What? What do you mean?"

"Watch."

The agent's hands did their magic with the control pad. The air lit with new pictures.

"These are from Bionational security monitors at the Lima complex. Note the date."

Orona looked at the red numbers in the corner of the image. Yesterday. Last night, from the hour.

"Apparently Salvaje had Pindar under a loose surveillance. Or perhaps an informant in the local police. Whatever. He must have found out we were closing in on him. Before Pindar's questioning had been completed, this is what happened at Bionational's Peruvian labs."

The scene was of a fenced perimeter. A guard kiosk. Two men sat inside.

"Hey, look at that!" one of them said.

Both guards jumped up. The road camera caught the approaching vehicle. An old-style windjammer thirty-ton cargo truck approaching the gate. At speed.

"Stop, you asshole!" one of the guards yelled.

The truck slammed into the gate. The gate was durasteel mesh and solid wrist-thick bars and had not been designed to withstand the impact of a multiton cargo truck moving at fifty kph. The metal bent, bolts tore loose, wire stretched . . . but even so, it held. The truck slewed to a halt against it.

From the ruined cab of the vehicle, a single battered woman crawled out, managed to stand. She wore a robe. The security computer locked a wide-angle camera onto her. Her face was bloody. Her hands were empty but she had something strapped to her chest, a blocky circular device about the diameter of a dinner plate.

One of the guards hit the panic button and the alarm Klaxon started hooting. The other guard pulled his sidearm and ordered the woman to halt.

She kept coming. As the guard raised his weapon to fire, the woman exploded. The image washed white.

"Buddha," Orona said.

"We IDed the bomb as a five-ton building demolition charge," the agent said. "It took out the kiosk, the truck, and twenty-six meters of fence."

A patrol robot provided the next segment of recording.

The POV shot as the robot approached the destroyed entrance to the compound was a little shaky, despite the minicam gyros in the bot, because of the rubble it was traversing, the agent said.

Orona watched, fascinated.

The bot broadcast its security warning as a stolen passenger bus stuffed full of people roared past it. Since a security alert had been called the bot's guns were armed and it was authorized to fire upon intruders. It sprayed the bus with twin 10mm machine guns; its cameras picked up the holes as the rounds pierced the heavy plastic sides of the bus. People were dying inside, that was apparent, and the bot continued firing, aiming for the operator. A warning light began flashing on the bot's proximity detectors, and the bot reacted to the new target, shifting on its axis, just in time to be smashed by a speeding aircar. The driver, who died in the subsequent explosion as he and the car and the bot were engulfed in a yellow flash, died smiling.

"This next piece we got from a spysat we had footprinting the area," the agent said.

The view was from overhead, and had that too slick look that an augmentation computer added to a pixilated image. Three buses approached the large building centered in the frame. Security robots fired on the vehicles, and return fire came from the buses at the defensive bots.

The first bus reached the complex's entrance. Ten or twelve robed figures scrambled out and ran for the door. From the angle, Orona couldn't tell if they were men or women, but it didn't matter, because they were cut down by gunfire from within the building.

Another dozen figures boiled forth from the bus.

Yet more from the next bus that arrived, and a fourth wave from the final bus. Nearly all of them were slaughtered, too.

Nearly all of them.

One of the figures tottered to the door.

The spysat's filters cut down the white blast as the figure blew apart. Smoke and debris sprayed from the building.

"Got the door and the guards there," the agent said. He spoke as if he were talking about what he had for lunch.

More figures emerged from the buses.

The images wavered.

"Spysat moved out of range there," the agent said. "We didn't have anything else we could shift over for another few minutes. This piece is from the building's security comp. Watch."

A lone guard, one of his legs missing, lay on the floor, a suppressed machine gun in his hands. He fired the weapon, waving it back and forth.

The wounded guard's targets were robed figures, men and women, smiling as they walked into the hard sleet of bullets. Ten, fifteen, maybe a score of them fell before the guard's gun ran dry.

The camera caught perfectly the woman who bent over the wounded guard and put a thin knife blade through his eye. She was smiling as if this were the funniest thing she had ever seen.

More figures moved into view.

"Freeze frame," the agent said.

The moving figures turned into an oil painting, clear, sharp, still. "Nice optics," the agent said. He pointed at the hologram. "See that one, second from the right?"

Orona nodded.

"Salvaje."

Orona regarded the bearded man. He didn't look like a fanatic. But then—what exactly *did* a fanatic look like? Was he supposed to be drooling and foaming at the mouth?

"Resume play."

More robed people arrived. Orona estimated there must be at least thirty-five or forty of them who had survived the attack.

"Thirty-seven passed this camera," the agent said, as if reading Orona's thoughts.

The image cut to a view of a door. DANGER, it said in ten-centimeter-high letters, BIOLOGICAL EXPERIMENT. Authorized Personnel Only.

A pair of dead guards lay on the floor. One of them had a thin knife stuck in his eye. Five robed figures sprawled near the guards.

"Thirty-two of them left," the agent said.

Another angle. Inside the chamber. Orona recognized the ropy exudate on the walls. A translucent mist fogged the ground, partially covering rows of eggs.

Some of the attackers stripped off their robes, showing themselves naked underneath. They each had a tattoo of a drone alien on their bodies, extending from neck to pubis.

"God*damn*," Orona said.

"We found the tattooist, he was one of them. Been making house calls for months, apparently. It gets better," the agent said. "Check this part."

The queen alien lumbered into view. She stared at the people, twisted her head to one side, then the other, as if puzzled.

Salvaje faced her. He said something, but only a few words were audible.

"—be one with you, Messiah!"

"Sorry about the sound," the agent said. "We're lucky we got this much. We found the blue box almost six klicks away."

Orona looked at the agent. "What?"

"I'll explain. Watch."

Some of the eggs began opening. Half of the invading people now stood naked, arms outstretched, eyes closed, waiting. The others remained well outside the room, one angle showed them. "We've cut together several views here," the agent said.

The first one to open was in front of Salvaje. He stood with his arms wide, as did the others, but his eyes were open. He leaned down over the egg. The flaps glistened with strands of shining slime. Fingerbonelike legs emerged and caught the edges of the opened egg, hauling the primary-embryo stage of the alien's crablike body onto the lip. It leapt at Salvaje, wrapped a muscular tail around his neck, jammed its ovipositor into his startled mouth, and clutched his face with the legs, pressing itself flat against his face.

Orona could see the terror grip the man, and he realized that in this final moment of truth, the reality was more than he had bargained for, for Salvaje tried to scream.

The sound was choked off by the tube rammed down his throat.

The scientist in Orona was intrigued, but the human part of him recoiled.

Other eggs splayed wide their fleshy openings, other primary-embryos leapt upon waiting faces.

The queen watched it all impassively.

Then, when all of the naked humans had been infected, the outermost eggs hatched and depleted of their inhabitants, the remaining robed people darted in and dragged their comrades away, adroitly avoiding, save for one, being attacked by the remaining eggs.

The queen did not approve of this, but she was anchored to her huge egg sac and could not move quickly enough to catch the scurrying humans.

"Normally there would be drones to hold them," Orona said.

"What?"

"Never mind."

The door shut. The queen raged.

As the attackers hauled away their fellows, one of them spotted the watching camera. He pulled a handgun and fired at it. He missed three times, but the fourth shot wiped the screen.

"What happened?"

The agent shrugged. "The security system was overridden at this time. We have no more images of the fanatics."

"Overridden?"

"One of Bionational's chief security people sent a coded squirt to the system. Self-destruct code."

"What?"

"Ninety seconds later the security system destroyed itself—along with the entire complex. Blew it to bits."

"No! What about the alien? The eggs?"

"Scattered about the countryside in pieces the size of your little fingernail, Doctor."

"Oh, no!"

Orona was stunned by the news. What a waste! He'd sent a ship halfway across the galaxy to obtain such specimens and if they'd been a few hours quicker, they could have had one right here on Earth! *That* explained the dreams people had been having! Damn! Damn!

Wait. Ninety seconds. Could that mean—?

"What about the fanatics? Did any of them get away? There were at least a dozen of them infected!"

The agent sighed. "We don't know. Our people have been combing the country looking for them, but there's no sign of them. The explosion was in the half-megaton range. There's no way to tell from the wreckage how many people died in it, whether anybody got away."

For a moment hope flared in Orona. There might be a chance.

"We hope none of them did," the agent said.

"What? Are you crazy? These life forms are priceless!"

"Think about it, Doctor."

Orona was a brilliant man; he had always been at the top of any class he was in. It hit him, what the agent was trying to say. Yes, the aliens were priceless. But under controlled circumstances. Bionational knew that. That's why the complex was rigged to blow up if there came a breach in security. If the alien somehow escaped, got free of captivity, that could be disastrous. Even a single egg was potentially dangerous. Given how quickly they could breed and come to maturity, given how they could change into queens if the need was there . . .

Orona nodded. Yes. He saw it.

A dozen queen aliens, hiding out, laying eggs, that could be a problem.

That could be a major problem.

17

Billie stood in front of one of the "viewing ports," watching the streams of light strung like thin, crooked tubes of bright neon across the dark background. She hadn't spent much time in space, not since she had been a child, and this kind of travel was new to her. She stared, trying to remember her parents during happy times, but their bloody end kept jamming itself into her thoughts. Since Wilks had come to see her that first time, the reality the doctors had tried to wipe kept bobbing to the surface like floats on a pond. The truth was rising and would not be denied. All the dreams that had been real . . .

"That's an illusion, you know," came a voice from behind her.

Billie turned and saw one of the marines, Bueller, standing there.

"The improved gravity drive means we can spend less time in hypersleep, but the multidimensional matrices of the butterfly field turn dots into lines. Something to do with some esoteric particle, chronons, or impiotic zuons or some such."

"I wonder what Easley saw in his last seconds?" she said.

It was a rhetorical question, but Bueller shook his head. "I don't know. I can't imagine why he would have gone EVA and taken a grenade with him."

"Some kind of depression, the colonel says. Maybe Easley was running from monsters."

Again Bueller shook his head. "I don't think so. We were pretty close. It doesn't make any sense that he would suicide. Besides, there are a lot easier ways."

Billie nodded. Blowing yourself to bits in deep space was not her choice of an entry to the final chill.

"I don't trust Stephens," Bueller said. "He doesn't have any command experience in the field and I think he wanted to hush the whole thing up. If we're successful in our mission—whatever it *is* exactly—then up-levels will overlook a few bodies. But if we fail, then the little things will count."

"I hate to disillusion you, Bueller, but if this mission doesn't succeed, we'll get eaten by things with big teeth, or else turned into puppy chow for the baby things with little teeth. We'll all end up on the cold ground as lumps of alien dung for the bugs to fight over."

"How colorful," Bueller said.

"Telling it like it is. I've seen these things work."

"You sound like Wilks." He stood there for a second and she could see he was uncomfortable.

"Come on," Billie said. "I'll buy you a cup of what passes for coffee."

"Okay. Yeah."

In the mess hall, Ramirez was waiting for a self-heating meal packet to cook. He grinned at Billie and Bueller when they came in.

The two of them sat at an expanded plastic table with their paper cups of the vile ship's brew.

"Wilks must really think a lot of you to bring you along. You know Stephens will hang him out to twist when we get back, no matter what face-saving shit he's telling us now."

Billie sipped the coffee, made a face. "Yeah. Wilks and I, we understand each other."

"I'll bet," Ramirez said as he put his tray down on the next table. "Wilks, he's an expert on cradle-robbing, hey?"

"Shut up, Ramirez," Bueller said.

"Hey, man, I'm all for a little pussy myself, but not so green—"

Bueller came up, caught Ramirez under the chin with the V of his thumb and fingers, and shoved him back against the wall. "I said shut the fuck up!"

Ramirez's voice was choked when he tried to speak. "Hey, man, fuck, let go!"

Billie saw the tendons in Bueller's hand standing out. He was practically holding the bigger man off the floor, pinned to the wall like a struggling insect. He seemed too strong for a man his size.

Abruptly Bueller relaxed, pulled his hand away.

Ramirez rubbed at his throat. "You're crazy, man,
you know that?" He turned and walked out of the
room, leaving his steaming dinner behind.

"Why did you do that?" Billie asked.

Bueller looked flustered, embarrassed. "He's got
a big mouth and he shoots it off too much."

"That's it?"

"Yeah."

Billie let it alone. There was something else here,
but she wasn't sure what it was. She wasn't sure
she wanted to know what it was.

In his quarters on the chase ship, Massey sat
seiza and concentrated on his breathing. He had
never learned to meditate as the masters did, but
he could use it to calm his system. Sure, he exercised his body, practiced fighting techniques,
drilled over and over again with weaponry, but these
things brought him no joy. They were to keep him
crisp, to maintain his cutting edge, nothing more.
Being in top shape was part of the business, necessary, and he trained himself as if he were a prized
show animal, proper diet, enough rest, technical
mastery as required, no more, no less. He was the
equal of any serious athlete, and against the few
who might be in better physical shape or with faster
reflexes, he augmented himself with drugs or figured ways to cheat. If you wanted a man dead, it
was better to shoot him in the back from long range
than to stand facing him like some holovid hero.
That was a fool's game, and since the last man
standing was the victor, it was always better to slant
things your way when possible.

Soon another test would come. He must be ready for it. So he sat, but it was not mindless meditation but mindful scheming that filled him. In a contest like this, there could be no second-place winner. To be second was to be last and to be last here was to be dead.

"Have you got a first name?" Billie asked as they toured the magazine. Here were racks of carbines, canisters of gas, grenades and other hardware, all securely stored under the QM's seal.

Bueller said, "Yes. Mitchell."

"Mitchell," she said, testing the word. "Mitch?"

"If you like."

Billie turned to look at the racks of small arms under their kleersteel cases. Bueller put a hand on her shoulder, to point her toward the display model.

"Don't touch me," she said.

He snatched his hand away. "Oh. Sorry. I didn't mean anything by it."

"It's okay. In the hospital, when somebody put their hands on you it almost always meant you were in trouble. After the hand came a derm-patch or an injector, to fill you with chem that made you sluggish and stupid."

He sighed. "Yeah, I can understand that."

"Can you? Do you know what it's like living most of your life in a medical unit full of crazy people?"

"No," he admitted. "But I've spent my share of time in hospitals. Not fun places."

He changed the subject. "Here, here's the basic weapon we're using on this mission." He pulled the demo model, a dummy, from the rack. "This here

is your four-point-eight-kilo-fully-automatic-elec-
tronic-blowback-operated-caseless-ten-millimeter-
M41-E carbine," he said, as if reciting a litany.
"It has an effective range of five hundred meters,
holds either a one-hundred-round magazine of
antipersonnel, a one-hundred-round magazine of
armor-piercing, or a seventy-five-round magazine of
rainbow tracer ammunition, and mounts a thirty-
millimeter pump-operated grenade launcher under
the barrel with a range of one hundred meters.
Officially."

He grinned. "Unofficially, you can't hit anything
smaller than a subway car past a couple hundred
meters 'cause the sights are for shit, and if the
grenade goes farther than fifty meters before it hits
the ground, you must have a god who likes you.

"At close range, however, this is a mean machine
and you don't want to be on the receiving end in
anything less than full class-VII spidersilk armor or
you get turned into bloody mush."

He held the weapon out. "Take a look. It won't
bite."

Billie held her smile in check. The model number
had changed, but the basic weapon was not that
different from the one she had dreamed about. No,
not dreamed about, *remembered*. This part of the
dreams had come back to her dozens of times over
the years, the instructions that Wilks had given her
were burned into her as if branded by white-hot
metal.

She took the carbine, thumbed the magazine
catch, and popped the dummy, checked to be sure
it was empty, then slammed the magazine back

into place. She cycled the action twice to make certain the chamber was cleared, then stroked the grenade launcher's pump twice to make sure the loading tube was empty. She pulled the weapon to her shoulder, sighted at the far wall, both eyes open, and dry fired the piece. The electronic trigger was rigged to make an audible click for such practice and did so. She lowered the weapon, twisted it to present arms, and tossed it at Bueller. It had been more than a dozen years, she had not touched such weapons in all that time, but it was like she knew it would be. Except that the weapon felt so much smaller and lighter now than it had when she was ten.

He was surprised, but managed to catch the carbine without dropping it.

"Trigger's a little stiff and it's got some creep," she said. "Your armorer should run a diagnostic on it when he gets the chance." She was showing off, but what the hell.

He laughed. "I'm impressed. Where'd you learn to do that?"

"I ran with a rough crowd when I was a kid." She paused, then said simply, "The things we're going to go hunt, they killed my family and everybody I knew."

"Buddha," he said. "I'm sorry."

She shrugged. "What about you? You have family?"

"No. The marines are my family."

Billie thought about that for a second. Well. Other than going off to get killed they had something else in common. No family.

"Listen, about Sergeant Wilks," he began. "If you've got something going with him—"

She cut him off. "When the aliens took over our colony, Wilks and his squad came down. He and I were the only ones left who got off-planet before they sterilized it. He saved me. I was ten years old. That was the last I saw of him until a few days before we left Earth."

"I'm sorry, I don't mean to pry—"

"Sure you do. That's okay. I've been pried open by experts. I got used to it."

He stared at his feet.

"Let me ask *you* something," she said.

"Okay. That's fair."

"Why'd you really grab Ramirez in the mess hall?"

He sighed. "What he said about you and Wilks. I didn't want it to be true."

"Why not?"

He shook his head, stared at his feet again.

It hit her why all of a moment. Buddha and Jesus in a hammock, Billie, you been taking stupid pills again? This guy *likes* you! Not like one of the orderlies who felt you all over when tucking you in bed, or who took out their dongs and jacked off on you when you were lying there so stoned you couldn't move, he's *concerned* about you!

We're going off to get killed and here's this marine falling for you. How about that.

Suddenly she saw him in a new light. He was her age, he had nobody but the marines and they were sending him off to die. He was lonely. She knew what that felt like.

She reached out, touched him on the shoulder. "Hey," she said. "Mitch."

He looked up from his boots, his gaze bright, pale eyes clear and searching. "Yeah?"

"Why don't you show me some more of the ship?"

He grinned, like a kid with a new toy. "Yeah. I'd like that."

Billie was fairly certain she was going to like it, too.

18

The agent said to Orona, "No. Nothing new on possible survivors of the explosion in Lima. There are some rumors floating around about a cult talking over a ranch in New Chile; we're checking it out. Other than that, nothing." He shrugged.

Orona merely nodded. In this case, no news was bad news.

Massey checked his timers for the fifteenth time. Soon. Very soon. The last squirt update said they were within a light-year of their destination. Practically there, as fast as the new gravity drives could move the ships. Getting close. Getting ready.

Wilks had given Billie a couple of make-work chores, checking systems, cargo manifests, like that. When he arrived at the midship comp terminal kiosk, he expected to see her there.

He didn't expect to see somebody with her. Somebody like Bueller, with his hand possessively on the girl's shoulder, kneading the muscle gently.

"Bueller," Wilks said. "You have business in here?"

The marine jerked his hand away from Billie's shoulder.

Billie turned. "Wilks. Mitch was only—"

He cut her off. "Yeah, I can see what *Mitch* was 'only' doing. Take a hike, Bueller."

"Dammit, Wilks!" Billie said. "Who the hell do you think you are?"

"Me? I'm the guy who pulled you out of the chemical fog you were living in, just before they were ready to strain your brain and throw your mind out."

Billie flushed, stared at him. She owed him, he knew that, and he knew she was holding her comment because of it.

"I thought I told you to take a hike."

Bueller smoldered. He was on the edge of swinging at him; Wilks could feel the rage like heat from a furnace. He hoped Bueller's sense of duty was stronger than his anger: if he let go, Wilks wouldn't be able to take him—Bueller was younger, faster, stronger, better-trained. He would have to shoot him and Wilks wasn't sure that would stop him in time, given the tightness of the quarters.

But Bueller stalked out, not saying anything.

Billie rounded on him. "All right, Wilks, I owe

you, but that doesn't give you the right to tell me who I can talk to!"

"I saw you," Wilks said. "You were doing more than talking."

Billie's eyes went wide. "Are you jealous? Damn, Wilks!"

"Not jealous, kid. Just trying to save you grief."

"I'll handle my own grief, thank you! I'm not a child and you aren't my father!" With that, she turned and marched out.

Wilks stared at her as she left. He shook his head. Maybe he was too burned out. Maybe she just liked having somebody pay attention to her. Maybe he should tell her the rest of it.

No. Maybe none of them were going to ever get home; even if Billie did, the whitecoats would be waiting for her. Maybe she should enjoy whatever free time she had left.

Lotta maybes there.

So, no. He wouldn't tell her. He'd tried to warn her, that was the best he could do. Like she said, she'd have to handle her own grief.

One way or another, grief was coming, that was for damn sure.

They'd dragged a cushion into the forward storage compartment, between two rows of hex cartons that effectively formed corridors in the room. It was dim, quiet, and nobody was going to happen across them accidentally. There was a door alarm rigged to chime if anybody even stuck their head into the room.

They sat facing each other on the cushion, and

Billie rubbed her hand against the hard muscle in Mitch's arm, feeling the smoothness of it. His strength appealed to her, it made her feel safe.

"I'm sorry about Wilks," she said. "He was out of line."

"Maybe not," Mitch said. "Maybe I don't know what I'm doing here."

"I know," Billie said. She reached up with both hands and caught his face. It was smooth, his beard depilated so close that his skin felt softer than her own. She urged him to her, kissed him. Slipped her tongue into his mouth.

The heat of his passion flared, and he circled his arms around her; she could feel the power of him even though he held her loosely. The kiss grew more intense. Billie felt her heart speed up, her breathing turn ragged.

He slipped one hand under her shirt, cupped her breast.

Oh, yes!

Eagerly she tugged his coverall tabs open, the *critch* of the cro separating loud in the quiet room. Felt his hairless chest, the thick muscles bunched under her touch. Slid her hand down, and found a different kind of hardness.

He moaned, a soft, wordless sound of desire.

He slid his mouth down her neck, pulled wide the tabs on her shirt and pants, moved farther down, kissing his way over her breasts and belly and beyond.

"Oh, yes!" she said. She could hardly breathe.

After another moment she didn't worry about breathing anymore.

* * *

Afterward, Billie and Mitch lay in a tangle of arms and legs. She was sweaty and her pulse had slowed some, but she wasn't tired. Just . . . fulfilled.

There had been others. Even in a hospital they couldn't watch you all the time, and Billie had been with a male patient once, and another time an orderly. And there had been a couple of women, too. But nothing like this. It had never felt so good, seemed so right, been so joyous as this linking with Mitch.

Mitch said, "I've never done this before."

She smiled. "Really? Could have fooled me. You were terrific."

"Was I?"

"Well, not that I have all that many guys to compare you to myself, but, yeah, you were."

He laughed softly. "Good. I wanted to be, for you. I—well, I love you, Billie."

Billie drank it in, the feeling, the touching, what he said. Yes. She'd been waiting her whole life for this, had never expected it to happen, never really believed such a thing was possible for somebody like her. But here it was.

"I'm glad. I love you, too, Mitch."

He shifted slightly and she felt his renewed interest poking at her. "My, my. Potent, aren't we?"

He bit at his lip. "There's something I need to tell you," he said.

"Showing is better than telling," she said. "Why don't you show me how this works instead?" She touched him lightly with one hand. "We can talk later."

"Okay. I take your point."

"No, sweetie, I'll take *yours*. . . ."

Jones was taking her turn at the proximity sensor board. Ten minutes into her tour, a bogie began blipping at her.

"Well, shit," Jones said. She wasn't deep in this kind of work but since the computer did most of it, all she had to do was ask. "What do we have here, folks?"

The computer ran a crawl across the hologram.

Jones shook her head. "Can't be, pal. There ain't supposed to be another ship out here."

"Problem?" came a voice from behind her.

Colonel Stephens stood there.

Jones said. "Sir, the PS says there's a vessel out there only a hundred klicks back and closing. The thing musta blown a circuit or something, right?"

"Could be an echo, that happens," Stephens said. "Run a diagnostic."

"Affirmative, sir." Jones touched a button.

The image gridded, words sprayed across it, and the result came up almost immediately: DIAGNOSTIC CHECK COMPLETE, ALL SYSTEMS FUNCTIONAL.

"Damn," Jones said. "Excuse me, sir. There *is* a ship out there. I'll sound General Alert." She reached for the red button cover, started to flip it up so she could reach the alarm control.

"No," Stephens said.

"Sir, if that's a ship we have to assume it's hostile to our mission, that's SOP—"

By now, Jones had turned enough to see that

Stephens had drawn his side arm. An issue softslug pistol.

"Sir!"

He shot her. Through the left eye. Gore spattered on his coverall as Jones's head snapped back and smashed into the sensor board. She slid from the chair, dead before she reached the deck.

"Sorry," Stephens said, reholstering his weapon.

The colonel waved his hands over the com unit. "Stephens here," he said. "We are go for mating."

"Copy that," came Massey's voice from the com. "We are on the way."

Wilks was in the rec room working out on the myoflex full range-of-motion gear when the ship shook. He didn't know what, but something had hit them. Damn! Anything smaller than an asteroid should have been deflected by the shields!

Wilks jumped from the machine and grabbed his clothes.

There was a General Alert button near the door. Wilks broke the cover and slapped it with one hand, hardly slowing as he ran.

Billie was putting her shirt back on over tender breasts when the vibration rocked her hard enough to knock her from her feet. She hit one of the hex cartons and bounced off, managed to land on her butt without doing any damage.

Mitch absorbed the rocking with his legs and stayed up.

A klaxon began screaming, *reeh-aww, reeh-aww*, over and over.

"That's General Alert," Mitch said, tabbing his coverall shut.

"It's a drill, right?" Billie said, getting up.

"Maybe," he said, "but I don't think so. Something hit us."

"Maybe it was an engine going out?"

"No, we'd all be atomic dust, that happened. I can't believe they'd run a drill this close to the destination. Something is wrong."

He started for the exit, then stopped. "Listen, Billie, stay here, okay? Until I see what it is."

"Wait a minute—"

"Please? This is a pressurized area, if there are leaks anywhere, you'll be okay here. Please. I'll be back as soon as I can."

Billie nodded. "Okay. Listen, Mitch, be careful!"

"I will. I love you."

"I love you, too."

He grinned, then turned and sprinted away.

Ramirez came out of the shower wrapped in a towel as Bueller ran past. "What the fuck is going on?"

"Got me," Bueller said. "We've got to get to the armory and load up; our stations are next to the APC; we're supposed to be locked and loaded in a GA."

"I know, I know." Ramirez grabbed a coverall hanging on the door and tried to run and put it on at the same time. He didn't manage either very well.

"Jones is on watch, right?" Bueller said, glancing at his chronometer.

"Got me, man."

Mbutu stepped into the corridor ahead of them and started toward the armory.

"You seen Wilks?" Bueller yelled at her.

"Nah, ain't seen nobody, I was sleepin'," she hollered back at him.

They reached the armory. Chin had armorer duty and had already lifted the kleersteel covers. He started handing out weapons. Half of 2nd Squad was there, most of 3rd. Bueller didn't see any of 4th or anybody else from his own, 1st.

"Shit!" somebody from 3rd Squad said.

"What?"

"This piece is missing the feed ramp, asshole!"

Chin looked at the carbine he was about to hand to another trooper. "Sah! So is this one! Weapons check, marines!"

It only took a few seconds.

All of the carbines were missing the feed ramps.

Electronic feed ramps were critical. Without them, the only way anybody was going to do any damage with one of these pieces would be to whack somebody over the head with it.

"Oh, shit," Chin said. "We got a big problem."

"What about the grenades?" somebody asked.

"Buy a brain, stupid," Chin said, "you want to set off a fucking grenade on a *starship*?"

Somebody else waved a handgun. "These are rascaled, too. Somebody don't want us to be shootin' nothin'."

Bueller said, "You got hands and feet, marines, you been trained to use them. Get moving."

The intercom came to life. "This is Colonel

Stephens. All marines report to the aft loading bay immediately. Repeat, I want all marines to report to the aft loading bay immediately."

Wilks still had his unregistered civilian stunner, and he had it in hand when he heard boots clattering through the lock. Company coming, and not anybody he was expecting. He lit the target laser. The first few through the hatch were his. He took a deep breath, lined the laser's dot up on the hatch at eye level, and waited.

"Put your weapon down," came a voice from behind him. "Try to turn around and you're dead."

Stephens!

Wilks said, "Sir, we're being boarded!"

"I know all about it. Drop the stunner."

Whatever this was all about, Stephens had him cold. He'd never get around in time. Wilks dropped the weapon.

The hatch slid up and assault-suited men sprinted through the opening, splitting into two groups, one heading fore, the other aft. Two of them brought their hardware to bear on Wilks: these were automatic shotguns that fired frangible epoxy-boron-lead pellets. They didn't have much penetration, but against an unarmored human target, they were deadly enough. They didn't call them splatter-guns for nothing. Wilks raised his hands.

The last man sauntered into the ship proper, an antique 10mm recoilless Smith DA-only pistol in one hand. He waved the gun at Wilks. "Hello, marine. New in town?"

"Right on schedule, Massey," Stephens said.

"Of course. I've got him. You can put your piece away."

Wilks felt his guts twist. Stephens was a traitor. He didn't know who this Massey was or who he represented—one of the war cartels, maybe, some corporation—but Stephens had sold them out.

Wilks turned. "You killed Easley, didn't you?"

Stephens was holstering his sidearm. "It was necessary."

"Bastard."

"Life is hard, Wilks. A man has to do things to get by."

The one called Massey grinned. "Glad to hear you say that, Colonel." He pointed his gun at Stephens. "Move to the side there, would you, Sergeant?"

Stephens blinked, his mouth gaping in shock. "Wh-what are you doing?"

"A man who would sell out his command can hardly be trusted, wouldn't you agree?"

"W-w-wait a second! We had a deal! You *need* me!"

"The deal is off. And I don't need you anymore."

He fired the pistol.

The gun made a loud *whump!* in the corridor. Wilks's ears rang with the noise.

Stephens grew a crater in his chest. As he fell, the crater turned bright red. Arterial blood from the shattered heart, Wilks knew. Dead meat.

Wilks looked at Massey.

"No, don't worry, Sergeant, I'm not going to kill you, unless you do something foolish. You and your marines will be useful. You know anything about, ah, fishing?"

Wilks stared at him as if he had turned into a giant lizard.

Massey laughed. "If you want to catch a fish, you have to have the right kind of bait."

Massey laughed louder, as if at a private joke, but Wilks understood exactly what the man meant.

Because Wilks knew exactly what the aliens ate.

19

fter waiting for an hour, Billie crept to the comp panel inset next to the storeroom's door and carefully switched it on. She managed to activate a monitor after a little effort, and what she saw was three marines being herded down a hall by two strange men with guns.

Billie sucked in a fast breath. What was going on?

A few minutes with the computer gave her very little more. The ship was in the hands of some invading group. Who were they? Why had they attacked the ship? How had they managed to overcome a military vessel full of armed marines?

What about Wilks and Mitch?

She couldn't find Mitch, but some switching did give her an image of Wilks. He was being held at gunpoint by a tall, fair-haired man.

Oh, gods! What was she going to do?

The man talking to Massey was strange, Wilks saw, and after a moment he realized why—the man was an android, one they hadn't bothered to do a full cosmetic on. Must be an expendable. And, Wilks also realized, one that didn't worry fuck-all about the First Law for robots and androids, never to kill a human. How in the hell had the pirate managed to pull that one off?

"Is everybody accounted for?" Massey asked.

"Yes, sir," the android replied. "We lost two units during the operation. Four marines died as a result of wounds incurred during takeover; two more are seriously injured. Two marines were killed by Stephens previously. We have all the remaining marines and ship's crew in custody, cross-checked and matched, although there is an anomaly."

"What's the problem?"

"The initial marine head count after hypersleep arousal shows plus one."

Massey turned to look at Wilks. "Well?"

"Stephens miscounted. He was a stupid asshole."

Massey said to the android, "Double-check the names and ID numbers. We don't need any loose cannons onboard."

"Sir."

"You got balls, whoever you are," Wilks said. "To attack a government ship. What's the point?"

"To keep a greedy competitor from stealing my company's money."

"Competitor? If you represent a company you

should know the government doesn't compete with private concerns."

"Sure it does. They want to round up some of these valuable aliens and develop them as weaponry. You don't think they'll sell the results to anybody with the money to pay for them?"

Wilks shook his head. "You don't know what you're fucking with here. These things have wiped out a couple of colonies."

"I know more than you think, Sergeant. You see, we already *have* one of these things. On Earth. Our mission here is to make sure nobody else gets one before we can exploit our advantage. That, and gathering whatever information we can to help things along. Their favorite food, lighting, environment, like that. For all we know, these things aren't the top dogs on their world. They could be like mice."

"You have an alien? On Earth?"

"Yep. I haven't seen it myself, but I understand it's an ugly beast."

"Buddha!"

"He can't help you, Sergeant. I'm your god now."

Billie huddled against a crate, thinking. She could probably hide here for a long time without anybody finding her. She wasn't listed on the crew or marine manifests. Somebody might tell the invaders about her, of course, but maybe not.

Then again, staying here wouldn't help things. Mitch could be dead or wounded—she'd seen bodies being spaced last time she'd tried the monitors. Sooner or later she'd have to find water and food.

If they didn't know about her, she might be able to do something to help. The ship's ventilation system was big enough in places for her to move through it. She had experience in hiding, from when she was a kid and the aliens had taken over the colony. If you were quiet and quick, you could survive. She'd done it befcre.

And she had to find out what happened to Mitch. If he had been killed, then nothing mattered anymore. If he was still alive, she could find out, could do something to help him.

She stood. Yes. She wasn't going to spend whatever remained of her life cowering in the darkness waiting to be found and eliminated like some vermin. At the very least she could go down fighting.

In the APC bay, Massey and Wilks watched the landing craft being loaded. The marines were herded into the vessel by the guards, all of whom were androids.

"You'll stay here," Massey said to Wilks.

"Why?"

"Because I wish it so. We have enough worms for our hooks."

"You're sending my men to be slaughtered."

"Yes. But my forces will cover them from the air pods as best they can. They're already down there, buzzing around, setting up cover patterns. Live bait works better than dead, according to my information."

"Bastard."

"Not true. Both my parents stayed alive until I was nine. Then I killed them."

Wilks watched the squads marching onto the drop ship.

"The atmosphere is marginal down there," Massey said. "Little short on the oxy side, long on the CO_2 and other trash gases, got some methane and ammonia that'll probably make eyes burn and noses run. Extended exposure will be fatal, but I doubt anybody'll be there that long."

Wilks said nothing. They were in deep shit. The only bright spot seemed to be that Massey and his thugs hadn't found out about Billie. They would, eventually, when they strained enough of the ship's logs to get to Stephens's personal stuff. And she was probably on a monitor recording. Sooner or later somebody would ask the computer the right question and it would give them Billie.

He hoped she found a good place to hide and stayed there.

Inside the APC, Bueller sat at his station, waiting for the ship to drop. He'd been prepared to meet the aliens, but not like this, not unarmed and marched across the ground by enemies in air pods. They wouldn't have a prayer against those things, even if only half of what Wilks said was accurate.

Still, there was nothing to be done about it. A direct confrontation with the androids guarding them would mean a fast death. As long as they stayed alive, there was a chance they might be able to do something to survive.

He thought about Billie. He hoped she kept hidden. If he could be sure of that, then dying wasn't so bad.

Amazing that somebody like him could fall in love. Amazing, but true enough.

The whine of the repellors cycling up and lifting the ship free of the grapples for the drop interrupted Bueller's thoughts. I love you, Billie, he said to himself.

Good-bye.

Billie crawled through a stacked-plastic tube only a few centimeters bigger than she was. It was hard, slow, rough on her hands and arms as she dragged herself along. But it wasn't as if she had a whole lot of choice.

Wilks found himself in one of the forward storerooms alone, the door locked and guarded by a pair of Massey's androids. Things didn't look good for the home team.

Massey sat in front of the telemetry array, watching the feeds from the APC and helmetcams the marines wore. The usual life-systems input wasn't there. The Colonial Marines must be on a tight budget these days. Well. That didn't matter. He didn't care if they died, he only needed another specimen or two and whatever information he could gather on the aliens' homeworld. Plenty of that coming in. The APC sensors gathered it up, gravity, atmosphere, lighting, weather conditions, all kinds of readings, and spewed it into the *Benedict*'s recorders. Offhand, it didn't look like a world that was going to become a vacation spot anytime soon. Gravity a bit higher than Terran Standard, maybe a gee and a quarter, so fat people and those with heart conditions would not like it much, even if it happened to look like Paradise, and in no way did it look inviting. The local star made most of the planet tropical, at least weather-wise. There were small ice caps at the poles, but even the more temperate regions would give you body heat plus a couple degrees. Vegetation was sparse, the oceans were full of nasty salts, and there didn't seem to be many places where an unprotected human could survive even *without* killer locals prowling for supper. The poisoned air would require full-time filters or implants. Looked like a place to dump garbage to Massey.

"Commander, we are breaking through the overcast, " came the android pilot's voice.

"I hear you."

Massey switched to the nose cam in the APC. The hologram lit the air to his left, showing a swirl of clouds that flew past and thinned. Under the cloud cover, the land below was dull and gray, scraggly trees or what passed for them, lots of young igneous rock exposed to the air, sharp edges, and dirty colors.

"Got a big thunderstorm forty klicks ahead," the copilot said. "Tops up to twenty thousand meters, look at the voltage on that lightning."

"Go around the storm," Massey ordered. "Find me a nest of the things and put down within a couple of kilometers. Don't want our marines to get too tired on their walk."

"Copy, Commander."

Massey watched the shifting pictures. So far, this

mission had gone exactly as he had planned. Right on the nose. It was almost boring. Maybe something would happen down there to spice things up a little.

Billie found that the ventilation tube opened into one of the small kitchens. Nobody seemed to be around, so she slid down the shaft and wiggled her way onto a microwave oven top. She quickly climbed to the floor.

Most of the food preparation on the *Benedict* consisted of heating and opening SMPs. That didn't require anything more than pulling and twisting a tab. Nobody produced wonderful meals for dinner here, but there were some special occasions when something a bit more elaborate than field rations might be called for. Visiting officers, an ambassador, perhaps. So the kitchen could be used to make a soypro cutlet or a stew, maybe even a pie or cake, and therefore there were implements.

Billie dug through all the cabinets until she found a combination knife and vegetable peeler with a U-shaped slotted extrusion pointed for coring. The edges were serrated on one side and sharp on the other; the blade was only as long as her forefinger. Not much of a weapon, but she could stab somebody with it if she could get close enough.

A better find was a tapered hollow plastic tube that could be filled with liquid and frozen, to make a rolling pin. Billie triggered the freezer in the handle and in about twenty seconds the liquid inside turned solid. It was cold in her grip but heavy and solid; she could bash in a skull with it. Again, it wasn't as good as a gun, but it was better than nothing.

She hefted the rolling pin. Now all she had to do was sneak up behind a whole shipful of armed men and whack each one on the head. Simple, right?

She chuckled to herself. You've lost your mind for sure this time, kid. Still, it felt better to be doing *some*thing.

Massey watched from the remote hovercam as the marines marched out onto the surface of the alien world, in full gear except for weapons. Six of his own troops floated in three small open-air pod craft over the walking marines. The androids in the pods were armed and the marines below knew they could either do as they were told or be cut down.

Sensors watched and listened and smelled and tasted and fed the results to Massey. He monitored his androids as they spoke to each other on their coms.

"—move pretty well for men who don't have enough oxygen to breathe—"

"—we in jeopardy here?"

"That's a negative, the alien life form is ground-based."

Massey mentally tuned out the chatter. His plan was simple enough: he would march the marines into the nearest hive where the aliens could grab them and implant eggs in them. Then he would send his androids in to retrieve them. Stephens had been instructed to refuse to allow plasma rifles on his ship, but Massey had enough such weapons and chargers on the company vessel to outfit a small army. However tough the aliens might be, they couldn't stand up to energy blasts that would blow holes in durasteel armor plate easier than a man could poke his finger through damp tissue paper. No, that wasn't going to be a problem. Once he had a specimen or two and all the information he could collect, he would head back to Earth.

Maybe after that the company could find him something *difficult* to do.

He laughed aloud. It was tough being the best. You had to invent your own challenges. Maybe he would quit the company, go to work for some smaller, hungrier concern. Turn against the people who now fed him and bite their hand a few times, just to show them he could do it. Yes. That had a certain appeal to it.

Ah, well. Best not to get too overconfident. One mission at a time. You didn't get to be the best by making mistakes, and counting embryos before the eggs were fertilized was unwise. He turned back to the holograms and information flow in front of him. One mission at a time.

20

Bueller and 1st Squad approached the mound cautiously—unarmed as they were, and walking knowingly to their deaths. The mound—nest? hive? whatever—loomed like an apartment-building-sized anthill. The surface was ridged and convoluted, a dull blackish-gray with bits of lighter color here and there. As they drew nearer, Bueller saw that the lighter bits were bones, a lot of them skulls, all blended into the surface.

"Damn," somebody said quietly.

"Some kind of secretion, all right, with a little organic stuff mixed in for the hell of it."

There was an oval-shaped entrance with a beaten path leading to it maybe a hundred meters ahead.

"I ain't going in there," Ramirez said. "Fuck this."

But the trio of air pods buzzing back and forth

overhead like dragonflies meant otherwise. As if to confirm this, Bueller's com came to life. "Move in," the voice said. And to punctuate the command, a thin green plasma beam splashed against the ground behind the squad, digging a small smoking crater into the stony surface.

"Wonder how the other squads are doing?" Chin said.

"Who cares?" Ramirez said. "We're about to become history here."

"This is what we came for," Bueller said.

"Fuck that," Ramirez said. "We are supposed to be marines, not bait!"

"I'm open to other ideas," Bueller said.

The six of them moved toward the entrance of the mound. Once they were inside the place, maybe they could just squat down and not go in any deeper.

Right, Bueller. And the guy on the monitor'll go blind and not see from our cams that we're standing still.

So, what can they do about it?

They can fry us with a reflected plasma beam, that's what they can do about it.

Oh, yeah. Right.

Or they can send one of the expendable androids down to hose us. Probably won't even have to get out of the air pod. Like Ramirez said, we're history.

The group reached the entrance. Bueller flicked his shoulder light on and took a deep breath. He stepped into the mound first.

Whatever was gonna happen was gonna happen.

* * *

Billie wound her way slowly from the kitchen to the hallway that led toward the ship's armory. A rolling pin and a peeler weren't going to get her very far against a shipful of armed men. She needed a gun. And a whole lot of good luck. Maybe even a miracle or two.

Massey was staring through the holographic readouts when a tiny chime called for his attention. He focused on the screen. The three air pods were holding over the entrance to the first mound; the other marine squads hadn't made it to their destinations yet. What was—?

Doppler showed aircraft closing on the air pods.

Impossible! There wasn't any civilization on this world. The aliens didn't have, couldn't have flying devices!

Then he realized what was wrong with the images. No heat signatures, no power leakage, no radio or radar or Doppler. Either the craft were so primitive they had to be gliders, or . . .

Massey blinked. "Team One," he said. "Alert!"

The first wave of flying creatures dived on the air pods. The cameras caught and recorded the images. They looked reptilian, with grayish, scaled skin. They had delta-shaped wings that spanned at least ten meters, short, sleek bodies and elongated heads with rows of pointed teeth. Carnivores, definitely. There were a dozen in the first group and they attacked soundlessly the three pods.

The androids were good, Massey had to give them that. The plasma rifles lit and lines of green swept the air. The creatures fell and died as the high-energy beams cut off wings, slashed bodies, lopped heads. Nine of the things went down in the first three seconds as the six androids fired their weapons repeatedly, dodging in the agile little pods.

But the second wave arrived and there were too many. One of the things took a beam in the chest, was probably dead instantly, but slammed into a pod and knocked it sideways. Another attacker flew in while the pod was tumbling and showed how well those big toothy jaws worked when it bit an arm from one of the androids. The one flying the pod. The pod spiraled down toward the ground, four or five of the beasts following it in controlled dives.

The other two pods were also in trouble. Flapping wings buffeted the androids as the things darted in and snapped at the heavy plastic, tore at it with taloned claws as if the pods were themselves alive.

Plasma beams flashed, the flying monsters died under the flares of energy, but those who weren't hit kept attacking. One of the pods looked like a popcorn ball beset by a flock of starving crows; the plastic was pocked with gouges and bite marks, dented from impacts. The androids fought on, but they were losing.

The first pod splatted against the ground, shattered, and hurled the two androids away from the impact. Almost instantly the flying creatures were upon the androids, tearing at them, ripping limbs from torsos, spraying circulating fluid up in thin white fountains.

They tore the androids apart but didn't eat them.

Apparently they didn't much like the taste of artificial flesh.

Massey watched, amazed, as one of the pods landed in a controlled dive and one of the androids leapt out and sprinted toward the mound. While the flying animals fell on the other android still trying to exit the pod, they did not pursue the fleeing one. They must have known what the aliens in the mounds were capable of. The running android neared the entrance.

The third pod burst into flame while still thirty meters above the ground. By the time it crashed, both the passengers inside had been mostly consumed in the fire. One of the plasma rifles went critical in the heat and a blinding green flash turned the pod into dust, along with four or five of the attackers who had followed it down too closely.

How interesting, Massey thought. Surely there was a market for these things. Perhaps he could capture one. A baby, perhaps.

But first, he had to protect his primary mission. He called the pods shepherding the other marines. "Go immediately to the 1st Squad coordinates," he said.

"What about the marines here?" one of the androids asked.

"Who cares? Do as I order. Keep a ground-hugging flight path. There are flying aliens here who will attack you. Get moving."

He broke the com and leaned back in his form-chair. Yes. This was turning out to be more interesting than he had anticipated.

* * *

Bueller heard the explosion and stopped.

"What the hell?" Chin began.

They were only fifty or sixty meters into the nest and the devil they knew suddenly seemed less dangerous than the one they didn't. "Let's go see," Bueller said.

"I'm with you, pal," Ramirez said.

"I'll watch our rear," Mbutu said. She held a fist-sized rock in her hand. She waved the rock.

Bueller had to laugh. Mbutu was crazy if she thought a rock was going to do her any good. Then again, any weapon was better than none. Bueller looked around for a stone of his own. Better to go down trying than riot.

What they saw was amazing. There were some kind of flying things flapping around like giant bats out there. All three pods were down, only one of them intact, and one of the androids was hauling ass toward the mound, moving at Olympic speed as he broken-stepped the rugged ground. He carried a plasma rifle in one hand.

"Move back," Bueller said. "I think maybe some luck just went our way."

"Maybe," Smith said from behind him. "What I want to know is how come the things who live here haven't swarmed all over us by now."

"Don't look a gift horse in the mouth," Chin said.

"What does that mean?"

"It means be glad you're still sucking in the air," Chin said. "Such that it is."

They watched the android run. One of the flying things made a half hearted pass at him, swooping down like a giant raptor seeking prey, but the

android dived flat and the thing missed by ten
meters anyhow. By the time it circled around for
another try, the android was nearly at the mound's
entrance. The flying thing must have decided it had
business elsewhere. It soared upward, caught a
thermal, and lifted away.

"Get ready for company," Bueller said.

The android reached the entrance and ran inside.
He never had a chance. All six of the marines hit
him, and he sprawled under their combined weight,
helpless.

Now they had a weapon. It wasn't much, but it
sure beat the alternatives.

Billie returned to the armory where she and
Mitch had been only a few hours past. There were
weapons aplenty, but after examining several of
them, she realized that they were all missing the
same part. She mentally shrugged, and slung one
of the carbines over her shoulder, collected a couple
of spare magazines and a flexbelt of grenades.
Maybe she could find the part to fix it. Or maybe
she could bluff somebody into thinking it was work-
able. Or threaten to blow up the ship with a grenade. If she was up against it and going to die
anyway, what the hell, she'd have nothing to lose.

Especially if something had happened to Mitch.

Bueller said, "All right. Blake, you're the best shot
in the squad, you get the plasma rifle."

She nodded, took the weapon, and did a quick
inspection. "Got almost full charge," she said.
"Thirty, thirty-five shots."

"If you have to use them, make them count," Bueller said.

"He's got a sidearm, too." That from Smith.

"Better let me have it," Bueller said.

"No offense, Bueller, but who died and left you in charge? We're all the same rank here since Easley bought it."

"I outscored everybody in pistol qualification."

"Yeah, Smith," Mbutu said, "you couldn't hit a tank at arm's length with a sidearm."

"Yeah, well, okay, fine," Smith said. "I was just checking, you know."

Bueller took the pistol, a standard 10mm caseless slug thrower. It used ammunition close to that of the carbines, except it was less powerful, and in a pinch could be made to fire the heavier stuff—if you didn't mind risking that the pistol would most likely blow up after five or six shots.

"Okay, pal," Bueller said to the captured android, "let's you and us talk."

"Wasting your time," the android said. "I'm no good as a hostage, I'm expendable, and my clock is running down. I'm dead in a couple weeks no matter what."

"You could have a real miserable couple of weeks, though," Mbutu said, hefting her rock.

The android shook its head. "I don't know anything, either. Massey runs the show and he keeps it to himself. We get what he wants us to get, nothing more."

Blake kicked the pinned android, hitting his hip with her boot. "Fine," she said. "Let's kill him now.

Go ahead, Mbutu, bust his head with your rock, no point in wasting a bullet or a charge on him."

"Ease off, Blake," Bueller said. "This guy came out of the vats and got programmed for this. It's not his fault. Not everybody gets a choice."

Blake stared at Bueller. "Yeah. I guess I hear that."

"I hate to point this out, but *I* hear something coming this way from inside the nest," Smith said. "And even a plasma rifle won't stop a whole herd of these bugs. What say we go play outside?"

Bueller glanced down the corridor. He heard the rattle of alien feet and claws on the material. "Let's move it, people. Get to the downed pods, there might be more guns or supplies, something."

"And then go where?" the android asked. "You're trapped on the planet without pods or an APC."

"Maybe so, pal, but we *ain't* trapped in this ant-hill. Let's go, marines."

Nobody needed to be told again.

Billie moved carefully through the ship, hiding when she heard people approaching. She had the carbine over her shoulder and clutched the rolling pin and peeler in her hands. She kept moving away from the voices and bootfalls until she realized she was in the ship's crew and commanding officer's quarters. She snaked her way around doorways and stayed flat against the walls, edging along, trying to stay invisible. If somebody should see her, she would be in deep shit in a real hurry.

Ahead was Stephens's cabin, and something drew Billie that way. He wouldn't be using it—one of the bodies she'd seen spaced had been the colonel. Surprised her, that he would die defending the ship, but maybe she'd read him wrong.

As Billie approached the door, it started to open.

Damn, somebody was inside!

She glanced up and down the corridor. She'd never get clear in time. Whoever came out of Stephens's cabin would see her before she could get to cover. If he was armed, she'd catch one in the back.

Billie raised the rolling pin, triggered the freezer, and flattened herself against the wall to the right of the sliding door. She hoped it was only one of them.

As the man stepped out into the corridor, Billie swung the rolling pin. The liquid inside hadn't solidified yet, but the pin was still heavy.

She smashed the pin into the man's head, angled just over his left ear. She put her shoulder and back into it, it was a good swing, powered further by her fear. The thick plastic shattered as it met bone, probably cracking the skull as well. Viscous blue coolant splashed from the broken pin, covering the man's face with cold globules.

He didn't go down. He staggered, slammed into the doorjamb, and wobbled, but he didn't go down.

Billie stepped in and drove her left hand at the man's belly, just below the sternum. The peeler sank into his flesh all the way to her hand.

White fluid sprayed from the wound onto her as she jerked the peeler out.

Android blood, she realized, as she tried for the second stab. He was an artificial person.

The android managed to twist and slap at her hand, partially deflecting the second thrust so it missed his solar plexus and skidded over his ribs, gouging chunks of his uniform and flesh out, leaving a shallow ditch that stretched from the center of his chest almost to his shoulder.

The coolant from the rolling pin clouded his vision, though, and his own punch missed Billie by a hair. As he wiped at his eyes, it gave Billie enough time for one more shot. If she didn't drop him with it, he would have her. Even a wounded android was still stronger than an ordinary human.

Billie jabbed, a long stroke, aiming at his eye. Growing up in a hospital you learned something about anatomy. The eyes were the easiest path through the skull to the brain.

The peeler hit just under her target, bounced up, and sank through the softer eye tissue. Jelly oozed from the ruined eye as the peeler went in.

The android jerked away from Billie, reached up with both hands, and jerked the peeler out. The serrated edge brought most of the eye out with it, clearing the socket until milky white circulating fluid welled and spilled.

He stood here for what seemed a long time, then collapsed. He didn't say anything, not even a groan, just dropped as if his bones had vanished, and died.

Billie's heart raced, pounding as though trying to dig its way out of her body. She still held part of the shattered rolling pin in her right hand. She let it fall. The clatter it made seemed loud in the corridor.

Her first reaction was to turn and run, but she didn't. Instead, she wondered why the android had been in Stephens's cabin.

Inside, she figured it out. The parts missing from

the carbines were stacked neatly in rows on the colonel's bed. Who would have put them there? Somebody had sabotaged the weapons, and it looked like she had found out who. Why had he done it? It didn't matter, she could worry about that later. Right now, she had other things on her mind.

Billie picked up one of the feed ramps, stripped the receiver on her weapon, and replaced the missing part. She snapped the connector into place and the ramp toggled through a diagnostic code and then clicked into place. She shoved a magazine into the carbine, touched the bolt control, and cycled a round into the firing chamber. The magazine's counter showed ninety-nine antipersonnel rounds remaining.

Billie smiled. It was tight, but she felt a lot better. If the headshrinkers in the clinic could see her now, they'd really have something to worry about: good God, it's a crazy woman with a gun!

Damn straight. And if anybody gave her any shit, she was going to invite them onto the dance floor for a fast and deadly tattoo tango.

Wilks. She would go find Wilks and get him loose. He'd know how to handle this. And once she got Wilks, they could collect Mitch and get the hell out of this mess. Maybe it wasn't the best plan in the universe, but it would do for now.

She hoped.

21

Massey watched as the other six air pods arrived in the vicinity of the 1st Squad's hive.

Watched the various angles the cameras gave him as the marines began shooting the pods out of the sky.

Well, well. They must have gotten hold of some of the downed weaponry. At least two plasma rifles were working from the ground, spearing his troops with brilliant green spikes.

His androids were pretty good, but they were general-purpose expendables, strong and quick, not extensively trained for formal combat scenarios. In this kind of thing the marines had the edge, even though they weren't armed very well. Three of the six pods flamed out and crashed; the other three quickly pulled out of range and hovered over the area.

"Commander," came the query from the com, "we have a problem here."

"I'm not blind," Massey said. "Hold your position. Keep them in sight."

He leaned back in his chair and rubbed at his chin. He turned away and called to the android standing guard at the door. "Go get Wilks and bring him here."

The android left.

Hmm. Yes, this was much more challenging than he had expected. Still, it was a minor setback. He had uploaded a raft of information about the planet, and his primary mission, to keep the government from securing an alien specimen, was accomplished. Should he continue this, or cut his losses and go home? On the one hand, he'd done pretty much what they wanted him to do—he could tell the company that the surface teams had been destroyed by alien wildlife and they would shrug it off as nothing. The company had its specimen, another one would only be backup. On the other hand, he hated the idea of even a partial failure.

Yes, it was an interesting question. He'd have to think about it a little more.

It was blind luck that let Billie see the pirate moving Wilks along, a gun jammed into the marine's back. Wilks had his hands crossed behind him and held with a thin carbon-fiber cuffstrip. The man—or was it another android?—herding Wilks along didn't glance down the corridor as he passed, his attention being on his prisoner, so he didn't see Billie crouched down by a radiator heat sink.

When they had gone by, Billie stood and cat-footed to the end of the cross corridor. She peeped around the corner in time to see them turn toward the control deck. Well, she had wanted to find Wilks and now she had. She slipped into the main corridor and started after the two.

Wilks had a feeling that wherever he was going, he might not be leaving under his own power. What the hell, he figured. He'd been living on borrowed time for more than a decade. He should have died with his squad back on Rim. It had all been gravy since, and not real tasty most of the time anyhow. Fuck it. If his number was up, then his number was up. He was going to go down like a man.

Bueller had the squad dispersed and shifting positions every few seconds. They were lucky the air pods hadn't been designed for anything other than quick and dirty transportation—the little craft didn't have much in the way of sensing gear, only basic radar and Doppler, no sniffers or IR. And no weapons except what the passengers themselves carried. Since the androids flying the pods had to rely on their own senses for targeting, the camo suits the marines wore made it difficult to see them. *They* were hard to see but the *pods* weren't. And the two plasma rifles the squad had would reach the same distance as the ones in the pods. So if they came down within range to splash the marines, they risked getting smoked themselves. And since they were much bigger and better targets, so far the score was marines three, pirates nada.

Then again, they couldn't sit here on the ground much longer. Sooner or later the bugs would come swarming out of the mound and that would make things more than a little worse for the squad. They couldn't afford to be pinned down here.

"Okay, everybody listen up," Bueller said, using his scrambled opchan. "We got to move out before company comes looking for dinner, everybody copy? On my signal, we rocket, magnetic south. Ramirez, you take point, Blake you cover. Everybody else keep your head down and give me asses and elbows."

Bueller didn't think the pirates could tap their opchan, but he remembered the lesson he'd learned from Wilks when he and Easley had gotten nailed during a practice assault back on Earth. "On my signal, marines, gainsay prior."

The last was a code. It meant move at 180 degrees to the last order. If the pirates *did* have an ear tuned to their private line, they'd be looking for the marines to move south. The squad would be going north, however, and it might buy them a few hundred more meters.

"Go!"

The captured android had been listening to Bueller give the order. Bueller didn't think about it until they were moving—the android didn't know their codes. When the marines scrambled, the pirate android went the wrong way.

"Hey!" Bueller yelled.

Too late. One of the pods swooped down to the south of their position, a plasma rifle on full auto. Its charge wouldn't last long firing that way, but hosing could cause a lot of damage in a short time. The ground smoked and cratered; rocks screamed as they shattered under the blasts of energy; the pirate android tried to stop but ran into the dancing lines of green death. His internal fluids boiled and he exploded like a water balloon stuck with a sharp knife. Well, it was quick. He wouldn't have suffered much.

Blake pulled up, spun, and sighted at the pod. The craft looped from its dive and started to lift.

"Too far," Bueller yelled. "Don't waste your shot!"

Blake grinned, her smile wide. She kept both eyes open as she aimed, followed the pod with her rifle, then squeezed off the plasma bolt.

It was five hundred meters if it was a centimeter, a fast-moving target. Not much chance of hitting it, Bueller thought.

The green beam drilled the pod dead center. The energy bolt coruscated against the heavy plastic, ate its way through in less time than it took a nervous man to blink, and burned out the pod's repellors. The pod seemed to hang motionless for a heartbeat, suspended in time and space, then it fell like a fat lead ball dropped in heavy gravity. Without the repellor, an air pod had the aerodynamics of a round brick. They were close enough to hear the atmosphere whistle across the hole the plasma bolt made. The thing hit the ground hard enough to make the hard dirt splash.

"Nice shot," Bueller said.

"Like duck hunting," she said. "Got to lead the target a little, that's all."

They ran.

The remaining two pods circled high overhead, keeping well out of range.

"Where are we going?" Chin yelled.

"To the APC."

"It's the other way!"

"I know. We'll circle around. Let them think we're lost. Once it gets dark we can lose these slush-brains."

"Yeah," Mbutu said, "but can we lose *them*?"

Behind the running marines, aliens began to emerge from the nest.

Massey dismissed the android. He turned to Wilks and said, "Your marines have proven quite adept down there. Seems they managed to get their hands on a couple of weapons and now they're making a run for it."

Wilks grinned. "That's too bad. I hope that hasn't upset your little plan any."

Massey pulled his antique pistol from its holster and stuck it under Wilks's chin, shoving the barrel into his flesh. "Here's an idea: Why don't you call them and tell them to surrender?"

Wilks managed to grin even wider. "You gonna do what, *kill* me if I don't?"

Massey laughed, backed off a little with the pistol. "It's nice to work with professionals after all the scum I usually have to deal with. You know I'm going to kill you no matter what."

"I sort of suspected that."

"It's necessary, you know. But you can go hard or you can go easy." Massey holstered the gun and pulled a thin boot knife. The stainless steel glittered in the overhead lights. The knife was only about seventeen or eighteen centimeters long, half of that handle, but it didn't take much in the hands of an expert. Wilks didn't doubt that Massey knew how to use it.

"Hell, my dick is bigger than that," Wilks said.

"Not for long."

Wilks gathered himself. His hands were bound behind him, but he could use his feet. Doubtless Massey knew hand-to-hand, but better to die trying than not.

The com chimed.

Massey moved back, outside of Wilks's range, and touched a control. "Commander, the marines have shot down another of our pods. They are moving north, away from the APC coordinates."

"They aren't that stupid," Massey said. "Stay with them. Targets of opportunity." He glanced at Wilks, then back at the com. He touched other controls on the board. A timer lit the air in one corner of the standard screen projection. It began to count down.

"Better safe than sorry," he said.

Wilks went for it. He took a couple of quick steps toward Massey.

Massey laughed and snapped up a sidekick. The move was almost lazy, a contemptuous strike. His boot caught Wilks in the belly and knocked him down. He hit hard, unable to use his hands to break his fall. He dug with his heels in a futile effort to get up. He'd never make it.

Massey twirled the knife in his hand. "This game is being called on account of rain," he said. "Time to take my winnings and go home. So long, Sergeant Wilks." He started toward the helpless marine.

"Drop it!" came a woman's voice from behind Massey.

Evening threw long shadows over the alien landscape, and as the sun settled for the night, Bueller and his squad started their circle toward the APC. It was harder to see the air pods trailing them, and therefore it would be harder for the pirates to see them, too.

"What about the aliens?" Bueller asked.

Mbutu shook her head. "They must have lousy senses of smell," she said. "When we cut left back there, they kept going straight. Crummy trackers."

"That's good."

"Maybe," Ramirez said. "Or maybe there's something in this direction they don't want to run into. Something meaner than they are."

"That's what I like about you, Ramirez, you always look on the bright side of things," Blake said.

"Fuck you, Blake."

"You wish. If you had anything bigger than a toothpick I might consider it."

Bueller grinned. They might all die out here, but if they could make jokes, then morale was higher than it had been since the pirates had boarded them.

"Let's hustle it up, marines. We got places to go and things to do."

* * *

Billie had the carbine aimed at the pirate's heart and if he made any sudden moves she was going to carve it out of him.

The man grinned as he let the knife fall. He looked like some of the psychotics Billie had seen in the lockdown section of the hospital.

"Well, well. What have we here? You the ship's mascot?"

"Stay real still."

"So that explains the extra on the head count. You can't be one of those ugly marines, you're too pretty. Crew smuggle you onboard for fun and games, maybe?"

Wilks said, "Shoot him, Billie. Shoot him now!"

The man glanced at Wilks. "Ah. Friend of yours, eh, Sergeant? You have nice taste." He turned back toward Billie. Slid a half step toward her, hands outstretched wide, trying to look harmless.

"Another step and I punch your ticket," she said.

"Come on. Sweet little thing like you? You don't want to kill me. Think about what it would be like, being responsible for the death of another human being. It'll give you bad dreams, honey." He slid another half step forward.

Billie swallowed, her mouth dry. This man was a killer, she had seen the bodies get spaced. And he had done something with Mitch. But his hands were in the air. Shooting somebody down like this, it was different from thunking the android on the head.

Billie shuffled back a step. "I'm telling you to stop right there."

Wilks managed to lever himself to his feet by leaning against a bulkhead. "Billie, this guy is a murderer! You have to put him down! Shoot!"

She glanced at Wilks.

A mistake.

As soon as her attention left the pirate, he leapt. God, he was fast! Billie pulled the trigger on the carbine, but he was already twisting, dropping under the line of her fire. Half a dozen rounds shattered a computer console, the noise was awful, lights flickered as the power surged and shorted in the plugged console—

She tried to realign the weapon but too late. He hit her above the knees, and she did a half flip forward and landed on her back—

"Stupid bitch!" he said as he rolled up and caught Billie by the shoulders. "Point a goddamn gun at me!" He snatched her from the floor and threw her against the bulkhead.

Billie went gray as her head slammed against the wall. Even as she bounced off, he was on her, one hand grabbing her shirt, the other slapping her face. "I don't need a weapon, you stupid cunt, I could tear your throat out with my fingers!" He slapped her again. Billie felt a tooth cut the inside of her lip. Blood sprayed from her mouth as he slapped her the third time. He shoved her back against the wall, lifted her feet clear of the deck by her shirt. Pulled his pistol from his holster. Grinned like a maniac.

"But I don't dirty my hands on nothings like you."

As he raised the gun to kill her, Billie saw a blur behind him. She couldn't stop her gasp.

The pirate tried to turn, but she locked both her hands around the wrist of the hand he held her with. It slowed him enough so that Wilks hit him with one shoulder just above his hip. Billie felt her shirt tear as the pirate was knocked away.

She fell to the floor and scrabbled on all fours.

Toward the carbine where it had fallen. Five meters. Four. Three—

The pirate roared and Billie twisted enough to see him. He had lost his pistol, but he was up and diving for it.

Two meters to the carbine. One—

"I'll kill both of you!"

Wilks was sprawled on his side, pushing himself along with only his left foot. Toward the pirate.

Billie reached the carbine. Grabbed it. Rolled onto her back. Wouldn't be time to get to her feet—

The pirate's gun went off, but she was rolling and she felt the slug hit the deck where she had just been. No time to aim. She pushed the gun out as if it were her fist punching and pulled the trigger. The fire selector must have been jiggled when the gun had fallen. It went off once. Billie, expecting full auto, couldn't figure it out. She held the trigger back, waiting for more fire. Nothing. She'd have to let it go and pull it again, she realized. Oh, fuck!

But one was enough.

The caseless 10mm round caught the pirate just below the shoulder of his gun arm. Blew a hole through him. Billie saw him tumble, the gun falling from his nerveless fingers. The entry wound was the size of her fingertip, but when he fell she saw the exit wound, high on his back, was as big as her fist.

The pistol slid two meters away from the fallen man's fingertips. He raised his head, saw the pistol, crawled for it. Stretched his good hand out for it.

Billie came up, carbine held ready, and jumped for the pistol. Kicked it across the room. Pointed the carbine at the downed man.

He rolled over onto his back. Blood poured from his wound, spreading under his head in a coppery-smelling pool.

"Stupid fucking bitch," he said. He reached for something at his waist.

"Don't move!"

"Fuck you." He slid his left hand into a vertical slit on his coverall over his right hip. She saw him smile as he gripped it.

"Billie!" Wilks yelled.

"Stop!" she screamed.

He started to pull his hand out—

She squeezed the trigger.

The explosion was loud in the enclosed room, it lapped against the hard walls and splashed back at her. The smell of burnt propellant filled her nostrils. Her ears rang.

The round hit him square in the mouth. Chopped out some front teeth and blew the back of his head all over the deck and wall behind him. Whatever he had intended to do wasn't ever going to happen.

She bent, tugged his hand out. He death-gripped a grenade. The safety cap had already been snapped up and his thumb was on the detonate button. Carefully, Billie pried the grenade loose from the dead man's hand and closed the safety cap. He would have blown them all up, ruined the control room, sent the ship spiraling down to burn in the atmosphere.

"Billie, cut me lose."

She looked at Wilks, blinked as if she'd never seen him before. "What?"

"He's set some kind of timer going. Hurry!"

Numbly, Billie obeyed. She found the fallen knife, used it to cut the strand binding Wilks. The knife was very sharp.

Free, Wilks ran to the com board. Looked at the screen. A bullet had shattered the projector. He couldn't see how much time was left. He started tapping controls on the console, swore, then moved to another screen.

"What is it?"

He shook his head. "I think it's a bomb set on the APC. 1st Squad got loose. He was afraid they'd get to the APC and come back."

"What about Mitch?"

"I don't know."

"Call him! Find out!"

"Billie—"

"Goddammit, Wilks!"

"Let me see if I can stop this timer. They'll need a way off the planet. Go guard the door! There are still a couple of the androids running around loose!"

She stared at him.

"Go, do it! If they get us, we all die!"

Billie moved. She pushed the selector to full auto, looked out into the corridor, didn't see anybody. She stood at the doorway, watching.

"Wilks?"

"I don't have enough time! There's got to be a failsafe, a break-off command but I don't know the code. I'm trying to bust the APC controls open to shut the power down, maybe the destruct is run off of its systems. It's all I can do."

"How long?"

He shrugged. "Could be a minute, could be an hour. I can't tell. The system won't access it from here."

Billie turned back to watch the corridor. If Mitch was alive, she'd go down and find him. If not, then it didn't much matter.

"Damn!" Wilks said. "Damn, damn, damn!"

22

Fortunately for the squad they'd been issued IR viewers. The pirates had known the marines would be going into a dark hive, so they let them keep their red eyes.

So they could move in the dark.

The air pods might be buzzing around up there somewhere, but for now, the marines were better equipped and effectively invisible.

They approached the APC in the moonless night, guided by the landing craft's heat leaks. Ramirez had the point; he was several hundred meters ahead of the rest of them. Bueller had told Ramirez to pull up short, scout the area, and then report back. It was likely that there were guards on the lander and Bueller had to figure a way to take them out without damaging the craft.

Bueller was looking away from the lander when all of a moment the night turned to blinding day.

"Shit!" he said. He flipped the IR flat screen up and turned, using his own vision.

The fireball from the APC was still spreading, dimmed somewhat and growing darker as it expanded outward and upward. They were far enough away so that the shock wave was fairly mild; it was like a hot wind, a sudden breeze off a desert at midday. Bueller dropped flat, but realized even as he did so that his reflexes were too slow. If it had been dangerous they'd already be past tense.

After a second pieces of wreckage began to patter down, some of it hit nearby, a solid *chunk!* as a heavy object dug into the rocky soil. A bit of flaming debris arced past, still climbing, and other burning shards fell like a holiday fireworks display, a hot rain that pocked the dirt and went dark or bounced and stayed lit even after coming to rest.

"Oh, *man!*" Chin said.

Bueller spoke into the com. "Ramirez? Respond."

The opchan was quiet.

"*Adios*, Ramirez," Mbutu said.

Bueller stared at the smoking ruin ahead of them. Ramirez must have gotten caught in the explosion. Damn!

He was sorry to lose Ramirez, but another cold fact lay in his belly like a bar of dry ice: with the APC destroyed, they were all fucked. End of mission. End of squad.

Damn.

*　*　*

Billie said to Wilks, "Can you contact the marines?"

The com board was alive with incoming calls, but all of them from the pirate androids, who were stranded on-planet when the APC blew. Wilks waved his hand over the cutoff control and the board fell silent. He touched another control.

"Fox Platoon, this is Sergeant Wilks. Anybody copy?"

For what seemed a long time to Billie there was no response. Oh, gods, Mitch!

"This is Bueller, 1st Squad."

"Mitch!"

Wilks waved her to silence. "Bueller, what's your situation?"

"I've got Blake, Smith, Chin, and Mbutu. We lost Ramirez when the APC went nova. How are things there?"

"Billie got the drop on the head bad guy. He's no longer with us. There are probably some of his troops still loose on the ship but we're armed and in the control center. I think we can clean them out okay."

"Interesting that his androids aren't First-Lawed," Bueller said.

"Yeah, ain't it, though. Listen up. I'll light the other APC and come down after your squad. This mission is going to be an abort, Bueller. The bad guys already have one of the bugs back home. Once the government hears that, they'll grab it. We don't need a specimen anymore."

"Copy that, Sergeant Wilks. We'll find a safe place for the APC to land—"

Suddenly a voice cut in over that of Bueller's, bleeding across a wide spectrum of the radio band.

"Help, somebody help! This is Walters, Second Officer. The androids put us down next to one of those fucking anthills and the things are coming out right toward us! Help us!"

Wilks said, "Dammit!" He fiddled with the com controls. "Walters, this is Wilks! Where are you? Give me a transponder beacon!"

"Jesus and Buddha! They're all over us! No! Leave me alone! Aaahh!"

"The beacon, Walters, trigger the beacon!"

Billie stared at Wilks.

"There it is!" he said. "He managed to kick it on."

Billie shook her head. "The things will take them into the hive. They'll web them up in the egg room."

Wilks nodded. "Yeah. Even with the beacon, we can't get to them before they get implanted. They're dead men." He blew out a short sigh. "I'm gonna nuke the planet from breakaway orbit," he said. "At least it'll be quick. We've got enough hardware. While Stephens was bitching about the plasma rifles, I was moving bomb components past him disguised as spare parts. I can put a ring of fire down there that'll trigger a thousand volcanoes. Between them and the nukes, they'll scour the place like a sandblaster. Sterilize the whole fucking planet."

"Sergeant Wilks," came Mitch's voice. "We heard the distress signal. It's only a dozen klicks from here. We're on the way."

"Negative on that, mister. The mission is an

abort, repeat, it is an abort. You find a spot for the APC and wait for it to collect you. That's an order."

"Sergeant, you know we can't leave those men in there."

Wilks's jaw muscles danced as he ground his teeth together.

"We'll call for the APC when we get them out," Mitch said.

Billie didn't understand what was going on. "Mitch! This is Billie! You can't save the crew; they are as good as dead! Wait for the APC!"

"I—I can't explain it, Billie, but we can't just let them die."

"Dammit, Mitch! What is this, some kind of marine honor thing? They're gone! They might be breathing for a while longer but they're dead if they get implanted! We couldn't do anything for them even if you could get them out! It isn't worth the risk!"

"I'm sorry, Billie. I love you."

"Mitch!"

"Save your breath," Wilks said. "You can't stop them."

"Why?"

But Wilks had nothing to say.

"Anything from the other squads?" Chin asked.

"No," Bueller answered. "I expect if any of them made it and still have coms working we'll see them at the hive."

Smith shook his head. "Damn, I don't like this."

"Tell me about it," Bueller said.

They moved off through the night.

* * *

There were four of Massey's First-Law-less androids on the ship. Wilks and Billie found and killed them all.

"I don't understand," Billie said. "I didn't think androids could hurt people."

"Close," he said. "They modified Asimov's First Law of Robotics for androids. They can't *kill* a human or even stand by and *allow* a human to be killed without trying to help. Otherwise there couldn't be android surgeons; they wouldn't be able to hurt somebody a little to save them from a bigger hurt or death. Apparently nobody told this group. Massey's backing must be very high up in the scheme of things to have pulled that one off."

Wilks programmed the remaining military lander, as well as the one from Massey's ship. The company ship would hang in standby orbit in case it was needed; he could pilot it by remote from the planet. Massey had dropped the little pods with their crews in what was called snowball wrap—it burned off going down—but the pods couldn't reach escape velocity to make it back out of the gravity well.

"I'm going down with you," Billie said.

"Not a good idea. I'd rather have you on the ship."

"I don't much care what you want. I'm going."

Wilks looked at her, shook his head. He'd tried to warn her, tried to keep her from getting involved with Bueller. It hadn't worked. Now she was having to pay the price. The cost was steep. He hurt for her, but maybe it was the best way. Bueller and the others were probably history, no better off than those of their crew the monsters had dragged into their mound for baby food. None of the other squads had answered his calls. The mission was a fuckup from the first. Damn.

"All right. You can go." What else could he say?

The squad had a stroke of good luck. Just before dawn they happened on one of the air pods. The little vehicle must have run low on fuel and put down next to a stream to try to recharge the converters. It would take a long time for the stream's water to power up the flywheel batteries—the thing wasn't much bigger than a ditch and the current was slow-moving—but it was not as if the passengers had a lot of choice. Running dry of power at a hundred meters in the air would guarantee a landing nobody would walk away from.

Using her red eye, Blake spiked the two androids from two hundred meters out, one shot each.

"So, do I get a medal or something?"

"Sure, Blake. When we get back to Earth, I'll put you in for the Marksmanship Badge."

"Aw, I already got that one, Bueller. I was hoping for a Platinum Star, at least."

"What the hell, that, too," Bueller said.

They grinned at each other, but the expressions were tight, whistling-past-the-graveyard humor. Their chances of getting out of this alive were as slim as those of a spitball in a supernova.

But they were better off now. The pod held two more plasma rifles and chargers, a 10mm carbine, and two softslug pistols. Everybody was armed, a plasma weapon for everybody except Bueller, who took the carbine and a belt of grenades.

"How's the pod's charge?" Bueller asked.

"Almost dead," Smith answered. "It'll take sixteen hours at the stream's flow rate to give it enough to lift. Even then, two passengers would be reaching."

Bueller shrugged. "Let it keep charging. Maybe it'll be useful when we get back."

" 'When'?" Smith said. "My, ain't you the optimist."

"Let's move out."

Dawn lit the eastern skies with the first reddish glimmers of day.

" 'Red sky in the morning, sailors take warning,' " Smith said.

"We're marines," Bueller said. "Let the Navy worry about that shit."

They marched toward the alien mound.

As the APC fell from the *Benedict*'s belly into space, Billie held her breath. Outside the ship's faux gravity field, she and Wilks were suddenly weightless, and that cold, pit-of-the-stomach flutter made her want to throw up. She swallowed the bile that threatened to spew and took deep breaths through her nose. Mitch was down there and still alive. If they could get to the hive before he went inside, she could maybe stop him. If they were too late for that, then she would grab a gun and go in after him.

"How long?" she asked.

"If we're lucky, maybe an hour."

"And if we aren't lucky?"

"We've got to skip through the atmosphere at a bad angle to make the rendezvous," he said. "If we do it wrong we could fry inside this can."

"What happens to the planet if we die?"

"If I don't put in a call to the ship in six hours, the computer drops the atomics and heads for home. Anybody left down there had better get their affairs in order real quick."

Billie looked at Wilks.

"You know what those things can do where there's only a few of them," he said. "I'm not taking any chances on leaving a whole planet full of them lying around for some other poor sucker to stumble on."

She nodded. He was right. If they died, it was best to take the entire world with them. It was the only way to be sure.

"There's the entrance," Mbutu said. "What's the drill?"

"I'll take the point," Bueller said. "Move in after me in a two-and-two, Mbutu, you and Chin in front, Blake, you and Smith covering our asses. We have the signal from the transponder, we go straight to it, recover the crew, come straight out."

"Easy as falling down a grav-shaft," Smith said.

"You got a warped sense of humor," Blake said. "Somebody must have jiggled the tech's arm when he was installing your brain matrix."

"Fuck you," Smith said.

"If we get back to the ship, I'm all yours, lover."

"That's great, Blake," Mbutu said, "give him a reason to die quicker."

"Let's move in, marines. People need our help in there."

They were two hundred meters into the mound when the first wave of aliens came at them. A dozen of the things, moving impossibly fast, fangs bared, claws extended.

"Aim low!" Bueller ordered. "Take out their legs!"

He snapped off three three-round bursts, waving the carbine in a short arc to his left, leaving the center and right of the corridor clear.

Green beams flashed past him and burned limbs from bodies. Several of the things fell and skidded on the ridged floor and others tangled with them.

Bueller pulled the softslug pistol from his belt. The exterior armor would stop the handgun's rounds, but when the things opened their mouths to extend those toothed rods, he fired his sidearm into the openings. The softslugs tore through the tissue inside the heads very nicely, and the projectiles stayed inside the harder skulls, doing enough damage to be fatal. Rattled around like a mad bumblebee in a jar.

It was over in five seconds, and the twelve attacking aliens lay burned or shattered, smoke rising where the blood touched the hive. Not that something that acidic could really be called blood.

"Don't step in the liquid," Bueller ordered.

"Stuff's not eating into the floor much," Blake said.

"Makes sense that it wouldn't," Chin said.

"Wouldn't do to have holes burned in the building every time some drone cut its finger."

"We're still five hundred meters away from our quarry," Bueller said. "Let's move."

The APC bounced, the ride bone-jarring despite the seat restraints. The atmosphere was cloudy, and visibility was nil. Wilks hoped the computer controls knew what they were doing. The hull temperature was hot enough to melt silver and climbing. The belly, nose, and underwing tiles on the APC were designed to take a lot more friction than they were getting, but if the lander slewed too much one way or the other, the heat could be a problem. If the skin burned through, it could cause fatal damage to the occupants in a matter of a couple of seconds. At least it would be fast.

"A-a-ar-are w-w-we g-g-gonna m-make it?"

Wilks looked at Billie. His own voice chattered with the vibrations when he answered. "M-m-maybe."

Another wave of monsters clattered toward the squad, hissing as they moved. Bueller's carbine rumbled, a giant tearing heavy canvas, and the armor-piercing rounds punched through the bodies where they hit straight on, ricocheted off when they struck at an angle, making sparks like flint on steel.

Chin was right behind Bueller and his plasma rifle flared, the pulses making the walls glow with a sickly verdant gleam.

One of the things tumbled, legs seared off at the

knees. It skidded into Bueller, knocked him to the side against the wall.

Bueller slammed into the surface, his head protected by the helmet but his shoulder hit hard. The force of the impact twisted him so as he fell away he saw what happened to Chin as if watching it on a holoviewer in slow motion.

—The legless alien spun, scrabbled with its taloned hands, and slid in at Chin under his line of fire. Chin tried to lower his aim, but too late. The alien opened massive jaws and bit, latching on to Chin's thigh—

—Chin screamed. He slammed the butt of the plasma rifle uselessly at the thing's armored skull—

—Blake yelled, "Don't move!" and slid over a step to shoot the alien that had Chin in its teeth—

—The alien's legs were gone, but it still had its tail. It speared Chin's belly, jammed the pointed tail through him so it emerged between two ribs on his back. The ribs broke through the skin, showing splintered bones—

—Blake fired, hit the alien behind the hinge of its jaws. The thing convulsed and the teeth sheared through Chin's leg completely. For a second he stood there on one leg, the monster's tail helping him stay up. Then he fell—

—Smith moved in to tug at Chin, the thing's tail still through him, and another alien flew past Bueller, blocking for an instant his view. He managed to raise his weapon, even though it had all happened so fast he was still falling after his impact with the wall—

—Bueller fired. One of the slugs *spanged* off the

alien, knocked its head sideways so it looked straight at Bueller. The other two rounds missed the alien. One of them found Chin and blew the top of his head off—

—Smith was close to the alien. As it twisted back to find him, Smith fired. He was too close. The focuser on the end of the plasma rifle nearly touched the thing. The beam pierced the alien's armor, but it also partially splashed. The plasma sprayed and hit Smith in the face. It cooked the flesh, boiled his eyes into steam. He fell back as the alien collapsed on him, its acid blood spewing onto Smith, eating through his armor and body, stinking smoke rising in a hot blast—

—Bueller hit the floor. He heard the hums of more plasma beams, saw the reflected green on the walls, came to his feet . . .

The second wave was over, maybe twenty more of the things lay dead, but both Smith and Chin also gone.

That left only three of them to save the crew.

Bueller looked at Blake and Mbutu. They nodded at him. Without speaking, they started deeper into the hive.

23

A hard jolt shook the APC and it dropped in free-fall for a second. Billie felt a moment of nausea. She'd never done particularly well in zero gravity; her stomach always twisted in what felt like a continuous drop from a great height. Then the little ship's wings caught the atmosphere again, weight returned, and she swallowed as her belly recovered its composure.

"That's the worst of it," Wilks said. "We're on a long glide path to the place now. Might hit a few clouds on the way, get a little chop, but that's pretty much it."

Billie nodded, not speaking. Would it be too late? Would Mitch still be alive? As much as anybody, Billie knew the dangers of the enemies her lover faced. Whatever their motivation, they were killing machines, and if they cared about their own deaths, it never showed. Survival of the species was the thing; individuals didn't seem to matter much. Not like people. Not like people at all.

"How long?"

"Thirty minutes, give or take. We have to glide in so we'll have enough juice to achieve escape velocity and make it back to the ship."

Billie nodded again. There was not much to say about that.

There was a side passage to Bueller's left and he put thirty rounds down it as he drew level with it, hosing the carbine back and forth at waist level. He really couldn't afford the ammo, he had only one more magazine, but the side corridor was dark and he didn't want any nasty surprises.

He got one anyhow.

The automatic fire should have chopped any of the aliens standing between the knees and hips; probably it did. But one of them must have been hanging on the ceiling or stretched out on the floor. As soon as the burst of fire ended, the thing jumped out.

Bueller wasn't taking anything for granted, so he still had his weapon held ready, but the thing leapt as he fired again, flew like a missile at him.

Bueller's reactions were fast. It wouldn't matter how many rounds hit the damned thing, inertia would keep it coming. Bueller didn't have time to think. He dropped, slammed flat onto the slimy, hot floor, and the alien missed him by centimeters.

Mbutu yelled as the thing barreled into her. Blake fired, but the monster and Mbutu were entwined, and as good as Blake was, she couldn't stop the acid flow her shot caused. The spewing wound drenched Mbutu's face. She instinctively opened her mouth to scream. The thing was dying but it pumped enough of the corrosive blood onto Mbutu so she would join it shortly. Maybe she might have survived were she in a full-ride military medicator, but she'd never make it that far. Her cheeks and nose were a smoking ruin, her throat and lungs already being eaten away.

She would drown in her own fluids.

Bueller scrambled up. Mbutu made a strangled noise halfway between a moan and a plea. He knew what she wanted. He couldn't ask Blake to do it. Bueller pointed his carbine, tapped the trigger once.

The bullet in her brain ended Mbutu's suffering.

Blake nodded. "Thanks," she said.

Bueller had trouble drawing enough air to breathe. He shuddered.

Two of them left.

"There it is," Wilks said.

The front view screens gave a better picture than the ports, but Billie stared through the clear shields, preferring the reality. The mound sprawled upon the ground like a malignant tumor, dull gray in the light of the local sun. It was a desolate landscape, cleared around the hive of everything but dust and rock.

"I'm going to put down on that little ridge," Wilks said. "We can use the ship's guns better on the high ground and we'll be able to see them coming. And anything that might be chasing them."

She looked at him.

"Still too much interference," he said. "Something in the walls is blocking the com's signal."

"I could go—" Billie began.

"No. You can't."

"Man, oh, man," Blake said, "I'm definitely crossing this place *off* my vacation list. It stinks in here."

The winding corridor had provided them with more attackers, but it was wide enough that the red eyes let them see in time. Bueller and Blake took the aliens out as soon as they spotted them, and it had almost gotten to the point of target shooting for Bueller. He'd switched to semiauto to conserve ammo. He had about eighty rounds left, but also had Mbutu's plasma rifle slung over his shoulder. Things could be worse.

A large archway loomed.

"Signal is coming from in there," Blake said. "Less than fifty meters."

"The hatching room," Bueller said.

"Yeah."

"Let's do it."

The heat intensified as they neared the archway, the air thickened even more with stench and high humidity. It felt like the inside of a steambath full of rotting corpses.

Bueller darted through the opening, Blake backing in behind him, her rifle pointed to the rear.

"There they are," he said.

Four people, three men and a woman, webbed to the walls in that gauzy, spidery goo the things used.

The garbage-can-sized eggs sat impassively on the floor. There was no sign of the queen, no other drones around. It was quiet enough so Bueller could hear his own breathing.

The two of them moved quickly.

"This one is dead," Blake said, her fingers on the carotid of one of the women.

"This one, too," Bueller said.

One of them was alive, though. The marines tore away the sticky webbing. The eggs next to the man were still closed, he hadn't been implanted yet.

He came to as they were dragging him free of the web. He screamed.

"Easy, easy!" Blake said. "It's okay, we got you!"

Fear had stolen his words. The man tried to speak, stammered, gave up.

"Can you walk?"

He nodded, still mute.

"Then let's make tracks, fast, understand?"

He nodded again.

The three of them started for the chamber's exit. When they reached it, Bueller stopped.

Blake raised an eyebrow at him. "What?"

"I'll just leave them a couple of grenades for a going away present," he said. He hip-pointed his carbine and launched three rounds, fast, so the first explosion was still expanding as the second and third rounds flew. The sound was deafening, despite the spike muters the marines wore.

"Go, go!"

They ran.

* * *

Wilks touched a control on the sensor board. "Got seismic activity in there. Looks like somebody fired some explosive armament. M-40s, probably."

"They're still alive," Billie said.

"Maybe."

"We have to *do* something!"

"We *are* doing something. We're waiting. Won't help anybody if we don't have a way off this damned rock. In five hours the whole planet is going to get hammered flat as the oceans on Jupiter. We don't want to be here then."

"To your left!" Bueller yelled.

Blake, cool as liquid oxygen, turned and painted the corridor green with her plasma. The withering beams cooked the onrushing alien drones like crabs under their shells. Fluid boiled from their joints in deadly steam, but far enough away so there was no danger to the marines or the crewman.

"Eat hot plasma death, alien scum," Blake said.

Bueller stared at her.

"I always wanted to say that," she said. She smiled.

He shook his head. But he shared her feeling; against all the odds, they were nearing the exit to this nightmare. Less than a hundred meters away the harsh daylight of the planet spilled into the mound, giving them a light at the end of a very dangerous tunnel.

"Almost there," Bueller said. "Can you make it?"

The crewman finally found his voice. "I'll make it. Just keep those bastards off us."

The last thirty meters were the worst. It was clear,

no drones in front of them, but the run for the way out filled Bueller with hope—they might really make it after all—and it was too soon for that kind of optimism.

Still, they reached the mouth of the tunnel.

"Hel-*lo*, sunshine!" Blake said as they stepped out of the mound. Bueller had the tail, he kept his weapon and his gaze behind them, but the pressure of the light on his bare skin felt as good as anything ever had.

Blake said, "Sonofa*bitch*, our ride is here! There's the APC!"

Bueller spared a glance. Yes. There it was, on a slight ridge five hundred meters away.

Blake laughed. "Let's go home, folks!"

Bueller managed a chuckle. There was something wonderful about the air, bad as it was. And aside from Billie, he'd never seen anything quite as beautiful as that combat-camoed drop ship perched almost within spitting distance. "I hear that," he said. "Move out, I'll cover our asses."

Blake led the crewman down the incline from the mound along the dusty trail.

"There they are," Wilks said, his voice quiet and edgy.

Billie jerked around. Too far away to tell by direct visual who they were. Three of them. Two moving down the slope to the mound's entrance, one standing guard behind them.

Billie reached for the view enhancer, tapped the magnification up, looked at the screen.

The one in the entrance was Mitch.

Alive!

"Only three of them left," Wilks said. "Two marines and one crewman."

Billie didn't care. One of them was Mitch, he was okay, that was all that mattered.

"1st squad, this is Wilks. You copy?"

A woman's voice came back. "Glad you could drop by, Sarge. But I think the party's over. What say we pack it in and junk this place?"

"Yeah," Wilks said. "Hurry up, Blake, the meter is running."

"On our way."

Mitch heard the com and grinned. He stared into the darkness of the mound's gaping mouth. He started backing away, weapon still trained on the entrance. "Hey, Billie," he said into his com. "Hope you kept it warm for me."

"Come and get it," Billie said.

He half turned to look at the APC, the smile bright and happy.

A mistake.

The alien must have been waiting in the darkness for some break in Bueller's attention. It came clattering out, claws scraping and digging into the rocky surface as it cleared the entrance, arms extended, teeth revealed in a moray eel's needle grin.

Bueller twisted, swung the carbine around. Slipped on a loose piece of rock. Shifted, off balance, to his left. The carbine's barrel dropped, just a hair, as he fired.

Fired, and missed.

He tried to correct his aim, the thing was almost

on top of him and he only needed to pointshoot, but he was too slow. It crossed its hands, grabbed him, digging one steel-hard claw into his ribs, the other on the opposite side, just under his hip. Talons bit deep. The carbine flew from Bueller's grip. He tried to draw the slug pistol.

"Mitch!" Billie screamed from his com.

The alien flexed muscles hidden under its exoskeleton, cords filled with power a score of times stronger than a man could manage. Bueller felt the pain burn through his waist, a shattering bolt that short-circuited all his systems, filling him, like a sudden plunge into molten aluminum. He managed a scream, then felt the unendurable shock as—

As the thing tore him in half at the waist.

Billie saw the parts of Bueller fall. Saw his hips and legs fly one way, his upper body another. Tumbling, and the white circulating fluid—not red blood, white, *white!*—spraying like a milky fountain into the air under the alien sun.

24

Wilks watched the alien rip Bueller apart.

He yelled into the com. "Blake, get down!" He slapped the fire controls for the robot guns trained on the mouth of the alien hive. He saw the edges of the entrance light with tiny flashes as the 20mm expended uranium slugs chattered against the walls inside. Having a specific target, the robot gun hosed it in bursts of twenty, S-shaped patterns from top to bottom, stopping a meter or so short of the ground.

The gunfire chopped the alien into pieces, blowing the shattered parts back against the hive like a swat from a giant steel broom. The fire computer locked in the shape of the alien and shut the gun down, waiting for more targets that looked like him.

Billie screamed. She was looking at the viewer

and it was dialed up so she couldn't miss what Bueller was. The ancillary nodes of his digestive system hung from his torso; white polymer circulating fluid oozed over everything. Where a human would be soaked with blood and painted bright crimson, Bueller was drenched in milky froth. Tubules, shunts, circulatory lines, all splayed from the ruined android body.

Billie screamed again, a wordless cry. Wilks knew then she'd never suspected.

"Billie!"

She kept yelling.

He didn't have time for this. Over her din, he yelled into the com. "Blake! Move it! Stay low, you're clear to one meter only!"

The computer triggered the robot gun again. Wilks only saw the aliens for a second before the things were punched back into the mound.

Blake moved, but the wrong way. She crawled back to where Bueller lay, staying under the gun's field of fire.

"Blake, goddammit!"

Billie screamed again.

Wilks slid the control chair over a meter, reached out, slapped Billie's face. Her scream stopped as if cut off by a laser harvester.

"He's alive," Blake said over the com. She hoisted the terribly wounded android onto her back and crawled back to where the crewman lay.

"Oh, God, oh, God, oh, God," Billie said.

Wilks lost it. "I tried to fucking warn you! I tried to keep you away from him! You wouldn't listen to me! Yes, he's an android. The whole platoon, all of them, they're *all* androids! Created for a mission like this. How do you think they managed to breathe that thin air and keep going?"

Billie stared at the screen, not blinking, not moving.

Blake zigzagged, cleared the APC's gun line, and stood, Bueller still on her back. Half of Bueller. The crewman was right behind her.

"That's why they had to go back into the mound," Wilks said, feeling very tired all of a sudden. "They couldn't let the humans die. It's the First Law."

Billie stared straight ahead.

"They're faster, stronger, cheaper than we are to maintain. Some people didn't like working with them, so the new experimental models were made to pass for human. They eat, drink, piss, act, and even feel like humans. They can hate, fear, love, just like we do. From the outside, even an expert can't tell. Everything external looks just the same. But I guess you know that, don't you?"

Finally she turned to look at him. He could see her pain, it went all the way to her core. She had fallen in love with an android, had slept with him. For some people, that would be the same as falling in love with a dog or a farm animal and having sex with it.

"The pirates didn't know," he continued. "That's why the aliens weren't in any hurry to attack the marines and use them for incubators. Their flesh wouldn't support the babies. They look the same, feel the same to the touch, but apparently they don't *taste* very good.

"I'm sorry, kid."

When she spoke, her voice was as cold as deep space. "Why didn't you tell me, Wilks?"

"I tried. You didn't want to hear it."

"You never said anything about androids."

"By the time I realized I should, it was too late. What was I supposed to say? You're in love with an artificial person? He was born in a vat and put together like a puzzle by a bunch of androtechs? You wouldn't have believed it."

"You should have told me."

"Yeah, well, my life is full of things I should have done and didn't. This mission is screwed, and we're leaving. The rest of it we sort out later."

Billie turned back to the screen. Blake and the crewman had what was left of Bueller cradled between them and were approaching the APC at a quick jog. Behind them the mouth of the aliens' nest erupted with dozens of the things. The robot gun worked its deadly magic, hammering the creatures with chunks of armor-piercing death, battering them to pieces; still, they boiled forth like angry fire ants, ran into the wall of metal, and shattered against it. Dozens, scores, hundreds of them—they kept coming.

The robot gun was state of the art, it locked on to the acquired targets, calculated for local gravity, windage, movement, then fired efficiently and dispatched them. But no matter how efficient a weapon, it could only live as long as it was fed.

The last of the ammunition ran through the electronic machinery. The control panel lit with a flashing red light. The gun, said the computer, was empty. Since further identified-by-image targets were in evidence, the computer hereby advised the primary operator that reloading was now required for continued operation. Since the spare ammunition module had already been expended, the primary operator was hereby notified that additional modules would have to be manually inserted for continued operation. Meanwhile, the system would remain on standby, identifying and tracking i-b-i targets.

Wilks shook his head. Bad news. The APC had shot up all the ammunition it carried. Nobody had figured a lot of air-to-air combat would be happening on this mission. And the aliens kept bounding out of that damned nest like giant black termites stoked on steroids and amphetamines. Must be fifty of them heading toward the ship, despite all the ones the gun had blown away. More of the things climbed over the piled bodies as he watched. Time to leave.

Blake and the crewman and Bueller were only fifty meters away from the ship. Wilks ordered the outer hatch open.

"Triple time, marine," he said to Blake. "There's a shitload of company behind you coming up fast and I want to shut the door real soon now!"

They were close enough so Wilks could see their expressions now. The crewman turned and looked over his shoulder, and apparently didn't like what he saw. He was the limiting factor, Blake could run probably twice his best, even carrying Bueller. The crewman speeded up, and Blake matched him.

For no reason he could think of, Wilks was reminded of an old joke, one that he'd heard as a kid, about sheep herders. Come on guys. What say, let's get the flock out of here. . . .

Billie was numb, all the way to her soul. Wilks had slapped her, but she couldn't feel anything but a little heat where his palm had struck.

Lies. It was all lies. Everything. How could Mitch have done it? Why hadn't he told her the truth?

Bootsteps clattered up the entry ramp. They were here.

Blake entered the cabin. She squatted and carefully eased Mitch onto the deck. There was an aid kit on the wall, but Blake passed it and pulled a plastic box from a cabinet instead. Of course. A human aid kit wouldn't help.

The crewman said, "Go, man, get us the hell out of here!"

Wilks was in the pilot's seat. "Strap in," he ordered.

Only the crewman hustled to obey. Billie stood over Mitch. His eyes were closed. He ended at the waist and what spilled from his torso was ugly to look upon.

"Sit down, Billie!"

She still didn't move.

Mitch opened his eyes. For a moment they were unfocused, but then she saw him recognize her. "I—I'm s-s-sorry, B-Billie," he said. His voice bubbled, as if he were talking underwater. "I—I w-was going to t-t-tell you." He gasped, trying to get more air to work his voice.

Blake had the box open. She pulled several small electronic devices out and slapped them against

Mitch's shoulder and chest. Another one on his
neck, yet another to his temple. She ran a tube
from a plastic bag of clear fluid into the device on
his neck. The liquid began to flow through the
tubing. Blake pulled a plastic can out and sprayed a
bluish foam all over the torn waist. The foam crack-
led and bubbled and quickly settled into a thick
film that changed from blue to a bright green,
coating all the exposed nodules and tubing.

"Is he going to die?" Billie asked.

"I don't know," Blake said. "His system valves
have shut down all the torn circulators and the self-
repair programs are running. It's a lot of damage,
but we're designed to withstand a lot."

"Sit the fuck down!" Wilks roared. "We've got to
lift, now!"

Billie moved to a seat, still watching Blake work
on Mitch. Blake hooked one hand under a stanchion, the other she put against Mitch's chest. "I'm
anchored," she said. "And I've got him held stable.
Go."

Wilks cycled the hatch closed and initiated the
lift program. The ship's repellors cycled up, whin-
ing as they came on line. "Sequencing for lift off,"
he said. "Stand by—"

Something slammed into the APC, hard enough
to jolt the vessel, to make it ring with the impact.

"Shit!" the crewman said.

More impacts. Three. Five. Ten of them.

"They are all over us!" the crewman yelled.

"Fuck 'em," Wilks said. "We're gone." He
punched a control.

Nothing happened.

"What the hell?" the crewman began.

"One of them is blocking a thrust skirt tube," Wilks said. "The computer won't fire it. I'll have to go to manual—"

There came a screech as metal tore.

"They're digging through the hull," Billie said.

"That's impossible!" the crewman said.

Another *grinch!* of metal being clawed by something harder than it was.

Wilks tapped controls. The APC shook, but lifted, wobbled a little, but rose slowly. Went up a couple hundred meters, Billie could see through the forward screens.

"All right!" the crewman yelled.

"We're too heavy," Wilks said. "We'll have to shake the fuckers off—"

The ship lurched, dropped, twisting to port as though a heavy weight had landed on that side. A siren began screaming from the control panel. Wilks worked frantically, hands dancing rapidly back and forth. The APC began to level but it continued to settle. "That's the left repellor," Wilks said. "Emergency brake-lock. Something is inside the housing. I can't override."

"But—but the housing is armored!" the crewman said.

"The intake is protected by a finger-thick wire mesh," Wilks said. "But something went through it. The computer knows the danger. The carbon-boron blades are supercooled, they're brittle. They hit something bigger than a few grams, they'll shatter and blow us to pieces. I can't compensate enough with the other repellors to get us into orbit. We'll have to land and clear the housing."

"You mean go *outside*?"

Wilks stared at the crewman. "Unless you got a better idea."

"Oh, man!"

Thumping continued on the hull, more squeals as the metal bent or gave up the fight.

Billie stared at Mitch. He looked at her, his eyes clear. She didn't know what to say. She'd lain naked with this man—no, not a man, an *android*—had shared her body with him, had told him her secrets. Had given him her truth, for whatever it was worth. And he had responded as a man, but he had also kept from her the biggest truth of all.

As she watched him lay there, possibly dying, she felt outraged, felt sick, felt that if she never saw him again it would be too soon. And yet.

And yet, another feeling stirred deep inside her mind, at the threshold of her perceptions. It was a feeling she could not deny, despite what he had done. She didn't want to look at the thing looming there, didn't want to know about it, didn't want to acknowledge it. She tried to close the door between her and that stirring, to make it go away, but looking at him, she couldn't.

Well. It didn't matter. They were all going to die here. It wouldn't be long before the aliens clawed their way in. Billie looked at the weapons Blake still carried. Wilks wouldn't let the things take them alive. It would be quick, if it came to that. So it didn't matter what she was feeling about Mitch. No. Nothing mattered. Her short and mostly unhappy time was about to come to its end. Except for the few hours when she'd thought Mitch was other than he turned out to be, it hadn't been much of a life. Maybe she should tell him that, since they were going to die.

Or maybe not. What difference did it make?

The APC reached the ground, settled unevenly.

"Maybe we crushed a couple of them underneath," Wilks said.

Billie stared at him. That didn't matter either.

They were all going to die. The way she felt at the moment, it would be a relief.

25

The thumps against the hull increased. The external pickups were mostly blocked by the alien forms as they mindlessly beat against the ship, as if it were alive and they were trying to kill it.

Wilks looked at the others. Billie was sunk into a stunned silence. The crewman was so frightened he had wet himself. Bueller drifted in and out of consciousness. Blake was the only one he could depend on for help; she was the one to guard his back while he went outside to clear the grid.

Wilks smiled wryly. Right. Opening the hatch would be fun. They didn't have enough firepower in the APC to keep the things off him long enough to do what had to be done. He'd been too rattled to think earlier. The reasonable thing was to get the ship into the air again, move it ten or fifteen klicks away from the nest, and deal with the few aliens that hung on to them once they landed.

Except that they didn't have much fuel to play around with here, and a miscalculation would leave them shy of what they needed to reach the ship in orbit. He had locked the *Benedict*'s comp into the nuclear scenario; it wasn't going to be altered from the APC, couldn't be. He'd wanted to be sure, in case something happened to them.

Well, looked like worst had come to worst.

"Sarge?"

He looked at Blake. "No, going outside isn't real swift. I'm going to take it up again, do a roll, and move us far enough away so we can put down without company."

Blake nodded. "Makes sense."

"If we're light on fuel after that, we'll gut this sucker and toss out everything that adds unnecessary weight."

Wilks worked the controls. The ship trembled, but didn't go anywhere.

"Oh, shit!" he said.

"Sarge?"

"Either too many of 'em on us or they've jammed up the other grids. Looks like we're back to plan A."

Metal screeched.

"Damn."

"I wouldn't want to bet on us pulling this off, Sarge."

"Yeah, me neither. I don't see as how we have any choice. Listen, Blake, if they get me alive, you punch my lights out, you copy?"

"I can't, Sarge, you know that."

"Oh, yeah, right. Never mind. I got Massey's grenade here. I'll pull my own plug, it comes to that."

"Billie."

She looked at him, her eyes dull. "What?"

"Take this pistol. If we don't come back . . ."

She nodded, understanding.

The ship rocked. Raised up on the starboard side, fell back.

"Uh-oh," Wilks said. "They're working together. Enough of them will tip us over. Get to the hatch, Blake."

She nodded. Unslung her plasma rifle and switched off the safety.

The ship rocked again. Slammed back into place.

"Billie. Look, I'm sorry for getting you into this."

"It's okay, Wilks. I didn't have anything better to do."

For a second their gazes locked and they smiled at each other. The borrowed time they'd both been living on was about to expire.

Fuck it, Wilks thought. He took a deep breath. "Let's do it—"

The ship *thrummed,* a sound unlike anything Wilks had ever heard washed over them, vibrating every surface in the APC, battering at his ears like padded pugil sticks. He dropped to his knees and clapped his hands over his ears. He felt the vibration to his core; it made the marrow in his bones hum.

"Chreesto!" the crewman screamed.

Abruptly the sound died.

Wilks stood, shaken. What the hell had that been?

"Listen," Blake said.

"I don't hear anything," the crewman said.

Wilks nodded. "That's right. The aliens have stopped attacking us."

It was as quiet as an isolation chamber.

They all looked at Wilks.

"Let's take a look, Blake."

Wilks took a couple of deep breaths, then moved to the hatch. He held the carbine ready, Blake with her rifle right behind him. The hatch went up.

"Oh, man," Blake said.

Wilks was speechless. At least fifty of the aliens lay sprawled on the ground around the ship. They looked . . . melted, as if all their edges had run together. Dead, Wilks didn't doubt it for a second. That was pretty incredible. But what he saw standing a dozen meters away was even more incredible.

"What the hell is that?" Blake said.

Wilks just stared.

Some kind of suited figure stood there. It was easily seven or eight meters tall, bipedal, with a clear helmet on the E-suit it wore. Wilks could see the thing's face behind the bubble covering, and it looked like nothing so much as an elephant might appear, were it to evolve to a two-legged animal. It had pinkish-gray skin, a ridged nose or maybe a trunk that vanished in a long chamber down the front of the suit, with what seemed to be a pair of small tentacles, one to either side of the larger trunk. It had a short extension of the suit behind it, and Wilks guessed that it had a tail in the tube, shaped like a skinny pyramid. A closer look and Wilks realized the thing wasn't exactly standing.

The heavy boots it wore had a central split, as if the thing had hooves, and they didn't quite touch the ground. It was actually *floating* a couple of centimeters above the surface.

It was close enough so he could see its eyes. The pupils were shaped like crosses, wider than they were high. They looked dead, those eyes.

The thing held a device in its gauntleted hands and Wilks would bet ten years pay against a toenail clipping it was some kind of weapon.

The air was thin and Wilks had to take big gulps of it to get enough oxygen. He glanced over and saw that Blake was slowly bringing her rifle around to bear on the thing.

"Negative on that," he said softly. "I think this thing just flattened all the local bad guys with whatever that gear is it's holding. I don't want it to think we mean it any harm. If it can knock down that many of those suckers all at once, we're way outgunned here."

Blake let her rifle droop, to point at the ground.

The thing—another alien, and sure as shit not from around here, Wilks knew—pointed its own weapon downward.

"Hello, spacer," Blake said softly. "You must be new in town."

Behind them, Billie screamed in terror.

Billie was back on Rim.

She was a child, sitting in the front of her father's scout hopper, watching the near featureless gray pass by the observation port. So far the ride had been dull, but her father had said there was something out there they had to go look at and he brought her and her brother Vick along. Her father's assistant, Mr. Zendall, was also there. Her father called him Gene, but she wasn't supposed to call him that. And her mother was there, too.

"Holy Sister of the Stars," her father said.

"Russ? What is it?" her mother said.

"Our detectors just went off the scale. There's something huge down there, in the Valley of the Iron Fingers."

"How can that be?"

"I don't know. But we're talking about megatonnage, a mixed signal. Got to be man-made. Gene?"

"I got it, Russ. Lord, Lord. I can't get a configuration ID on it. Look at the specs."

It didn't mean anything to Billie, all the numbers and stuff, but she knew it must be important because her parents and Gene—Mr. Zendall—were all excited.

"It's shaped like a giant horseshoe."

Billie didn't know what that meant, she'd never seen a horse except in edcom and that one hadn't been wearing any shoes she could see.

"Gene, Sarah, I think we've got an alien ship here."

They landed, and even through the swirling murk Billie could see what had her parents so excited. It was like a big U, the ends pointing up at an angle. It was real big, you could put a lot of scout hoppers in it and have room left over.

"No match to anything on record," Gene said. He laughed.

"How could colony tracking have missed it?" her mother said.

"Magnetic interference from the iron, maybe," her father said. "And the weathersats probably don't footprint this spot. Who cares? We found it, we've got salvage rights on it. This might be our ticket back to Earth. It could be worth a fortune!"

They landed the hopper. Her father and mother and Gene put on E-suits. "You stay here and watch us on the monitor," her father said. "Don't let Vick touch any of the controls. We're going to go look at the ship. If you get hungry, there are ration packs in the storebox. One each, no more, okay?"

Billie nodded. "Okay."

So then she watched. All three of them had cams on their suits and she knew how to switch around so she could see from one or the other or all three at once, if she wanted to.

At first it was dark, outside was stormy like usual, but pretty soon they got into the big ship and it got better. They had floodlights and turned them on.

The inside was spooky, weird, it didn't look like anything Billie had ever seen. It took her parents and Gene a long time to get to the control room—she knew that was where they wanted to go because she could hear them talking on their suit coms.

And when they finally got there—Billie had gone to the toilet twice and already eaten her meal pack and half of Vick's because he didn't like the green paste and she did—there was a dead thing sitting in the control seat.

It was real big, and it looked strange. Kind of like the edcom of a big terran animal called an elephant.

It had a big, funny nose and overall its whole body was as long as four men, but it was dead, lying on its back. There was a hole in its stomach or its chest or something, with bones sticking up from the hole. Yuk.

Her parents went around the thing a few times, talking to each other and to Gene. And then they went down the hall. To a big room. And on the floor of the big room were these things. . . .

Billie screamed, and Wilks was there, holding her by the shoulders, shaking her gently.

"Hey, hey, it's all right. We're okay."

The memories bubbled in her, and she fought them. But there was a pressure in her brain, a kind of malevolent presence.

"Billie?"

"It's that thing out there," she said. "I can read its thoughts. More like its feelings. It's inside my head."

Wilks glanced at Blake.

"I'm not crazy," Billie said. "It just killed all the aliens outside our ship, right? Because it hates them. It—its kind—have been here before. Collecting specimens. I, oh, God!"

"Billie!"

She shook her head, as if that would clear the intrusion by the stranger. "It somehow can feel my thoughts, too," she said. "It knows."

"Knows what?"

"I—on Rim—my parents . . ."

"What about them?"

"Oh, God, Wilks! My parents found a ship there.

An alien ship. The pilot was some kind of scientist, maybe. It had been to this world. It had taken specimens of these things. Eggs. It must have been infected, implanted. They killed it. The ship crashed on Rim. The things survived inside it, I don't know for how long. My—my parents found it. They went into the ship. . . ."

Wilks hugged her. "Easy, kid. Let it go. We know what happened."

Billie sobbed. Tears flowed. That was one of the memories she had buried the deepest. Not even the worst of her nightmares had dredged it up before now.

Hate filled her brain, but it was not her own emotion. It was from the space traveler floating outside the APC, the giant whose fellow being had died and crashed into Rim.

She didn't want to remember, but the space traveler pulled at it, drawing it into view. The child she had been, watching the monitors. Watching her father lean over one of the eggs. Seeing all over again the opening and the crablike embryo that flew out and latched on to her father's face. Seeing her mother and Gene drag him out. Listening to the screams . . .

"No! Get out of me! Go away!"

Hate. Gut-churning, black, molten hate, sloshing over and filling Billie to her toes. How this thing hated these creatures!

"It saved us," Wilks said.

"Not because it likes us," she said. "Because it can't stand them."

Blake said, "Sarge, we've got to get the ship spaceworthy. We've got what? three hours?"

Billie thought about the bombs that would drop, what would happen to the planet when they did.

She felt a sudden interest from the spacesuited figure. It understood her thoughts well enough to hear that message.

"The thing is leaving," the crewman said. "Just floating away."

"It knows about the bombs," Billie said.

"Yeah, well, while I'd like to be an ambassador to a new species and all, we have to get the APC fixed or we're going to be atomic dust ourselves."

Wilks stood, leaving Billie sitting on the deck of the little craft. Next to her, Mitch opened his eyes. He didn't speak, and Billie had nothing she wanted to say to him. The alien presence left her suddenly, a sharp sensation as if a knife were pulled from her brain.

It was hard to breathe, their eyes burned and their noses ached and dripped, but the repairs took only an hour.

The APC lifted, made orbit, and managed a safe rendezvous with the *Benedict*. Wilks made very certain there were no unwanted passengers on the APC before he pulled into the bay, and even then, he had the cleaning lasers scorch every bit of the landing craft's exterior before he let them leave the docking area.

Blake plugged Bueller into some kind of life-support system designed for androids.

The crewman—Billie didn't know his name and

didn't care if she ever did—went to do checks on the ship.

Wilks went to do something, he didn't say what.

Billie sat at a table, staring at the wall. It was over. They had come to the aliens' world. They had survived pirates and attacks by the creatures; they were about to smash the planet back to a pre-life stage. They were going home.

It was all over.

And she didn't give a damn.

26

Orona sat in his office, watching the three corporation executives seated across from him. The doctor was named Dryner; he couldn't remember the others' names, but thought of them by the clothing they wore: Red and Green.

The room walls were shielded, even the windows were lined with breakup softwires so a laser listener couldn't pick up conversations from outside. Orona suspected that at least one of the three corporation men carried some kind of scrambler to block electronic eavesdropping, maybe they all did. They'd been scanned, but there were some remarkable plastics around these days that could mimic just about anything. A shoe, a kneecap, whatever. Conversations held at this high a level were best done with great care. Nobody would be collecting Orona's words, either.

"All right, gentlemen, let's not do an elaborate mating dance all around it. We all know why we're here."

Green and Red exchanged quick, shielded glances, no expressions to read. They'd be good poker players, Orona figured. The medical VP was also cool, but a bit more nervous. He tapped a finger lightly against his thigh.

"Perhaps we should reconsider having attorneys present," Red said.

"Nobody is talking about prosecution," Orona said. "Let's not insult each other's intelligence. I'm government and you're private, my hammer is bigger, and I'd play hell whacking you with it, we all know that, too. At least right now, anyway."

Red and Green smiled, identical expressions. They knew that.

"So let's skip the scat and get to the bottom line," Orona said. "You had one of the aliens tucked away down in your SA lab and some religious fanatics broke in and got themselves impregnated by the thing's embryos. We all know that.

"Your specimen got cooked in the explosion that destroyed the lab. The fanatics got away. We know that because we are still getting reports of the nightmares, so some of the damned things are still alive.

"Am I telling you anything you don't know?"

Red and Green smiled slightly, as one. Men of the world had certain sources. No point in denying it.

The doctor, Dryner, shook his head. "We, ah, are aware of this."

"I thought you might be. Got a tap in our main-frame. But you don't have a line tied to our Tac Unit."

He looked at them. Red shrugged, the barest hint of a moment. Orona read that as a "no."

"Well, we've found one of the attackers."

The doctor leaned forward, eager. "With the implanted embryo?"

"Unfortunately, no. This man's chest had been burst from the inside. He'd been dead for half a day when our team uncovered him in New Chicago. There was no sign of the newborn alien."

The doctor leaned back. "Shit," he said. His voice was soft.

"I share your sentiments, Doctor. We would very much like to collect these things ourselves. But I'm afraid our worry is now larger than simply who'll be the first to get a potential weapons system, no matter how valuable that might be."

Green and Red perked up. Green said, "What do you mean?"

Orona stood, turned to look through the window at the city lights kicking on as darkness gathered in the dusk. Traffic zipped back and forth in the airlanes, glittering in the final rays of the setting sun. "Doctor, you understand how these things reproduce. Each one is a potential queen, is it not?"

Dryner looked at the other two company men. They gave him those tiny shrugs. Go ahead.

The doctor said, "Yes, that is possible."

"We don't know how many of the fanatics escaped. Could be as many as a dozen. We've lost one of the newborn aliens. The others will all be hatching from their human 'eggs' shortly, if they haven't already done so, is that not correct?"

"Well, it would depend on which eggs delivered their implants. The queen laid them over several days."

"But at the most, several days plus or minus is all, correct?"

"I'm afraid so."

"Doctor, if there were, oh, say, five of them implanted, and each of them produces a queen and they all begin to lay eggs as soon as they reach maturity, how long do you think it might take before the damned things are swarming all over the place?"

Dryner swallowed dryly. "I—there's no way to be certain, that is to say—"

Orona turned around. Felt the weight of the entire government on his shoulders. He was the expert, though these men might know as much as he did. He needed every scrap of knowledge he could get. "It's rather like the hamster problem. If one mother and her litters all come to term and keep mating and having more babies who all survive, in a couple of years we're knee-deep in hamsters.

"Of course, that doesn't happen. Some are killed by the mothers, some are eaten by natural predators, some get stepped on by things with big feet. But these aliens don't *have* any natural predators on this world.

"It takes armor-piercing military-grade weaponry to kill one and even then it isn't easy. We have the reports from our Colonial Marines' encounters with them. A Chinese farmer with a pitchfork, an Australian bird hunter with a shotgun, they'll be wasting their time trying to stop a full-grown alien with either of those weapons, correct?"

The doctor swallowed again. The question was rhetorical.

"In fact, just about anybody who comes against one of these things is going to regret it. They reproduce like hamsters, the queens don't even need mates, they come of age real fast. We don't know where they will start to pop up. The fanatics have spread out, we've gotten reports of them all over the globe. Some have to be discounted, of course, but if a tenth of the material is correct, we are going to start seeing these things making themselves known in both hemispheres from the equator to the poles. Chicago is a long way from Lima.

"And, gentlemen, that means we will all be in very deep shit. I expect your cooperation in every way to stop that. Because if we don't stop it, making that big end of the year bonus is going to be the last thing you have to worry about. These things will be killing so many people that you'll hear the survivors' outraged screams on Mars. And every one of them will be calling for heads to roll. I'll give them yours. Then the government will give them mine."

The doctor licked dry lips.

Even those two cosmopolitan men of the world, Red and Green, looked unhappy with that idea.

Good. Orona had them. Now, he hoped it wasn't too late. He didn't express his own worst fear: that the things would get well established enough so the very survival of mankind on the planet would be in

jeopardy. Of course, that was worst-case scenario,
he didn't really think that would happen, it was just
a nightmarish worry.

He hoped.

27

The giant elephantlike creature had gotten away, they saw the ion trail of its ship dispersing in the vacuum before they broke their own vessel out of its ellipse around the aliens' world. Funny, the place didn't even have a name, at least not one Wilks knew about. Not that he worried about it.

There wasn't anything down there to worry about.

So. The hard rain began to fall upon the aliens' planet, courtesy of the Colonial Marines and delivered by Sergeant Wilks. The chain-link nukes seeded from the *Benedict* dropped from their computer-designed orbits and drizzled across the harsh land; some fell into the sea, though the water harmed them not in the least.

When the nukes chained and went off, they

smashed at the planet as might a raging god grown angry with his creation.

Sheets of atomic fire scoured the surface. Shock waves pounded trees and bushes and even some mountains flat. Volcanoes long dormant were shaken to life by the explosions, adding their blasts and lava spews to the chaos. The land groaned and responded with earthquakes that shook the surface harder than any man-made scale could register. Oceans boiled, steam rose; life in the sea, land, and air cooked where it swam or walked or flew. The world rattled to its very roots and whatever might have survived the initial devastation would fare poorly under the ensuing pall of the nuclear winter and radioactivity left by the deliberately dirty bombs. The aliens were hardy; they could survive in conditions that would kill most forms of life, but even they had to eat. Food was going to be scarce here for a long, long time.

Wilks watched on the monitors, the cams shielded by filters, as the aliens' planet spasmed and died. And he felt real good about it, too. He hoped they all lived long enough to starve. Slowly.

He didn't think he would be bothered much anymore by the nightmares he had lived with for so many years. He had struck back against the hellish things, and his punch had been a lot bigger than any they could throw. He had destroyed them. The last laugh was his.

Yeah, there was the one left on Earth, but when he got back, he was going to see what he could do about that one, too.

He wondered what the penalty for blowing up a

whole planet was? Why, he might be court-martialed.

Imagine that.

It was worse than Orona had figured.

The first infestations seemed easy enough to deal
with. His Tac teams were primed for sudden mass
disappearances, and whenever an area starting
missing people, they went in. He mobilized transportation so that a fully equipped team could
launch and parabola down to any spot on the globe
in under three hours.

The first nests were small, no more than fifty or
a hundred eggs and a single queen. The Tac teams
took no chances. They sterilized the area. The nests
were razed, surrounding areas destroyed, suspected
carriers picked up and detained. Those with implants were killed quickly and their bodies burned.

New Chicago, Lesser Miami, Havana, Madrid—
those nests were quickly discovered and eliminated.

At first, Orona felt a certain smugness. True,
there would be a lot of damages to cover and a
certain amount of political heat to be endured, but
the Planetary Security Act gave him a great deal of
latitude. The things weren't very bright; they were
like termites or ants or bees; they built their nests
and set up egg chambers and sent workers out to
gather food. The behavior was instinctive; there was
no great intelligence behind it. It had apparently
worked for the things on their homeworld, but there
they didn't have such clever competition. For a time,
Orona rested easier. He was the expert, and the
military trusted him implicitly.

Weeks went by. Months.

More nests were kicked open: Paris, Moscow, Brisbane, Antarctic City. The things had spread far and wide as he had feared, but still they were easy enough to find and destroy. The infection was bad, but controlled. Like a staph boil lanced and cleaned, it would heal.

But then things began to change.

The Tac teams were getting good at their jobs, practice making them better, and maybe they started to get sloppy. Or maybe it was some kind of forced natural selection. Like rats or roaches who have been hunted and poisoned or smashed flat, the aliens began to vary their nest making.

The hives got smaller and more numerous. The Tac teams would find only ten or fifteen eggs in a tiny chamber, and such places were harder to locate. And there were more of them. An area of Greater North Africa in the old Ivory Coast yielded no less than eighty small nests inside a fifty-kilometer circle. Some of the hives were in Abidan, in the basements of skyscrapers or old warehouses, but some of them were in the surrounding countryside, under the ground. Tac squads discovered implanted cattle, horses, and even goats in some chambers. Anything large enough seemed to work. And while people in civilized countries who went missing were usually reported, a farmer and a few dozen cattle in some rural area might not be noticed.

It was as though the aliens were becoming smarter as a survival characteristic.

Six months after the escape from the labs in

Lima, Orona had to order a division-sized attack on a giant nest in Diego Suarez, on the northern tip of Madagascar. It was actually a series of several hundred smaller nests that had been tunneled and joined together.

Eight months into the war, Orona was responsible for the nuclear destruction of Jakarta.

A year after the war began, the continent of Australia was considered too infested to allow any travel to or from, and a full quarantine was instigated. Any ship, air vessel, or spacecraft trying to leave was shot down by Coast Guard laser satellites.

It was no longer a matter of Tac units seeking alien hives to destroy. It was a matter of establishing perimeters and checking to make certain no carriers crossed into safe territories. It was truly war.

Martial law was declared. All national boundaries were suspended. The Military Alliance came into being and civil liberties were put aside for the duration of the conflict. Suspected carriers of alien embryos could be legally shot by the command of any military officer above the rank of colonel. Then it dropped to majors and captains. Then sergeants. Pretty soon, any soldier with a gun could shoot anybody he damned well wanted to, and if the scan came up negative later, well, too fucking bad. War was hell, wasn't it? A few civilians here and there to save the planet? Yes.

Alien drones that were captured—a rare event— seemed to have gotten a little brighter. The smartest could barely keep up with an average dog, insofar as intelligence was concerned. But the single queen captured in a battle that destroyed half of San

Francisco's downtown district tested out to nearly 175 on the Irwin-Schlatler scale. That made it smarter than most of the humans ever born.

The nightmares had come true. Whatever Orona had felt before was nothing compared to the sinking, twisting coldness in his gut when *that* little bit of information arrived in his computer. They *were* getting smarter. Too smart.

And humans were responsible for it.

Onboard the *Benedict,* the survivors of the trip prepared for hypersleep.

Bueller lay in his rigged device, alive and stable, according to Blake. Billie had avoided him, but she couldn't get into her sleep chamber without a final confrontation. She had to speak to him.

He was shrouded in a hyperbaric sleeve from the chest down to where the rest of him had been. From there up, he looked as he had before. He was awake when she entered the room. They were alone.

"Mitch."

"Billie. I—I would rather you didn't see me like this."

"Well, that's too goddamned bad! How else would you have me see you? Like a man?"

"I'm sorry, Billie. You can't know how sorry."

"What was I, Mitch? A glitch in your programming?" She moved closer to him. She could have reached out and touched him. Could have. Would not.

"No," he said.

"Then what?"

"I should have told you. I tried, but I just couldn't. I was afraid."

"Afraid?"

"Of losing you."

She laughed, a short, sharp, bitter sound.

"I can't help what I am, Billie. I didn't have a choice in how I was born."

"Right, but you decided to fool the stupid human bitch, didn't you?"

"No. Whatever I am, wherever I came from, I eat, I feel, I hurt. And, I found out, I love."

Billie bit at her lip. She didn't want to hear this.

She wanted to hear it more than anything.

"I'm not like you," he continued. "I didn't have a mother and father, never grew as a child, never had a life before I was created for the Colonial Marines. But I grow, after a fashion. I learn. I became more than I was. And I experienced love. I don't know if it is the same as you feel. For me, it's a hollowness that only being around you fills, an ache when you are away, a fever that only you can cool. I feel lust for you, tenderness, I want to touch you, hold you. Even now, when I'm only half alive."

He stopped. Sobbed.

Oh, God. Don't let him cry, she thought. She couldn't bear that.

"And I deceived you," he said. "But when that thing grabbed me, when it tore me in two, that wasn't as painful as what I felt when I saw you look at me. Saw you look at me and hate me—" he stopped. Turned his face away.

And Billie realized that what she had felt was real, whatever Mitch was. That she had loved him

as he had loved her, for what he described was what
she had felt.

What she *still* felt.

"Mitch . . ."

"Go, Billie. Turn off the machines. Let me die."

Now she did reach out and touch him. His bare
shoulder was warm, the skin alive, the muscles
solid. He loved her, she was convinced of that.
Whatever else he might be, that counted for a lot.
Nobody had loved her since her parents.

"Mitch," she said.

He turned to look up at her.

She bent. Kissed him softly on the lips. Felt his
pain, and felt it ebb as he realized what she was
doing. His arms came up, encircled her.

"Oh, God, Billie!"

"Shhh. It's all right. It's all right. It doesn't matter."

And it didn't matter. Not at all.

It was war, and men were losing.

Orona marveled at this, that it should come to be
this way. Man had the superior technology, it was
man's world, man had the advantages. Except—

Except that the aliens had a stronger drive to live.
They would sacrifice all for that, for the survival of
the species. Only a few rare men were willing to do
that. A mother would die to protect her children; a
saint would walk into the fire for his fellow men or
his god, but the instinct of self-preservation was too
strong in most humans. The aliens didn't care. If a
hundred drones had to die to save one egg, then
they would. And did.

The things sprang up everywhere, in places where a rat would have trouble living, in spots where no one would have guessed they could spawn. Buried in the arctic ice floes, in deserts, in the tamed jungles, on barges, anywhere there was room for a nest. Nobody knew how many of the things there were, there were only guesses. The estimates ranged from hundreds of thousands to tens of millions. Private ships left Earth in droves, so many the military couldn't stop or even inspect them all. Most only fled as far as Luna or the Belt, some could reach the far planets of the system. A few wealthy souls banded together and bought private starships before the government clamped down and made such ownership illegal. Thousands ran, because on Earth, there were few places left to hide.

Orona was in one of those places, a heavily guarded military complex in Mexico. The perimeter was ringed with force fences, the ground mined, every car or air carrier that entered or left scanned, every passenger fluoroviewed for parasites. It was as safe as anywhere left.

In the end, Orona finally realized that the aliens were like a disease, not like an enemy army. The only way to save the patient was to cut off the cancerous parts and sterilize the wounds. And it was too late for that, it had metastasized and the knife and radiation and drugs would not be enough. It had all happened so *fast,* a wildfire that started with a match and only moments later was a conflagration. Nobody could have predicted it would erupt so quickly! A year and a half ago, men were supreme on their homeworld, top of the food chain, the king predator. But now . . .

The military minds were not brilliant, they never were, but those in charge were smart enough to know they were losing. All remaining starships were confiscated. Hastily laid plans began to be implemented. There would be a regrouping of key military personnel to the outer colonies, there to develop new plans for combating the aliens.

Sitting in his information center, a cool and clean place of technological miracles of communication, Orona laughed. The Earth was being abandoned. He wouldn't be leaving with them. Oh, he could have gone, but what would be the point? He would survive, but he would have lost the most important battle of his life. There was an ancient custom that sailors had once observed: if a ship sank, the captain went down with it. The aliens had been his project. His work. Someone had spilled a retort of crucial fluid, and the lab had been contaminated. It was his responsibility. He should have foreseen it. Even if everyone else forgot, he never would.

He was going to stay here, win or lose.

The hypersleep chambers stood ready.

"See you in nine months," Wilks said to the others.

The computer locked the ship into its return home. They would be going back faster than they had come, a few months. Wilks hoped things had been kept clean with the alien specimen they had on Earth. They'd be careful, he hoped. And it was only one of them, one couldn't cause too much trouble.

The chambers closed on their patients, lulled them into a rest nearly to the borders of death itself, then held them there in a perfectly balanced stasis.

By the time the first subspace messages of the horrors on Earth finally arrived in the flux of the ship's voyage through the Einsteinian Warp, the remaining few passengers of the *Benedict* were all hard asleep. The ship's computer recorded the cries from Earth, but the computer did not care.

28

Orona stared straight ahead, his face drawn, his expression more tired than anything else. "So, that's the way it is here on Earth," he said. "The military has pulled most of its highest-ranking officers and best remaining troops out, and they are offworld and well into hyperspace by now. A few more installations remain left to evacuate.

"The situation here has deteriorated steadily. Land communications are mostly down, satellite bounce is still working in areas where enough power remains to access it.

"Things are in chaos. In the past months, the aliens have increased their numbers at a rate that seems impossible.

"There are only a few enclaves where security is

holding them off. Perhaps a billion people have died in the last year and a half."

Something pounded on the door behind Orona.

"Even this place, which should have been able to hold out forever, is compromised. Amazing."

The pounding increased.

"I don't know if anybody will see this transmission," he said. "Or that it matters if you do. Such a comedy of errors this whole thing has been. Were I a god, I would be laughing myself silly at man's stupidity."

Thick plastic began to shatter under the force of the hammering.

Orona managed a half smile. He reached into a drawer, came out with a stubby pistol. He looked to his left. Shards of black plastic flew past him, from the unseen fury off the screen. Orona chambered a round in the pistol. Put the muzzle into his mouth. Pulled the trigger.

The back of his head sprayed red and white and he fell forward just as a clawed hand grabbed at him. The talons missed. The alien corrected, then jerked the dead man from the chair like a puppet whose strings have been cut. Shook him.

Another shape moved into view, blocked the camera.

After a moment, Orona was taken away. The room was now empty. The camera ran on, giving a view of the blood and brains and skull spattered onto the wall.

*   *   *

"Oh, fuck," Billie said, staring at the screen.

Next to her, Wilks nodded, his face grim. "It was all for nothing," he said. "We blew their fucking planet up but it was too late. They were already on Earth. The stupid bastards brought them home and they got loose."

Blake and the crewman stood there, also watching, Bueller lay on a gurney behind Billie.

"What are we going to do, Sarge?"

"Do? What can we do? We're in orbit. We're going down."

Nobody had any better ideas.

Then, the crewman—Parks, his name was—said, "Wilks, we've got company."

"What are you talking about?"

"Check the Doppler screen."

Wilks glanced at it. He swore softly.

It was the elephant-alien's ship, hanging in space only a couple of hundred kilometers away.

Impossible as it was supposed to be in the Einsteinian subspace, the thing had *followed* them.

How?

Why?

"You are cleared for touchdown at these coordinates, *Benedict*. Your computer should do fine, but keep a hand on manual just in case. You veer too much and you land in enemy territory and if you do, you're dinner."

"Thanks a lot, Control," Wilks said into the com. If the computer failed, they were dead; nobody on the ship could pilot a star hopper accurately in atmosphere, certainly not to a pinpoint landing.

"We'd rather you get down in one piece. We need the hardware. Outside of preprogrammed troop carriers, we don't have a lot of birds that can even make orbit."

"Copy, Control. We're on the glide."

Wilks leaned back. Things sounded even worse than the recordings they had seen and heard. Orona's supposedly safe installation had been overrun weeks ago. There didn't seem to be much left to come back for, but Wilks had to see it for himself. His victory on the aliens' homeworld was meaningless now.

When the ship landed, there were dozens of soldiers waiting, guns leveled at them. An officer, a colonel or a general, Billie guessed, strode up and nodded at Wilks.

"We're glad you brought the ship back, Sergeant. We need it. This is the last secure compound remaining. We're bailing out."

"What's going to happen to Earth?"

The man shrugged. "I can't say. I'm supposed to take the rest of my men to the outpost we've established; High Command will sort it out from there."

"You're just going to *leave*? What about the people here?"

The man shook his head. "What I think is, the aliens will overrun everything. Then someday we'll come back and try again. Develop some way to kill 'em from orbit without damaging the land or sea too bad, some kind of biological or chemical thing. We'll start with a clean slate."

Wilks looked as if he were going to punch the man. "There are billions of human beings here!"

"*Were* billions, Sergeant. The aliens have taken a lot of them, a lot have been friendly-fired, a lot died in experiments designed to stop the creatures. There are maybe five, six hundred million left, and going fast. We can't save them. If we're lucky, we'll get clear before this place goes up—"

As if on cue, a junior officer leaned over to the commander. "Sir, pickets report a surge from the southeast. Several thousand bugs attacking. They are through the minefield and approaching the fences."

"Check out the *Benedict*," the officer ordered. "And send C Company to help the pickets."

The armed soldiers swarmed into the ship.

The officer said, "When you think about it, maybe it's not all bad. Earth was on the edge of destruction for a long time. If it hadn't been this, it would have probably been something else that set it off. This way, we can maybe get it right next time."

"What about us?" the crewman asked. Parks, his name was Parks.

"I'm sorry," the officer said, "but there is only so much room. I have my orders."

"Wait," Wilks said. "There's another factor. We had help on the aliens' homeworld. Another space-faring species. He—it saved us."

"So?"

"It followed us here. In its own ship."

"Look, Sergeant, this is all very interesting, but what difference does that make? You think this thing can wipe out all the bugs on the planet?"

"I don't know, but it might help—"

The officer glanced at his chronometer. "If we had the time, yes. But if our intelligence is right, we have got a day, maybe only a few hours before we are overrun. We've set nukes to take out the complex after we've gone. We've lost this war, Sergeant. It's time to retreat."

"Dammit!"

The officer drew his sidearm. "Don't do anything stupid. You can die right now if you do."

Wilks held his hands wide.

Blake, standing between Billie and Bueller on the gurney, moved over a hair. The officer swung his gun to cover her. "I can't let you shoot anybody, General," Blake said.

"Listen, marine, I've been shooting people for months. A few more won't matter."

Blake smiled, and moved toward him.

"Blake, don't!" Wilks said.

But she kept going.

The general fired, his bullet taking Blake square in the chest. Blake hardly paused. The man cursed, fired again—

Wilks jumped. Slammed the heel of his hand into the general's temple just as he swung his pistol around and fired a third round. The bullet *spanged* into the side of the *Benedict*.

Wilks followed the hand strike with his elbow, and a kick as the general fell. He twisted the gun from the man's hand, spun to face the hatch to the ship.

A soldier stepped out. Wilks shot him in the head.

Blake went down. Parks ran off, screaming.

Billie went to the downed android. The downed *woman*.

"Blake . . ."

"Couldn't let him . . . shoot you," she said. She smiled. "Be . . . sure I . . . get my medals, okay, Sarge?"

Wilks glanced at her. "Yeah, kid. No sweat."

Blake's eyes dilated suddenly as Billie watched.

Wilks shook his head. "Damn. Hit her in the main pump. One chance in ten thousand, it's supposed to be caged and almost bulletproof. Must have ricocheted."

Billie said, "Blake!"

"She's gone, Billie," Wilks said. "And we'll be gone too if we don't move our asses, fast! I just killed a general. Go!"

He pulled her up, but she twisted away and grabbed Mitch from his gurney. She slung him onto her back.

"Billie, goddammit!"

"I'll keep up," she said.

Mitch said, "Billie, don't do this—"

"Shut up, Mitch. Otherwise I'll stay here with you and they'll kill me. If you don't want me to do that, then you have to hang on and go with me."

Wilks sprinted away, Billie and her passenger right behind him.

29

When they stopped for breath, Billie said, "Why are we running? There's no place to go. They're going to blow this place up when they leave. Even if there weren't any aliens outside the defenses, we can't get far enough away on foot to escape the blast."

"I don't plan for us to be on foot," he said.

"If what they said is true, nowhere on Earth is any better," Bueller put in.

The three of them were leaning against the inside of a stanchion, a support post that ran from the ground up through the level they were on. Wilks guessed they were on the third level, probably fifty meters above the surface.

"I don't plan for us to be on Earth, either," Wilks said.

"What are you talking about?" That from Billie.

"Remember what the controller said when we left orbit? There are programmed troop carriers here. When they leave, we'll be on one of them."

"How?"

Wilks hefted the general's pistol. "By doing whatever it takes."

Bueller looked uncomfortable. "I'm not supposed to allow that," he said.

Wilks laughed. "How you gonna stop it, gimpy? Besides, I see a basic flaw in your programming here. If they are gonna kill us, me and Billie, and we are gonna kill them, who do you worry about the most?"

Bueller chewed on that for a second. "Billie," he said.

"Ah. So some folks are more important than others, eh?"

"Yes."

"They didn't teach you that in the vats."

"No."

Wilks laughed again. "You just stopped being an android, pal. Welcome to the human race."

Billie allowed Wilks to take Mitch; they could move faster that way, Wilks said. And even as they ran, she marveled over what Mitch had said. He had outgrown his programming. His body might not have been born of a woman, but as far as she was concerned, he was a man.

Wilks led them into a storage area that had a computer terminal. He began punching questions into the system.

"What are you doing?"

He didn't look up at Billie. "Finding out which of the drone ships are carrying crew and which are only lugging cargo. Some will have troops; some will be hauling supplies. We can find a supply ship; we can dump some of 'em and replace the weight with us."

"We don't even know where they are going," Billie said.

"Who cares? Can't be any worse than being fried by atomics or eaten by the monsters."

"Wilks—"

"I know what you are gonna say," he said. "I thought my job was over when I blasted the aliens' homeworld, that I could come back, get stuck away in some nice quiet prison or brainwiped and that would be it. I was looking forward to it. But now, no. I can't quit until every one of these alien bastards is dead."

"Is it worth it?"

"It is to me. A man's got to have a reason to get up in the mornings. I spent years trying to decide if I should just shut my own lights off. Something always kept me from doing it. I never knew what, exactly, but I'm glad it did. I might die, kid, but I am going to go down swinging."

He was as happy as she'd ever seen him. He had a purpose, and that was more than a lot of people had.

"Ah, here we go. A cargo drone, number three-oh-two, nicknamed *The American*. Bay sixteen, level five. Here's the overlay map. . . ."

* * *

They approached the docked ships cautiously. Wilks put Bueller down carefully and drew the handgun. "I'll just wound the guards," he said, "I won't kill them."

"Thank you," Bueller said.

"Stay here. I'll be back when I'm done." He started to leave. Paused. "Hey, Bueller, I never got around to telling you how good a job you and your troops did. You did okay."

"For an android?" Bueller said.

"Nah, for anybody."

Wilks eased his way onto the dock, using the supports as cover. In the end, it was easy. There were four guards, they had their weapons slung, they weren't expecting trouble. When he was close enough and still covered, Wilks took a deep breath, brought the pistol up, and quickly fired four times. The suppressed barrel cut most of the noise.

He hit each of the four guards once.

Right between the eyes.

Head shots were the best way for an instant knockdown.

So he lied to Bueller. Life was hard.

Billie saw Wilks coming back. "Our ride is here, people. Let's go."

He led them past the bodies of four soldiers who had been guarding the ship.

Mitch looked at the dead men.

"Sorry. My hand must have slipped," Wilks said.

Mitch shrugged. Once they were dead, his responsibility ended. Wilks had to know that.

Behind them, small-arms fire rattled. It didn't sound close, but it wasn't too far away, either.

"Looks like company has come calling," Wilks said. "I'd bet the schedule is going to be advanced just a tad."

The ship was a rectangular module with heat tiles on the bottom and a small control cab that looked vaguely like the head of a giant insect stuck on the front. It seemed almost an afterthought to Billie, the way the cab joined the brick-shaped body of the ship.

Wilks caught her look. "Cobbled together out of spare parts," he said. "We'll be lucky if it doesn't come apart when we lift. Come on. We've got to move some gear around. This bird is loaded with food supplies and frozen sperm and ova, regular little Noah's ark. We have to install an oxy plant and recycling and recovery system so we can breathe and have a way to clear wastes. And since I don't know how long we'll be in flight, some sleep chambers would be nice, too. Take us a couple of hours, I've located the stuff we need on the ship next door."

"What about the passengers on that ship?" Mitch asked.

"They can double up in the chambers if they have to. This bird doesn't have any 'cause it's meant to be crewless. We need 'em more than they do."

It took almost two and a half hours to get the proper gear installed, and would have been impossible without the dumbots Wilks rounded up.

The sounds of combat were drawing much closer

as they finished. He could hear the occasional rico-
chet *ching* off the alien armor, and whoever had
taken over from the dead general would probably
be hauling ass real soon now.

Every now and then, Wilks heard a man or
woman scream.

Yeah. Real soon now.

"Let's lock it up," he said to Billie. "I have a
feeling we'll be going for a ride any minute."

The control cabin still had acceleration couches
in place, they hadn't gotten around to stripping
them, so Wilks helped Billie cinch Bueller into place
before he went to his own couch. He didn't know
exactly where the retreat was going, but he had
rigged the sleep chambers so they could climb in
when they hit hyperspace; the automatics would
shut the things down when they dropped back into
normal space. After that, well, they'd see.

No sooner had he fastened his own restraints
than the ship's board lit up with launch readings.
Close.

"Hang on," he said. "Looks like somebody just lit
the fuses."

30

The ship lifted, and the high-gee force shoved at the passengers, pressing them deep into the cushioned seats. Wilks supposed that if he had a viewer operational, he would have looked back, although it would surely be a depressing sight. Watching your own planet being overrun by monsters wasn't what he would call fun.

There was nothing to be done for it, now, at least.

The first rule in winning a war was to survive. If you lived, you could fight another day. Dead, you couldn't do shit.

And Wilks planned to stay alive as long as it took to kill those things. As long as it took.

Whoever had programmed the ships had figured on using Earth's gravity to help sling them into deep space. The cargo drone reached high orbit and the drives pulsed, pushing them into an ellipse. The monitors showed that there were at least fifty ships in the loose formation. Plus one unidentified vessel whose configurations Wilks recognized.

"Hey, say good-bye to old longnose," he said.

Billie looked at him. Went blank. Then screamed.

Somehow Mitch managed to unhook himself from his seat and walk on his hands to where Billie was still strapped into her chair. He climbed up, held her, tried to reach her.

"Billie! What is it? Billie?"

It was inside her brain again, that alien presence she'd last felt light-years away. The thing that had saved them from the monsters.

It was laughing.

The force of its thoughts overwhelmed her, she couldn't stop them, it was like trying to halt an ocean breaker with a bucket. The feelings were mixed: it gloated, it was filled with snide joy, it lusted, it felt superior, it hated, it raged, and among all those were things she couldn't identify, feelings for which there was no human reference.

But she got enough of it to know what it wanted her to know.

Oh, God!

"Billie?"

She managed to focus on Mitch. Mitch, who loved her. Her feelings for him became like a wall, against which the alien spacefarer's emotional sea splashed. Some of it slipped past, but enough was stopped so Billie could recover her senses. Somehow it knew this. The tide stopped.

"It—that thing. It talked to me."

"What did it say?" Wilks put in.

"It has no more use for us than it did the aliens. It followed us here to see our world, to see if there was anything here worth taking. It wants to conquer us."

"Won't have a lot of opposition, will it?" Wilks said.

"It plans to wait and let the aliens kill all the humans. Then when the soldiers come back—it knows their plans—it will be waiting. Maybe with others of its own kind. To take Earth from the winners."

"Damn," Wilks said. "If it isn't one thing, it's another. Out of the hurricane and into a tornado."

After that, there wasn't much any of them could say.

Wilks had the sleep chambers cycling on line; according to his instruments, the ship was about to enter subspace. None of them knew for how long or how far they would travel while dancing in the nowhere and nowhen of the Einsteinian Warp. It didn't really matter.

Billie helped Wilks install Mitch into his chamber. Wilks moved away to check his own bed for the long sleep. Billie stood over Mitch, smiled down at him.

"You okay?" he asked.

"Yes. I am."

They embraced, a long, soulful hug, then she stepped away and triggered the system. The lid clamshelled down and sealed. Mitch kept his eyes open, watching her, until the gases put him under.

She watched him sleep for a moment, then turned toward her own chamber.

Wilks was already climbing into his. He waved at her.

Well. She had come a long way in her life. From one destroyed planet to another, to yet another. But she was still alive. Not so long ago, that wouldn't have meant much to Billie, but things had changed. She had Mitch now, somehow they would find a way to repair him, bring him back to what he'd been before.

No, that wasn't true. He was already more than he'd been before, even if his body was half-destroyed. But there were ways to fix that, easier because of what he was. And even that wasn't really important.

Billie climbed into her chamber. Touched a control. Watched the lid fan slowly down. No, what was important was, she wasn't alone anymore.

And she knew as sleep claimed her, she would not dream of the past and of monsters. Rather she would dream of the future. Whatever that might be. After all, they hadn't done too bad so far. A war was fought one battle at a time.

Billie smiled, and closed her eyes.

ALIENS

BOOK TWO

NIGHTMARE ASYLUM

For Dianne of course;
And for John Locke, who probably would
have written it a bit differently...

Thanks go to: Mike Richardson, for the work and his input therein; to Janna Silverstein for her input and green pencil; to Vera Katz and Sam Adams for their oblique support. Couldn'ta dunnit withoutcha, folks.

"Now this is the law of the jungle—
as old and as true as the sky;
And the Wolf that shall keep it may prosper,
but the Wolf that shall break it must die."
Rudyard Kipling

10

Outside in the dead vacuum of space there was no sound; but inside the robot ship, the steady drone of the gravity drives vibrated like a low note played on some deep-throated musical instrument. It went through the flesh, to the bone; right to the soul; it had been there since the sleep chambers clamshelled up to expose their inhabitants to it. A mechanized *om* that lulled, as if calling them back into the long sleep, no chambers needed.

Billie sat in the makeshift kitchen, staring at what passed for coffee. The color was right, but that was about all. The taste was almost nothing, hot water with some vague taint to it. She watched it cool, stuck in the post-hypersleep lethargy, her own animation still feeling somewhat suspended. It was like the flu, you couldn't cure it and it just

1

seemed to hang on forever sometimes. The coffee vibrated, making tiny ripples that lapped against the circular wall of the cup.

Behind her, Wilks said, "Tastes like shit, don't it?"

"That would be an improvement," Billie said. She didn't turn to look at him as he moved into the room. He sat on the bulkhead roll-out to her right and watched her for a few seconds before he spoke again.

"You okay?"

"Me? Yeah, I'm fine. Why shouldn't I be okay? I'm on a robot ship going God knows where, leaving behind an Earth overrun by alien monsters, in the company of half an android and a marine who is probably a borderline psycho."

"What do you mean 'borderline'?" he said. "Hey, I'm certifiable on any world you want to name."

Billie glanced at him. Couldn't stop the grin that matched his. Shook her head. "Jesus, Wilks."

"Hey, cheer up, kid. It's not as if things are really bad. We got each other. You, me, and Bueller." There was silence for a moment. Then: "I'm gonna go monitor the 'casts. You want to come along?"

Billie shifted on the crate she was using for a chair. Looked at Wilks. The burn scar on his face was something she almost never noticed anymore, but in this light, it gave his features a kind of wry malevolence. Like some minor demon out to play practical jokes. "No," she finally said.

"Suit yourself." He stood.

Billie sipped at the tepid liquid. Made a face at the nontaste. "Wait. I changed my mind. I'll go along."

It wasn't as if there was an awful lot to do on this tub. Since they'd awakened, a week had gone past, with no sign of stopping. Their monitoring gear was crappy, but even so, if there were any human-inhabited places around, they should have spotted them. The gravity drive was a lot faster than the old reaction sprayers, but if there was a planetary system, Wilks couldn't find it. There were better ways to die than starving on a ship going nowhere.

She should go and see if Mitch wanted to come with them. *Mitch.* She had trouble with that even now. Yeah, she loved him, but what a can of worms that turned out to be. Maybe not worms exactly, but whatever plumbing androids had installed sure looked verminlike. She loved him, but she also hated him. How was that possible, to have two such opposing feelings at once for someone? Maybe the medics in the hospital where she'd spent all those years were right. Maybe she *was* crazy.

The ship was fairly large, most of it was given over to cargo. They hadn't really gotten around to exploring all the nooks in it yet. Billie supposed that if they were stuck in it much longer, she'd get around to serious poking about, but the urge hadn't really come upon her; she wasn't quite bored enough. Why bother? Who gave a shit?

The control room was tiny, barely space for two to wedge their way into it. The designers had only to leave enough room for a repair tech, since the thing had been built to be run by the computer and a few service robots. The 'cast screens were blank, save for the two running ship data in computer language.

"Showtime," Wilks said. He wasn't smiling.

A man who looked like Albert Einstein at sixty said, "Have we got it? Have we got the uplink—okay, okay, listen, anybody out there, this is Hermann Koch in Charlotte; we're out of food, we're almost out of water, we're overrun! The damned things are killing or kidnapping everybody! There are only twenty of us left alive—!"

The man went away and abruptly there was another place. Outside, a bright and sunny day, spring flowers in bloom, bright green leaves sprouting on the trees. Only something hideous wrecked the scene:

One of the aliens carried under its arm a woman, as a man might carry a small dog. The alien was three meters tall, light gleaming from its black exoskeleton; its head was shaped like a mutated banana; it looked like some obscene crossbreed between an insect and a lizard. Boney, notched spars protruded from the thing's back like exposed ribs, three paired sets. It walked upright on two legs, a fact that seemed impossible given the way it was constructed, and a long, vertebrae-flanged, and pointed tail swept the pavement behind it as it moved.

A bullet spanged off the thing's head, doing no more damage to the hard surface than a rubber ball bouncing on a plastecrete sidewalk. The alien turned and looked at the unseen shooters.

"Aim for the woman!" somebody screamed. "Shoot Janna!"

Before the alien kidnapper could flee with its prey, three more shots boomed. One of them missed completely. One of them hit the alien's chest, flattened on the natural armor, did no harm. The third bullet hit the woman, just above the left eye.

"Thank God!" the unseen speaker said.

The alien sensed something wrong. It lifted the woman up, held her at arm's length, turned its head from side to side, as if examining her. The thing looked at the shooters. It dropped the dead or dying woman onto the sidewalk as if she were yesterday's garbage. Began to run directly toward the shooters. Made a hissing, burbling sound as it came—

Here, what was once a school classroom: but the rows of blank computer terminals were powerless; the only light was that which slanted in through a broken window. A human body lay on the floor, parts of it gone, eaten away, leaving a fly-blown swollen mass. Maggots squirmed in the rank remains, and the putrefaction had drawn ants and other small scavengers. The corpse was too far gone to say what sex it had been. Above the body, spray-painted on the wall in letters half a meter high the words: DARWIN ESTIS KORECTO.

Darwin was right.

Had the dead person written those words as a final statement? Or had the human arrived later, to contemplate them, to seek after truth—before the higher link in the food chain came for its due? Words like these had power, but in the jungle, the sword, the tooth, the claw, were mightier than the pen. Always . . .

A young man, maybe twenty-five, sat in a church, in the front pew. Religion hadn't been doing so well on Earth in the last twenty years, but there were still places of worship. A soft glow from beneath a cross mounted behind the altar illuminated the young man, who sat in the first row of the otherwise empty church with his eyes closed, praying aloud.

". . . And lead us not into temptation, but deliver us from evil," he said. "For Thine is the kingdom, and the power, and the glory, for ever. Amen."

Almost without pause, the young man began the prayer again, speaking in a monotone. "Our Father which art in heaven, Hallowed be thy name . . ."

A dim fuzzy shadow loomed suddenly on the wall at the end of the pew.

". . . Thy kingdom come. Thy will be done . . ."

The shadow grew larger.

". . . in Earth, as it is in heaven . . ."

There came a faint rasping on the floor, and if the young man praying heard it, he made no sign.

". . . Give us this day our daily bread. And forgive us our debts, as we forgive our debtors . . ."

The alien rose from behind the praying man, clear slime dripping in jellylike strings from its jaws. The lips cleared the sharp teeth. Its mouth opened, revealing an inner set of smaller teeth, more like a claw in their function.

". . . And lead us not into temptation, but deliver us from evil . . ."

The inner set of teeth was mounted on a greasy

ridged pole. The rod shot from the thing's mouth with incredible speed and power. The sharp teeth punched a hole in the top of the praying man's skull as if it were no thicker or harder than wet paper. Blood and brain tissue splashed. The praying man's eyes snapped open in a final surprise and he managed one word: "God!"

The alien caught his shoulders with its taloned hands and lifted him clear of the pew, the claws piercing flesh and drawing gouts of blood from a heart that didn't know it was dead yet.

The alien and its prey disappeared from view, leaving only a small puddle of congealing blood and a few flecks of gray matter on the pew to show they had been there.

The pew stood empty and silent.

God, it seemed, wasn't taking deliver-us-from-evil petitions just now.

Wilks leaned back and stared at the empty church on the screen. "Automatic camera," he said. "Probably set to catch thieves. Wonder how the signal got this far?"

Next to him, Billie's face was streaked with fresh tears. "Jesus, Wilks."

"Amazing how people keep sending the 'casts out. Like they really expect help. Or maybe it's like an old grave headstone, you know? The signals will go into space forever. Immortality as a radio wave. Maybe they think a million light-years from Earth somebody will pick them up and give a shit. You know, buy a bag of popcorn and watch the end of man, maybe on a double bill with a nature special."

Billie stood. "I'm going to see Mitch," she said.

"Give him my love," Wilks said.

She tightened, he could see her go tense, and he thought about softening it, but said nothing as she left. Fuck it. It didn't matter.

Wilks scanned the 'casts, looking for something different, but found only more of the same. Death. Destruction. Bodies rotting in the streets, animals feeding on them. A pack of dogs worried over a human arm. There wasn't any sound, probably a traffic cam, but he could tell they were growling and snarling at each other. The arm was bloated and slug-belly white. Been out in the sun too long, Wilks figured. Well. Whoever had owned it probably didn't have any use for it, might as well let the dogs eat it. It was just carrion now.

He shut the feed from Earth off. It was all history now. Whatever he was looking at had happened already, was over with, done.

He played with the scanners again, looking for wherever this ship might be bound. It was a crappy situation, the ship having been designed without passengers in mind. He'd managed to rig a few programs to get a read on the screens, which were only there for emergency backup anyhow, way he figured it. Probably cobbled together after things went bad on Earth, and as such was built with fence wire and prayer. After seeing the guy in the church, Wilks didn't have a lot of faith in prayer. Not that he'd ever had much to begin with.

The ship knew where it was going, maybe, but that didn't help Wilks. There must be a planet or wheelworld out here somewhere; there was a G-class star less than two hundred million klicks away, but if it had satellites, he hadn't spotted them yet. Had to be there, otherwise why would the sleep chambers let them out?

Could be a malfunction, asshole, the little voice in his head said with a smirk. *Could be you're all gonna die.*

Fuck you, Wilks told the voice. I got business to finish before I die.

And you think the universe cares about your business?

Fuck you, pal. You and the id you rode in on.

The voice rewarded him with a nasty laugh.

2

Mitch rested in the cradle they had improvised for him, and from behind it appeared that he was sitting up. Given that there was nothing left of his body from the waist down, sitting wasn't exactly possible. He stopped in the middle, almost literally half a man—half an android—a ragged medifoam blob sealing his innards shut. He had done the repairs on his circulatory tubules himself, shunting, reconnecting, so that he was once again a closed system. That was how he'd put it, a closed system. The other half of him had been left on the aliens' homeworld, torn off by a maddened drone protecting its nest. That alien was killed and likely it and most of the others there were vaporized by the subsequent atomic explosions Wilks had left them as a going away gift.

A man torn asunder as Mitch had been would

have died on that hellish planet, from blood loss or maybe shock. Androids were built better.

He heard her come in. This was the starboard computer access compartment, smaller even than the place where she'd just left Wilks. He heard her, but pretended he had not.

"Mitch?"

He shook his head. "I can't get past the operating system," he said. "Navigation access code is sixty-five digits, backed up by a second code of forty numbers. It would take forever to get it, given the hardware I've got. And where are the other ships? We left Earth in the middle of an armada. They should be somewhere around here, but they aren't. We're alone. It doesn't make any sense."

She moved to stand next to his cradle. Resisted the impulse to stroke his hair. "It's all right—"

"No, it *isn't* all right! We don't know where we are, where we're going, if we'll get there alive! I have to, it's my function to . . ." he trailed off. Shook his head again.

Billie wanted to cry, something she'd done more of in the last week than ever in her life. His *function*. She'd fallen in love with an android. Worse, maybe, he'd fallen in love with her. He was having more trouble dealing with the feelings than she was. When they'd gone into the sleep chambers, she'd accepted it, believed it would be all right, somehow. But when they'd come out, something had changed. Some of it was him. Some of it, she had to admit, was her.

She didn't think she was one of those people who carried her prejudices around like a club, bashing those who disagreed with her. She'd always paid lip service to equality. A person is a person, no matter if they're born of woman, incubated in an artificial womb, or made in the android vats. Where you came from wasn't important, only where you were going. Spend too much time looking back, you'd run into something and brain yourself, right? She'd always said that. Androids were people.

Yeah, but would you want your sister to marry one?

Or would you want to marry one yourself?

Jesus.

He hadn't told her, that was his main crime. She'd only found out after they had become lovers, after she had let him into her heart. That hurt. She hadn't thought she could ever get past that, but amazingly, she had. Or so she had thought. But now?

It wasn't just that he was less than he had been. With the proper facilities, Mitch could be made whole again. As good as new. Meticulously designed muscles, perfect skin, all the right equipment in the right places . . .

Stop it!

No, there was something else going on here and Billie didn't know exactly what. The man—artificial or not—she had fallen in love with wasn't the same as he had been. Something inside his mind was different. She wanted to understand, wanted to give him all the slack he needed, but he had become someone else, a cold, fearful person who wouldn't let her in. Somebody who didn't want to hear about her love or anger or needs. Hiding behind his wall, hands over his ears.

Still, she kept trying.

"Mitch, listen. I—" Now she did reach out and touch his hair. It felt as real as her own, was real in that it had grown from his scalp the same way, was made of protein so similar only a microscope could see the differences.

"Don't, Billie," he said.

She felt the words like a blast of frigid air, so cold it took her breath away. How could he do this? Not talk to her?

"Billie, please. Try to understand. I—I'm not trying to hurt you. It's—it's just that I don't—I can't—I . . . I'm sorry."

"I'm tired," Billie said. "I'm going to try to get some rest now."

She walked away, nearly tripped as the faux grav fluctuated a hair. They'd had problems with that, nobody thought a robot ship really needed gravity in transit and that system, like many of the others, had been rigged by Wilks before they lifted. To hear him tell it, if somebody sneezed too hard, the ship would break up.

The storeroom she used as her sleeping quarters was private, a three-meter-by-two-meter box, but since it was next to the ship's internal power and heating system, it was also hotter than most spots onboard. She stripped to her undershirt and panties, lay down, and leaned back against the bulkhead that served as a pillow. Sweat slid down her bare skin, dampened her clothes, and made her feel sticky. Still, it wasn't unbearable. And it was damnsure better than the company she'd have to endure otherwise.

She was dozing when Wilks appeared in the doorway. She hadn't bothered to slid shut the hanging curtain she'd rigged. His sudden presence startled her.

"Make some noise when you move, Wilks. You scared me."

He stepped into the room, his feet nearly touching hers. She sat up, drew her feet in. He'd seen her naked, but something about the way he stood there made her nervous.

"Everything scares you, Billie," he said.

She blinked sweat away, wiped at her eyes. "What are you talking about?"

He moved closer. Knelt. Reached out and caught her shoulders. "When you were a kid you were scared of dying. Later, you were scared of living."

"Jesus, Wilks, back off—"

He slid his hands under her shirt before she could react. Cupped her breasts. "And you've always been scared of me," he said.

Her shock turned to anger. She grabbed his hands, pulled them from under her shirt. "Goddammit! What the hell do you think you're doing!"

He grabbed her wrists, leaned against her. His face was only centimeters from hers now. She could smell his sweat, his . . . musk.

"You really prefer that *thing* in the computer room? Wouldn't you rather be with a real man? One who has all the right equipment?"

She felt something hard poke into her belly. Christ, was he going to rape her? "Wilks! Stop it! Why are you doing this?"

He jerked back, his face gone slack for a beat, eyes closed. The lids snapped up and an infernal light shined from his pupils at her. He grinned.

"Why? Because I'm going to make you face yourself. What you're afraid of. Love. Passion. Caring. People."

Billie looked down, and saw that the bulge she'd felt wasn't what she'd thought. It was his belly—

"Aagghh!"

With his scream, his abdomen burst outward in a spray of flesh and gore and a full-size adult alien came forth. Impossible, it wasn't physically possible! It smiled at her, showing the sharp carnivore's teeth. Slime and blood dripped as it reached for her . . .

"Wilks!"

Billie sat up, alone in her cubicle. Her shirt and panties were soaked with sweat, her hair hung limp.

Oh, fuck. A dream. Only a dream!

But she knew better. It wasn't a dream. It was a vision. A . . . communication. It was too real, it went too deep.

They were here.

On the ship.

Billie grabbed her clothes and ran.

Wilks was fiddling with the program that ran the external pickups, hoping to figure a way to magnify images visually when Billie rushed in. She was half into her coverall, drenched in sour sweat. There wasn't much water on this tub, they probably all smelled a little overripe. Even Bueller, who had sweat glands that did a fair imitation of human ones. He was in the other seat, having hand-walked in earlier, dragging his little plastic cradle behind him like some beggar from the streets of West L.A.

"Wilks, they're here. On the ship!"

She grabbed at his shirt. "Take it easy, take it easy! You saw one?"

"She dreamed about it," Bueller said quietly.

Billie turned and glared at him, as if he had violated some secret between them.

"It wasn't just a nightmare, Wilks. I *felt* them. Remember the spacefarer alien who saved us, how I could feel his hatred?"

"Yeah, the elephant man. Scavenger of doomed races."

"It was like that. I can still feel them. It's like some kind of light touch against my mind. I can't quite put my finger on it, but it is there!"

Wilks shook his head. The kid was stretched too tight. They all were, cooped up on this bucket. They'd been through a lot. The stress had to come out somewhere. He'd been doing sets of push-ups and chin-ups and squats every day until he couldn't move anymore, trying to burn it out of himself.

"Look, Billie, it doesn't make sense—"

"Where is the gun, Wilks? If you won't help me find them, I'll do it myself!"

Wilks looked at Bueller. The android looked away. Dealing with emotional women was out of his territory, Wilks knew that. Like it was something he knew how to do. Christ, women were like another species sometimes. He didn't understand them at all.

"Well?"

"All right. You want to play marine? We'll play

marine. But I'll keep the gun. We've only got part of one magazine left."

He stood, moved to the locker where he'd stored the carbine. He'd locked it securely away, along with the pistol he'd had before they went into the sleep chambers. He should have collected more ammo, maybe another couple of M-41Es before they lifted from Earth, a good marine armed himself as best he could when he could, but time had been a little tight. When your choice was hurrying to catch a ship leaving or staying to face either an atomic fireball or a hungry monster, you didn't dick around looking for spare ammo. He did have a couple of grenades for the under-the-barrel launcher of the carbine but those weren't much use on a vessel cruising through hard vacuum. Bust a hole in an external wall and the cold emptiness outside would suck your air out and freeze it into nice little crystals for you. Only a madman wanted to make something go *boom!* on a spaceship. Even the AP rounds from the 10mm could be a problem, but at least the hole they might make would be real small. Toss a Gum-sparrow into the stream and it would plug the leak okay.

He pulled the locker open, reached in, removed the carbine. Toggled the battery-saver off and saw the LED light. Five rounds left in the magazine. Shit.

Wait a second here, Wilks. It's not as if we're gonna need even five rounds. The kid is just tense. We do a run-through and show her we're alone and that's it.

He turned to Billie. "You want to take the handgun? It won't do shit to the armor, but maybe if it opens its mouth . . ."

"Give it to me," she said.

Wilks tendered the pistol, a slicked-up version of the standard army-issue Smith auto. He'd taken it from the general back on Earth, after the bastard had shot Blake. The general had gotten off three rounds, then Wilks had shot five more times. Eight. This model didn't have a counter, fucking regular army was too cheap to install them, but it was a fifteen-round double-stack mag, so it had seven shots left, eight if the general had kept an extra one in the chamber.

"Got seven rounds," he said.

She checked the gun. "I only need two," she said. Then she glanced over at Bueller. "Three."

"Okay, let's go find the monsters," Wilks said. "Bueller, you want to tag along?"

"Do you really think there is any danger?"

Wilks looked at Billie, then back at Bueller. "Truth? No."

"Then I'll stay here and continue to work on the computer."

Wilks could almost see Billie's anger smoldering. If he had said he thought there were aliens on the ship, then Bueller would have had to go along, being an android. To try to protect the two real humans.

"Let's move out, Billie."

Her jaw muscles danced and she nodded. "Fine."

What the hell, Wilks thought, it was something to do. So far, it had turned up exactly what he thought it would, zero. They'd been through all the ship big enough to hide a small dog and so far hadn't seen even an insect. Sometimes you got a few bugs on a ship, despite the zap fields supposed to keep 'em off. Some guys made pets out of them.

"That's it, Billie. End of sweep. Nobody home."

"What about the aft cargo storage?"

Wilks leaned the carbine against the wall and scratched a sweaty itch on his shoulder. "Can't get into it. Coded lock. We can't get in, nothing can get out, either."

"Come on, Wilks. I've seen these things operate. So have you."

"We could take a look at the door, that'll make you happy."

"It won't make me happy, but we have to check."

He shrugged. He could cut her a little slack. She hadn't exactly had a great life. Both parents killed by the aliens or, worse, webbed into hatching chambers as baby alien food. Years in a mental hospital on Earth where they thought she was nuts because the mind-wipe they'd tried broke down and let her remember it. And all the shit they'd been through since. What the hell.

The corridor leading to the aft cargo hatch was narrow and dimly lit. But Wilks could see down its length that the hatch door was shut and the LED on steady red-lock. Like all inner doors, it was air-tight and proof against sudden decompression or hammering of fists—if somebody got on the wrong side of it during an emergency. Standard duralloy plate, six or seven centimeters thick. Even the aliens could have trouble clawing through that.

"Knock, knock," Wilks said, "anybody home?"

The pair of them stood in front of the hatch for a moment. "Sorry, Billie. Looks like the hunt is over."

"What's that smell?" she asked.

Wilks sniffed. Something burned. It smelled acrid, like . . . cable insulation. A short somewhere? Could be easy enough, given how this ship was put together.

"It's stronger over here," she said, pointing toward the side corridor they'd just passed.

"Better check it out—"

A lazy wisp of smoke crawled from the corridor, a heavy vaporous snake that stayed low, hugging the deck.

"Better grab an extinguisher," Wilks said.

Billie pulled one of the portables from the wall.

Suddenly there came a loud metallic scream, the blare of a Klaxon. Foam from a ceiling fire suppressor sprayed into the corridor ahead of them, gushing from the cross-corridor.

"Shit!" Wilks said.

In his cradle Bueller saw the FIRE alarm visual flash onto the screen in front of him. "Shit!" There wasn't a PA system onboard. He couldn't call Billie and Wilks.

Using his hands, he flipped himself out of the cradle, hit the deck on his palms, and began to "walk" as fast as he could. It was awkward, but quick, as a man might move if he were late for an appointment but didn't want to embarrass himself by running.

• • •

The foam shut off and the Klaxon followed it a second later. Wilks sighed. That meant the fire was out. Or else the suppression system had given up the ghost. But he didn't feel any heat pour out of the corridor.

"Stay here, I'll check it."

"Fuck that. I'll be right on your ass."

He had to grin. "Okay. Watch it, deck's slippery."

They were walking parallel to the aft cargo compartment, and it only took a couple of meters to find the source of the smoke. A dangling cable, burned through, still smoking a little even though covered with fire foam.

"Wilks."

He turned to see what Billie wanted. There was a hole in the wall between the corridor and the aft cargo hold. A ragged, melted gap big enough for a man to walk through without touching the edges.

Melted by acid.

"Oh, shit," Wilks said.

Billie nodded. "Yeah."

3

Billie let the fire extinguisher drop as she hauled the handgun from her pocket. She clutched the pistol in hands gone sweaty and cold. Fear turned her bowels into a gelid lump. She wanted to run and hide, but there was nowhere to go.

"You were right," Wilks said. "I stand corrected."

He catfooted his way through the hole in the bulkhead, being careful to avoid touching the edges. "Careful," he said.

Billie followed him. The room was dark, a faint gleam from the corridor on the remnants of the fire foam the only light. No, wait, there were instrument diodes . . .

Wilks found a lume control and dialed the lights up.

"Jesus."

22

Billie nodded, her mouth too dry to speak.

Lying on the floor was an alien. Part of the deck beneath it was eaten away by its blood, a fluid so acidic as to defy belief. One theory Billie had heard in the 'casts was that it made the things taste bad. That was fairly horrifying. What kind of creature could possibly eat these monsters?

Along with the dead alien, the main cargo in the hold seemed to be four hypersleep chambers. Each had once contained a person. What was left of the four bodies wouldn't add up to one full-size corpse. The lids of the chambers were cracked and blood-spattered, human blood from the look of it, and long dried.

Billie felt like vomiting. She fought for control, won, but barely.

Wilks examined one of the control panels next to a ruined chamber. He turned back to Billie, who was glancing quickly around, expecting an attack at any second.

"These four were deep into it," he said. "Iced as cool as you can get without killing them. I think maybe somebody knew they were infected. Trying to keep the things growing inside the humans dormant. Looks like it didn't work."

"Why? Why would somebody do that?"

Wilks shook his head. "Dunno." He looked around, the carbine held ready. "Politics. Profit. We can talk philosophy later. Way I figure it, there were four aliens. Three of them killed the fourth and used its acid blood to eat themselves an exit. They've finished off breakfast"—he waved the carbine at the mostly eaten bodies—"and they'll be out looking for dinner."

"Mitch!"

"Don't worry about Bueller, they don't much like the flavor of android. We figured that out on the trip to their homeworld."

"But if they find him, they'll kill him."

"Yeah. Him and us, too. They must have left just before we got here. The acid triggered the fire foam. Come on. We need to get back to a section of the ship we can fortify."

Something rattled behind them in a dark recess of the cargo hold.

"Wilks—"

"I heard it."

He turned, brought the carbine up, flicked on the sighting laser. The tiny red dot danced in the shadowy corner.

Something hissed.

"Billie—"

The thing stepped out into the light. Three meters tall, gleaming black. If the monster had eyes, they were hidden from view as always, but whatever senses it used, it knew they were there. The external jaws opened and drool dripped from the rows of finger-thick needles that were its teeth. The spiky tail lashed back and forth like that of a cat about to pounce.

"Wilks!"

"I got it." He raised the carbine to his shoulder slowly. Billie saw the laser's red spot move up the creature's chest, over its chin, to shine on a lower tooth.

The thing's mouth opened wider. The red dot disappeared.

"Adios, motherfucker," Wilks said.

The *boom!* of the carbine was loud in the cargo hold, a blast that bounced from the hard walls and hurt Billie's ears. The alien fell backward, Billie saw the top of its head ten centimeters behind the jaws burst outward, tiny chips of armor flying as the bullet tore through. A thin stream of yellowish liquid spewed, painted the floor. It seemed to fall in slow motion, collapsing into a heap onto a hatch set flush into the deck.

"You got it!"

The hatch began to smoke where the stream of acid landed. More liquid pooled from the punctured skull.

"Out, Billie, out! That's a dump hatch, it leads to a lock between here and the hull! If that shit eats through the outer door—"

Billie didn't need to be told. She jumped for the alien-created door in the bulkhead behind her. Wilks was right on her heels. "Move, move!"

The fire alarm went off again, the hooter filled the corridor with noise. Foam sprayed inside the cargo hold behind them as they slipped and slid along the corridor still wet with the dregs of the earlier foam.

"Go, go, we've got to clear the next hatch!"

Billie was two meters ahead of Wilks when another alarm, more strident, began to blare. That would be the hull breach warning. The floor-to-ceiling hatch five meters ahead began to slide down, a light next to it lit and flashed red. Unless something plugged the hole in the hull, all the air on this side of the hatch was going to piss itself into the vacuum. Anybody on this side of the hatch was going to die trying to breathe nothingness.

Billie dived at the closing hatch, made it
through, hit the deck. She skidded on her belly, felt
the skin on her arms and hands scrape and abrade,
but she was through! She rolled over. Saw that
Wilks wouldn't make it.

He tried. He dived, stretched out full length, slid.
But the door came down across the small of his
back. Billie saw it press into his flesh.

"Aaggh!"

"Fuck!" Billie scrabbled on her hands and knees.
She had to get something under the plate! A fire
extinguisher, something! But there was no time,
the door would break Wilks's spine in another
second—

The gun. Billie still held the pistol. She shoved it,
twisted it. Almost, not quite—"Breathe out!" she
yelled.

Wilks couldn't see what she was doing, but he
obeyed. She shoved as hard as she could and the
barrel of the weapon touched the underside of
the descending plate. When Wilks exhaled, it
bought her a half centimeter. The back of the pistol's receiver skidded on the deck, got almost directly under the door, then stopped. The heavy
plastic and steel of the gun creaked, began to bend.

Billie slid back, grabbed Wilks's wrists, and
pulled.

"Come on, Wilks! Pull!"

The thin fabric of his pants snagged on the door,
tore. The underside of the door scraped skin from
his buttocks away, dug into the muscle, but he
moved.

The pistol made a sound like a nail being pulled
from wet wood as Wilks's thighs cleared the portal.

Billie shoved her heels hard against the deck,
leaned back, and Wilks crawled up her, grabbed
her shoulders, and pulled himself into a frantic
hug, his feet sliding under the narrowing gap just
as the pistol bent and shattered like a crystallized
steel spring. Something sharp hit Billie's face just
under her left eye. The descending hatch slammed
into the deck as she fell backward with Wilks
sprawled full-length on top of her.

Billie felt the muscles in Wilks's upper back relax
under her hands. They lay pressed together for another second. Then Wilks drew a ragged breath
and rolled off her to lie on his back next to her. After a moment he said, "Thanks."

Billie fought to slow her breathing. "No problem.
I don't usually go this far on a first date, though."

Wilks shook his head. Managed a weak grin.

When the hull breach alarm went off, Bueller
was halfway to the aft cargo bay. He had gotten
fairly efficient at walking on his hands, but the
sound made him hurry even more. Billie and Wilks
were in danger. He had to save them. Especially
Billie.

Wilks saw Bueller padding toward them, a distorted version of a man gone from the waist down.
From the angle, it looked like somebody wading
through the deck.

"Billie! Wilks!"

"We're okay," Wilks said. "Just another wonderful
day on the exotic starliner cruise vacation. Come
on." He extended a hand.

Bueller leaned to one side, resting all his weight

on his left palm. He reached up with his right arm. The two locked into a wrist grip, and Wilks pulled Bueller up onto his back. Bueller said, "Billie . . . ?"

"We've got company," she said. "Maybe next time you two will listen to me when I tell you something."

Back in the computer access room, Wilks began playing with the internal video cams. They weren't much, basic and cheap bottom-of-the-line Cambodian units. Terran regulations required such equipment, even on robot ships, and for once, Wilks was glad to see union politics doing something useful. No motion sensors or infrared, but something was better than nothing.

Bueller sat cradled in the operations chair. His reflexes were faster and he knew the systems better.

"We figure there are two of them left," Billie said. She leaned against the back of Wilks's chair, watching the monitors as Wilks brought up the various views.

Nothing in the main corridor.

"How did they get on board?"

Wilks said, "Somebody had four demi-stiffs in chambers in the aft cargo hold. Infected."

The midline cargo bay was clear.

"Why would anybody do that?"

"Good question. Fuck if I know." He winced. "Ah, shit."

"You okay?" Billie asked.

"Muscle spasm in my back. I'm not going to be running the marathon for a few days." He looked at Bueller. "Billie hadn't stopped it, the pressure hatch would have made me into your twin brother."

No monsters in the makeshift head.

Wilks brought up another view, this time of the kitchen they'd rigged. Nobody home.

"That's it," Wilks said. "Cheap bastards put in the minimum required, we're blind everywhere else. Damn."

Nobody said anything for a few seconds. Then: "I can maybe give us some more eyes," Bueller said.

Wilks turned. Pain shot down his spine, hurt all the way to his goddamn feet. He bit his lip. "What are you talking about? You aren't going anywhere."

"No, that wouldn't be very efficient in my present condition. But there are a couple of mobile cleaners, battery-operated dumbots. If we can rig a cam to one, we can program it to do a search."

Wilks managed a smile. "That's good, Bueller. And here I thought your brains were in your ass. Let's do it."

It took a couple of hours for Mitch to wire the things, but when he was done, they had a portable camera. Billie didn't know what they could do about it if they found the aliens, but she figured it was better to know where they were. They still had four shots left in the carbine.

The dumbot and camera were together as big as a medium-size dog. The unit rolled on six fat little silicone wheels and should be able to go anywhere a person could walk.

"Okay, puppy," Wilks said, "go find us the nasty monsters."

• • •

It took them nearly two hours to spot the aliens.
They were on the ceiling of the corridor just outside the midline cargo section. If Wilks hadn't
known they could do that, latch themselves to the
ceiling, he wouldn't have had the camera doing full
pans, but he'd seen the things come off the walls
and ceilings of their nests. They weren't moving
and if he hadn't known better, they looked like
some kind of sculpture hung by a modern artist.

"There they are," Wilks said.

Billie leaned forward for a better look. "Now
what?"

"I'm open to suggestions."

"I could take the carbine," Mitch began. "If I can
get close enough before they move—"

"No," Billie said. "Can you make the robot make
noise?"

Wilks and Mitch looked at her.

"Put it into the midline lock," she said. "If we
can lure them into the lock . . ."

"Yeah," Wilks said. "We could blow them out
into vac. Maybe."

"Better ideas?" Billie said.

Wilks and Mitch looked at each other. Shook
their heads.

"Let's do it."

Bueller was good at taking over the dumbot with
the remote. He got it through the inner hatch to
the lock and started running it into the walls. They
didn't have a sound pickup, but it must be thumping pretty good.

"Move it next to the outer hatch," Billie suggested.

Bueller did so. He trained the cam on the inner portal. Less than a minute later, the two aliens moved into view.

"Let's give them something to chase," Wilks said.

The dumbot moved back and forth in front of the outer hatch, Bueller had it going in jerky stops and starts.

"They probably know they can't eat it," Wilks said. ' ·

"They're both inside," Billie said.

"Shut the fucking hatch," Wilks said.

Bueller abandoned the controls to the dumbot and slapped the override button for the hatch. Before the aliens could react, he grabbed the controls to the mobile unit again and sent it at the aliens. The little machine crashed into one of the aliens' legs.

The picture canted wildly as the alien kicked the robot.

"Grab hold of something, I'm shutting the gravity off!"

Wilks felt that familiar pit-of-the-stomach lurch as his body told his brain he was falling and would soon be smashed flat.

"Blow the outer hatch!"

Bueller hit the control. The ship wobbled.

"Can we get the camera?" Billie asked.

Bueller's hands did their dance, fingers wiggling impossibly fast. The picture spun. "It's outside the ship," he said. "Tumbling—there, there's one of them!" He froze the picture. One of the aliens floated past, its horrible expression made more so by the realization it was leaving the only sanctuary for millions of klicks. Or maybe that was just Wilks's imagination. .

"Where is the other one?"

"I don't see it," Bueller said. "But I've got a shot of the inside of the lock." He pulled up another image.

The lock was empty.

"All *right*!" Wilks said. "*Hasta la vista*, fuckheads!" He turned to look at Billie. "Score another one for the good guys, kid."

Her hair floated up around her head in the zero gee. She closed her eyes and nodded.

Bueller turned the gravity back on and Billie settled into herself—

Then something started banging on the hull.

4

The pounding that vibrated through the ship changed to a scraping noise. Like giant claws scratching on metal.

"Sounds like the cat wants in," Wilks says. "I'll get it."

He tried to stand. An invisible karate expert slammed a steely fist into Wilks's lower back. The spasm and pain nailed him into stillness. Any movement was too much. He collapsed back into the chair, and that hurt, too.

"Or maybe not," he managed through tight lips. "He probably hasn't had time to pee yet and we don't have a litter box."

"I'll go," Bueller said.

"Wait a second," Billie said. "Why does anybody have to do anything? It's outside. It doesn't have any air, it will freeze, it will die!"

Wilks shook his head. Damned if that didn't hurt, too. "It's not human, Billie. We don't know what kind of oxygen or energy reserves it has tucked away. It might survive a long time. Any of us would already be history out there."

"So? Fuck it, let it croak slowly."

Bueller picked it up. "This isn't a combat ship, Billie. No armor. There are things it could damage out there. Heat tiles and hydraulic sheathing will protect against atmospheric burns and space dust, but not against what that creature can do."

"What are you saying?"

"It jabs a finger in the wrong spot, bends the wrong flange crooked, rips the wrong hose, it might wreck the ship," Wilks added.

"I don't believe it."

"Trust me here, kid. A human in a suit with a half-kilogram reactionless hammer could do it. If it knew where to hit us, that thing could blow us to eternity and it wouldn't even work up a sweat."

Billie shook her head. "Great. Just fucking great."

"We have a couple of inspection suits," Bueller said. "Umbilicals. I'll see if I can rig one to fit me."

Billie stared at him. She took a deep breath.

Wilks saw it coming.

"No," she said. "I'll go."

"Billie—" Bueller began.

"A spacesuit has magnetic boots," she said. She stared at Bueller. "Is that right?"

"Yes, but—"

"So how are you going to move around and carry a carbine, Mitch? Hold the gun in your teeth while you clump around with boots on your hands? Wilks can't, you aren't in any shape to do it. That leaves me."

Wilks and Bueller exchanged looks. "She's right," Wilks said. "I hate that, but she's right."

Billie stripped to her undershirt and panties. The lock was chilly, the suit stiff and bulky as she stepped into the bottom half and worked it up her legs. Chill bumps frosted her skin; her belly felt as if it had been flash frozen from the inside out. Wilks had drilled her half a dozen times in how to put the suit on, how to test the seals, make sure everything was in working order. If he could have moved, he would have been here checking it. Of course, if he could have moved, he would have gone himself.

The suit had a voxcom; Wilks's voice came over it as Billie lowered the hard plastic helmet into place.

"Listen, kid, we can't be of much help in here. The internal cameras would freeze outside and this piece of shit isn't equipped with hull scanners. I might be able to rotate one of the long-distance sensors, but even so, it'd be fairly myopic."

"You want to watch it eat me?"

Mitch came on the com. "Billie . . ."

"Just a joke, Mitch. Don't worry. I'll find the damned thing and shoot it. I've got four shots left, that should be plenty."

She wished she felt as brave as she tried to sound. The odds were in her favor. She knew what she was dealing with, she had a gun that could kill it, she was brighter. The drones were like big ants or bees, they were nasty and deadly, but stupid.

That's what everybody said. Relentless, yes; smart, no. Faux grav was confined to the inside surfaces of the ship. Outside, the thing would float away if it wasn't very careful. Billie could walk on the hull with her boots; the alien would have to have something to hold on to. And it wasn't going to be her.

"Okay, I'm in the suit. The air is coming through, the heaters and valves and all are green, according to the little panel under my chin. I'm going to close the inner hatch and depressurize the lock."

"You sure?" Wilks said.

"Yes, Mother."

"Billie. Be careful." That from Mitch.

She could hear the love in his voice. She thought. She nodded, realized he couldn't see it. "Don't worry. I'm going to be *real* careful."

The pumps cycled online. The heavy suit expanded as the pressure dropped in the lock. God, she felt as if she were in a thick balloon. She could bend her arms and legs, but it was not easy. The carbine had been built with combat gauntlets in mind so she could reach the trigger okay in the suit's gloves. She made sure the fire selector was in single-shot mode. The LED number 4 on the magazine readout gleamed redly at her. Four shots should be enough. Should be plenty.

Another red light went on, this one a bar showing the lock's air pressure was effectively zero. Billie swallowed, her throat dry. "I'm going to open the outer door," she said.

"Copy. Go."

The hatch slid up. The stars were hard pinpricks against the dead black curtain of space. The local sun was shining, but on the opposite side of the ship. Billie moved to the entrance. Leaned out and looked to the sides. The ship had running lights and the faint glow was enough for her to see the immediate area was clear. A faint dusting of dreg-air blew out, becoming visible as it froze.

"Nobody in sight. I'm going out."

"Don't forget, your boot controls are on your hips, they're toggles. Put one foot out and light the magnetics on that side first."

"I remember."

Billie put her right foot outside the ship, lifted the protective cover over the button on her hip, pressed the control. The boot stuck to the ship's side without sound.

"The magnets are stronger under the arch of your foot, weaker at the ball and heel," Wilks said. "Walk as normally as you can and the boot will peel up and replant okay. It'll feel like you're stepping on something real sticky. Just take it slow, keep one foot down at all times."

"Wilks, you already said that. It wasn't that long ago; my brain hasn't gone dead yet."

Billie moved her other leg outside of the ship, triggered the magnetics on the left boot. Felt a sudden dizziness as she stood "up," extending from the side of the ship like a thorn stuck into it. She attached the magnetic ball of the umbilical to the ship as a backup.

"You'll probably feel like you're falling," Wilks said. "That's okay, don't let that bother you, you'll adjust in a little while."

Billie looked around. God, it was so *big*! Despite the fear she felt, a sense of wonder flowed into her. There was a kind of razor-edge beauty to it. The suit's heaters were on, she was comfortable enough, but the cold was so deep she could almost hear it sing. She sighed. It was a rush, being out here in the middle of nowhere, millions of klicks away from anything. It made her realize how small she really was, compared to the vastness of the cosmos.

"It's a real E-ticket ride out here."

"Ain't it, though," Wilks said. "You never forget your first EVA."

"Assuming you survive it," Billie said.

Walking was, as Wilks said, not too hard. A little awkward, but not bad once you got used to it. There was a little light on top of her helmet, and she switched it on. She felt as if she were the only person in the entire universe.

Wake up, Billie, she told herself. Don't forget why you're out here.

"I'm by the big dish-shaped thing," she said.

"The main antenna," Wilks said. "See anything?"

"Nope. I'm going to walk toward the back of the ship. I'll stay near the right edge so I can look down the side."

"Copy."

Billie started moving. She held the carbine ready to fire, her finger on the trigger. You weren't supposed to do that, you weren't supposed to touch the trigger until you were ready to fire the weapon, but she wasn't going to risk fumbling in the damned gloves when she couldn't feel anything through them. She'd heard the scientists were working on nanopuke suits that were thinner than paint and stronger than spider silk, you could see right through them, but the alien infestation no doubt put a stop to that fast enough.

She passed the parabolic dish, a couple of meters away on her left, glanced over to make sure nothing was crouched down behind it. The umbilical ball rolled soundlessly along behind her. She started to turn back and peer over the side of the ship when she caught a glimpse of movement in her peripheral vision.

Billie twisted back toward the dish, pivoting slowly on the balls of her feet. Her left boot peeled up from the deck.

The alien flew toward her like some malignant retro-bird, arms extended, taloned hands spread wide to catch her. It must have been flattened against the back of the dish, she thought. She should have looked higher. Bad mistake—

She screamed, something wordless and primal, and snapped the carbine up. Her vision tunneled, and she was vaguely aware of her yell echoing in the suit, of Wilks rattling something incomprehensible at her through the com. A single heartbeat later even those sounds vanished as all her attention focused on the black death sailing toward her. The distant sun glittered on the thing's armor, cast a long shadow over her, as it loomed, a living eclipse. Nothing existed for Billie in that moment save the thing's teeth, frozen spittle and slime crusting them as they came for her. She had the carbine up now, no time to aim, just point it and shoot—!

The recoil from the first shot peeled the other boot free of the ship. She couldn't tell if she hit the alien or not. The second shot's recoil spun her backward in a flip, her lower body and feet blocked her view of the onrushing monster. The umbilical created drag; the magnetic ball held. Instead of finishing the flip or sailing straight back, she arced downward toward the ship. Went over the side, still connected to the hull.

The alien flew at her, a meter away, but rising. One of her shots must have hit it, a stream of liquid sprayed from the top of its head, the fluid glittering and freezing into crystals as it spewed forth. The impact of the bullet had spun the monster slightly, but the spray of its blood coming out under pressure seemed to be pushing it back the other way. Toward her—

Billie fired the carbine again and again. She couldn't hear it, but she could feel the electronic click under her gloves as the weapon cycled empty. It was all so deathly silent—

Both rounds missed, as far as she could tell, but the recoil drove her away from the flying monster. It soared past her, missing by a good half meter. It did not go easily into the void. It twisted, tail lashing, inner jaws shooting out and snapping in what she thought must be rage. The thing turned slowly and continued onward into the vast emptiness.

Billie managed to tug on the umbilical and keep herself mostly facing the alien as it moved off. It was only when the thing was the size of an ant, a real ant, that she became aware of the com blasting at her again.

"Billie, goddammit, answer me!"

"Okay, okay. It's all right."

"What happened?"

"I found the cat," she said. "It didn't want to

come in after all. It wanted to go prowl the neighborhood."

"Buddha. And Jesus, too."

"It may run into Them where it's going."

"You okay?"

"Yeah."

"Come on in."

"Yeah. I hear that."

She hauled herself up the umbilical until she could stick her boots to the hull again. Oh, man.

As she was heading toward the hatch, she saw something glittering in the sunlight. The angle was just right, anywhere else she probably would have missed it. "Hello?"

"Billie?"

"Wilks, there's something floating next to the ship."

"The alien?"

"No, it's long gone. This looks like a contrail. Runs right toward the rear of the ship, but at an angle."

"Stray vapor, maybe," Wilks said. "From when we blew the aliens out. Or the dregs from your EVA lock-open."

"I don't think so. I can see some frozen air here and there. This looks like a jet trail. Real thin, but it seems to make a loop out in the distance. I can't tell at this angle."

"So it's an anomaly. Forget it. Come inside."

"I ought to go check it out, long as I'm here."

"I said forget it."

"Yeah, well, you say a lot of things, Wilks."

"Billie. Maybe it's alien piss. Or puke. It doesn't matter."

"Maybe. Maybe the other alien could pee hard enough to shove itself back to the ship."

"Come on. The things aren't that bright."

"You ever hear of anything that could survive hard vac without a suit? That could pound on a deep-space ship from the outside when it didn't have any air or protection from cold down around Absolute Fucking Zero? They might not be bright, but they die hard, Wilks."

The com was silent.

"I'll go see. Probably it's not anything."

"How many shots do you have left?" Bueller put in.

"Uh, actually, none."

"Dammit, Billie—"

"Doesn't matter," she said. "I don't have anything to shoot with, anyhow." The carbine was gone. She couldn't remember when she'd let it go.

"What are you gonna do if there is another one of those things there?" Wilks asked. "Insult its mother?"

"I'm just going to look. One thing at a time."

Bueller started to leave his cradle. "Where are you going?"

"Outside."

"Cancel that thought, mister. Not gonna happen."

"Sergeant, if there's another one of those things out there Billie won't have a chance against it unarmed."

"And you will? Last time you went up against these suckers you lost your ass, Bueller. And you are a bottle-bred marine and were armed."

"Wilks—"

"Civilization may be down the tubes but you're still a marine assigned to my command until you hear otherwise, ain't that right, Bueller?"

"You know it is."

"Then stay right where you are. We don't know anything is out there and therefore Billie is not in any clear danger."

Bueller bit down on his anger; Wilks could see him fight the desire to disobey the order. The programming won out. "All right."

"Good boy. Now, see if you can figure out something we can do if she gets to a place she does need help."

Billie walked down the rear of the ship until she was at the docking thruster. The gravity drives didn't use this thing; they were tuned to waves that ran completely through the ship, as she understood it, but for close order drill, the ship had rockets for maneuvers. As long as the gravity drives were operating the rockets wouldn't budge the vessel, that's what Wilks had told her.

The main thruster was a hollow tube a good three meters across, and it went far enough in so the other end of it was in complete blackness. The only way she was going to see that far was to lean over the rim and use her helmet light. Which meant that if anything was in there, it was going to see her when she peeped over the edge.

She told Wilks and Mitch what she was going to do.

Her breath was loud in the suit, the no-fog plastic of the helmet's faceplate was beaded with little

drops of condensation, perfect, round spheres, un-
affected by gravity, held together by surface ten-
sion.

"Okay. Here goes."

Billie pressed herself flat against the ship, using
her hands to keep her steady, her boots touching
only at the tips of the toes. She edged forward and
leaned over the rim of the thruster, the lip of which
was some slippery ceramic material. Managed to
keep her grip as she was looking into the black
hole.'

Nothing. Least not from this angle. She edged
farther out, to give herself a better view, all the way
to the back of the thrust tube.

The little pool of light from the helmet splashed
on the smaller reaction tubes that formed the rocket's spray controllers. Nothing. She started to relax.

Then she saw the alien. It was crouched against
the reaction tubes, ready to spring. As if it had
known she was coming.

"Oh, shit! It's in the thruster!"

Billie scrabbled backward, trying to get back over
the rim. Her gloved hands slipped on the ceramic
liner. Her right boot came free of the ship.

"Turn over!" she yelled at herself. "Get your
fucking boots down!"

The monster raised its head and seemed to smile
at her. It crouched lower. It was going to spring,
and if she wasn't out of its way when it got here, it
would catch her.

"Billie, get clear of the thruster!" Mitch yelled.
"I'm going to fire it!"

"I'm trying!"

Time stretched, seconds became days, months,

eons. Billie twisted, tried to put her foot down, but had nothing to shove against. She pulled on the umbilical. It was loose, it didn't help.

"Billie!"

The alien sprang. It seemed all teeth and claws . . .

"Billie!"

In desperation, Billie realized she was trying to do the wrong thing. There wasn't any gravity out here. She didn't have to crawl backward on the ship, she just had to get out of the thing's way. She was thinking in two dimensions, but now she had wings. She shoved, as if she were doing a push-up. Flew away from the ship at a right angle—

"I'm clear!"

Fire blossomed, yellow-orange heat and light that nearly opaqued her faceplate as the polarizers turned the plastic dark against the wash of brightness.

She imagined she could hear the alien scream as it pinwheeled away from the ship, wrapped in a mantle of burning fluids, cooking within its shell. She took joy in watching it roast. Found herself grinning wolfishly. Yes. Fry, you son of a bitch, fry.

"Billie?"

"Nice shot, Mitch. Score another one for the good guys.

"*Now* I'm coming in."

5

Two days after Billie blasted the last alien into space Bueller picked up radio transmissions. The signals were on the military band and coded, so they didn't know what was being said, but from the strength, they had to be close. Unfortunately, the ship did not have any transmitters they could use, only receivers.

It didn't take Wilks long to figure out where the signals originated. "Hello," he said. "Lookie here."

Billie leaned over his shoulder as Wilks played with the computer screen. "Got us a planetoid. Not much bigger than a moon, but in direct orbit around the local primary. Been on the opposite side of the sun from us pretty much since we left the chambers, that's why we couldn't see it."

Numbers crawled up the screen. Wilks did something and the tiny blotch expanded and took on a roughly spherical shape, overlaid with grid lines.

"Colonial Marine base?" Bueller said.

"Yeah, that'd be my guess. Inflate a few pressure domes, pump 'em full of breathable, bury a couple gravity generators, and you got all the comforts of home. Provided you grew up in a barracks. Military has hundreds of these bases scattered around the galaxy. Or did have."

"Is that where we're going?" Billie asked.

"I don't see anywhere else, kid. If these crappy range finders can be believed, we'll be there in a couple more days."

The three of them stared at the computer-augmented image. Billie wondered if they were thinking the same thing she was: Was this a place of refuge? Or were they leaping from the frying pan into the fire?

It looked as if they were going to find out soon.

These damned gravity drives were something, Wilks had to admit. They were moving at speeds the old reaction ships couldn't touch. As they approached the planetoid—it was about the same size as Terra's moon—the constant drone of the engines shut down. The ship turned and began to retro, slowing their descent toward the only sizable chunk of real estate around for a hundred fifty million klicks. There was some rumble from the rockets, but compared to the thrum of the gravity drives, the ship was quiet. He had tuned the vibrations out, but now that they were still, he missed them.

"Might as well use what water we have left to

clean up," Wilks said. "We want to look good for the party."

"Yeah, especially since they aren't expecting company," Billie said.

He shrugged.

Despite his banter, Wilks was nervous. They were a long way from what any of them knew as home. Their reception was questionable.

The ship fell toward the tiny planet. The gravity increased as the military-industrial-strength generators on the base enveloped them in their fields. Bueller shut off the ship's faux gee and it got a little more comfortable.

The landing was rough; the ship fell straight in on its tail, the retros firing. Apparently it navigated some kind of gigantic hatched roof and wound up in a bay. The ship vibrated as compressors pumped air into the bay; when there was enough atmosphere, they could hear the machinery.

His back was still pretty tender, but Wilks could walk on his own. Bueller rode in his cradle strapped to a wheeled hand truck Billie had found. The aft cargo bay registered breathable air, and the three passengers made their way into it as the loading ramp was lowered from outside. The hydraulics whined as the back of the ship yawed wide and the ramp grated to a halt. It was cold, but the air felt fresher than what they'd been used to.

A quad of Colonial Marines in combat gear stood there, carbines held ready. At the sight of them, the four marines snapped their carbines up. Behind them, an officer sat in an electric cart, a fat cigar stuck in his mouth. He wore duty fatigues, and the gold braid on his visored cap identified him as a light general, a brigadier.

"At ease!" the general yelled. He stepped from the cart. He was medium height, but powerfully built, with the body of a weight lifter. He wore an opchan command headset, the bonephone and mouthpiece a single sculptured unit. He had an antique stainless 10mm auto pistol with full santoprene grips in a hip holster. The sleeves of his fatigues were rolled up to reveal several tattoos on his forearms: on the left, a rampant screaming eagle and chains; on the right, the Colonial Marine emblem and a dagger-and-banner. A rainbow holopatch shimmering on his left breast said T. Spears.

The general moved to stand in front of them. "I didn't expect to see you ambulatory," he said.

Wilks blinked. Nobody knew they were on the ship. If the general was expecting to see somebody *not* ambulatory, then he had to know about the human cargo.

"If you're talking about the four people in the freezers, that isn't us," Wilks said. "Sir."

The general raised one bushy eyebrow. "Say what, marine? Download it."

"We just came along for the ride," Wilks said.

The general nodded. "All right." To the marines standing by, he said, "Maxwell, Dowling, go check on the cargo."

"If you're talking about the four men in the sleep chambers, you're wasting your time," Billie said. "They were infected by aliens."

Billie wasn't slow. Wilks realized she also understood what the officer meant.

" 'Were' infected?"

"The aliens ate their way out. The men are dead."

Wilks could see the general didn't care a lizard's ass about the men. The general frowned. "What about the aliens?"

Before Wilks could stop her, Billie said, "We killed them."

The general's jaw muscles bunched. Wilks thought he was going to bite his cigar in half. "What? You killed my specimens?"

It was Billie's turn to blink. "*Your* specimens?"

"It was them or us," Bueller put in.

The general stared down at Bueller. "Listen, vatscat, I've got a base full of people, I don't need any more. What I *needed* were those Terran-bred specimens! I *needed* to have my R&D people studying possible mutations! There's a war on, mister, in case you haven't heard. You just fouled up a Priority One mission. I could have you shot for that."

Wilks stared at the general.

He pulled the cigar from his mouth, tapped ash from it. "Put these three in isomed and scan them," he said. "Maybe they're infected and trying to hide it. We might salvage something yet." He tapped the command headset. "Powell! Get down here, we got a snafu."

The barrel of the carbine jabbed Wilks in his tender back. He fought the urge to spin and smash the marine who'd prodded him. He managed to keep a grip on himself. No point in getting blasted by one

of his own after coming all this way. He'd go along.
Maybe later he could figure out what the hell was
what.

One of the marines pushed Bueller's carriage,
the other kept his weapon trained on Billie and
Wilks. Billie didn't understand what was going on.
They went down a descending corridor. When they
rounded the end, they were on the edge of a large
room.

Billie gasped.

Against the far wall was a row of clear cylinders.
The six tubes were four meters tall, perhaps two
and a half meters in circumference. There was
some kind of pale bluish, transparent liquid in the
containers.

Each of the cylinders contained a full-size alien
drone.

Billie found that she was digging her fingers into
Wilks's arm.

"Jesus," Wilks said.

The marine with the carbine pointed at him
said, "Not to worry, Sarge, those babies are in suspension. That's fluropolymer fluid. They're alive,
but they ain't going nowhere."

Billie saw a dozen smaller containers lined up on
a long table nearby. Each of those had one of the
crablike alien hatchlings in it, ovipositors drooping
limply under the fingerbonelike jointed legs. Several techs in osmotic clean suits stood or sat at the
table. Billie, who had spent years in hospitals, recognized microscopes, surgical lasers, autoclaves,
and other medical impedimenta.

Billie felt a wave of nausea. They were doing research on the aliens. Why? To learn how to kill
them better?

That had to be it, didn't it? Why else would they
be doing it?

6

The forklift rolled across the floor, thick slunglas tires silent on the smooth sheetcrete. The powerful electric motor hummed louder as the driver slid the special hoop clamps around the specimen container and lifted it. Carefully—the driver knew that breaking a container was a shooting offense—she backed off slightly, then pivoted the fork and headed for the queen's chamber.

Spears watched, nodding to himself as the specimen was carted away. The driver was good, she deftly avoided the hoses and power lines connected to the bases of the other containers in the vast storage room. Spears had more than a hundred of the alien drones undergoing suspension here, each of which had a complex chemical bath being pumped into it full-time. According the R&D scientists, the hypnotic chem flowing through the special drones should match their particular chemistry enough to affect them. To make them more amenable to outside suggestion.

Spears grinned, chewed on the end of his cigar. It was real tobacco, vat-grown and illegal as hell, but that didn't mean shit. Out here, he was the law. The cigar wasn't as good as those made from sun-raised and barn-dried leaf, but it was what he had. Oh, he still had six of the precious Jamaican Lonsdales left, *maduros* and dark as they came, each sealed in its glass tube of inert gas. But those were worth a fortune, he could get ten thousand credits apiece if he wanted to sell them.

He chuckled. As if money meant anything. Money was nothing, money was only a means to an end, the only reason you needed it at all was for supplies, equipment, to get things done. Here at Third Base, they didn't even use the stuff. The troops took what they were given and liked it or lumped it. The cigars had come from a vault in Cuba, a gift from a rich man who had been grateful to Spears for saving his ass in some dinky banana republic revolution. There had been eight of the valuable smokes. He'd smoked the first on the day he got his stars and command of Third Base. He'd smoked the second when his tame medicos had succeeded in bringing forth an alien queen and establishing her in a controlled hive. He planned to smoke the third after he won his first battle against the wild-strain aliens back on Earth.

Thomas A.W. Spears had plans, big plans, and they amounted to no less than the retaking of man's homeworld, using the deadliest soldiers a man had ever commanded.

He turned and strode toward his office, trailing smoke as he walked. A military man was bred for war, and in his case, it was truer than usual. He'd been among the first to be incubated in an artificial womb—he proudly kept the middle initials he'd been given at his decanting signifying just that— and it had been on a marine base where the first live births of AW children occurred. He'd been raised in a creche with the other children, nine of them, and all but one had become Colonial Marines. The other one would have, if he hadn't been killed in an accident when he was still a prepube. Sure, the bulge-brains had come up with androids later, but he wasn't vat-scat, he was a real man, all his chromosomes in place, not a stray gene among 'em. A man who knew what he could do. What he *must* do.

The general paused next to one of the specimen containers. Put his hands on the thick Plexiglas. It was cold to the touch. The alien inside didn't move, but he imagined it could feel him, was aware of him, even in its suspended state. *Mark me,* Spears thought at it. *I'm your master. You live or die at my whim. Obey and live, disobey and die.*

He moved away from the container, took another look at the killing machine within. Hell of a soldier, this thing. Would destroy or die for its queen without hesitation. He nodded at the alien, then walked away.

He rounded the corridor's end and marched to the small office from where he ran the base. Damned civilian authorities on Earth had bollixed

it up, just like they always did. Tried to fight a forest fire with little buckets of water, tried to extin-
guish a raging conflagration with spit and prayer.
The only way to kill a big fire was to use a bigger
blaze. Burn its fuel, choke its oxy off, eat what it
would eat and starve it. Sure, you could punch
holes in the aliens with armor-piercers, could blow
'em up with bombs, but that was wasteful. What
better way to fight a beast than with another beast
of equal ferocity? Something that could hunt the
enemies down because it knew how they thought,
because it was like them? Like a king snake will kill
a poisonous viper or tame dogs will track a wild animal, the solution to the problem was painfully ob-
vious. He hadn't believed that at first, until he got
to know how the aliens operated. Now he was the
strongest believer. The powers-that-were had been
eliminated; now, it was up to him to carry on alone.
No problem.

Spears reached his office, opened the old-style
hinged door, stepped inside.

Major Powell, his first officer, stood next to the
gunny running the computer terminal, peering
down at the holoprojection that floated above the
desk. Spears could read the words, even reversed
and backward, if he wanted, but his first reaction
was surprise and a little anger.

"Powell, I thought I told you to get to docking
and clean up that snafu."

"Sir. It's as clean as it is going to get, sir."

"In my sanctum," Spears ordered.

The major nodded, said, "Continue, gunny," and
preceded Spears into the inner office.

His office was spare, a chair, desk, comp terminal, couple of plaques on the sheet plastic walls. Spears circled the desk so that it was between him and Powell, but did not sit in the chair. "Well?"

"The ... specimen containers were ... destroyed, sir. Apparently the lowest survivable setting on the sleep chambers was insufficient to keep the specimens themselves dormant. The, ah, *containers* were dead, usual exit mode, to judge from the blood spray patterns, and mostly consumed. The adult-stage specimens apparently killed one of their own and utilized its blood to burn free of the area in which they were contained."

"Very resourceful," Spears said. He took his cigar from between his lips and looked at the cold ash on the end. He put the cigar down into the ashtray on his desk. "Continue."

"There were no signs of the other three—we assume all three survived—specimens. Acid burns in various places indicated a battle between the stowaways and the aliens. I have done a preliminary debriefing of the CM sergeant and from this report determined that one was killed by weapons fire onboard and the other two were ejected into space."

"Damn."

"Apparently the female stowaway went EVA and battled the remaining pair, who survived for some minutes in hard vacuum without apparent ill effect."

"The female did? Why not the marine?"

"He suffered an injury during the fight."

"Hmm. Well, the space stuff, we already knew they can do that. The in-head compression chamber and the—what's it called?"

"Pseudohypothalmic regulator," Powell answered.

"Right. Heats up the acid and keeps 'em from freezing."

"The corpses of the two killed on-ship were ejected."

"Too bad. We might have gotten something from the DNA." Spears looked at his dead cigar, thought about relighting it. "Two humans and half an android against four aliens in a close environment. I wouldn't have thought they could survive. Their tactics might be interesting."

"Apparently the stowaways have some prior experience with the aliens."

"Oh?"

"We don't have anything on the woman—the bounce from Earth is shut down—but the military bibliocom is bringing up records on the marine and android. The android, by the way, is Issue."

"One of ours?"

"Affirmative."

"Interesting. Are any of them infected?"

"Not according to the scan, no."

"Too bad. Let me see the squirt from bibliocom when it arrives."

"Gunny will have it in about eighteen minutes, sir."

"That's all, Powell."

"Sir."

Once Powell was gone, Spears sat. He leaned back, put his orthoplast boots up on the desk. Picked up the cigar and relit it. Took a deep drag and blew the smoke out in a blue-gray cloud. The ventilators whirred and sucked the smoke from the air. Maybe there was something to be gained here after all. It was a truly bad battle if nothing was gained; even the illest of winds sometimes blew a breeze or two of good. He'd see what the library had to say about this marine and android. And if they didn't have anything to offer, well, the techs could always use a couple more bodies in the hatching rooms . . .

"You okay?" Wilks asked Billie.

"Yeah, fine."

"You shouldn't have stomped on that guy's foot. He was just obeying orders."

"Yeah? So was the guy who nuked Canberra during the '82 Food Riots."

"How about you, Bueller?"

"No new damage," he said.

Wilks looked around. The room was bigger than some cells he'd been in. Five meters by five, foldout bunks now flush against the wall, reinforced sheetplast, a double-thick door with a simple snap lock. A chemical toilet rested in one corner, bare white, no seat, a roll of wipes perched on a sink with a single water tap next to it. Nice place. A guy handy with a sliver of spring steel or stacked carb could pop the lock easy enough. Thing was, on a world where everybody lived inside a pressure dome, where were you gonna go even if you did get out? They might steal another ship, but without some knowledge of navigation, not to mention knowing which human settlements were still untainted by alien infection, they wouldn't have a clue about where to go.

"Did you see the monitors we passed?" Billie asked.

"Yeah. They've still got spysats in place, military view only. That major who stopped and questioned us? He told me they could keep tabs on the war. He seemed like an all right guy. Almost apologetic. We'll probably be hearing from him again."

"I don't have much experience with the military mind, Wilks. What is going on here?"

"Hell if I know. The general looks like a lot of RMs—that's regular marines—I've known. Eats, breathes, and shits the Corps. Probably runs the base so tight it hums. Probably doesn't matter to him that Earth is down the tubes, he's got his orders and that's what he lives by. Or else he's got delusions of godhood—lot of generals get that way—thinks he can do anything. Hard to say which it is."

"What do you think he's going to do with us?"

Wilks shook his head. "Dunno. He's obviously running some kind of experiment with the aliens. My bet's it's—or was, when still it mattered—very hush hush. Top-secret stuff. We're sand in this guy's well-lubed machine."

"You take me to the nicest places, Wilks."

He laughed. "Can't say it's been dull, can you?"

Billie managed a smile. "Nope. That's a word that never crossed my mind. So, what now?"

"Ball is in their court. We wait and see what they do with it. Get some sleep." With that, Wilks unfolded one of the cots and climbed onto it. Bueller did the same, pulling himself up easily and sprawling onto the thin material. After a moment, Billie pulled a third cot loose and lay on it.

Wilks had been in the military long enough so he could sleep pretty much whenever he wanted. Whatever was going to happen was going to happen. He'd deal with it when it got here. Within a few moments, he dropped off.

7

The three marines were in one of the third-level *inodoros*, crowded into the space designed for a single toilet and sink. The walls had eyes all over Third Base but they figured the crapper ought to be safe enough. The room was made yet tighter by the backpack one of the men had propped on the white plastic HWDS-C— human waste disposal system, chemical, in military parlance.

"How much did you get?" one of the marines asked. That was Renus, Wolfgang R., Private First Class.

"Three days, if we stretch it," the marine balancing the knapsack said. He was Peterson, Sean J., Corporal.

"Shit," the third marine said. "It's four days to

the civilian terraforming colony, five if we stick to the canyons." Magruder, Jason S., also PFC.

"So we'll be hungry when we get there," Peterson said. "Listen, I was pushing to get this many meals. Spears has everything on this fucking base inventoried, down to the paper clips. Besides, the crawler will have E-rations, carbocons."

"Great, if you like greasy sawdust," Magruder said.

"Hey, you can fuckin' stay here if you'd rather."

Magruder shook his head. "Like hell."

Renus said, "You think the civilians will take us in and keep quiet about it?"

Peterson shrugged. "They've dealt with Spears. They know he's over the edge. They'd be worried about him thinking they had a hand in helping us, if they did or not. My guess is, they'll hide us and tell him they never heard of us."

"Still risky," Magruder said.

"Like I said, you can stay here. Sooner or later you'll stumble over some reg you never heard of and you know what that means."

Magruder nodded. "Yeah. Baby food."

"How long you figure we got?" That from Renus.

"Couple–three hours, maybe," Peterson said. "Spears and Powell will play mad doctor with the stowaways. Our general likes to watch the implants, I think it gives him a hard-on when those things shove their eggs down somebody's throat. If we can get to the Thousand Canyons and the heat faults, they won't be able to see us on IR. The crawler's cammo should cover us from visual."

The three men looked at one another.

"At least it's a chance," Peterson said.

They filed out of the *inodoro* into the hallway.

At the South Lock, Patin, Robert T., PFC, was on security. He leaned against the wall, his carbine propped at an angle next to him. He looked up, saw somebody approaching. He smiled, but didn't bother to assume any kind of guard-ready position. Sloppy work, but he doubtless had the same attitude about lock-duty as most marines: You couldn't get in from outside unless you had the admit codes and if you did, you were okay; you could get out, but—who would want to? The planetoid wasn't what you'd call a pleasure dome, now was it?

"Hey, Renus. You come to keep me company?"

Renus drew near. "Take some more of your money playing cards, you mean? Nah, I wish. Decker sent me to relieve you. Circulating pumps on Four are showing red in the backup chamber. Guess who is the only qualified pump-tech on duty?"

"Fuck," Patin said. "Red means automatic suit-up. Why didn't somebody call when the cocksucker went yellow?"

"Don't ask me, Bobby. I don't run things around here."

Patin pushed away from the wall, stepped across the hallway toward the computer terminal inset into a panel at chest level. "I'll punch it into the security com and it'll be all yours, pal. Can't be too careful these days."

The guard couldn't see Renus pull what looked like a sock full of something heavy from under his shirt. "Sorry, Bobby," Renus said.

"Huh—?"

Renus slammed the sock down on Patin's head. It made a sound like a thick rope slapping a plastic barrel full of liquid soap. Tiny slivers of gray flew from the sock on impact. Lead shavings, sparkling like glitter under the overhead lights, drifted onto the unconscious man's downed form.

"Let's go!" Renus yelled.

Peterson and Magruder came running up. Each of them had a carbine. Renus grabbed Patin's weapon. They had the codes for the inner lock door and cycled it open quickly.

The outer door's codes were something else. While Peterson took a stab at the computer override, Magruder pulled climate suits from the racks. He and Renus shrugged their way into the suits.

"Not gonna happen," Peterson said. "Security seals are dogged down tight. We'll have to burn the sucker. I'm trashing the alarms."

Magruder, his helmet in place, the suit tabbed shut, nodded and moved to the door. He pulled the plasma cutter he'd stolen from Supply and thumbed the cutter up to full. "Watch your eyes," he said.

The brilliant plasma jet spewed, turning the inside of the lock into noon on a desert. Peterson kept his eyes covered until he got his climate suit on and the polarized faceplate snapped down.

It didn't take long. The security bars were designed to keep people outside from getting in, and the plasma jet ate through them almost as fast as Magruder could move the welder. Durasteel went bright orange, then flowed molten and fell in fat drops.

"That's it, that's the last one!"

"Go, go, go!"

The lock door started to open, then ground to a stop with a shriek still audible in the escaping air, stuck where a flange of partially melted metal caught the frame. But it was wide enough for the men to get through. They clambered from the station into the cold darkness, and ran toward the motor pool. The gravity generators extended the field outside the domes for a hundred meters around, so they didn't bound into space.

The trio of deserters piled into the first crawler they reached. After a moment the multiwheeled machine lurched into the darkness and was gone.

Spears leaned back in his chair, watching the video on his holoproj. "Replay, security cam 77, 0630 hours."

The air above his desk lit with the images of the three marines in the loo. "Increase volume one-eighth. Continuous tracking."

He watched it again, listened to the three marines plotting their desertion. When they left the toilet stall, another hidden cam just outside the *inodoro* picked them up without missing a beat.

The scene at the security station played itself. The downed guard didn't get any sympathy from Spears. If he'd been doing his job, he would have stopped the deserters. Well. There was a place for men like the guard. Down in the hatchery.

Spears watched with interest the burn-out through the lock door. They moved well as a team, the trio. Too bad they chose treason instead of duty.

"General?"

Spears glanced up from the projector to the door. "Come."

The door opened and Powell stood there. Spears waved one hand and shut the projection over his desk off. "Yes?"

"The squirt has arrived from bibliocom. In the system."

"Query number?"

Powell gave it to him.

Spears tapped it manually into his terminal. "What's the marine's name?"

"Wilks."

He tapped that in.

The air blossomed again with the infocrawl. Images fluttered into life to join the words and figures. A practiced speedreader, Spears scanned the material.

"Well, well. We sure this marine is the same one in isomed?"

"Got a positive ID from his magnetic femur implant. It's him."

"This sergeant has had more hands-on experience with wild-strain aliens than just about anybody except that civilian, whatshername."

"Ripley, sir."

"Right. Nobody knows where she is but we got Wilks right here. How's that for luck? Fate smiles on us, Powell."

"Sir. And if you'll scan the android's file, you'll see another coincidence, sir."

"Give me the gist."

"He was one of a Specials Unit, bred to travel to the aliens' homeworld. Under the command of Colonel Stephens, prior to Terran infestation."

"Stephens, I remember him from MILCOM HQ A desk jockey, couldn't find his dick with both hands."

"The primary mission, retrieval of a specimen, was apparently a failure, sir. Records of the trip are incomplete; by the time the survivors reached Earth, the infestation was in the advanced stages."

"And the woman?"

"No records on her. She's not military, and we can't pull up any history." Powell shrugged. "You know how civilians are about record keeping in the best of times, sir."

Spears nodded absently. "Well, our sergeant and the vat-boy have got actual combat experience against the wild strain. Much too valuable to turn into incubators, at least until after we find out what we can from them."

"That's what I thought, sir."

"Let's go have a little talk with them."

"Sir."

Billie felt a coldness grip her legs, bands of rough steel encircling her ankles, pulling her knees apart. She blinked, glanced down, saw she was naked.

Something wet and slimy dripped onto her bare belly. A clear, ropy jelly. She looked up, but couldn't see the source, there was a kind of fog hovering over her, only centimeters from her face, a feature-less gray.

I need you, came a deep voice. No, not a voice, the words were unspoken, they were in her mind. They were the thoughts of a lover, but not a human lover.

The fog swirled away, and teeth glittered under a

coat of clear slime, white needles set in a massive black jaw, on a long, impossibly long head that flared into wide, flat, branched antlers.

Billie gasped, fear filling her, every cell in her body straining to contain it.

Lean back.

Unable to resist the command, Billie arched her neck, saw just behind her a massive, fleshy egg, easily the size of a garbage can. Flaps at the top of the egg opened, spidery webbing stretching and breaking. It was like the blossoming of some obscene flower, petals spreading wide in a photographic time-lapse hurry.

Crablike legs reached over the folded flaps, long, fleshless finger bones with sharp tips, questing, exploring. Looking for something.

Looking for Billie.

She opened her mouth to scream, and a glob of the slime from the monster above her fell onto her chin, oozed into her mouth, over her cheeks, into her eyes. Billie tried to swallow, but it was too much.

I need you. The monster's thoughts tried to soothe. *Do not be afraid. It will be good.*

"No!"

Billie came up on the cot, yelling the word.

"Easy, easy," Wilks said. He was next to her, holding her shoulders. And on the floor, balanced on one hand, the other hand on her leg, Mitch.

Billie blew her breath out in a big sigh. Shook her head. There was no need to say it. Wilks knew. He dreamed, too.

She looked at Mitch. Did androids dream?

"Up and at 'em, people," came a voice from the entrance to the cell.

A pair of armed marines stood there.

"General wants to see you," one of them said.

"Tell him our calendar is full," Wilks said.

The marines grinned. The same one said, "Not me, Sarge. You tell him. Move out." He waved the carbine.

Wilks looked at Billie and Mitch, shrugged. "Well. Since you insist."

With Billie pushing Mitch on his cart, the three of them left the cell.

8

The table was, nearly as Wilks could tell, black glass. Expensive for an officers' mess on some back-rocket planetoid. Course, it could have been made from local mineral and not brought in on-ship; even so, it was not something you expected to see. The chairs were some kind of basic fold-out issue, but they'd been padded and spiffed up by somebody with skill and time.

Billie sat to his left, Bueller to his right, the three of them occupying one end of the table. Another dozen people could sit along the sides, but those chairs were empty. Spears sat at the other end, alone. A platter of what looked to be roast meat sat in front of him, aromatic vapors wafting from it. A long knife and double-tine fork were stuck in the meat.

"It's not real beef, of course," Spears said. He

pulled the knife and fork from the roast and ran
the edge of the blade back and forth against the
fork tines, as if sharpening the knife. "Protein
hard-jell and soy, but our mess sergeant has a deft
touch with seasonings. It's not bad."

With his hat off, Spears was as bald as an egg.
Nothing but eyebrows and lashes, from what Wilks
could see.

Spears stabbed the roast with the fork and began
to slice the ersatz beef.

An orderly, dressed in kitchen whites, came from
the doorway behind Spears. By the time the general had the first slab of roast carved free, the orderly arrived and shoved a plate under it. The
timing was perfect. Half a second later and the
"meat" would have flopped onto the black glass.
Spears never looked to see if the plate was there.

The general repeated the carving. A second orderly scooted from the doorway and arrived in time
to push another plate under the falling slice of
roast.

The third slice, yet another orderly.

It was offhand, but every bit as impressive as a
precision drill team tossing carbines back and forth
at speed. Spears knew it, too.

When the plates had been delivered to Wilks,
Billie, and Bueller, along with glasses of red
liquid—wine?—and eating implements, the general carved himself a slice.

The fourth orderly was a bit slow. He thrust the
plate out, caught half the roast. For a second, it
looked as if the fake meat would flip from the plate
and smack onto the table, but the orderly juggled
his cargo and managed to slide the slab back into

place. It left a smear of gravy on the white plastic, but stayed put.

Spears's jaw muscles tightened once, then his face relaxed into a somewhat forced smile. He nodded at the orderlies. "At ease, troopers."

The four orderlies filed out via the door by which they'd entered.

Wilks would not want to be the last one, the one who had nearly bobbled the general's own meal. He had very nearly made the general look bad. On a military base, that was as dangerous a crime as a soldier could commit.

The general raised his glass. "To the Corps," he said.

What the hell, Wilks thought. He lifted his own glass. Noticed that Billie and Bueller did the same, albeit without much enthusiasm.

The wine wasn't bad. Wilks had surely drunk a lot worse.

"Eat," the general said.

The cook was inspired, Wilks had to admit. The counterfeit beef was as good as any he'd ever had. Right texture, right flavor—if Spears hadn't told him, he wouldn't have known the difference. Not that he got a lot of real meat on the money he made anyhow. Rabbit now and then, fish, even chicken on special occasions, that was about it. Last time he'd had what was supposed to be certified beef had been at his old top kick's mustering-out party couple years back, bio-time. Given all the suspended animation travel since then, it was a lot longer in realtime.

Whatever was going on inside Billie's head,

Wilks could see she was enjoying her meal, too. As for Bueller, who knew? His model of android could eat, even cut in half as he was now; whether he enjoyed the food in the same way a basic-stock man did or not was something else.

"Food okay?" the general asked around a mouthful of it.

Wilks nodded. "Very good."

Billie and Bueller also nodded and mumbled something. This was strange territory and wherever this conversation was going, they'd decided to play along. For his part, Wilks was pretty sure this guy's wingnuts were dogged down too tight. It didn't make sense to set him off until they had some idea of what he was all about.

"You'll have to excuse my somewhat abrupt manner when we met," Spears said. "There's a war on, one can't be too cautious." He smiled.

Jesus, Wilks thought, it looks as if his face might crack from the strain. This cocker wanted something from them, that was plain enough. What?

"It has been brought to my attention that you have had considerable experience with wild-strain aliens, Sergeant Wilks."

Wilks chewed on the beef. Swallowed it. "Yessir."

Spears popped another chunk into his mouth and chewed it thoughtfully. "Been in combat against them in several theaters, correct?"

"That's right, General."

The man nodded. His eyes seemed to take on a brighter gleam. "Good, good." He looked at Bueller. "And you, Issue, your injury was sustained in combat as well, was it not?"

"Yes, sir."

"These men are military, marines, I know about them. What about you, little lady?"

Wilks saw that Billie couldn't bring herself to speak. "Sir," he put in, "Billie was on Rim during first contact with the aliens. The only survivor."

The general raised one of his thick eyebrows. "Is that so?"

Dumbly, Billie managed a nod.

"She survived on her own for more than a month," Wilks said.

The general's other eyebrow went up. "Really? Most resourceful. How old would you have been then?"

"Ten," Billie managed.

Another of the face-threatening smiles. "Excellent." He ate another bite of the meatless meat. "I envy you three, you know. You've been in combat against the toughest enemies, the most dedicated soldiers men have ever faced. Perfect troops, fearless, tough, almost unstoppable. Your survival is quite an achievement. A fluke, really, but no less heroic for that."

He pushed his plate away, less than half of the meal eaten. An orderly zipped from the doorway, removed the plate, refilled the general's wineglass, and vanished almost without a sound. Spears leaned back, sipped at the freshened wine. "The only way to beat an enemy as hard as the one man now faces is to use troops of equal vigor. Ones who can match the ferocity of the opposition."

That got through to Billie. "You're trying to raise tame aliens here?"

"With the proper leader, my troops could spearhead the retaking of Earth," Spears said. "Think about it. What better way? The wild strain behave like ants. With troops of equal caliber plus proper strategy and tactics, they wouldn't stand a chance."

Billie started to say something. Wilks kicked her under the table. She closed her mouth.

"Great idea, sir," Wilks said.

The general nodded, pleased. "I knew you would see it so," he said. "You've been up against them, you know how little chance humans or even specially bred androids have." He nodded at Bueller, gestured with his wineglass.

"How can we help, sir?" Wilks said.

Billie looked at him as if he had lost his sanity. He kicked her under the table again without changing his expression.

If Spears noticed Billie's look it didn't seem to register. "Your experience, Sergeant. I have computer-generated scenarios, recordings of battles on Earth, theories. You three have been there, you know the reality. I want your advice, your knowledge. My troops must be as well prepared as they can be when I formulate my strategy."

"Certainly, sir," Wilks said. Stretched his own scarred face into a smile. "Bueller and I are marines before anything else. And Billie wants to help, too, isn't that right, Billie?"

Billie nodded. "Right."

Spears was practically beaming now. He raised his wineglass. "A toast, then—"

But before the general could offer the toast, the major came in via the same door the orderlies had used.

Spears frowned. "What is it, Powell?"

"Sorry to disturb your meal, sir. A security breach. The guard on the South Lock has been assaulted, the outer door burned open. One of the land crawlers is missing."

The general waved one hand. "Oh, that."

Powell blinked. "Sir?"

"This is my base, Major. I try to keep up." He looked at Wilks. "You have to stay on top of things when you're the CO. Enjoy the rest of your meal. You are free to go anywhere on Third Base; you have full clearance. If you have any questions, Major Powell will be happy to answer them. I suppose I should go and see to the malcontents who have destroyed military property."

With that, he stood, gave Billie a military bow that was barely a nod, and left with Powell.

Wilks stared at the general's back as he left. Wished he had a gun at that moment.

In the hallway, Spears said to Powell, "Keep an eye on them. Put the android in rehab, see if we can give him mechanicals or whatever so he can be ambulatory."

"Sir."

"And that guard from South Lock, put him in the egg chamber. He fucked up."

Spears felt a happy satisfaction at watching Powell swallow dryly when he gave him that order. The universe had become a place where only the strong, the ruthless, could survive. Sentiment was for another time. In the past and, someday when he had won this war, in the future. Meanwhile, somebody had to make the hard choices and Spears was the man to make them.

Billie found she was shaking. She wasn't sure if it was because she was afraid or angry. She stood, but Wilks was right there. He hugged her, and before she could do more than stiffen and start to pull away, he whispered, "Play along, Billie. They probably have a cam on us and a voice recorder."

She relaxed a little. "What?"

"If we don't do what this guy says, he is going to feed us to his monsters. Play along."

The thought of that turned her bowels to lumps of dry ice. For a moment she couldn't even breathe.

A marine private entered the dining room and started to wheel Mitch away. Billie turned quickly. "What are you doing?"

"Major's order, ma'am. Taking the AP to Rehab."

"Why?"

"Don't ask me, I'm just doing what I'm told."

"It's okay, Billie," Mitch said. "It's like putting your flitter into the shop for repairs."

Billie stared at him. The marine wheeled him away.

"Relax," Wilks said, his voice at normal volume. "The general just wants to make sure his troops are cared for properly. I don't know what kind of facilities they have here, but my guess is they can fit Bueller into some kind of lower body exoframe, at least, so he can get around on his own."

Billie couldn't think of anything to say. This was all so damned weird.

"Come on, let's explore a little. Might as well get

acquainted with our new home, eh?" He winked at her.

Billie nodded. She understood. The more they knew about this place, the better. "Yeah," she said. "Good idea."

9

Days passed; Wilks and Billie explored the base. It was like a dozen such places Wilks had been on in his career, standard hardware from the lowest bidder, as cheap as it could be and still work. The one thing he noticed that bothered him wasn't the gear, but the people. There didn't seem to be enough of them for a base this size. If anything, the military usually had too many troops for the work needed, a larger command being what officers liked to wave at each other. Warm bodies meant more than cold rock. Given the extent of the base, almost as big as a very small town, there ought to be several hundred more people staffing it.

Eventually, Wilks and Billie worked their way into places not so easy to find or reach.

"What's in there?" Wilks asked the guards posted in front of a large double door.

The two troopers, one male, one female, wore holstered sidearms but they didn't seem particularly worried that they would need them. The man, who looked to be almost two meters tall, smiled down on Wilks and Billie.

Wilks said, "The general has given us the run of the base. You want to open the door?"

Now the woman grinned. "You don't wanna go in there, Sarge. Show him, Atkins."

The tall man touched a control on the wall.

Billie gasped.

"Fuck," Wilks said.

"Hell, she don't even have to do that," the woman said. "She's fertile all by herself."

The projection floated in front of the wall. A queen alien occupied the center of a huge room, a monstrous sac jutting from her rear like some obscene, translucent intestine. The sack, webbed with supports that ran to the convoluted ceiling and walls, was obviously full of eggs, and as they watched, the queen deposited yet another onto the floor already thick with the things. A pair of attendant alien drones stood in a puddle of fluid near the sac's sphinctered opening, and they gently moved the fresh egg to one side as the queen began to lay another one.

"Still want me to open the door?"

"Why are you even guarding it?" Wilks managed.

"Pan right," the woman said.

The taller guard stroked a slide control. The holoproj shifted as the camera panned.

Webbed against a wall in front of a neat row of

eggs were ten humans. The cottony material holding them in place hid most of them, leaving only the faces bare. Some of the people were awake, eyes wide. Were they already infected, or still waiting for the horror yet to come?

"Turn it off," Billie said.

As Wilks and Billie walked away from the stomach-turning scene, the tall marine, obviously enjoying himself, said, "Have a nice day, folks."

They weren't there to keep anybody from getting in.

They were there to keep anybody from getting out.

Spears watched the image of Wilks and the woman as they turned away from the projection outside the egg chamber. They were weak, like most people were weak. But he could use them. That was the important thing.

He looked at his chronometer. "Ah, the mice are about ready. Time for the cat to wake up and move." He touched a control on his desk. "This is Spears. I want First Platoon, A Company, saddled up and ready to ride ASAP. Full combat gear, full field rations. I'll be at the South Lock in ten minutes. Better not keep me waiting, marines."

Wilks went to shower, water being one of the few things they had plenty of on the station. Piped up from some deep underground cave as ice chunks and melted on the way up by heaters in the slurry conduits, SOP for this kind of operation. One of the few perks even grunts got.

Alone, Billie wandered down narrow hallways,

feeling as if she were being watched. God, this was all so insane. Having spent years in a mental hospital because the authorities thought her memories were hallucinations, Billie had some experience with madness. This was right up there. Spears ought to be in a silicone room somewhere, doped to the hairline, scheduled for a full mental revision. Who were those people in there with the queen alien? What had they done to deserve such a fate? No crime could be so awful as to rate that kind of sentence. Spears was bug-fuck crazy and he should be put away. Instead, he commanded troops and had a personal nest full of the deadliest things man had ever encountered. What kind of deity would allow that kind of lunacy? Only one that was crazy itself.

She came to a door marked Communications. It slid open as she approached.

A tech sat, a comhelmet covering half her head, staring at a series of flat screen monitors. The tech looked over, saw Billie. "I heard we got visitors. Come on in, I got a notice says you're cleared for this area."

Billie stared at the woman. Why the hell not?

The door closed behind her.

Wilks sluiced the cleaner from his body, enjoying the feel of the hot water against his skin. They were in deep shit here, no doubt about it, but you had to take it as it came. He had expected to fertilize the flowers on the alien homeworld. Hell, he'd been living on borrowed time since the first time he'd run into these fuckers on Rim all those years ago. He should have died with his squad then, it was a miracle he hadn't. And the years of trying to hide from it and from the nightmares that wouldn't go away since hadn't been all that pleasant. He had been ready to pack it in, to take the Big Jump and the hell with it, but before that happened, he got pissed off. He'd blown the aliens' homeworld flat and that hadn't been enough. Somehow, for some reason, he was still alive. It didn't make any sense. He'd never been a religious man, but it was like he had some kind of higher purpose driving him. He'd been too lucky, as if somebody had looked out for him. He was tired, he wanted to tube the whole mess, but he couldn't. It was as if he had been given the responsibility to take care of this little problem—the extermination of all those monsters that had nearly wiped out humans.

It wasn't fair, nobody could expect one broken-down chem-head marine to do that, but while he couldn't pin it neatly to any logical wall, Wilks felt as if that was exactly what he was supposed to do: save mankind.

Damn. And he couldn't even float very well, must less *walk* on fucking water . . .

The old man was white-bearded, his left arm bandaged crudely from wrist to elbow, his clothes dirty and torn. A dark and grimy baseball cap was pulled down over his head and whatever hair he might have left. He had an antique rifle lying next to him, something that appeared to be blued steel and worn wood, an old-style bolt-action piece, probably a hunting weapon from a hundred years past. Back when people hunted for sport and not for survival. He sat cross-legged, leaning against a pile of rubble, mostly broken furniture and shattered building material; a small campfire burned in front of him, the flickers from it painting the old man's face yellow-orange.

A girl of about six leaned against the old man's side, her face dirty, long hair matted.

"Here comes Air Sammy," the old man said. He pulled a vial from his jacket pocket, sprinkled a powder from it into the campfire. The fire sputtered and the flames turned a bright blue-green. "I hope the bastards have their spookeyes on."

Overhead in the night, the running lights of military attack jets appeared, red and green against the smog that was mostly smoke. The rumble of their engines increased.

"Will they see us, Uncle?" the little girl asked.

"I hope so, honey. They should." He waved at the blue fire.

The fiery lance of a missile erupted from one jet, then other rockets followed. Like meteorites, the missiles streaked and died quickly, to be replaced by a brighter flash of light followed by artificial thunder as the rockets exploded.

"Stupid fucking airheads," the old man said.

The little girl covered her ears with her hands as more explosions rocked them. A blast wave streamed the little fire as might a man blowing gently on a candle.

A woman moved into the circle of firelight. She looked a worn fifty, her clothes were smudged with ashes and dirt, and she had an airpump shotgun on a sling over her shoulder. She squatted next to the little girl. "Hey, Amy. You okay?"

The little girl looked up. "I'm okay, Mom. Did you find anything to eat?"

"Not this time, honey. Maybe Leroy did. He should be back soon. Damn!"

This last followed a louder boom and brighter flash of light. Dust and small bits of debris swirled over the trio, and the fire flattened briefly under the blast.

"Why do they bother?" the woman asked. "They hardly ever kill any of them and the damned things just don't get scared."

"Fucking airheads," the man said. He glanced around. "We'd better move out, Mona. The things will probably start their sweep after Sammy shears off."

"What about Leroy?" the little girl asked.

"Don't worry about him, baby. He will meet us at the reservoir. He knows we can't stay here."

The old man looked across the fire, and spoke as if there were an unseen watcher sitting there. "That's it for now, sports fans. Tune in again tomorrow, same time, same satellite, for another exciting episode of *Life in the Ruins of Earth*. We'll sign on at 1900, if the bugs haven't eaten us. Summer's over and it'll be getting dark sooner. That's a dislink and endit—"

He pointed an old-style IR remote control at the unseen watcher and the three people vanished . . .

Billie gripped the arms of the plastic form-chair tightly and found she had been holding her breath as the image on the viewscreen went blank. She forced herself to relax. To breathe.

"They're regulars," the tech said. "Amy, Mona,

Uncle Burt. Sometimes Leroy—he's Chinese, we think. The kid looks to be about six. Our guess is that her mother is in her late twenties, some of the stuff she talks about. The old guy is maybe seventy, probably not related, though the kid calls him Uncle."

"God," Billie said.

"I don't know why they bother 'casting," the tech said. "It's not like anybody is going to drop down and help them."

Billie shook her head. "Maybe it's all they have left. It matters that they try. People do that."

The tech shrugged, scanning for another image. "Or *did* it. This base location is classified information," she said, "but I can tell you that the 'cast we just saw is history. Even in cold sleep and with full race gee drives going through the hypercut we are a long way from Earth. The little girl could be years older by now. That, or worm food. It's a message in a bottle."

Billie's insides clenched. She knew just how that little girl must feel.

Something about being clean and in fresh fatigues made a man feel better. When you faced death as often as Wilks had, minor shit like crazy generals didn't seem so bad. While he couldn't say he felt the same detachment about the Long Nap some of the Zen martial arts boys had, Wilks had looked Death square in the face enough times so it didn't scare him. You lived or you died, that was how it went, and when your number came due, you got collected. He'd thought his was at the top of the pile several times but Death had only grazed him when he reached for another. Fuck it. A hot shower and clean clothes, however, were tangible, something you could relate to in the here and now. The ground might open up and swallow you next step, a stray comet could zip in and squash you like a bug, one of the aliens could hop from behind a garbage can and eat your face off, but those were in the unseen future. Right *now*, Wilks felt pretty damned good. One second at a time.

Being cooped up on that drone ship hadn't given him any love for it, but Wilks found himself walking toward the vessel because he had an idea. The thing had been unloaded and it would need new fuel cells and probably some repair before it had any chance of being spaceworthy again. It sat in the middle of one of the big prefab storage areas, a mostly dark and very cold room that apparently wasn't worth spending more than the minimum on for light and heat.

Wilks's footsteps echoed hollowly as he walked across the sheetcrete flooring toward *The American*. The cargo bay door was still open, and the ship's internal lights were off. He walked up the expanded-metal incline and slapped the light button. It was a little warmer inside the ship, the fuel cells' heat sinks radiating their excess warmth into the air.

Wilks moved deeper into the cargo hold, found an empty hex storage crate, and sat on it. It was very quiet, only the low hum of power units audible. After a few seconds Wilks heard what he expected: boot steps outside the ship.

Whoever was following him was approaching.

Wilks flexed his hands, rolled his shoulders. Prepared himself to move, if he needed to move.

The footsteps drew nearer.

Billie worked her way toward the medical section. She wanted to see what they were doing to Mitch, if she could.

On the other side of a clear door inside a smallish chamber that looked like an anteroom combined with an airlock, there was a short, fat man dressed in a lab cloak and what looked like white paint. She touched the plastic wall and it was very cold. He spoke to her through an electronic passthrough. "This area is Clean," he said. "You want to come inside, you have to be deloused first."

Billie blinked. "Deloused?"

"Chem- and electro-instillation," he said. He waved at a horizonal cylinder about the size of a coffin on a metal frame against one wall. "All your internal and external flora and fauna get zapped. No stray bacteria allowed. Then you get spraysuited." He rubbed his leg with one all white hand. "Osmotic, lets your skin breathe air, keeps everything else in—including sweat."

That would explain why it was so cold in the room, maybe. "Seems like a lot of trouble."

"Regulation sterile technique. Can't have some wild micro-animal messing up experiment protocols. Even though the UV overheads usually catch any we miss, you never know. If you're just planning to satisfy idle curiosity, better you should look at it on the holoproj. That'll save you a lot of B-time."

"B-time," Billie said.

"As in 'bidet.' When all of your intestinal bacteria get fried, it tends to do interesting things to your bowels. After your first delouse treatment, you tend to get a real fulminant diarrhea that lasts about a week. Cuts down on your personal mobility, it does."

"Ah. I'm looking for the Artificial Person who came here with us."

"The 'droid? He's in mechlab. They're molding him for an exobase and walker. Won't take all that long. I can connect you on the com."

Billie thought about it for a moment. "No. That's okay. I'll talk to him later."

"No problem. You need anything, just ask. I do what I'm ordered, no mistakes."

As Billie wandered away, she thought about what the fat man meant by that last remark. It had been another long day. She was tired. All she wanted to do was lie down and sleep.

No, not sleep. Not with the aliens here to infect her unconscious mind and make it churn out nightmares.

She had thought the hospital awful. Had feared for what they planned to do to her mind, the chemical lobotomy the medics had decreed.

Given all that had gone on since she'd escaped, a mind-wipe didn't sound so bad.

10

Wilks saw the man step into the cargo bay, but not who he was—the hangar lights were dim and the ship's standby lamps were not much brighter. The man looked around.

"Over here," Wilks said.

The man tensed, dropped his hand toward his hip and the handgun clipped there, then froze. He straightened, then moved closer.

"I thought it might be you," Wilks said.

It was Powell.

"What do you—?" Wilks began.

Powell gave him a cut wave. Wilks shut up. Watched as the major pulled some kind of electronic sniffer from his belt and touched a control on it. A green LED lit on the little black plastic rectangle. "Okay, clear."

"Walls have ears?" Wilks said.

"And the ceiling has eyes. Everywhere on the base, except in here. Another few days and this ship will be bugged, too."

"Spears."

"He's as paranoid as they come. Crazy as a spider on a hot griddle, you know."

"Yeah, I figured."

"He lives for his scheme of retaking the Earth and being the hero of the millennium. He thinks everybody is out to get him. He runs a poison scan on his food and still makes an orderly taste it first; he sees conspiracies everywhere. In normal times the mindbenders would be lining up to write books about him."

"Normal times," Wilks said. "Been a while since then."

Powell nodded. "Yes." The man paused, sighed, seemed to gather his thoughts. "Maybe we're beyond reason as a species. Maybe what mankind needs is a sociopathic psychotic killer to match the aliens." He shook his head.

"But you don't believe it," Wilks said.

"No. It would be a step backward, a return to the caves. We're . . . better than that. We have achieved civilization, the stars. We can't go back."

"Not to defend Spears, but dialogue doesn't seem to work too well on these things."

"I understand that. But the queens are intelligent. They *can* be communicated with—we've done it here. Our queen is cooperating, after a fashion. They want what we want, to survive, to thrive."

"If you're preaching the 'Brotherhood of Life' line, Major, you're wasting your time. I've seen my friends slaughtered by these fuckers. I was on Earth just before they nuked a big chunk of it rather than get eaten alive."

"I know, I know. I'm not saying we should hug the aliens and expect smiles all around. Sharing the same world with the aliens isn't likely, they're too much like we were half a million years ago, too egocentric to think of life forms other than their own. No, I'm not suggesting any such thing. But we are supposed to be intelligent, to be civilized. War is stupid, annihilation of an entire species is barbaric."

"Funny, coming from a major in the Colonial Marines."

"Not all military men are killers, Sergeant. Neither are all officers automatically savage morons."

"Could have fooled me," Wilks said. But he grinned. Powell was somebody with a conscience, and he was obviously trying to do something here. Wilks wasn't sure just what, yet, but he had a feeling he was going to find out.

"They didn't nuke it, you know."

"What?"

"Earth. Didn't happen. No major atomics, nothing but tacticals, according to our feeds."

"Probably because your friendly neighborhood aliens ate the guy supposed to push the button."

Powell shrugged.

"Okay, so, what's the scat, Major? Why are you telling me all this and risking your own ass?"

Powell nodded, and took a deep breath.

The atmosphere plant was never going to produce a surface nitrogen-oxy mix thick enough so unaugmented humans could use it for breathing purposes, unless they crawled in the bottoms of deep craters. True, the planetoid was big enough to hold some gases down with its feeble gravity but the term "terraforming" was something less than exact in this case. Unless you thought of humans as moles or perhaps prairie dogs.

No, the civilian colony was here because there were a vast number of underground caverns that could be sealed tight, filled with air, and used either as shelter or to grow enough food to sustain a permanent population. Once the tiny world became self-supporting, there were plenty of uses for it: expanded military bases, mining, an escape-proof prison. It was to those ends the terraformers worked. What the atmosphere plant produced was, save for venting, pumped into the ground.

The stolen crawler approached the plant, slowed. Came to a stop. Inside the small craft the trio of deserters were four days from a bath and out of food.

"We made it," Renus said.

"Yeah, so far," Magruder added.

The crawler's pilot at the moment, Peterson, nibbled at his lip, but said nothing.

"Radio's still quiet, 'cept for stray stuff from Third Base," Renus said.

"Spears would have them on a war footing, no transmissions—like there's anybody out there who gives a roach's ass."

"Yeah," Peterson said, "but we ought to be picking up suitcoms or Doppler or something this close."

"This isn't a place where people go out for a picnic, now, is it, dickhead? They're all underground."

Peterson glared at Renus, looked as if he were going to come up from the seat and take a swing at him.

"Bury it," Magruder said. "We made it, that's the important thing. Spears didn't even come looking in this direction; we didn't see any flyovers. We're home free."

"I'll feel better when I'm inside," Peterson said. "Be a hell of a lot easier to steal a ride offworld here."

"So what are you waiting for?" Renus said. "Move in."

The crawler started forward.

In the hold of *The American*, Powell said, "He's been feeding the experimental subjects all kinds of chem the scientists say might have some effect on the things. We don't know if it's working or not. The body chemistry of these creatures is astounding."

Wilks touched the scar on his face without conscious thought. He realized what he was doing, dropped his hand, said, "Yeah. I noticed. Acid blood probably fucks up your basic tranquilizer pretty good."

"We've done some conditioning exercises with the queen. She doesn't appear particularly concerned with the fate of individual drones—we've killed them and she doesn't display distress in any way that shows. But if we threaten or destroy any of her eggs, she becomes very agitated."

"Fetch the stick or we squash the babies?"

"Something like that, yes. It seems to work. And the queen controls the drones—we aren't sure how, some kind of telepathic or extremely low frequency radiopathic waves, something. We—ah—we've put a single human subject into a chamber filled with alien drones, given him an egg and a blowtorch with which to threaten it, the queen watching, and none of the aliens touched the man."

"Jesus, you're cold-blooded fuckers."

"It wasn't my idea, Wilks. Spears runs the show here."

"Why doesn't somebody put a bullet into him? Shove a grenade under his bidet?"

"He has his supporters. And like I said, he's very careful."

Wilks shook his head. "He trust you?"

"Not really."

"But you could put him away. Then you'd be in command."

"I'm not a killer, I told you that."

"Yeah. Go on."

Powell went on.

Billie was in the room they'd issued her, a closet-sized cube big enough for a bed and chair, the sink, shower, and toilet all in a walk-in space inset in one wall. She'd just finished cleaning up. She didn't want to sleep, but she was so tired she knew it was going to happen soon. One of the medics she'd talked to had given her a tablet he said would help. She wasn't the only one on the base who had bad dreams, so it seemed.

She was staring at herself in the tiny mirror over

the sink, wondering who this thin, hollow-eyed woman was.

"Billie?"

She turned. Mitch.

They had repaired him, after a fashion. He was held in a bipedal frame by shoulder straps and a wide band across his chest and waist. The platform began where his body ended, and extended into a pair of hydraulic struts, pistons and stainless steel and stressed plastics that terminated in oval pads nothing like human feet. They hadn't tried very hard to match his proportions—he was about eighteen or twenty centimeters shorter than he'd been with his own body intact, so his hands dangled at the mechanical knees of the legs. Billie's flash image was of a man who had been stripped of flesh from the waist to his toes, then had his skeleton chrome-plated and hung with cables.

"So," he said. "Is it me, you think?"

The joke fell flat and it broke her heart that he tried it. But if that was how he wanted to play it, she would give it a shot.

"I think the flitter salesman sold you a demonstrator. You should have held out for next year's model."

The silence began, stretched too long. He broke it, finally. "They don't have an AP vat-works here, this is the best they can do." Another moment stretched, a spiderweb made of silken time hit by an insect in slow motion. "You okay?"

"Now that you ask, no. My homeworld is in ruins, my love life is for shit, I'm stuck on a military base with a guy who thinks he can keep monsters in a kennel like pets. The galaxy is going to hell in a hearse, Mitch, or hadn't you noticed?"

She turned away, so she wouldn't have to look at him.

"Billie, I'm sorry."

"Why? None of it is your fault, except the love life part. In the grand cosmic scheme of things, that doesn't count for a whole lot anyhow. Forget it."

"Billie . . ."

"What, Mitch?" She spun around and glared at him. "What are you going to *do* about it? Did the technicians hide a nice little expandable dick in that thing?" She pointed at the exoframe. "Pump it up and it stays hard all night?"

He blinked. Raised one hand, started some gesture, then dropped it. Shook his head. Turned and walked away. The quiet whine of the hydraulics grew quieter, the thumps of the pseudopods faded away.

Billie sighed and it turned into a sob. Oh, man. She'd stepped over the line. Leapt over it like she was wearing rockets. She'd wanted to hurt him and she had. They apparently didn't teach him how to fight when it came to emotional stuff and she fought dirty, going for the throat. Oh, man. How could she do that?

How, came the little voice from deep within her mind, *how could he make love to you, make you fall in love with him and not tell you he was an android?*

Was there any doubt about whose sin was the greater one here?

Billie took the tablet the medic had given her,

swallowed it dry, and fell on the bed. Pulled the flat and hard pillow over her head. Life was so unfair.

What an original thought that was.

With the crawler docked, the three marines exited and found themselves in the antechamber of the air plant. The locks were coded but some helpful civilian had scribbled the admit number over the pad.

"Christo, what a bunch of fuck-offs," Renus said.

"It's not like they're gonna get a lot of company out here, now is it?" Magruder said as he punched in the code.

The inner lock slid open and the three padded inside. Once the door sealed behind them, they removed their helmets.

"They might not take too well to visitors waving guns," Peterson said.

"Yeah, well, until we know which way the hydrogen fuses, I'll feel a lot better holding on to mine." He waved his carbine. An armed marine should be worth thirty unarmed civilian air farmers.

"If they give us any flak, we go to plan B—the shuttle," Magruder said.

"Will that thing really get us anywhere else?"

"It got the farmers here, didn't it?"

"Yeah, but who'll fly it? Not you." That from Renus.

"Whoever flew it here," Magruder said. "We'll make him a reasonable offer." He patted his own carbine.

Peterson snickered.

The corridor was wide, dark, with high ceilings. The lighting was bad.

"Spooky in here," Peterson said. "And hotter than the Devil's dick, too."

"Some side effect of the gas generators," Magruder said.

"Who made you an expert on this shit?" Renus said.

Their footsteps echoed as the trio walked down the corridor.

"Where the fuck is everybody?" Peterson said.

"Maybe they're having a party," Renus said. "An orgy. I sure could use a little pussy right now myself."

"Little is right," Magruder said. "Hell, you couldn't make a mouse groan."

"Hey, fuck you."

"Like I said, with what? Way I hear it, you have to rent a microscope to find it when you want to piss."

Peterson laughed, and Magruder chuckled at his own joke. They were feeling better, to judge from the banter. They'd made it to safety, the general hadn't stomped them flat on the way. If the civilians didn't cooperate, fuck 'em. They could steal their transport and full-wing it to worlds elsewhere.

"What's that on the wall?" Peterson said.

"What? Where?"

Renus tapped Magruder on the shoulder with his carbine. "Over there, to the left."

The three men moved.

"Why the hell don't they have any lights in here? Christo, it's like a tomb."

Magruder pulled his flashlight and pointed it at the wall.

The circle of light thrown by the bright halogen

lamp showed a convoluted and ridged overlay on the wall, grayish, like flattened loops of intestine.

"Some kind of sculpture?" Renus said.

"Oh, fuck. Oh, fuck. Oh, fuck!"

Renus and Magruder turned to look at Peterson. "What?" Magruder demanded.

"I—it's—I've seen this shit before!"

"So?"

"When—when I was on guard duty at the queen's chamber."

"What the hell are you talking about?" Renus wanted to know.

"The fucking alien queen's chamber! This shit is all over the wall in her chamber!"

Magruder shone his light farther along the corridor's wall. The stuff continued, spread so it covered the entire wall from the floor to as far up as the light would shine, all the way to the ceiling.

"Ahh!"

Both Renus and Magruder spun, their carbines pointed at the third man.

"What?!"

Peterson wiped something from his face, a clear, slimy goo.

"What the hell is that?" Renus asked.

Peterson looked up at the ceiling.

Renus and Magruder looked up, too.

11

The miracle of modern chemistry failed to put Billie to sleep. She added to the medicine the relaxation drill she'd learned in the hospital but after three rounds of pleading for her muscles to relax she was still awake. Mitch had gone, where she didn't know. And she didn't care.

Right.

Fuck this.

Billie stood, exhausted but past the point where she could drop off. Washed her face and looked at herself in the small mirror over the basin. Her image stared back, hollow-eyed, her muscles taut with strain. When Wilks had broken her out of the hospital—so long ago it now seemed—her almost-ash hair had been shoulder length. The hair was still a pale-brown but she'd chopped it off short somewhere along the way. She couldn't even re-

member when she'd done that. During one of the
post-sleep lethargies. If there were an omnipotent
god out there somewhere who paid attention to
what people did, he must have one hell of a
warped sense of humor.

She dried her face under the blower, took a few
deep breaths, and left the little room.

Billie walked as though she were a passenger on
her own shoulders, along for the ride but not in
control. She observed almost distantly her feet taking her back to the communications room. Maybe
seeing how other people dealt with monsters might
help somehow. And she found herself worried
about the little girl she'd seen, a child billions of
kilometers and years away. What was her name?
Amy?

There must have been a shift change, a different
tech was on the board when Billie arrived, a man
this time. But he must have had his orders, too.

"Annie said you were here earlier," he said.
"C'mon in."

Billie nodded at the man and sat next to him.

The images shifted on the various screens, sometimes people, sometimes test patterns, sometimes
information blurring past so fast she couldn't begin
to read it. A montage of humanity calling out to itself electronically, sending its voices and pictures
out on invisible waves into the galaxy. Is anybody
listening? Is anybody there?

A woman appeared on the screen to Billie's left.
She was attractive, dark hair chopped short in a
spacer's cut, chiseled and even features, thin lips,
good cheekbones. She spoke rapidly, her image

without sound. Sweat beaded on her forehead, ran down her face.

"Who's that?"

The tech glanced over at the picture. He smiled. "That's Ripley."

"Ripley?"

He looked at her as if she were a not particularly bright child. "Ellen Ripley. *The* Ripley. She was on the *Nostromo* and the *Sulaco*. She was there at the beginning, on LV-426, first contact with the aliens. Holds the record for long sleep, as far as we can tell. You been living in a cave the last few years?"

"Yeah, you might say that. What happened to her?"

The tech fiddled with the control. "Can't get the sound, sorry. This is a real old 'cast. We catch a few of them now and then, light-speed being as slow as it is. Never know what you're gonna pick up. I can plug it into the computer lip-reader, you want."

"What happened to Ripley?"

The tech shrugged. "Dunno. She was the only survivor of the *Nostromo*. Basically a buncha truck drivers who sat down in the wrong place at the wrong time, got infected. She later went back out to the colony as an adviser with a crew of Colonial Marines. The colony was destroyed in a nuclear explosion. Probably they all died. There were some rumors . . ."

Billie, exhausted, stared at the tech. Waited.

"I had a buddy, used to work for a civilian biotech division of a major Terran company. He said Ripley managed to get offworld before the place blew. Wound up on an old prison world somewhere. They sent somebody out after her, but that's where the story ends. A lot of shit got lost after the invasion. Who can say?"

"You seem to know a lot about it."

"Not really. Spears—ah—*General* Spears studies everything available on the aliens. Bunch of it gets routed through here. You pick up stuff."

Billie stared at the woman on the screen. She felt a kind of kinship with her. How had she behaved when she faced the things? Was she alive somewhere? Or blown to atomic dust, the same way Wilks had blasted the aliens' homeworld with nuclear flames? Or worse, webbed to a wall and used as a human incubator for a baby monster?

The image faded. Billie leaned back in the chair and allowed the other vidpixs to wash over her. They were hypnotic, light strobing, low sounds droning her into a kind of somnolence . . .

Without realizing it, Billie dropped into a troubled sleep.

The glob of slime apparently marked Peterson somehow as the first target. He raised his carbine and started blasting, waving it back and forth, spraying a 10mm fan of steel-sheathed lead. The armor-piercing bullets sang as they struck the ceiling, the roar of the exploding propellent smashed against the ears of the three marines, deafening them.

Renus and Magruder brought their weapons up but not in time. The things dropped from the ceiling, peeled away from the convoluted resinous bas-relief sculpture, invisible until they moved.

The first alien fell on Peterson, slammed him to the floor, knocked his weapon away.

Peterson screamed, a wordless bleat, full of terror.

The thing bounded up like a giant grasshopper, Peterson held in its claws like a doll.

"Fuck! Shoot it!" Magruder yelled.

"I can't, Peterson's in the way—!"

"Out, out, get out, move—!"

"Help!" Peterson finally found a word to put into the scream.

The alien holding the man leapt toward the wall, reached it. Another alien—two, three of them—unfolded from the wall right in front of the marines and reached out to grab Peterson. They passed him from claw to claw upward.

"Oh, man!" Renus fired, and the closet alien shattered under the hail of hard metal, spraying yellowish fluid in all directions like a popped water balloon.

"Yaah!" Magruder yelled as some of the acid splashed on his suit, ate small holes in it. He turned, ran.

Renus didn't see Magruder go; he was busy waving his carbine back and forth, filling the corridor with noise and death. Another alien fell, cut in half at the hips. But Peterson was gone, moved up the wall out of sight.

More of the things dropped from the ceiling, sprang from the walls, charged Renus.

"Die, motherfuckers!"

The cyclic rate on the M-41E carbine was, in theory, nearly seven hundred rounds per minute. Slightly more than eleven rounds a second. With the weapon held continuously on full auto, therefore, a hundred-round magazine would be exhausted in a little over nine seconds.

It was the longest nine seconds of Renus's life.

Three heartbeats after the magazine ran dry, one of the things sprang at him, shot that efficient toothed rod from its mouth right down Renus's screaming throat. The scream turned into a choked-off liquid gurgle. The aliens had saved Peterson for implantation but Renus was nothing more than fresh meat. The last thing he did before he died was to trigger the grenade launcher on his carbine. The 30mm explosive shell hit the wall at an angle, bounced upward, and went off somewhere near the ceiling. The explosion washed the corridor with clean fire and deadly shrapnel.

Magruder ran, driven by fear and adrenaline, the acid burns on his suit trailing acrid smoke. The blast wave hit him, he staggered, nearly stumbled, but kept on his feet.

Ahead was a doorway marked Interior Life Support. Magruder reached the door, slapped frantically at the admit panel. The door slid open. He jumped into the room, pressed the closure control, held it until the door slid shut.

"Jesus, Jesus, fuck!" Safe, he was safe, for now. He had to find a way out of here, fast! He looked around frantically.

Something clattered, a rattle of claws on a metal grate.

Magruder looked up. Saw one of the aliens overhead on an expanded aluminum mesh ceiling plate. "Fuck!" He snapped the carbine up and fired. Half a dozen rounds hit the grate, some of them got through to the creature. It fell, a puppet

with its strings cut, collapsed on the grating. Acid
dripped, burned the grate, the floor beneath it,
raising smoke and a stench.

Magruder backed away from the acid rain,
slammed into the wall.

Something banged on the door. The thin metal
dented inward as if it were no thicker than foil.

"Oh, man!"

A claw came through the wall and stabbed Magruder just above his left kidney. He lurched away
from the pain, felt a piece of his back jerked out.
He screamed wordlessly in pain. The shock hit him
as the blood spewed from the hole in his back. He
stumbled through the pool of acid eating away at
the floor. His boots began to smoke. His feet took
fire, blistered, began to char.

He dropped his weapon, pulled at his boots,
burned his hands getting them off.

He leaned against another door opposite the one
the things tore at.

The door opened behind and he fell backward.

Looming above him, something. An alien! No, it
wasn't a thing, it was a man! Thank God!

Then he saw it was Spears.

"The wages of treason are death," Spears said.

He smiled.

Spears had watched it all. The initial desertion.
The frantic ride through the canyons. The entry
into the air processor plant. This fool thought he
could just steal a crawler and escape. Never even
looked for the hidden cameras onboard the stolen
property, the cameras that sent every moment of
the trip back for Spears to enjoy at his leisure. Ev-

ery word, every fart, every bump on the frantic ride. Just as the surveillance equipment had picked up the attack only moments ago. True, some of the network had been put out of commission by the drones, webbed over or covered by the resin secretions as they built their nest inside the plant, but plenty of photomutable gel eyes had remained. All of it had been recorded, fed to the computers at Third Base, where the tactics would be broken down and studied, used to extend his knowledge of his alien troops.

The three deserters had panicked, lost it, and that disgusted Spears. Real marines would have used controlled bursts, overlapped their fields of fire, and walked through the drones to safety. But humans were weak, filled with fear, and they lost control. Their emotions damned them. Had three aliens been armed as the deserters, the wild strain would not have been able to touch them. That was what a *real* trooper was, one without fear. One without the emotional entanglements that came from being born of woman. In a way, Spears felt a kinship with the aliens. He had come from an egg and sperm, but had been carried to term without the uncertainty of a living mother.

The marine at his feet—Magruder?—stared up at him. "G-g-general! Th-thank God . . ."

"You fucked up, son. Fouled your jets right across the tubes. Because you are weak. But you served your purpose. Every little bit helps. They'll be watching the recording of that chickenshit run you did for a long time. What not to do. A classic example of bad tactics built on an even worse strategy."

He turned. A pair of troopers in full combat gear

stood nearby. They were nervous, fidgety, the stink of fear rising from them. Not much better than this scum lying on the floor, but at least they obeyed orders. It was what he had to work with, for now.

"I'm done with this," Spears said, waving at Magruder. "The drones are hungry. Give them supper."

Magruder screamed. "No! You can't! Please!" He struggled to rise.

One of the guards opened the door. The aliens were about to break through into the next room, the walls shuddered under their blows.

"Please! Pleeaassee!"

The two marines shoved Magruder toward the door. He stuck his arms and legs out, trying to stop himself. Caught the doorjamb with one hand. His fear gave him strength. He stopped.

Spears kicked out with his boot and smashed Magruder's fingers. Magruder screamed as he slid through into the room. The door slid shut with a grating noise.

Spears watched through the plastic viewplate set in the door as the alien drones breached the wall and stormed into the room. Magruder's voice filtered through the closed door. He kicked at the first alien to reach him, but it was a wasted effort.

Spears turned away. "Let's go," he said. "We're done here."

The two guards practically leapt to obey. That brought another smile to Spears's face. A little example did wonders to keep the troops in line. Yes, sir. Indeed it did.

12

Powell paced back and forth in the hold of the cargo ship, his movements quick and nervous. "There were one hundred sixty-eight civilian terraformers," he said. "Men, women, children. Spears gave them to the aliens. The air plant is automatic at this stage, you see, so the people were . . . redundant."

Wilks found that he was standing, his fists clenched.

Powell stopped pacing, turned and faced the sergeant.

"You let him do it."

"I'm not a murderer," Powell said. "Not even Spears."

"I saw you reach for that pistol you carry when you got here," Wilks said.

"But I didn't pull it. I would, I suppose, if I truly thought my own life was in jeopardy."

"And you don't think it is? What the hell do you need, a formal declaration of war?"

Powell chewed on that for a second. "Listen," he said, "I joined the service to do my duty for my planet. I was studying for the priesthood at the time. I planned to finish my training and become a chaplain. It didn't work out. I got sidetracked. So I wound up here. What Spears has done sickens me, but the path to the Light is not by creating more darkness."

Wilks stared at the man. He'd run into guys like Powell before. The military had to have a certain number of medics and religious types. Their bent, because of what they did or who they were before they ever joined up, was usually pacifistic. If you were wounded in battle, you needed somebody to staple you back together, so a surgeon; if you were emotionally burned out, some kind of counselor, though Wilks himself hadn't ever had much use for those, psychologists or faithers. They were necessary, but you didn't want one next to you when the grill flamed on and the other side started shooting. And you didn't want one in charge when your ass was on the line. It wasn't that way with all of them—Wilks had seen medics who would just as soon carve your heart out as smile at you and men of various gods who would cheerfully burn a stadium full of small children if they thought that's what their deity wanted. But Powell wasn't one of those.

And, given the situation, that was bad news.

So what did the man want? Why was he telling Wilks all this?

Abruptly it dawned on Wilks exactly why. Powell was one of those who bought his meat flash-wrapped at the market, or pretended it was soypro—but still ate it. He wasn't a hunter himself but he wasn't above enjoying the taste of the game—once it had been sanitized and neatly pack-aged. Once the thing had been gutted and the blood drained. He would eat it, but he wouldn't hunt and kill it.

And he at least knew a hunter when he saw one.

Wilks nodded to himself. Fine. He could live with that. He was used to doing the dirty work himself.

The queen was a giant, bigger than other queens. A force of nature, unstoppable, irresistible, like something from an ancient mythos. She was the Destroyer of Worlds, she was the eater of souls, it was foolish to even think of resisting her.

The queen loomed large, four sets of inner jaws opening and extruding like a Chinese puzzle box, able to spear and eat anything from mice to ele-phants. But she wasn't interested in mice or ele-phants, she wanted other prey. She wanted—

Billie turned to run, but her feet were mired in the floor, she struggled and could only manage a glacial slow motion, as if she were shod in lead boots, as if she were on the bottom of a deep pool full of thick syrup.

She cried out, kept trying to run, but it was hopeless. She could smell the queen as she drew closer, the sharp, bitter, burned-plastic odor of her flowed out in waves to envelop Billie. The stench of bodies a-rot for years in some dead and fishless sea curled over Billie, a pustulent and blackened breaker with bloody red foam about to crash down . . .

Do not be afraid, the queen said. Her voice was soothing, a melody from childhood, the tones of a mother comforting a frightened baby. *I love you. I want you. I need you.*

"No!" Billie screamed. She'd heard it before. She knew it was a lie. She struggled to move in her personal amber, a prehistoric fly waiting for the hand of Death, a doomed insect waiting for Eternity to smother her.

I love you. Come. Let me touch you . . .

A cold claw gripped Billie's shoulder.

"No!"

"Take it easy!" the tech said. He stood next to her, his hand on her shoulder. "It's okay. You're just dreaming."

Billie blinked, trying to make the transition from *there* to here.

"I know how it is," the tech said. "I dream about her, too."

Billie stared, unable to bring up words.

"Tell the medics. They've got some stuff that helps."

"Nothing helps," Billie said. "I've been dealing with this since I was ten. It's only a matter of time until the dreams finally come true."

Outside the com room there came a sound as if someone were thumping down the hallway on metal boots. Billie was sure she knew exactly who it was.

Ah, shit. What was she going to do about Mitch? Even as pissed as she'd been when they fought, she still felt that pull, that energy. Fuck, call it what it was. That *love*.

Damn.

As they were leaving the complex, Spears took a short detour through one of the newer egg chambers. A mere dozen eggs rested here on the alien-constructed floor, all fairly fresh, only a couple of days old. He had surveillance gear everywhere; he knew there was no danger of these units hatching anytime soon. Plus, the doors, left open deliberately so the drones could move the eggs unimpeded, still worked. He had a trooper crank the doors shut, so he could be in the room for a few moments without interruption from nervous drone egg-tenders.

He liked to do this, visit the eggs. The rubbery, fleshy shells with the flower-petal lips still clenched tightly together, protecting their precious cargo, they touched something in Spears. He was not a man given to deep introspection, no navel picker to worry over the unchangeable past or unborn future, he was a doer, not a ponderer; still, there was a cold and merciless beauty to be found here. These were unborn warriors out of the greatest warriors man had ever met. And Spears was a man of war.

With two guards standing nervously alert, Spears walked to the nearest egg, squatted, put one hand out to feel the roughness of the living container.

You could drop this little closed barrel off a tall building in standard gee and it would bounce like a plastic ball without damaging the tiny occupant. Spears knew, because he'd had it done. In the variable gravity room the scientists had built, they'd done more than a few such experiments. The eggs were tough. Even under three gees they still maintained their integrity. They could be cut, were the knife sharp enough, but the wielder had best be very quick—piercing the outer wall of an egg would get the cutter a face full of acid spray even more potent than that in the grown creatures' blood. Nature had been lavish in her protection of the aliens' birth packaging. And the first-stage babies were hardy little devils, too.

Spears grinned, stroked the egg as if it were the head of a faithful dog. The alien queens could reproduce in a kind of modified parthenogenesis, and the drones were mostly neuters. There were some males—the labbos had found a few—and indications were that there could be a battlelike sexual intercourse between the two sexes. The available males, when they reached some critical number, fought each other to the death, leaving only a single survivor, who then lay claim to the queen. She made him work for it, slammed him all over the place, and if he survived this battering, worse than the fights with the other males, the queen would submit to his advances.

The male's triumph would be short-lived. Within seconds after this hard-contested mating was consummated, the queen would kill the hapless male. The scientists babbled on about genetic diversity and such, but it didn't matter. If there weren't any males around, the queen could do it herself. And if there weren't any queens around, one of the drones would undergo what the scientists called a hormone storm; when it was done, the drone would be a queen.

Spears shook his head. Goddamned efficient bastards. Just what a commander in the field needed. You could hatch your own army in a few months and as long as one of 'em stayed alive, you could start over again when those got killed.

The troopers moved around, Spears could feel their fear. He grinned again, partly because he knew they were scared and he wasn't, partly because growing down his uniform pants leg was a fairly solid erection. As long as he squatted here, stroking the egg, it didn't show. He chuckled at his own hormone storm. That didn't happen much anymore, he'd managed to sublimate his sexual drives into more important things, but the little head did rear now and again. Not that he found sex unpleasant, no, that wasn't the problem, just that it took too much time and energy to indulge in it these days. Course, when he'd been younger, he thought he would live forever and he would fuck anything with a hole and a pulse and even the latter wasn't strictly necessary. And he'd learned something from the very first time he'd ever done it, something very important.

He laughed at the memory. Ah, Gunnery Sergeant Brandywine. Whatever happened to her?

Colonial Marine Cadet Spears at fifteen was still two years away from his first hitch, though he'd already gotten three Corps tattoos. Gunny Brandywine was his small-arms instructor, she was probably twice his age, tough as a boot sole, and could drill the eye out of a ship rat at twenty paces with a carbine or a handgun, you pick which eye. She wore her black hair chopped short in a spacer's buzz, had a rangy, tight frame, flat pectoral muscles and no breasts to speak of, and abs Spears would die to have himself. A lean, mean fighting machine, Gunny was, a strong and deadly female. He'd watched her in the showers a couple of times, carefully keeping his back turned so she wouldn't see the short-arm salute she was causing. Christ, he was so hard sometimes it stood nearly straight up.

He didn't think she'd noticed, but one afternoon after a session in the gym with the autoboxer, he'd found himself alone in the shower with her. As usual, his dick was trying to go ballistic, and he kept fiddling with the water's temp control, as if it were malfunctioning, so he could keep his erection out of her sight.

She shut her shower off and started to leave. Good.

But her footsteps on the wet plastic tiles went the wrong way. He could see her peripherally when she reached out and slapped him on the shoulder. "Come on, cadet. You might as well learn how to use that."

Spears thought of himself as a marine already, tough, unflappable, cool under stress, but he felt himself go red. "Excuse me?"

"You've been wanting to stick that in me for weeks, kid. In my quarters, five minutes, you can give it a shot." She turned and padded away. He watched the muscular roll of her buttocks, unable to breathe he was so scared.

But it had been fine. Gunny was practiced, she had obviously broken in more than a few first-timers, and she was patient.

The first round took maybe three seconds until he discharged his weapon. Five strokes, no more. It was great, but he knew enough to realize it hadn't done anything for her. He started to apologize. "Oh, man, I'm sorry, I—!"

"Forget it, cadet. I know how you young guys are. Besides, that didn't even take the edge off you. Here. Give me that."

The next three hours were a wonder to Cadet Spears. Sure, he had beat-off plenty, but it didn't feel anywhere close to as good as what Gunny Brandywine taught him that afternoon. Amazing things.

In the end, the most useful thing of all was patience. He was a hot-shot cadet, always rushing, always in a hurry, like life was a race he had to finish first. He couldn't wait to be on active duty. Gunny taught him how to wait.

They were on her bed, reconnected for the fifth time, she on her back, one leg drawn up, foot hooked over his ass, he on his side, pumping fast.

"Slow down, mister."

"Huh?"

She reached out, caught his hip with one hand, slowed his movement.

"When you're on the handgun range and you get an in-your-face pop-up target, what do you do?"

"Pointshoot, triple tap, two in the heart, one in the head," Spears said, as if he were in class. Which, he realized much later, he was.

"Right. Slow will get you killed in that combatsit. But if you get a pop-up at fifty meters, do you react the same way?"

He continued his motion at the speed she had set.

"No, ma'am," he said. "You take deliberate aim using your sights and squeeze off two to the torso."

"Ah, that feels good." She grinned, looked at him. Raised her leg so her toes pointed at the ceiling. "Now, back in the combat scenario, explain your actions."

"Pointshooting is inaccurate at long range. Accuracy is more important than speed in that situation. Shoot too fast and miss, the enemy might not. Better to be slow and certain."

"Push a little harder now, and a little faster." She bent her knee, brought it down close to her face. "Good. Put your finger here. Rub this way. Mmm."

He was getting close again. But he forced himself to hold his pacing where she wanted it.

"Life is like the range, cadet. There's a time to hurry and a time to go slow. Learning when to do the right thing at the right time is as important as anything you'll ever learn, you got that?"

He nodded. Drawing close to his release yet again, he would have agreed with anything she said, but on some level, he did understand the lesson. It was a unique teaching method.

"*Now* you go fast. Move, cadet. Move!"

He obeyed. It was one hell of a teaching method.

•　　•　　•

Spears came back to himself. Patted the egg and stood, his sexual excitement cooled. A less patient man than himself might have missed this whole opportunity to develop an invincible army. If Gunny Brandywine were still alive, she'd be a crone, pushing eighty, easy, but it would be interesting to see her. To show her how well her lesson had taken. And what the hell, maybe to fuck her once for old times' sake.

"Let's move out, marines."

He wouldn't have to tell these men that twice.

13

"The queen has learned to obey the general," Powell said. He leaned against a bulkhead, staring at the floor.

"Obey him?" Wilks said.

They'd been in the little ship a long time, Wilks was beginning to feel stiff and cramped, but he wanted to hear as much of it as Powell could get out before they had to break this off.

"Oh, yes. Spears started training her like a dog. Used his cigar lighter. He'd have a trooper with a flamethrower roast an egg while the queen watched. After she calmed down, he'd put a human into the testing cage with her. When she went for the bait, he'd pop the cigar lighter on and hold it next to another egg. The queen picked it up fast. You could leave a man in with her and a dozen drones for hours and none of them would touch him. She's not stupid, the queen.

"It seems odd, though," Powell continued, "that the queen will sacrifice the drones without a second thought but that she'll obey Spears to protect the eggs."

Wilks shrugged. "She's an alien. What drives her doesn't drive us. Maybe her responsibility ends when the damned things hatch."

"That's what Spears thinks. But she controls the drones. Telepathically, empathically, we don't have the sophisticated gear here to be sure exactly how, but it isn't with sound or odors or any visual signals we can detect. We've run tests where the drone was a klick away in an airtight chamber, no possible way it could see or hear the queen, and Spears made it do what he wanted."

"You have more than one queen," Wilks said.

Powell blinked. "How do you know that?"

"Somebody is laying the eggs in the air processor. Unless you're ferrying the queen from here back and forth."

"No, you're right. We put one egg from this nest over there. Spears did it himself. There are a score of drones there now tending the young queen."

Wilks shook his head in disgust. "Spears doesn't know what the hell he is messing with here."

"He thinks he does. And he's done more with them than anybody else, Wilks. Last month he took a dozen of the things out and had them marching in close order drill. He's taught several of them how to hold a modified M-69 machine gun and had them shooting the weapon."

"Jesus."

"Yes. It's Maggie's Drawers for accuracy, they can't hit anything smaller than a wall even at close range, but still."

Wilks nodded. A monster with a machine gun. The only advantage men had in battle with these things was their weaponry. If they were armed as well as human troops, they'd be unstoppable.

"The drones are stupid," Powell said. "But even a chimp can be trained to shoot fairly straight. And we think the queen's connection with the drones gives her the ability to see what she sees. And the queen is probably as smart as we are, according to the psychologists."

"Buddha fucking Christ."

"Crude, but apt."

Wilks stood, paced across the room. "But— what's the point? Earth is history. When we left there, it was already nearly overrun. A few more years and everybody there will be dead. A few clean neutron bombs after that would sterilize the place. All this cowboy shit is stupid."

"This isn't about saving the Earth or anybody on it," the major said. "It's about Spears and his ideas of personal glory. Or something. I don't know what, for sure."

Wilks nodded. "All right. Let's get to the bottom line here, Major."

Powell sighed. "Enough people have died, Sergeant. This has to end. Spears is at the air processor plant. There's a magnetic storm heading this way, sunspot activity on the primary is up. Spears will be delayed some hours, maybe even a day or two before he can lift and return to base. We need to begin our preparations now."

Wilks nodded. "All right."

"Mitch?"

The door to his room was open. He was half machine now, but the android part of him was programmed for sleep, to enhance his human characteristics. He lay on a pallet on his back, a sheet covering him to the chest.

"Come in, Billie."

The room's lighting was dim, and he was barely visible as she approached the pallet. She stopped two meters away. "I'm sorry," she said. "I shouldn't have said what I said."

He remained lying down, his hands under his head. He stared straight up at the ceiling. "I can understand that you were upset."

"It didn't give me the right to behave that way. It's just that—" she stopped.

"Just that what?"

She turned slightly, so she was looking at the back wall and not directly at him. "It's all so confusing," she said. "I thought I had gotten past it, about your being an artificial person. That it didn't matter."

"But it does matter, doesn't it?"

Her sigh was almost a sob. "When we came out of the sleep chambers on the way here, you seemed so cold. So distant. I didn't understand it. I still don't understand it. What happened, Mitch? Did you change? Or was it me?"

Now he sat up, the sheet draping down around his waist, covering the metal skeleton and revealing his bare upper body. He looked human to her in this light. Was human, she reminded herself, but not quite the same as she was.

"They made us to be as much like humans as possible. We're as far away from first-generation synthetics as they were from robots. Almost human.

"Funny, there were rumors we heard when we were still damp from the vats—the next generation of synthetics could not only pass for human among wombfolk, they would be born thinking they *were* human. Memory tapes of childhood, family, full implant blocks of internal workings, anatomically perfect right down to a dye in the circulation fluid so it would look like human blood to a naked eye.

"They would not only look like naturals, they would believe they were naturals. There would be inbuilt Laws of Function, of course, but the new APs would simply think they were personal ethics. They'd have the same energy requirements, ability to process food, oxygen, normal elimination, same natural cycles. For all practical purposes, they would be people, save that they couldn't reproduce, and they would be stronger, faster, and more durable."

"Mitch—"

"Of course," he went on, ignoring her interruption, "the question that immediately arose was: What's the point? If you want real people, why not make them the old-fashioned way, parent or artificial wombs? And the answer was that they would be expendable. Able to do the dirty and dangerous work that real men didn't want to do. Radiation disposal, exploration on hostile worlds, pressure rescue, suicide missions for whatever reasons.

"The new androids would be perfect. Acceptable in polite society, able to move without upsetting the most delicate sensibilities, but throwaways. Instant third-class citizens—no, not even citizens, but property, slaves, loyal as dogs, ready to leap at the proper command."

"Jesus, Mitch—"

"I'm not finished yet. But to get to those happy models, they had to experiment. Stir in the proper emotions so the passers-for-human would laugh at the right spots, cry when appropriate, even fall in love when necessary. So, here we are, you and I. It worked. My fake hormones did what they were supposed to do and I fell for you. Only thing is, there's enough of me outside the emotional part that I can understand it apart from the feelings."

Billie turned and looked at him. "And you resent me for it," she said finally.

"No. Not you. See, I do love you. But I resent them for making me this way. They didn't give me any experience, any guidance, any way of dealing with this whole thing rationally."

Billie smiled, small, sad, but a smile nonetheless.

His eyes were better than hers. He saw the expression. "Something funny about this?"

She heard the anger in him. "In a way. Nobody ever gave me any guidance or way of dealing with this 'whole thing' either, Mitch. Love and logic don't go together. You're looking for a nice clean path to walk. It doesn't happen that way very often among us 'naturals,' either. Love is usually messy, cluttered, sometimes painful and just plain awful."

"At least you had a choice," he said.

"What makes you think so? We don't get to choose any more than you do in some things."

"You could have walked away. You didn't have to love me."

"I could have walked away from you but I couldn't walk away from my *feelings*. That's why I can't just bail out now. I could leave but what I feel for you would stay with me."

"This is beyond my capabilities to understand," he said.

"Welcome to the club."

The silence stretched long between them. If only he had told her before they'd begun. If only she had known. She wasn't a bigot, she could have gotten past it, could have accepted him.

Really? Are you sure about that, Billie? Are you?

There was the damning part of it. She wasn't sure.

Not at all.

Spears sat in the ship, waiting for the goddamned storm to pass. Stupid, he'd known the solar magnetic activity was up, there had been swirls forecast, he should have destroyed the traitors and hustled his ass back to base. They could have beaten it, if they had hurried.

Well. Done was done, no point in crying over a broken plan. Best he make use of the time. There were some combat scenarios he wanted to run; the compsim unit had the latest learned-commands the alien troops had assimilated logged into it. They weren't a crack fighting unit yet, not by any means, but they were getting there. It was just a matter of time. And when they were ready, nothing in the universe could stand against them. Spears's word would carry more weight than God's when he had these troops whipped into shape. Yes, indeed.

Just a matter of time.

14

man carrying a durasteel fire ax hurried across the open space, moving crouched. "Over here," he called out.

After a moment a second man came into view, this one carrying a small shovel with a green plastic handle. Both of them were dirty, their clothes torn and worn. The first man had on a leather jacket that had probably once been black but was now a sun-bleached pale gray. The second man wore a dark blue nylon or synlon windbreaker with a hood.

"You sure about this?" Nylon asked.

"No, I ain't sure," Leather replied. "But if it's true, we're in fat town for sure. C'mon, dig."

The men were next to a collapsed building. The arched doorway immediately behind them stood upright in the rubble and looked to be made of steel—there were patches of orange-brown rust on the metal and a few twisted rods extending from it.

"Man, it'll take hours to get down far enough," Nylon said.

"Yeah, but if there *is* a military food cache there, we're talking about maybe a ton of canned food and *barrels* of clean water. We can retire to the Hidden Underground and never have to worry about bugs again."

Nylon lifted a shovelful of debris and tossed it to one side. "Hidden Underground. You believe that shit?"

"I believe I can buy the prettiest woman in the burg with five cans of unspoiled edibles and ten armed guards with a hundred. With a truck full of military-issue protein, I can damn sure find out if there's an HU. Shut up and fucking dig." Leather used the ax as if it were a rake, moving shards of brick and stone aside.

"Okay, okay. Where's Petey?"

"Standing watch, moron. Up on the tower."

Nylon glanced up at a pockmarked building across the street. A segment of the structure extended up three or four stories, carved like some ancient rock formation, only not by wind and rain but by bombs and fire.

"I don't see 'im."

"You're not supposed to see him, he's supposed to see you, and anybody else who might come strolling along. You didn't think I was gonna be rooting around out here in the open without covering my ass, did you?"

Nylon shrugged, said nothing, went back to digging. With the two of them scraping at the rubble, anything they said was covered by the sounds of their work.

"Amy, what are you doing?" The speaker was unseen, his voice almost a whisper.

"Videoing, Uncle Burt. You can hear everything they say and they look real close in the camera, see?"

"You shouldn't be out here, Amy, you know that. Your mother would—uh-oh. Here give me the cam."

The viewpoint shifted, there was a quick disorienting flash of the ground and a small girl's leg, then the picture steadied on the two diggers again, the angle slightly higher.

"Nobody moves," came a deep and unseen voice. A second later, a tall man in GF camo gear stepped into sight, a softslug shotgun held at his hip. The soldier pointed his weapon at the two diggers.

"Oh, fuck," Nylon said. "Where the hell is Petey?"

"Look," Leather said, "there's plenty to go around. We ain't greedy, we'll split it with you."

The soldier laughed. Waved the shotgun. "There's nothing down there, scatcats. We put out that rumor to catch guys like you."

"Motherfucker," Leather said.

"Oh, man, oh, man!" Nylon said. "You're bug feeders! Fucking bug feeders!"

The soldier took a step and slapped Nylon across the temple with the barrel of the shotgun, hard enough to knock him to his knees but not so hard as to put him out. "Don't call us that, scum. Never say that. We serve the queens. It is an honor. An honor, you hear? But you wouldn't understand that. You aren't among the Chosen." The soldier glanced to his left. "Simmons, King, front and center."

Two more soldiers, also armed with shotguns, came into view. Walking ahead of them, a third man, his hands cuff-taped behind him.

"Oh, man, Petey," Nylon said.

"You're not feeding me to the goddamn bugs!" Leather said. He threw the ax at the first soldier, turned and ran.

Simmons and King snapped their weapons up. "I got him!" one of them yelled. "Cover the others!"

The speaker fired his weapon. The charge caught the running man's left ankle. He managed one more step and then collapsed when his weight came down on the shattered joint. He screamed.

The ax didn't do any apparent damage to the first soldier, who said, "Go get him. I've got these two."

The two soldiers moved to grab Leather.

"The queen will be pleased with these three," the first soldier said. "She will smile upon us." He looked around the clearing, what had once been a busy street in a major city.

The viewpoint shifted. "Go, Amy," the unseen Uncle Burt said, his voice urgent. "Go, go!"

The image vanished. The scanners cycled, looking for another broadcast.

Seated before the now-blank screen, Billie was drenched in sweat, her heart pounding.

"Lot of them went over like that," the female tech said. Annie, Billie remembered. "Not enough they have drones out hunting people. Now they got traitors doing their work for them, too. Hard to imagine why somebody would do that."

Billie sighed, and it was almost a sob. Yeah. It was hard to imagine, but there it was. Jesus. How could anybody sink that low? Jesus.

The familiar weight of the 10mm carbine in his hands felt good. He wasn't in field armor, but Wilks also had four spare magazines strapped around his waist. Five hundred rounds ought to be plenty.

Powell had gone off to the computer center to do the kind of thing he could do, fiddle with controls. Didn't matter, Wilks would manage the hot work, it was the one thing the marines had taught him well.

Ahead, the doorway to the communications shack loomed. Wasn't even closed. Of course, they didn't have any reason to worry about security. Or at least, they hadn't until now.

When Wilks stepped into the small room, he saw Billie sitting in one of the chairs, staring at a blank screen. Next to her was a female tech.

"Back away from the console," Wilks said.

Billie looked at him. "Wilks. What—?"

The tech started to touch a control.

"Unh-uh, lady, you don't want to do that." He waved the carbine at her. "Roll the chair back and stand up slowly."

The tech, unarmed, did as she was told.

"Wilks!"

"Come stand over here, Billie."

She shook her head in puzzlement, but complied.

He opened up on the console first, then shifted his hip point up and raked the screens. He was wearing canal suppressor buttons so the sound was muted for him, but the two women covered their ears with their hands. The tech screamed. Thirty rounds were plenty. The hard plastic chipped and shattered, delicate biocircuits shorted out, and the flat screens starred and ran out of image, turning a dark gray.

Long-range communications at Third Base were history, at least for a while. There would be radio and Doppler on the crawlers and ships, of course, some of it capable of reaching over the near horizon to Spears, but if he hurried, nobody would get to those. Or if they did, it wouldn't matter.

"Wilks, what the *fuck* are you doing?"

"Staging a coup. Or a mutiny. When Spears comes back, he is going to be relieved of command. Powell is taking over."

"Shit, that pussy?" the tech said. "Spears will chew him to pieces."

"If it was just him, yeah, probably. But there's a few troopers who don't want to become monster food, they're on Powell's side. And then there's me. Which team you want to be on, sister?"

The tech licked her lips. Sighed. "I'm with you. Sooner or later everybody fucks up. That happens, you go into the hive. I'd rather swallow a bullet than an egg."

Wilks nodded. "Come on, then. Tell me about communications elsewhere on the station."

"What is the situation on the storm, trooper?"

The man shook his head, obviously nervous. "Still swirling, sir. We can't hope to lift for at least another three hours." The trooper swallowed. "Sir."

Spears nodded. Not much he could do about the

weather here. On some planets, decent-sized worlds, there were measures that could be taken with surface meteorology. A climate-controlled world wouldn't have your troops bogged down in mud or freezing in snow at the wrong time. A good commander had to think of such things. Many a battle had been lost not to the enemy but to a freak rain or heat low. A kamikaze—a Divine Wind—had once saved the old Terran empire of the Nihonese from an invasion by sea; better weather at the start would have tilted major engagements of the Civil War toward the South; the Australian Wars, the Acturian Police Action, the Berringetti Conflict, the outcomes had been affected in all these by a capricious natural ecology. How galling it must be to know you were superior in strength and numbers, had tactical advantages in terrain and matériel, and were a better strategist, only to be defeated by a monsoon. Could make an atheist believe in gods, that kind of shit.

Spears nodded to himself. "What about communications with the base?"

"Negative, sir. Even the LOS transmitters can't punch through the swirls. Sorry."

"Not your fault, marine. Carry on."

Spears turned away from the communications man. They were in the plant's south dock, a fortified and secured area the alien drones were unlikely to be able to penetrate, even if their queen would allow them to try. The place rang hollow under Spears's gravity-augmented boot heels as he walked to the intercom sensor and waved it on. His men were clustered around their craft, talking in low tones. Scared shitless of the aliens. As well they should be. "Computer, put visual of the queen on-air."

The holoproj flowered in front of the general. Four cameras, four different views of the young queen, busy pumping out fresh eggs four levels below where Spears now stood. "Good girl," he said, smiling. "Just keep those troopers coming. Computer, ignite the floor burner in the chamber."

"Burner tube is blocked," the computer said.

Spears allowed his smile a bit more wattage. Had to give it to the queen, she never stopped trying. Her drones had paved over the burner, probably four feet of the rock spittle covered the training device. "Clear the burner tube."

After a moment, a faint orange glow began in one corner of the chamber, quickly climbing through the spectrum from dull to bright. A thin blue line flashed, speared through the overlay with the sharpness of a laser beam, hard-edged in the dim room.

"Tube cleared," the computer said.

The queen had noticed and Spears would bet megacredits to mouse turds she knew what was coming. "Light the burner. Half-second burst only."

A blast of flammable gas roared up to splash against the ceiling, a single hot ejaculation that cut off while the circle of fire still painted a yellow-orange circle on the ridged overlay.

The queen looked at the vanishing fire, then swiveled her great emplated head to look directly at one of the cameras focused on her.

Spears chuckled. She knew it was there, knew he was watching her. "Computer, give the queen an image of the pulse-paint room. And put me onscreen so she can see me, too."

The projection swirled into life in the chamber, the details hard to make out from where Spears watched his own holoproj. But he knew the queen could see it well enough. The queen looked at the image, then back at the camera. Opened her mouth, hissed an acknowledgment at the tiny version of the general floating in the air before her.

Spears nodded. "Very wise, little mother." He turned away from the screen, looked at his human troops. "Gizhamme, Ceman, Kohm, front and center. We're going to the ID room."

The three men traded glances, but hurried to obey.

Very good, for troops about to be outmoded. They followed their commander.

Billie followed Wilks down the corridor. "We'll get you a gun, Billie," he said. "Soon as we get control of the situation on this level."

"What exactly are we doing here?" she asked.

"Taking sides," he said. "Powell has given me a list of men and women we can depend on to lean our way. And the transponder coordinates of the troops who are likely to stay loyal to Spears. We're going to round up and detain the general's supporters. Then when he comes home, we won't have so much to worry about. We take him down, flush all this demented shit away, and live happily ever after."

"You've said that before," Billie said.

"I'm still working on it, kid. Give me a little time. Earth wasn't built in a day, you know." He grinned.

Billie returned the smile. She was tired and had a lot on her mind, but she had no trouble buying into this scenario. If they didn't do something about the madman running this base, he would kill them all sooner or later. Win or lose, this had to be better than the alternative.

"Do you know where Mitch is?"

"If he's where he's supposed to be, yeah. He'll be rigging an override in life support's auxiliary control by now."

"Why there?"

"Well, the base is military, so there are modular fail-safes all over for air and gravity and heat and light, but if the mains go down, the emergency doors shut tight. Our side has the new override codes, their side won't. They'll be bottled up unless we let them out."

"Nice trick."

"I thought so. Powell's idea. He's not much of a field soldier, but he's not bad behind a console."

Wilks pulled a small device from the cro-patch on his belt, looked at it. "Ah, here we go. There are five of the bad guys just ahead, in the queen's antechamber. Stay behind me until we get the field of fire on them."

"Copy that."

"Feels good to be moving, doesn't it?"

Billie nodded. "Yeah. I hate to say it, but you're right."

"Hey, that wasn't so hard. You should practice saying it more often, it'll get easier."

"First you have to *be* right once in a while, Wilks."

"I like you, too, kid. Come on."

• • •

Spears held the pulse-paint gun five centimeters away from the drone's skull. It had its mouth closed, but he could smell its carrion breath. It would just as soon kill him as look at him, he knew, but it would not. The queen understood what would happen to her and her precious eggs if any of her drones so much as laid a claw on Spears. It was all about control, about power, and Spears had both. It had taken time and effort to find the aliens' Achilles heel, but once he had found it, he kept his arrow aimed right at it. It was their only weakness, and he knew how to exploit it.

The general waved the paint gun back and forth. The paint was actually microencapsulated grains of tritium in an acidic solution. The gun was programmed and sequenced so it would spray the correct number. The gun hummed as it forced the glowing slurry out under pressure. The material's color was also computer-controlled; this trooper would become a member of the Greens in another two seconds. There were seven corps in his New Colonial Marines, one for each color of the rainbow. As of now, he had less than a score in each of the corps, not much of an army per se, but one had to start somewhere.

The number 19 etched itself into the drone's exoskeleton, deep enough so it wouldn't rub off, not so deep as to cause any damage. In the night, the radioactive tritium would be visible for a long way; in daylight, the number still stood out against the dark gray of the alien's skull. Under an augstrobe, the paint would pulse, like a sighting laser, each number blinking rapidly so a field commander in

the air could visually acquire and pinpoint his men
from even farther away than usual, if need be.

Spears would put a copy of the skull ID on the
back of the head in a moment. For now, he leaned
back slightly and observed his work. "Welcome to
the Colonial Marines, son."

The drone did not react, but Spears fancied that
on some deep if murky level, it understood.

Spears slapped the thing on the skull. It was
cold, smooth, slightly clammy to his touch. "Now
you stand still, marine, while I get the backside."

Spears was aware of his three human troopers
watching him as he moved around the platform.

"Jesus Christ," one of the men whispered. He
must have thought Spears couldn't hear him. But
the general heard. He made a mental note of it.
Disloyalty was everywhere. Even among the so-
called best of his human troops.

He put one hand out and touched the alien's
skull to steady himself as he brought the paint gun
up. Disloyalty wouldn't be a problem with these soldiers. They did what their queen said without
question, without hesitation. And Spears controlled
the queens.

Glowing green etched itself into the hardness of
his new recruit's head. *Semper fidelis,* Spears
thought. That was never more true—this marine
would always be faithful. It would be the perfect
soldier when Spears got finished with it.

Perfect.

15

One of Powell's supporters arrived right after Wilks and Billie, also armed with a carbine. Between the two of them, they had no trouble capturing the four men and one woman whose transponders IDed them as Spears loyalists. At least according to Powell. Wilks didn't much like trusting the major, but in this case, the choice was easy enough. At least Powell wasn't homicidal.

"What's the scat, Sarge?" one of the captured troops said.

"Changing of the guard," Wilks answered. "To keep it simple, here's the drill: Spears is out. Powell is in. Any problems with that?"

The five troopers glanced around. And at the weapon Wilks held across his chest in port-arms position.

"You breaking a few regs here, Sarge," one of the women said. "Spears will cut you a new asshole."

"Yeah? How long you figure before you trip over one of those regs and wind up feeding the general's little pets?" Wilks asked her. "You know some of the people webbed in there, don't you?" He waved at the reinforced wall to his left. The queen's chamber was on the other side.

He could see them weighing it. If Spears came back and assumed command, they would be in deep shit if they played along with this. He was not a forgiving man. On the other hand, if Powell was the new honcho in charge, he wouldn't give them to the aliens. A smart marine would sit tight and wait to see which way the current flowed.

Then again, Wilks thought, a smart marine would have figured out that it was only a matter of time before they all went into the chambers as protein supplies for Spears's new and improved troops. Like the three who deserted and ran, only to find themselves out of the intake and into the combustion chamber. And it wasn't as though Colonial Marine line troopers were galaxy-renowned for their high intelligence.

Then *again*, he had the gun. Even a stupid marine usually figured that possibly dying in the future was better than for sure dying right *now*.

"Looks like it's your show, Sarge," one of them said.

"That it is. Let's take a little stroll to assembly, what say?"

The lights blinked out, followed by the sound of pressure doors dropping into place. That would be Bueller. The emergency lighting popped on almost immediately. Half a second, no more. Unfortunately, that half a second was enough time for the largest of the troopers to think he could take advantage of the darkness. He jumped at Wilks.

Wilks's first reaction was to shoot the sucker. He was big, but slow, and he had plenty of time to cap one off into the man. But blowing away marines, however misguided their sense of duty, didn't appeal much to somebody who'd spent most of his life in the corps. He'd done it before, he hadn't liked it.

Wilks sidestepped to his left, swung his foot up in a spring kick, caught the charging man high in the belly. Stole his wind just long enough for the second kick, this one to the man's right leg, next to his knee. The attacker's leg buckled, the ligaments and cartilage torn, and he collapsed onto the deck, cursing.

The Powell-loyal trooper brought his weapon to eye level and prepared to fire on the other captured troops.

"Negative!" Wilks yelled. "Don't shoot! There's no need."

The armed man glanced at Wilks.

"My men are in control of life support," Wilks said, making it up as he went along. "If anything happens to me, you lose heat and air, you're bottled up here without the exit codes. Anybody want to choke to death, taking me out is the way to do it." To prove he wasn't worried, he lowered his own weapon.

The four troopers still standing looked at each other uneasily. It was one thing to catch a round in battle and go fast, another to lie on a floor sucking air that had gone foul with CO_2. Not a pleasant way to die.

"Nobody is gonna do nothin', Sarge. You call it."

"That's good. Help bimboboy up and let's move."

The four moved to help the wounded marine.

Well. So far, so good. He hoped it would all go so easy.

Wilks seemed to have things well planned and under control, Billie saw. As they moved through the station, Wilks used a magnetic card and a keypad code to open the pressure doors. Once, there were three men waiting on the other side of a door, but Wilks herded some of the captives through first, their hands raised, to advise the marines of the situation. The threat was simple: Surrender your weapons or freeze in the dark trying to breathe. He must have forgotten that he was going to give Billie a gun, because she hadn't collected one yet. Not that there were many guns around. A couple of carbines, some pistols from various guards. Apparently Spears didn't like his men running around the base armed. Probably a good idea, it would have been too tempting to take a shot at him.

By now they had collected about thirty people, about half of them loyal to Spears, according to Wilks, who seemed to know how to tell the difference with some kind of electronic device he carried. Interesting.

"Where are we going?" Billie asked him.

"Central Assembly," he said. "Gotta sort these guys out as to ours and his. Powell says there are a hundred seventy-five marines, forty-eight scientists and medicos, a couple of androids, and fifteen workbots here. Spears has a short platoon, twenty-five men, with him. We can't have anybody running around loose who might short-circuit things."

"A lot of people to find," she said. "Couple hundred and then some."

"Used to be more. Powell says there were almost five hundred marines assigned to this base. Want to guess where the other half of them went?"

Billie swallowed, her throat suddenly dry.

"Between them and the colonists, Spears has given the aliens more than four hundred people."

"God."

"More like the Devil, I'd say, if I were inclined to believe in such things, kid."

Billie blinked and thought about somebody who would give that many of his fellow humans up to such a horrible death. He had to be crazy.

"Yeah, he's that," Wilks said.

She hadn't realized she'd spoken it aloud.

"But don't worry about it. We're going to shut it down. Powell says the medicos on his side know how to put the corraled aliens down fast; we can shut them off like lights"—he snapped his fingers—"that quick. Soon as we get Spears's loyalists locked up, we turn this place into an alien graveyard. The air processing plant is a little harder, but we can work something out, worst comes to worst, we'll just nuke the whole place."

One of the captured marines overheard this. "You can't do that!" she said. "The air plant is worth billions! And we need the oxy!"

"Sister, this planetoid is a wash. Even if we cook the plant crispy, some of those things might be dug in. They can survive a long time without food, without water, even without air. They could hibernate for *years*, just waiting for some fool to come along and be dinner. The best we can do is kill all those we can spot and then bail out. On sterile ships, too."

"You would let the Earth be overrun by these things and destroy the only means of combating them?"

Wilks looked at the woman as if she had grown fangs. "You buy that shit?" he said. "You think Spears is gonna drop down and clean up the whole fucking planet with a couple of hundred tame monsters?"

"He knows what he's doing," she said.

Wilks just shook his head. "Move, sister. You believe that, you're as crazy as he is."

Spears had learned over the years that circumstances often dictated events in a way that was beyond human control. Since the magnetic storm had caught them, there was no help for it, save to make the best of the enforced grounding. He'd worked computer scenarios, painted new trooper IDs, and now stood in a makeshift shooting range, provided by an unused corridor with a soakplate at the end as a backstop. It wasn't state of the art, no holographic attackers who would crumple and fall realistically when hit by computer-tuned and augmented weaponry; still, it would serve. A trooper stood out of sight through an open doorway ten meters down the corridor from where Spears was. With his pistol holstered, Spears called out, "Throw!" and went for his weapon.

The hidden trooper tossed an industrial-sized food can into the corridor so it entered at eye level and climbed in a lazy arc toward the high ceiling. The can was bright red plastic, as big as a small wastebasket, and it rose slowly in the reduced gravity of the corridor—micromanagement of gee was possible if you had a good programmer working the generators and plenty of time on his hands to route the flux lines.

Spears fired. The caseless round punched into the can as it reached its apex. In the lowered gravity, the impact of the starfish round as it expanded and tripled in caliber size was enough to knock the can noticeably away from the general. He punched the can twice more as it tumbled away and downward. The faint odor of canned fruit reached him as syrup and fruit cocktail spewed from the holes in the plastic. The booms of the pistol filled the corridors, but Spears's hearing was protected by in-canal wolf ears, electronic suppressors that allowed normal sounds in but stopped anything over eighty decibels.

"Good shooting, sir," the unseen marine said.

Spears chuckled. Catshit. A half-blind soldier should be able to hit a target that big at this range. "Use the smaller one next time. Ready . . . throw!"

More booms lapped against the walls as his shots found the next target, a head-sized can of yellow plastic. Spam, it looked like. Now that wasn't bad shooting.

In the Main Assembly area, Powell came to join Wilks and Billie and the others.

"Major?"

"We've got all of Spears's men here except for those he's got with him," Powell said.

"You've lost it, Major," a top kick said. "The general will wipe the floor up with you and your mutineers when he gets back."

"Maybe, Top, but I'll risk that. I'm going to give you all a choice," he said. "Those of you who wish to remain loyal to General Spears and his demented vision, move over to the left there. Those of you who will obey my orders until we can contact SekCom and get an official review of the situation, assemble on the right, by the aft wall."

The docks and ship bays were much larger, but this room was the biggest space normally used for general assemblies. The two hundred or so people rumbled, a disorganized crowd walla, as they spoke to each other and to nobody:

"Powell's lost his fucking mind—"

"I don't wanna wind up feeding the bastards—"

"What's the legal scat here, Sarge—?"

"We're fucked either way—"

"Ah, hell, I'll go with the major—"

Wilks watched as the men, women, and androids chose sides. The bots didn't count, they weren't AI grade; the androids had no choice, really, they were programmed to obey the ranking officer and since Spears was gone, that was Powell. The human group gradually divided into roughly equal numbers moving toward each side of the room. Most of the scientists went with Powell—maybe their exposure to the aliens had taught them something. More enlisted troops went to the aft wall, too, while the line officers, a couple of captains and lieutenants, and most of the NCOs went to the Spears group. That figured. Sergeants mostly ran the day-to-day operations of any military organization and they trusted more in the military process than did the grunts. Officers usually stuck together because they were officers.

"I can't believe so many would still follow him," Powell said softly.

"Hell, I can't believe *you* got so many," Wilks said. "What will we do with them?"

"Put them in detention. It'll be a little crowded but they'll just have to make do."

"What about the crossovers?"

"We'll keep them supervised," Powell said. "Outside of you and a few others, there aren't any of them I would trust with a weapon just yet."

Wilks nodded. "I hear that."

"All right. You men and women on the aft wall, return to your normal stations. You'll be reassigned shortly, keep your coms open, you'll get a computer log telling you where to report. We'll be a little thin but we can keep things running."

Billie said, "What about the general?"

"Yeah," Wilks put in, "do you have any antisky-craft weaponry mounted in the base?"

"Negative," Powell said. "We didn't expect attack from that quarter. Some of the crawlers and hoppers carry light machine guns, 20mm EU slug cannons."

"Enough to bring down a small troop carrier," Wilks said. "Better get somebody you trust who can shoot suited up and into battery, PDQ. The best way to stop Spears is to knock him down before he knows he's in trouble."

"I would prefer to capture him," Powell said.

"With all due respect, Major, as long as Spears is alive he's dangerous. If he gets back here, into the base, he's got an army the same size as yours, plus he's got personal control of the aliens, isn't that right? You said the queens recognize him, didn't you?"

Powell took a deep breath. "That's correct."

"I don't like taking out marines; I've had to do it in the past and I would rather not, but this is what you hired me for, isn't it? The hot work?"

Powell closed his eyes, nodded, resigned. "Yes."

"Fine. You run your base, Major. I'll take care of Spears."

The man nodded again, and Wilks turned away. He wouldn't order anybody to shoot the general but he would stand aside and let Wilks do it. Fine. Whatever it took.

"Come on, Billie. I'd feel better if you stuck with me."

"What about Bueller?"

"He's okay. He's standing by the life-support controls until we're sure what's what."

"Where are we going?"

"To give Spears a welcome home party. Once he's gone, we're gonna put all his pet monsters to sleep."

Billie shook her head. "Thank God."

"Whoever. Let's go."

16

"**S**ir, the storm has passed. We can lift whenever you are ready."

Spears nodded, pointed one finger at the trooper in a kind of salute. "Load 'em up."

The men hustled toward the hopper, eager to get out of the place. The air plant belonged to the aliens now, and his human troops were afraid to be here. They didn't have anything to worry about, as long as Spears had a use for them. Soon they would, but not right now. A good general didn't waste matériel until he could see suitable replacement for it on the horizon.

Spears climbed into the trooper carrier and moved to the control cabin. The pilot had all systems online, doubtless had had them ready for some time. Spears grinned. "Lift it," Spears commanded.

The hopper rumbled with power and then surged up a hair, enough to clear the landing area floor. It began to move forward slowly. Once it was clear of the plant, the little ship would become like an arrow shot at a distant target, would hang a lazy parabola, decelerating against the faint gravity for the last portion of the flight. POC—piece of cake.

"I don't hear the beacon," Spears said.

"Probably some residual crosspole flurries, sir. Flux whirlpools causing interference. It's not uncommon after a big storm.

"Is our com working?"

"All systems are green, yes, sir."

"Call Third Base. Coded squirt, advising them of our status."

"Sir."

The pilot slid one finger across a motion-sensitive contact bar, then touched a keypad next to it.

The general watched. Waited.

"There's the response, sir," the pilot said. "Ackno, confirm, green and green."

Spears rubbed at his chin with his thumb. Missed a spot with the depil last time he'd wiped the whiskers off. Just a couple of hairs, but that was sloppy. Sloppy was bad. Sloppy could get you dead.

"Call 'em back. Punch in code 096-9011-D, that's delta."

"Sir? I don't recognize the code—"

"You aren't supposed to, son. Just do what you're told."

"Yessir."

The pilot tapped in the numbers.

The hopper had full holoprojics. After a moment the screen area over the console blossomed, swirled for a moment, then remained a pale and featureless blue. A clear signal.

"Well, well," Spears said. "We've got trouble at home."

"Sir? There's nothing there."

"Exactly."

The pilot looked puzzled. Spears said, "You don't know the story of the barking dog, do you, son?"

The pilot shook his head.

"Back on Earth, long time ago, there was a famous investigator working on a crime. While listing the clues, he said, 'And of course, there's the matter of the dog barking in the night.' His assistant, who had been compiling the evidence, said, 'But the dog did not bark.' 'Precisely,' the detective said."

The pilot might as well have been in suspended animation, midpoint in a fifty-year sleep. Spears shook his head. "The signal is not supposed to be clear," the general said. "That it is means there is a problem."

"Ah. I see."

Whether he did or not didn't matter. Spears was not so inept that he would leave his base without stringing a few noisemakers. Time to try another one. There was always a chance that the magnetic storm had damaged some electronics.

"Put the ship back down where it was," Spears said.

"Sir?"

"A little detour. Don't worry about it."

• • •

Wilks pushed the helmet back on the E-suit. The heaters in the crawler had the somewhat stale air warm enough to breathe and keep his ears from freezing. Billie sat in the co-operator's chair, waiting for him to tell her what he wanted.

"Okay, we have to assume that his hopper has got firepower equal to ours, so we have to shoot first. The weaponry here is like that on the APC we flew on the aliens' homeworld. Robot guns, computer-operated, 20mm expended uranium armor-piercing slugs. All we have to do is plug the target in, like so . . ." He tapped in the specs for a light military hopper. "Light the system, here . . ." He lifted a protective cover, pressed a button. The fire control screen flicked on. "Security code, courtesy of Major Powell, thus . . ." The screen flashed. ARMED, it said. SYSTEM READY.

"That's it. Everything is automatic from here on. The ship gets into range, our system hoses it."

"He's got twenty-five troopers with him," Billie said. "You ever hear the expression 'burning down the barn to get rid of the rats'?"

"Depends on how nasty the rats are, kid. The guys with him are on his side. You can't think about them or their families or anything like that."

"That's cold, Wilks."

"War is ugly, Billie. People die. Sometimes the choice comes down to you or them. If Spears gets back here and rallies the troops who might be loyal to him, the rest of us are going to wind up feeding mama bug and the little ones. In a perfect universe there wouldn't be any need for soldiers or marines. In this one, there is."

Billie nodded, despite her feelings. He was right,

she knew it. She had killed before, both APs and humans. She remembered the pirate who had attacked their ship, and how he would have blown them all out of existence. She didn't like it, but Wilks was right.

"But if the guns are automatic, why do we have to be here?"

He shrugged. "Like a pilot on a commercial arc ship. In case something goes wrong. A circuit could overload, something could jam, maybe the guns work fine but somebody gets clear of the hopper in an escape pod and keeps coming. We're backup."

Billie repressed a sigh. Humans, backing a death-dealing machine. She sometimes wondered if people were any better than the aliens. They were killers, but more like ants or bees. Beast of prey, they hunted to feed, not for sport. And she doubted if they ever planned an ambush of their own kind.

Then again, Billie had no desire to become dinner for the monsters. She had come too close too many times already. And people like Spears, like those turncoats on Earth who caught and gave their fellow humans to the aliens, those kind of people were psychotic. Whatever it took to stop them had to be done. She just wished she wasn't the one who had to do it.

"General? The hopper is ten klicks out."

Spears, looking at a computer read, turned toward the pilot. "Keep it on standard approach."

"Sir."

The hopper in which they rode smelled musty, the air stale, and while everything worked as it was supposed to work, the little ship felt loggy. Spears could understand that; the backup vessel had been in storage at the air plant for more than a year, parked and sealed, awaiting just such a use as this. The hopper on which they had flown from the base was five kilometers ahead of them now, empty of personnel, being piloted on remote by the man who normally would be flying this vessel. The copilot seated next to him kept the chase hopper on an even path, same altitude, same speed. Not that it was really necessary—*this* ship had a major advantage over the drone ahead of them; this ship wore a full stealth suit, would be invisible to radar or Doppler, and with the flat-black anodized hull damned near invisible to eyeballing against the dark of space. Still, if the hide-me suit somehow malfunctioned, a lazy radar operator would see a double blip and probably think it was a ghost. Since there weren't supposed to be any other hoppers the same size away from the base—this one didn't show on records anywhere, Spears had seen to that—then the operator who *might* see it, *if* the stealth gear failed, would not be unduly worried. And if, in this very unlikely scenario, the tech didn't scramble a code, he would be fed to the aliens when Spears got back. The general had no use for such troops, even if he was the one trying to fool them.

"Five klicks, sir."

"Steady as she goes, son." This could all be a waste of his trump, but Spears had learned it was better to be cautious than dead. Time was running down on this planetoid anyway. There were big things in the offing, worlds to conquer, glory to be reaped. Wars to be won.

Spears grinned. And victory begins at home, doesn't it?

"Here they come," Wilks said. "Right down the pipe."

The tiny green dot on the gunnery radar screen moved toward the center. After a moment, the dot began to pulse, alternating now between green and amber.

TARGET INITIALLY ACQUIRED, flashed across the bottom of the screen.

"It's a match," Wilks said.

The alternating dot continued to pulse, then went from green/amber to red.

TARGET CONFIRMED. TO ABORT FIRING YOU MUST ENTER CANCEL CODE.

Wilks glanced at Billie. Shook his head. "All yours," he said, knowing that the computer wouldn't understand the comment.

The pulsing dot expanded, became the outline of the hopper. A blue grid appeared on the screen in one corner, then expanded to cover the hopper. A bull's-eye ring lit in bright green, centered on the hopper.

SIXTY SECONDS TO OPTIMUM FIRING DISTANCE.

A timer began counting down from sixty toward zero.

Wilks watched Billie. She stared at the screen, blinked rapidly. Her breathing speeded up. At fire minus thirty seconds, she said, "Jesus, it's like watching an execution."

"Yeah, it is."

FIFTEEN SECONDS TO OPTIMUM FIRING DISTANCE.

Wilks tapped a control on the external monitor.

The tracking cam gave him a star-sprinkled black. "There it is," he said, as much to himself as Billie. A tiny dot, the running lights barely visible.

FIVE SECONDS TO OPTIMUM FIRING DISTANCE.

The hydraulics of the guns whined slightly as they moved the weapons, tracking the incoming ship.

OPTIMUM FIRING DISTANCE. COMMENCE FIRING.

The machine guns were recoilless so the vessel around them didn't shudder, but the weapons vibrated, shaking them as if they had developed a sudden palsy. And the vacuum outside didn't carry any sound, but some of the hull and air inside did. The reports were muted by the dampers, the noise almost like a thick sheet of canvas being ripped. Every tenth round was a tracer, and the guns fired so rapidly that there seemed to be a continuous line of colorful fire splashing against the incoming hopper. The fire computer had it all figured out: the target's speed, the gravity, the velocity of the incredibly hard uranium slugs that hammered the hopper. It couldn't miss.

It didn't miss.

The hopper's armor wasn't enough. The machine-gun fire punched through it. Wilks could see sparks as bullets hit the plating, sparks that blossomed as air from within spewed out and fed the tiny fires.

The tracers raked the ship, found the engine, smashed through and destroyed it. The hopper lost power, tumbled, out of control. Fell in the low gravity, a ruined and discarded toy from the hand of a bored child.

"God," Billie said.

Wilks watched. No escape pods popped out. It was almost too easy. See you in hell, Spears.

"Sir, the drone is drawing fire!"
Spears nodded, pleased. "Set your fire control to backwalk the attacking battery."
"We'll have to drop the stealth suit to use our targeting systems."
"That doesn't matter. We've got the drop on them. Punch them out."
The pilot and copilot hurried to obey.
Got to be Powell behind this, Spears thought. I wouldn't have guessed that you had the guts, you little no-dick bastard. But if you want to play with the best, you have got to be a lot sharper than a chickenshit ambush, Major. I am going to hand-feed you to the queen myself when I get down.

The hopper went down, streaming oxy-fed flames that winked out quickly in the vac. The ship hit, bounced high, hit again, shattered, and sent pieces flying. The light gravity let most of the debris sail quite a distance. Those chunks that entered the station's faux grav fell faster, bounced lower. The tracking cam stayed with the largest section. Wilks didn't see any bodies but he supposed they were all cocooned into their seats. Just as well. The sight of a ruined human body tumbling across the landscape wasn't one he particularly wanted to see anyhow.
Adios, General.
SECOND TARGET ACQUIRED, the computer flashed. OPTIMUM DISTANCE MINUS ONE THOUSAND METERS. COMMENCING FIRE.

Wilks jumped. Stared at the screen. It took a second to register, a second they didn't have to spare.

"Fuck! Close your helmet! Move! We've got to get out of here, now!"

He slapped his own faceplate shut, grabbed Billie's hand, and jerked her up. They scrambled for the exit. He hit the emergency hatch control, both locks snapped up.

They leapt for the opening as the first slugs began to punch holes in the crawler.

17

Spears watched the hard metal teeth of his machine guns chew the crawler to pieces. He felt a certain satisfaction in knowing he had outsmarted his enemy, had not fallen into the trap. Had not been outsmarted.

The crawler shuddered under the impact, vibrating, shaking. They were close enough so the combat belly cam picked up the two troopers abandoning the landcraft, running away from the doomed vessel.

"Cut them down," Spears said. If he'd thought about it longer, he might not have given that order, the new troops always needed unspoiled containers and food, but once an order was given, he was not a man to belay it unless he had good reason. Canceling orders given in the midst of combat reflected badly on a commander; it made him look indecisive. Nor did it matter that these men wouldn't be around to remember these orders much longer—Spears was not an indecisive man.

The crawler continued its bullet-driven dance, and the two troopers kept sprinting. "Was I unclear in my speech?" Spears said, his voice cool and tight.

"N-no, sir. But the computer is locked on the crawler. I'll have to reset it for human targets."

"Do so."

"Sir."

The pilot's hands fluttered. The machine guns whined on their hydraulic gyros, began to alter their aim.

Too late. The fleeing pair achieved the safety of the station, disappearing from view.

"Sorry, sir."

"Never mind. The crawler is dead, that was the primary threat. Hose down the other craft on the apron."

"Sir—?"

"Destroy them. We don't want to get shot in the back and we do want the only operating vehicles out here."

The pilot nodded. "Yes, sir."

One of the rules of combat was to do your enemy enough damage so he couldn't recover in time to damage you. Spears had control of the airspace and he intended to keep it. And while Powell might think he had the station buttoned up, there were ways inside that he didn't know about. A wise officer never let himself be caught without an entrance or an exit. Powell was not wise. Spears was.

•   •   •

Billie's breath came hard, the suit's tanks hadn't been designed to supply so much oxygen so quickly. But they were inside, and safe. For now.

Wilks was already halfway out of his climate suit, rushing toward a com mounted on the lock wall. He slapped the com.

"This is Wilks. We've got a fubar here, Powell. Spears sent in a decoy hopper. He's taken out our crawler, we're in the South Lock. Billie, what's going on out there?"

Billie moved to the lock, triggered the observation cam next to it. The little holoproj lit up. Dust puffed up in little spurts around the various vessels sitting on the ground. An occasional spark glittered on the craft, and as she watched, one of the hoppers canted wildly to one side, the support struts suddenly collapsed.

Billie turned back toward Wilks. "They're shooting up all the hoppers and crawlers," she said.

"You get that?" Wilks said into the com.

Powell's voice when it came through the speaker was nervous: "God. What are we going to do? He could peel open the station like a banana!"

"He won't," Wilks said. "He doesn't want to risk damaging the aliens. But he'll have an attack plan figured out. We underestimated him. If he knew enough to give us a decoy to shoot at, he'll know a way in we aren't expecting. Get whatever troops you can trust with weapons armed, fast, get a combat opchan working and cover every lock. And get anybody who might be loyal to Spears into a secured area PDQ."

Powell said, "That won't be easy, we can't be sure—"

"Listen, Major, we damn well *can* be sure that if somebody opens a door and lets Spears in we will be in very deep shit. Don't take any chances. If there is any doubt about a trooper's loyalty to you, put him behind a thick door."

"All right. I understand."

"I'll meet you in Command Center in five minutes."

Wilks turned to Billie. "The general is knocking out our ability to fight him in the air, or escape on the surface. He'll be occupied with that for a while. Come on."

"Where are we going?"

"Powell can issue the orders but he isn't a combat soldier. He is going to need somebody he can trust telling him what to do. I fucked up once, we can't afford to let that happen again."

"How bad is it?" she asked.

"It could be worse. We've got the high ground. Spears can spend all his troops at one spot and we've got to cover every entrance, so we'll be thin, but he's got to come in through a lock and we can watch all of them. As long as it's our troops on the doors, we should be able to keep him out. Powell will be scrambling the entrance codes and putting the station on full alert, soon as he gets the general's men dogged down. Odds are still in our favor, though I should have had Powell set this all up before we tried to pot Spears. I thought sure we could knock him down. I guess that's why he's a general and I'm a sergeant. Come on."

They ran.

•   •   •

"Status?" Spears said. His blood was up, he felt like a hunter tracking dangerous prey. There was some risk, to be sure, but no doubt that he would win in the end. Whatever the cost.

"Sir, all of the exterior landcraft and aircraft have been immobilized. All engines appear to be dysfunctional, power mains knocked out."

Spears nodded. "Good." Of course, there were the starships inside the base, but nobody was going to use those for flitting around on the planetoid's surface. And if Powell planned to run in the star transports, he had a big surprise coming. Spears had never bothered locking the crawlers and hoppers into his personal keycode—there wasn't anywhere to run *to* on the planetoid—but the offworld vessels wouldn't lift a centimeter unless he okayed it. No, Powell and his little band of insurrectionists weren't going anywhere. They were bottled up in the station and while they might think they had the edge, they were also mistaken about that.

"Put us down at these coordinates," Spears said. He rattled off the grid numbers. Without asking why, the pilot obeyed. There was a blind spot just east of the North Lock, a corridor not much wider than twenty meters that led right to the fusion plant's heat sinks. The big aluminum and ceramic plates could be used to radiate excess warmth away from the station, did there happen to be an overload the environmental pipes couldn't handle. A careful platoon could march along that no-cam corridor to the sinks, then duck the security scanners and go in either direction. Nobody would see them approach a lock; nobody would know company was coming until they knocked on the door.

True, the doors would all be scramble-secured and guarded, if Powell had any brains at all, but Spears had an answer for that.

Another big surprise for the mutineers.

No, there wasn't any doubt as to the victory. The main thing now was to do it clean, by the numbers. A hundred years from now they would be teaching tactics based on scenarios that Spears created. Might as well begin dazzling the future now.

Powell looked as if he were about to try to climb a wall, Billie thought, watching the man pace. His hands shook, he was pale, sweat beaded at his hairline and on his upper lip. There were a dozen carbines side by side on a table in the room, with boxes of magazines stacked next to them. While Wilks went to talk to Powell, Billie moved toward the weapons. Whatever happened, she wasn't going to be standing by helplessly.

A trooper with a carbine slung across his chest and held ready started to swing his weapon around as Billie approached.

"Wilks," Billie said.

Wilks turned away from Powell. "Let her have one," he said to the trooper.

The man didn't even glance at Powell for confirmation. He knew who was in charge, whatever the ranks involved. He nodded.

Billie picked up a carbine, racked the action, checked it over—the gun was empty—then pulled a magazine from an open box and loaded it into the piece. She took three more hundred-round AP mags from the box and put them into her pockets, one under her belt. With four hundred shots, she could theoretically kill a whole lot of things, if they didn't get her first. She slung the weapon over her shoulder. She felt a little better, now that she was armed.

Wilks and Powell went back and forth; it was easy to see that Powell was scared shitless. He was a man of peace, Wilks had told her, should have been a preacher or a medic and not a soldier. Civilized men didn't make very good warriors.

Billie moved to a wall-mounted com. Told the routing computer to connect her with Mitch.

"Bueller here."

There was no visual, Billie didn't know if that was on purpose or not, but he obviously couldn't see her.

"Mitch," she said.

"Billie. You okay?"

"I'm with Wilks in the Command Center," she said. "We're fine."

"I saw you escape from the crawler," he said. "I was worried about you."

"No problem. What are you doing there?"

"I'm going to stay in Environment Control until we are certain of a stable situation. If Spears or his troops get inside, I might be able to do some good here, shut down air or heating or lights and slow them up some. I wouldn't do much good on the line."

Billie nodded, realized he couldn't see that, said, "I understand." And she did. Wilks had told her that the APs designed for the run to the aliens' homeworld were crack marines, able to outshoot, outrun, and outfight ordinary men in virtually every combat scenario. The problem was that Mitch's conditioning, Asimov's Modified Laws, wouldn't allow him to kill humans. Unless he was certain a wound wouldn't do that, he couldn't shoot a man, even though he could put a bullet into one virtually anywhere he chose at combat ranges. A man might bleed to death from a shattered foot, after all, and androids weren't allowed to risk that. Except, of course, for those who had been built without the Laws inculcated into them. Which was supposed to be impossible, though Billie knew better. Most of the pirates who'd attacked them on that fucked-up mission had been such androids, able to kill.

"Listen, Mitch, when this is all over, we need to sit down and talk. I haven't been treating you very well, I don't understand everything about it, but I want to do better."

"Thank you, Billie. You don't know how glad I am to hear that."

"No guarantees," she said. "I mean, I don't know what exactly is going to come of it."

"Anything is better than nothing," he said.

She felt uncomfortable. She was still pissed at him, but the idea of dying or of his dying didn't feel good. Not at all. "Okay, listen, I've got to discom. I'll talk to you later."

"You be very careful," he said. "I don't want anything to happen to you. I—I—"

"Don't say it, Mitch. Not yet."

She shut the com down.

Behind her, Wilks and Powell had begun yelling at each other.

"Listen," Wilks said, his voice hard, "get the fucking locks covered! Weld them shut, especially the cargo doors! You don't know what kind of code-

breaking gear Spears might have. He might have
access to the mainframe from out there."

"Impossible, the system is shielded, the internal
modems are hardened—"

"Dammit, Powell, this man is a soldier, career
military, and he suckered us once. If he gets inside
and starts blasting, a lot of people are going to die.
You didn't know about the second hopper, did
you?"

Powell's jaw was set tight, his lips thinned and
white, but he shook his head. "No."

"You can tape it that he's got something else up
his sleeve. We're self-sufficient here, all he's got
outside is field rations and gear. If we can keep him
outside long enough, we win."

Powell blew out a short breath. "All right. I'll give
the order."

Wilks nodded. Looked at Billie. Billie didn't know
much about military matters, but it seemed as if
the next move was up to Spears. She didn't like
that very much. The man was crazy. There was no
telling what he was going to do. All they could do
was wait.

In his C-suit, Spears led his platoon along the
wall under the sinks toward the East Lock. The
traitors would have lost the hopper when it veered
north and would probably be expecting an attack
from that quarter. True, they probably could have
gone in at the North Lock as easily as the East,
once the fifth column struck, but Spears was
thinking about posterity now. If he could finish this
without losing too many of his troops, it would look

better to one viewing historical tapes. What an amazing commander, they would say. How adept.

Spears nodded to himself as he reached the hiding spot next to the East Lock. Nobody knew they were here. He had his demolitions expert set the explosive charges on the lock door itself, stressing great care, using only hand signals and helmet-to-helmet conduction, all radios were off.

The charges set, his men in readiness, Powell pulled the special transmitter from his tool belt and looked at the covered button. He had not expected it would ever really come to this, but no man would ever be able to say that General Thomas A.W. Spears had been caught with his pants down in this combatsit.

He flipped the button cover up with his gloved thumb and pressed the control once, hard. Grinned behind his faceplate. Powell and his little band of would-be heroes were about to have something to worry about in there.

Yes, sir, right now, the security door to the queen's chamber would be sliding up, along with the protective covers holding twenty-five of the drones captive.

And a tiny holographic image of Spears would be standing behind the queen, waving a torch in his hand, urging her out of her chamber.

Spears chuckled, imagining the queen's surprise. And Powell's surprise, too.

"Dinnertime," Spears said. "Come and get it."

18

"**M**other*fucker*!" a man screamed. Gunfire rattled.

In the CC, Wilks said, "Powell—?"

"It's the guard at the queen's chamber," Powell said, touching controls on the monitor. The picture splashed into life in full color, the holoproj of the security cam revealing the guard firing his weapon at something offscreen.

Powell fiddled with the controls; the view shifted slightly. Revealed the open door.

"Oh, man!" Wilks said.

The guard screamed again. The man who had been so nasty to Wilks and Billie when they'd gone to see the chamber.

A spiked tail shot into sight, impaled the screaming trooper, punched through his chest as easily as a needle pierces thin cloth. The man went slack, his weapon falling. The massive ridged tail snapped like a whip and the man flew out of the frame.

"Sweet baby Jesus," Powell said.

"He's turned the queen loose," Wilks said. "Spears."

Other reports began flooding in over the op-chan.

The queen had company.

"Get to the starships," Wilks said, his face grim. "This base is contaminated. We're all dead if we stay here." But at least the son of a bitch's plan was also shot. He'd play hell rounding up the monsters with the men he had left.

Five minutes after the queen and her brood were set free and encouraged to kill anything in their way, Spears nodded, and the demolitions man blew the hatch. The shaped charge was silent in the absence of air, but the metal of the lock peeled open and the oxy inside spewed out, freezing into powdery white crystals in the cold night.

"Go!"

Guards inside began firing, the ones who hadn't been knocked sprawling by the concussion, at least. Spears's men had the advantage of surprise, however, and only one of his troops went down before the lock was secured. They were in, the enemy was in disarray, and this mission was going as well as anybody could expect. All the feeds from his men were going into the hopper's recorder. He would edit them later, for the sake of continuity, of course. He would look heroic enough; after all, he wasn't an armchair commander, and the record would show him right in the thick of things.

And he wasn't done yet, oh, no. Those who had crossed him would regret it, assuming they lived long enough for that thought.

Inside the inner lock, he motioned for his troops to open their faceplates. "Let's move," he said. "Keep your suits patent, they'll probably try to mess with life support. Go to opchan six, scrambled. No point in radio silence now they know we're here." With that, he snapped his own faceplate shut. "Try to keep some of them alive," he said. "Shoot low."

Wilks ran, carbine held ready to fire, Billie and Powell right behind him. The station's battle alarm screeched, a high-low *wee-wanh* that repeated itself over and over. Red lights flashed at every turning of the hallway, and men and women ran in panic, fleeing something most of them knew about but hadn't encountered yet.

Most of the ones who'd encountered the aliens would likely be unable to flee, Wilks knew. Spears had let the goddamned things out, somehow, and they would be in a feeding frenzy, collecting every human they could get their claws on, given what he knew about them.

Billie had found a portable com and was using it. "Mitch! Mitch, answer me! Get out of there, meet us at the ship bay! The aliens are loose! Spears is in the station! Mitch!"

If Bueller heard her, he wasn't responding. Wilks didn't have time to worry about it at the moment.

An alien lurched out into the hallway from an open door, turned toward the three of them, and opened those hellish jaws. Slime dripped from the teeth in long strings.

"Fuck you," Wilks said. He popped the carbine up, found the manual front sight—no time to mess with the laser—and fired a quick burst.

The armor-piercing rounds smashed the alien's face, shards of its hard chitin flew, acid sprayed. It fell sideways and backward, hit the wall, slid to the floor.

The blast of the caseless rounds hit Wilks's ears like a flat slap from a heavy hand. His ears rang. Damn. Should have put his plugs in. Oh, well. If he lived long enough to worry about growing deaf in his old age, he could deal with that.

The liquid on the floor bubbled and sent up clouds of stinking smoke as it ate through the treadplate.

"Watch the blood, don't step in it!"

They ran.

A trooper came around the corner with his weapon up. Spears was the first one to see him. He drew his pistol, brought it up and smacked his gun-hand into the waiting palm of his other hand, hit a classic isosceles stance and fired three times. The technique was called the Mozambique Double Tap, the name having to do with some ancient police action in some African country before space travel. It was a standard pistol procedure: two in the heart, one in the head, always in that order. Spears guessed that it dated from a time when body armor was sometimes hidden under regular clothing and to make certain of a kill, a backup shot was taken at an unprotected target.

The unfortunate trooper wasn't wearing armor,

so any of the three shots would have been sufficient to kill him.

As the man fell, Spears felt that sense of
triumph, that rush of *survival* he always got whenever he killed somebody one-on-one. It brought
back old memories. All the way from when he'd
been a boy and had taken out his first opponent
ever—

Tommy hid in the supply closet, among the
brooms and vacuum cleaners and fragrant tubs of
cleaneze. The granular cleaning compound made
his nose itch, made him want to sneeze, but he
pinched his nostrils shut so he wouldn't.

Outside the dark closet, Jerico Axe prowled the
dim hall, looking for Tommy. It was past quench-
light, everybody was supposed to be asleep, the
adult marines and medicos would be in bed by
now, but not Jerico.

Jerico was a stupid asshole, Tommy knew, but he
was a big stupid asshole and he was mean. Tommy
had gotten on Jerico's shit list, he didn't know how,
and now every time the bastard saw him out of an
adult's sight, he would proceed to kick Tommy's
ass. Not that Tommy didn't fight back, he did, but
Jerico had been decanted first, he was older, ten
kilos heavier, and six months ahead of Tommy in
martial arts skills. Tommy got in a few licks now
and then, he'd broken the cocksucker's nose once,
but that had cost a broken arm of his own, plus two
teeth had to be reimplanted and fifteen staples
over his left eye.

What Tommy wished was that Jerico would take
a hike along the Deep Rim and trip, bouncing all

the way to the bottom where he'd rot in the hot sun and not be found until the carrion birds were finished with him.

Might as well wish for a commission while you're at it, dickhead, he told himself. Jerico wasn't that stupid.

Tommy sat in the closet, hoping Jerico wouldn't think to look for him in here. He was tired, he wanted to go to bed, to get some rest before drill at dawn, but here he was having to hide to keep from getting pounded.

Bare feet slapped the floor outside the closet. Jerico had taken his boots off, but he still lumbered like a broken robot, making plenty of noise. Tommy heard the bathroom door creak as the thug went to look for him in there.

Shit. He would look in here, too. There was no real place to hide, unless he wanted to climb into the cleaneze bag mounted on the roller bin. Sure, if he dug down through the dirty cleaner, crouched real low and buried himself in it, Jerico wouldn't see him.

Tommy stood, started to put one leg over the rim of the bag, then stopped. Abruptly a rage filled him, a hot anger that bubbled up through his legs and groin, flooded into his chest, swirled fluidly into his skull.

Fuck this!

It wasn't right! He shouldn't have to hide from dicklick Jerico Axe, just because he was bigger and stronger and better trained than Tommy. It wasn't right.

With only the glows coming from the instrument panels of the cleaning bot parked next to the door,

the room was dark, but there was just enough light
for Tommy to see the baseboard scraper mounted
in the bot's accessory rack. It was a little over half
a meter long, an aluminum rod nearly as thick as
Tommy's wrist, connected to a dull blade set at an
angle. The bot used the tool to clean the grit from
the baseboards, it looked kind of like a garden hoe
somebody had bent crooked.

Tommy peeled the scraper from the bot's rack.
Hefted it. It was fairly heavy.

When Jerico opened the door, Tommy was ready.

The larger boy had time to blink, his eyes going
wide, as Tommy jumped and buried the blunt corner of the blade in Jerico's skull. Hit him just over
the right eye. It made a satisfying *chunk!*

Jerico screamed—that was nice, too—and stumbled backward across the hall until his back
smacked into the far wall. He slid down, tugged the
scraper from his head, moaned as the blood poured
into his eye. He looked up at Tommy, stunned, as if
he couldn't understand what had happened.

Tommy moved toward Jerico. "Here, gimme
that," he said. He grabbed the scraper. Jerico let it
go. What he thought, Tommy didn't know, but the
fear he had felt, the shame of being afraid, his
rage, all combined into something he'd never felt
before. He felt a great strength now, a power, at
having defeated his enemy.

"I'm bleeding!"

"Not for long," Tommy said.

He raised the scraper again and moved in.

Tommy Spears was nine years old the night he
killed his first enemy—

• • • •

"Holy shit!" one of Spears's marines yelled.

The general snapped out of his memory fugue and looked past the fallen soldier. Amazing. The entire memory had flashed past, maybe five seconds in realtime, all jammed and compressed like a squeezed data file on a modem squirt.

One of the alien drones stood there, readying itself to attack.

Spears stepped forward so an overhead light shone directly down on his face. Saw the alien see him.

"You know who I am," he said. He pulled a control from his belt. "And the queen knows what this is." He waved the transmitter. The floor of the egg room was wired with explosives and this control would set them off. Spears had made sure the queen knew that. Of course, by now, she would have her drones hauling the eggs out, hoping to find a safer place for them, but she wouldn't have had time to move them all yet, and besides *that*, she couldn't know if Spears had wired the whole fucking station so he could blow it all into orbit.

What the drones saw, the queen knew.

The drone hissed, then turned and ran the opposite way.

"Holy shit," the trooper said again. "It was *scared* of you!"

"Damn straight," Spears said. "With good reason. Let's go."

The platoon never hesitated.

"Powell?"

"This way," the major said.

Wilks turned to look at her. "I'm fine," Billie
said, though she was out of breath. "But Mitch—"

"—tastes bad," Wilks said. "If he stands still,
they'll walk right past him."

"Spears won't," Powell said.

"Thank you, Major." To Billie, he said, "Look, he
knows where we're going, he'll do what he can to
make sure we make it and then he'll be along."

"I can't leave him here," Billie said.

"Fine. We'll wait for him. I promise."

Billie nodded. It would have to do. She didn't
have a lot of choice. She would have to trust Wilks.

Somebody screamed behind them, a sound that
trailed off into a liquid gurgle.

"The clock is running, folks."

It seemed to Billie that she had been running
most of her life. This was not the time nor the
place to stop and take stock. "Go," she said. "I'm
right behind you."

They went.

19

Wilks was not afraid to die. He ran toward what he considered the safest place on this tiny planet, but if he didn't make it, well, too bad. He'd been living on borrowed time since his first meeting with the aliens, so long ago. What had it been? Twelve, fourteen standard years? Billie had been ten, he'd have to ask her how old she was now. He should have died with his squad then, but he hadn't, and he'd spent a great deal of drink and chem trying to forget it. Fate hadn't wanted that, the powers-that-be in the universe, not to mention the Colonial Marines, had thrown it all back into his face. Somewhere along the way he had come up with a new purpose: to wipe the aliens out, down to the last drone, the last egg. Getting himself killed here would prevent him from accomplishing his mission, and *that* bothered him more than dying. Once in his life there had been personal fear, but those days were long gone.

A few years back during one of his two-week chem binges, Wilks had been picked up in an alley by civilians. He was naked and his ID implants had been fuzzed by the people who'd robbed and then tried to kill him, to keep the authorities from identifying the body. Not knowing he was military, the civilians had stuck him into a medicenter and given him the standard life-support treatment, which included sessions with psychiatric types. It had been a teaching hospital and there were plenty of young medics eager to work with such an obviously depressed patient; surely that unrevised scar on his face bespoke worlds of mental impairment?

It didn't take long for them to peg him as a career marine and diagnose his problem. But while waiting for the medical MPs to come and fetch him, they hustled to get as many budding headbenders as they could exposed to him. Chances like this didn't come along very often.

In one of these sessions, with an attractive young woman he would have tried to bed under other circumstances, he first heard about the Doc Holliday Syndrome.

Holliday, it seemed, had been some kind of medical man in the Terran frontier times, a dentist or some such. He developed a fatal and, at the time, incurable illness.

"So," the young doctor said, "he packed up, moved to a drier climate, which was supposed to offer some symptomatic comfort for his remaining days, and became a professional gambler and outlaw. He engaged in a number of gunfights, and although he wasn't a particularly adept shooter, always managed to prevail over his opponents. There is an instance, for example, where M. Holliday fired upon a man inside a public drinking establishment using a period weapon called a six-shooter. He was within seven meters of his opponent, emptied his weapon, and missed entirely. Given that the six-shooter was supposedly accurate to a range of fifty meters in the hand of an expert, this was considered poor marksmanship. He later switched to a weapon called a shotgun, which, I am informed, is dangerous over a somewhat wider area."

"How interesting," Wilks told the young shrink. Maybe he *would* try to fuck her, if for no other reason than to shut her up.

Before he could speak, however, she continued, obviously in love with the sound of her own voice. "From what our medico-historical researchers can determine, the primary reason Holliday won his duels was because he did not care if he did."

That brought a frown to Wilks's face. "What does that mean?" He was immediately sorry he had asked.

"M. Holliday was going to die soon, or so he thought. Actually he lived well beyond his predicted termination, the diagnosis having been somewhat erroneous. But because he *thought* his days were numbered and that this number was very small, he believed he had nothing to lose. Whenever he faced somebody in a duel—they called them shootdowns or showdowns or some such testosteronic euphemistic nonsense—he had no fear of dying. He was, in his own mind, already dead. Further, he regularly imbibed large amounts of alcoholic beverages and was thus further anesthetized. While this doubtless impaired his physical responses vis-à-vis his reaction time and weapons' prowess, these things in fact gave him a psychological edge. Most of the people he faced in such duels did *not* wish to die and thus their fear often caused them to hesitate or behave in a panicky manner. Against an opponent who sincerely did not care if he lived or died but whose only goal was to shoot them and be damned, such fears can be fatal. And apparently these encounters were fatal more often than not against M. Holliday, D.D.S."

Wilks shook his head. He wondered if she talked like that when she came. "Wonderful. You want to take off your clothes and screw a war hero before they come to get me?"

The young woman smiled, unfazed by his crude invitation. "I think not, Corporal Wilks. It would hardly be professional . . ."

Running down a corridor with alien monsters searching for him, Wilks grinned, the scar on his face doubtless making the expression hideous to see. I know just how you felt, Doc. When you live on borrowed time and don't give a dog's dick if you die, it makes things nice and simple.

Billie saw a man holding a carbine squatting behind a bulkhead extrusion, trying to hide. When he saw her spot him, he started to point his weapon at them.

"Wilks!" she yelled. She brought her own carbine around to cover the trooper.

"Don't do it, marine!" Powell called out.

But the trooper was rising, still swinging his piece toward them. "The general is back! You're all dead meat!"

Billie and Wilks fired at about the same time. The trooper did a twisting jig as he fell, his chest blown open, his blood splattering the wall.

Billie felt sick. Killing people never got any easier. But she kept moving. Self-preservation ruled.

Somebody had killed the lights and life support in the corridor but Spears was prepared for that. His troops were suited, in full combat gear. "Go to spookeyes, marines," he ordered. He clicked his own faceplate filters into Amplite mode, saw the corridor light up a ghostly green. Another control flicked on his lamps and the glow that would look a dim and almost invisible violet to unaided eyes splashed the walls with brilliant green, almost as bright as the normal overheads. "Stay sharp, troops! Overlapping fields of fire!"

Somebody stumbled into view twenty meters ahead. Spears saw the man waving his arms, heard him call out: "General! Is that you? Don't shoot, I'm on your side!" He couldn't see much, Spears could tell that, he wore station coveralls, didn't have a weapon or vision augmenters.

"Fire," Spears commanded.

The two marines running point opened up. The sounds were muted but audible. The man ahead fell as if his legs had disappeared. Many inside the station would be his allies but Spears couldn't take time now to worry about loyalties. One enemy with a grenade could cause a lot of damage. Better to clear the halls first and sort things out later.

Abruptly the gravity shut off. There was no warning, merely a sudden cessation. The running marines bounded high into the air, slammed into the walls or ceiling, or tumbled along the floor, out of control. Switching from nearly a full gee to a tenth or less between steps was not something a man could realistically train for.

"Switch on your boots!" Spears yelled.

There were magnetic strips under the floors, put there for just such a failure, and the combat boots would allow walking, albeit a much slower pace than in normal gravity.

When the confusion settled down, along with the troopers, only one man had been injured too badly to continue. The platoon medic said he'd broken his neck and would need full rehab.

"Can he move?"

"No, sir. He's paralyzed."

"Leave him, then. Somebody will come for him later."

Some *thing*, actually, Spears figured. The man was useless as a soldier now, save as fodder for the new troops. Might as well let them have him.

"Sir!" the wounded man cried out. "Please. Don't leave me here for those things!"

"They also serve who lie and wait," Spears said. "It's war, son. You fucked up, you pay for it. Let's move, troops."

They shuffled along, boots clumping on the deck. The cries of the injured man stopped when Spears had his unit switch radio freaks to opchan three.

Powell listened to the com he carried, shook his head. He and Billie and Wilks were in the ap-

proach corridor leading to the starship hangars.
They still had lights and power, though much of
the station had apparently been shut down. Panicky reports came over the com, voices blending
into a continuous and frightened walla:

"Life support shut down in D-2—!"

"It got Maury, it just took him—!"

"Air doors are down, air doors down—!"

"—are under fire, somebody is shooting here—!"

"Monsters, monsters—ahh, get away—!"

The sound of explosions, gunfire, metal on
metal, and other sounds of death and confusion
came, too.

For a moment Wilks felt himself grow heavier, as
if somebody had suddenly put a weight on his back.
Then the feeling vanished.

"Wilks?"

"Somebody is fiddling with the gravity," he said.
"Bueller, trying to slow Spears down, or throw the
aliens off stride, probably."

Powell was on the edge of full-blown panic himself, Wilks could see that. His face was pale, sweaty,
and he clutched at the com as if it were some kind
of lifeline. "The base is overrun," he said. "We're
fucked. I should have known better than to try
Spears. He's a killer. He's a madman. We're all
doomed."

"Listen," Wilks said, as if talking to a buzzhead
recruit or a small child. "Listen, we can get away.
We'll take one of the starships."

Powell shook his head. "Can't. It takes too long to
program a launch. They'll get us. They'll get us."

"We'll run an old program," Wilks said. "Take
one of the ships back to where it came from."

"Not a good idea. They came from Earth. All of them."

"We'll fix the goddamned program along the way! Move, Powell!"

Powell stared at him. Nodded. "Okay. You're in charge now, okay?"

Poor sucker. He should have gone into another line of work. Powell should be drinking high tea at some university, talking with other professors about modern art or ancient history. Only thing was, without killers like Spears and, yeah, like me, there weren't ever gonna be such places again. Maybe not anyhow.

Ahead of them, a pair of aliens stepped out of the shadows and hissed.

Wilks felt himself grinning. Fuck you, he thought. Don't you know me? You're messing with Doc Holliday, you stupid bastards.

He slid over next to Billie, who saw the aliens. They stood shoulder to shoulder and raised their carbines.

It got noisy in the corridor.

"Let's go, Powell. Stay with us."

The trio moved toward the hangar entrance.

20

The hangar was still patent, at least no aliens had managed to get in. After the two in the hallway, Powell's command override had admitted the trio through the lock without any other problems.

The vast space of the hangar was quiet, it seemed empty. If there had been work crews inside when the alert sounded, they were not around now.

"Which ship is the easiest to access?" Wilks asked. "Which one most likely to be fueled and spaceworthy?"

"Over there," Powell said. He pointed.

There might be other vessels elsewhere, but this particular hangar held four star hoppers, including the robot ship in which Wilks, Billie, and Bueller had arrived. Wilks was glad that the one Powell had indicated was not *The American*; he would prefer something with a little more human comfort designed into it. Then again, any port in a storm was a pretty good philosophy, and between Spears and the aliens, this place wasn't just a storm, it was a hurricane.

"All aboard," Wilks said. He waved his carbine at the ship.

The base was a wreck. Spears and his unit moved through the chaos, shooting whatever got in their way. Mostly, the targets were people; they did chop down a couple of the drones who were too slow on the uptake. What the hell, he thought, he was improving the gene pool. Attacking him was a nonsurvival characteristic, for certain.

There were few things to be salvaged here. He was going to have to cut his losses. True, he was going to win the battle and the war, pitiful and short as it was, but it would mean the base itself was a loss. Well. A good commander knew when to dig in or when to dump his tanks and leave the party. Third Base had served its purpose. He would have liked a little more time, but then, that was nearly always the case with commanders, wasn't it? You tried for perfect but you accepted what you had to and moved on. When the battle was joined, you had to deal with what *was*, not what you *wished* it was. In a perfect galaxy, you'd always have the troops and matériel you needed to wage the best battle plan. In this galaxy, it seldom happened.

The unit had lost a couple more troopers, one to gunfire, another to a booby trap, but it was moving well. The vault where Spears had his best drones stored, the cream of the crop so far, would be impervious to anything short of a nuke and only he had the key that would open the vault. Those being safe, the only other thing of value on this rock was the way off it. And he had that covered, too. It would be a poor general indeed who didn't keep his line of retreat open. Spears was not a poor general.

He led his troops toward the starship hangars.

Billie was beyond fear by now, her adrenaline surge no more than a trickle, just enough to keep her alert. It was odd to think that you could get used to something like this, but it seemed to be happening. Or maybe she was finally losing her mind. She was too tired to care which it was.

Next to her, Wilks said, "Well?"

He was talking to Powell, who frowned at the control unit he held. Powell tapped in a series of numbers on the small device, then looked at the ship the three of them stood in front of.

"The hatch isn't opening," Powell said.

"I can see that. Why not?"

Powell shook his head. "I don't know. This is the Command Override, it's supposed to open every lock in the base, right down to the beer coolers in the kitchen. It's the one Spears carries when he's here, it stays with whoever is the CO in the station. It has worked so far. It should work here."

"Are you sure you entered the correct code?" Billie said.

"Yes. I'm sure."

Wilks sighed. "Spears. He's fucked us again. We should have guessed it. As paranoid as he is, he wouldn't trust anybody with the ships if he wasn't around. We'll have to run a bypass."

"That'll take time," Powell said. "The access panel is armored."

"I don't see we have much of a choice," Wilks said.

Spears and his troops reached the outer hangar via the emergency escape tunnel he'd had built. The two transports in the huge room stood silent. He had half his platoon fan out and take up guard positions, but there was no need. They were alone. He almost felt sorry for the enemy. So outclassed. Powell never really had a chance.

"Okay, the rest of you with me to the inner hangar."

They moved down the interlink.

"I think that's got it," Wilks said.

The access panel for the hatch control had to be burned open, but once that was done, the circuits were fairly easy to reroute. Wilks bypassed the electronics entirely, shut off the power to the hatch, and used the manual crank to begin winding the hatch up. He had a fifteen-centimeter gap opened at the bottom when he heard the voice:

"Freeze frame it!"

Wilks turned to look, saw half a dozen marines in climate suits and full battle gear pointing their weapons at them. He spared a quick glance for Billie, and understanding passed between them. Better to go down shooting than to be fed to the aliens. "Good-bye, Billie," Wilks whispered. "Sorry."

He leapt for his carbine where it leaned against

the ship, saw Billie swing her weapon up to firing position. Wilks waited for the impacts of the bullets that would kill him, knowing there was no way he could get to his own piece before the marines cut him to pieces but going to go out trying. Fuck it—!

A blinding white light smashed into Wilks and took him away. Odd, he hadn't expected it to be like that . . .

When Wilks came to, he was lying on his back next to Powell, Billie sprawled on the other side of the major. Wilks blinked, not understanding.

"Nice try, Sergeant," Spears said.

Wilks rolled onto his side, found himself facing Spears. Half a dozen troops backed him, each of them holding stockstiks, essentially riot batons wired to stun a victim into unconsciousness at a touch.

"Concussion charges," Spears said, answering Wilks's unspoken question. "Mounted in the locks of all the ships. You'd gotten that hatch up another five or six centimeters, they'd have gone off without me having to use this." He waved a small electronic device.

Wilks looked at Spears, his mind still fuzzy. There was something he was going to do. What—?

"No point in doing anything heroic, Sergeant," the general continued. "I'll just have you stunned. You don't get to die, yet."

Spears looked at Powell, who had yet to awaken. "I might have known dickless there wouldn't have the balls to try something like this on his own. Was that you in the crawler shooting at my decoy?"

Wilks managed a nod.

Spears returned the gesture. "Thought so. You get credit for trying, but you picked the wrong side. Too bad. I admire a man with guts, even if he's an enemy."

Billie moaned in her sleep.

"Win some, lose some," Spears said. He turned away. "All right, men. You know the drill. Get the cargo loaded, collect your gear. Sort out the prisoners and free the loyalists, I'll give you a list."

"What are you going to do?" Wilks said. His head hurt and he felt as if he were going to vomit, but he maintained, taking slow and deep breaths.

"Well, it doesn't really concern you anymore, now does it? But because you gave me a decent fight, I'll tell you. I'm going home, to Earth. I'll be taking a small corps of the aliens and we'll have ourselves a little sortie. Once I demonstrate how effective my troops are, we'll get support to build a full-scale army of trained aliens. We're going to kick ass, son, and when I show the recordings of how we did it to the powers-that-be, we'll get what we need to *win* this war."

Jesus. He really *believed* it. The guy was a few kilograms short of fission mass, crazy as a stepped-on roach.

"What about us?" That from Powell, who had managed to sit up.

"You and your allies are up for court-martial, Major. I don't have time to fool with such piddly shit now, so you'll stay here until I can send the appropriate legal teams back to handle it."

"You can't leave us here! There are aliens loose in the base! We'll be slaughtered, eaten!"

"You should have thought about that before you played at sedition, Major." He turned away and moved off.

Wilks made as if to stand, but two of the troopers stepped toward him, stun wands held ready. Wilks settled back. Jumping them would only get him another headache when he woke up in half an hour. If he woke up at all. Right now, it seemed a lot more important to stay awake. Whatever happened to them, he wanted to see it coming.

21

Mitch was on top of Billie, moving slowly and with great power, thrusting, filling her. Sweat beaded on his face and he held himself up with his arms, muscles corded in his triceps, connected to her only at the groin, the juncture of their sexes.

Naked, connected, they danced.

Billie had never felt so fulfilled, so complete, as a woman, as a human being. This was what she had always hoped for but never expected to have, someone who loved her, someone she could love in return, giving and receiving totally, becoming not less, but more than two—

Becoming one.

He moved faster, nearing his peak, and she moved with him. Yes. Yes. Yes, yes, yes!

He screamed.

Billie stared at his open mouth, saw the claw tear past his lips. But it did not reach for her, the taloned hand, it extended in a half circle on an arm too thick and long to have possibly come from Mitch's mouth, extended to his belly and tore into the skin and muscle, ripping him in two and hurling his top half away, leaving his hips and legs on her. White fluid spurted from the torn body, android blood the color of milk splashed over her in an obscene bath, hot, salty, even as he began to throb within her . . .

"No!"

Billie felt the pressure on her legs; she struggled to move from under the weight—

"Billie. It's me, Wilks. Wake up."

She blinked her way into consciousness. Her head ached, nausea filled her throat with a sour burning. Soldiers stood nearby, staring down at them from behind sealed faceplates, long rods held in their hands.

"Wilks?"

"Spears. We were hit with concussion grenades."

Billie didn't know what he was talking about. Where were they? The last thing she remembered, they were running. It seemed as if they had always been running.

"Billie."

"What?"

"Are you okay?"

Pieces of it came back to her. The aliens in the corridor. The ship door that wouldn't open. Men

with guns pointed at them, the unspoken decision
she and Wilks made together to fight.

"Yeah. I guess. What is going on?"

Powell, seated with his back to the wall, his
knees drawn up to his chest, said, "Spears is going
to load his tame monsters onto the largest transport ship and lift. He says he's going to Earth. We
get left here, along with all the other marines and
scientists."

"Hey, fuck that noise," one of the troopers standing next to them said. "*You* get left here with the
other traitors. Those of us who stuck by the general
are going with him."

Powell laughed, a sound on the edge of hysteria.
"Are you really that stupid, marine? He doesn't
need you anymore, you're excess baggage. You get
dumped."

"No way, Major," a second guard said. "Spears
takes care of his own."

"His own? Christ, he thinks he is fucking *God*,
you moron! You're nothing more than used toilet
tissue to Spears. You've served your purpose;
you're going to be flushed and compacted with the
rest of us."

The guards looked at each other. The leader, an
older sergeant Billie had talked to once, shook his
head. "Bottle it, boys. The major here is just trying
to divide and conquer. The general has taken care
of you so far, ain't he? Don't let this fubbie rattle
you. Didn't you hear the man tell you to pack your
gear soon as we get the traitors stocked away?"

The other five guards murmured. Billie thought
they still sounded unconvinced but it didn't seem

to matter. They weren't about to let the three of them go.

"Okay," the leader said. "Now that sleeping beauty is awake, let's move it, people."

Wilks got to his feet, helped Billie up. Two of the marines jerked Powell upright.

Billie saw Wilks gather himself. He was going to try to fight his way out. She didn't think he would make it, but she would follow his lead.

The lights went out.

"What the fuck—?" somebody yelled.

There was a zapping sound, like an electrical spark, and somebody moaned.

"Spookeyes," the sergeant in charge hollered. "Turn on your spookeyes!"

A long moment hung there, time suspended like a spider on a strand of glistening silk . . .

"Eyes on? Everybody see? Report!"

A chorus of assents.

"Nobody moves," the guard in charge said. "We're spookeyed and can see you like it was noon on the Equator."

The lights went back on, three times brighter than they had been before.

The soldiers screamed, almost with one voice. Their hands went up to slap against the closed faceplates. One trooper tore open the clear plate and dug at his eyes.

"What—?"

"Bueller!" Wilks yelled. He kicked one man in the belly, caught the baton he dropped before it hit the deck, whipped the stick against another man's throat. Even through the suit that must have hurt.

"Go, go! This way!"

Billie followed Wilks, Powell right behind her.

"What happened?!"

Wilks said, "They're blind. They got the hangar lights all of a sudden amplified a couple of million times by the spookeyes. Ordinary C-suits don't have blast shields in the faceplates; the military is too cheap to spend the money. It must have been like looking right at an atomic flash. Go!"

Once again, they ran.

Spears was personally overseeing the loading of the alien modules onto the transport truck from the vault when the frantic call came over the com.

"General, Powell and the other two have escaped!"

Spears felt a stab of irritation. He held it in check. "It doesn't matter. Penned up or running free, they are still going to be left here when we depart. Maintain watch, shoot them if you see them, but otherwise, let them hide."

After he discommed, Spears watched one of the modules picked up by the big hoop lifted and carefully stacked on the other modules on the truck. He was the only one who knew the access codes to the starships. Two of the vessels would be making the voyage in tandem, one with cargo, the second with but a single passenger—himself. The other starships would remain here. Terrible waste of matériel, but he couldn't worry about that. Sacrifices had to be made in war, be it flying stock or troops. A man who couldn't do the hot work didn't deserve to command. The engines of the ships that remained behind would be slag thirty seconds after

Spears departed. Whoever was left behind was going to stay behind, unless somebody came to take them off. And, given the unreasoning hunger the drone aliens had, it wasn't likely there'd be anybody left if anybody ever did show up here again.

He'd be taking the queen, of course, she was necessary to his plan. Control her and he controlled the drones. Some of the techbrains thought that a new queen could develop from a drone if there weren't any other queens around, but that wasn't likely here. The food supply on this mostly airless lump was pretty limited. The marines and scientists still alive wouldn't go a long way, unless the aliens had their own version of Jesus to do the loaves and fishes routine.

Spears smiled at that thought. The idea of the aliens with a messiah was funny. Then again, come to it, this group of creatures, of soldiers, might well consider *him* their messiah. It was true enough. He was going to lead them to a better world, to a kingdom of power and glory. Why wouldn't they think of him like that? Not that they did much thinking anyway, but then again, neither did human marines.

"Easy with that cargo," Spears said. "Don't want to hatch it before its time."

Not much longer. Too bad about the others at the air station, but that was how it went sometimes. The old adage about the best of battle plans not surviving the first engagement could apply here; still, it was a minor setback. Nothing a decent commander couldn't take in stride.

Spears grinned again. Soon as he lifted, he decided, he was going to smoke one of the special

cigars. Hell, he deserved it. He'd just won his first
battle in the war against the aliens. He'd still have
plenty to toke up once he won his first encounter
on Earth itself.

Yes, by God, he would.

"Now what?" Powell asked.

"Seems like I've been here before," Wilks said.

They were in an unused cargo area, empty cartons stacked in neat rows, forming a maze in which
they could stay lost for a little while, at least.

"We can run, but we can't hide," Wilks said.
"We've got to get off this planetoid or we're dead."

"How?"

"Spears will be taking the largest ship, my guess.
Maybe another one locked to it. We've got to find a
way to get onto one of the ships before he buttons
them up."

"How?" Powell said again.

"Do you know where the aliens he'll be taking
are stored?"

"A special vault, yes."

"Let's get to it."

"If anybody sees us—" Powell began.

"They'll shoot us?" Wilks finished. "Big fucking
deal, Major. Let's do it."

Spears rode with the first truckload of his precious cargo while his men continued to load the
next transporter. Nothing could go wrong at this
stage, he had to see to it personally. He had recap-
tured the queen easily enough, all he'd had to do
was find the place she was trying to hide her eggs
and wave a flamethrower at them. Once she was

caged, the wild aliens running around the base would calm down—at least until they realized she was gone. He had the walls of the queen's cage opaque so she wouldn't know where he was taking her until it was too late.

Everything was under control.

The vault was heavily guarded, the men loading the truck parked in front of the vault were heavily guarded, but the next empty truck fifty meters up the corridor had only the driver and two troopers sitting on it, doing nothing but waiting.

"That's it," Wilks said.

"That's what?" Powell said.

"Our ride. We can hide on that transporter, it'll take us straight to the ship Spears is using."

"You're crazy. We'll never make it."

"I'm open to a better idea."

Powell stared at him, then looked at Billie. She shook her head. "Wilks is pretty good at this stuff," she said. "He's saved us before. Whatever he says."

Wilks nodded at her.

"Okay. This is how I see it . . ."

Spears watched the containers being loaded onto the ship. All his plans were about to come to fruition. It was a glorious day for the Corps.

Billie, naked, stepped around the corner where the three men on the empty truck could see her.

"Jesus Christ," one of the men said. "Check this out."

Billie smiled, wet her fingertip with her tongue,

and touched her left nipple so it pebbled up and grew hard. Then she stepped back out of sight.

"Hey," one of the three troopers said, "wait up, honey!"

"You crazy?" the second marine said. "Spears will chew you a new asshole if he catches you gone!"

"It'll only take a minute," the first marine said.

"Spears—" the driver began.

"Fuck Spears," the first marine said.

"Nah," the second marine said, "I'm with you, I'd rather fuck her. Come on."

The two marines jogged toward where Billie had disappeared.

When they rounded the corner, they saw her standing there, legs spread wide, arms open, a big smile.

How could men be so stupid? she wondered. Did they really believe that a woman who'd never even *met* them would be so overcome with lust at the sight of them she'd strip to the skin and beckon to them, all wet and ready?

Apparently so. The two marines moved toward her, already dropping gear and untabbing their coveralls.

Wilks stepped out behind them and bopped each on the head with the wand he'd taken from the other guards. Both men fell, out before they hit the floor.

"Now we have guns and uniforms," Wilks said.

"Jesus, Wilks, are these the guys who have been protecting the civilized galaxy? No wonder the aliens are ahead."

Wilks grinned and shook his head. "What can I

say? If you can find the way to the test site, the galaxy's finest will let you join up. Get dressed."

"That was quick," the driver said when he saw the two marines approaching the truck five minutes later. "How was she?"

"I was great," Billie said, lifting her head and giving him a good view of her face.

The driver reached for his sidearm, but Wilks had his newly acquired carbine pointed at the man's heart. "You don't want to do that," he said. "Let's take a little walk."

Three minutes later, with Powell in the driver's clothing and the driver asleep and tied with the two marines in a closet down the corridor, the crew chief waved the empty truck into the loading area.

The chief knew Powell by sight, so the major kept his face more or less hidden. But the chief didn't know Wilks or Billie, they were just two more marines as far as he was concerned.

Spears watched the opaqued cage containing the queen being loaded. If the mother alien was upset, it didn't show, she was quiet inside the kleersteel box.

Once she was secured, Spears felt better. He spoke to a second lieutenant supervising the loading of the drones. "All right, once the last truck of cargo is loaded I want you to assemble the troops in B-hangar, gear packed and stacked and begin loading the *Grant*. I want every loyal marine onboard by 1600 hours, clear?"

The lieutenant's face brightened. "Yes, sir!"

"Carry on."

Spears walked toward his quarters. He had some items he wanted to pack himself. Once that was done, he would be ready. He smiled at the old adage he'd learned in his first tour. Once you leave a place, don't look back. There might be something there and it might be gaining on you. In this case there would certainly be something behind him, but it wasn't going to be following him, much less gaining. He was going to the glorious future; here was nothing but the dead past.

Victis honor, he thought. Let's hear it for the losers.

22

"What about Mitch?"

Wilks scanned the wide corridor as Powell drove the loaded truck, looking for somebody who might recognize them. So far, nothing.

"I don't know," Wilks said. "After that last stunt with the guards in the hangar, he'll have bailed out of the life-support control room—Spears would have sent troops to secure it. We're lucky he stuck around as long as he did."

"You promised we wouldn't leave him."

"Look, Billie, he's brighter than nine tenths of the troopers on this base and that probably includes me. He'll know we have to get off this planet. We don't know what Spears has in mind, exactly, but once he's lifted, whoever is left behind is history, probably pretty quick."

"We haven't seen any of the aliens lately," Billie said. "Maybe they're all dead."

"You don't believe that."

Powell cleared his throat. "Spears has probably gotten them back under control using the queen," he said.

"But Mitch—"

"Has got himself some dandy new metal legs and enough sense to know where they need to take him," Wilks finished. "He's probably hiding in one of the hangars already."

Billie fell silent. She wasn't sure how she felt but she didn't want to leave Mitch behind, that much she knew.

"We aren't going to just drive up to the ship, are we?" she said.

"I don't see why not. You keep your head down, nobody'll notice you. They're in a hurry, nobody is going to expect to see us driving the truck. We park, hop off, get lost in the shuffle."

"It seems unlikely."

"You don't know marines very well," Wilks said.

"He's right," Powell put in. "Everybody will be so nervous about screwing up and getting left behind they won't be working by the numbers."

Billie shook her head. She didn't think it would work but she didn't have any better ideas.

Pretty much everything material that Spears valued could be tucked into a single hardshell case. There was the pair of matched Smith & Wesson snub-nosed stainless-steel revolvers with custom wood grips, antiques that had belonged to a former South American tinpot dictator who'd set himself up as ruler on Lebanon II in the Khadaji System. Spears had pulled the weapons from the man's belt after he'd shot him in the head. Here were the carefully packed cigars, snug in their inert gas containers inside a padded plastic box. Next to the cigars, a reader and a small collection of read-only infoballs, military manuals and histories. A hologram of his basic training class on completion day. Probably most of them were dead by now. He had other things, of course, but nothing that couldn't be replaced. A soldier traveled best who traveled light, after all.

His packing done, Spears left his quarters and started for the ship. He did not look back.

Despite what he'd told Billie, Wilks was nervous. The hangar was huge and there was a lot of scurrying activity, but if something was gonna go wrong, it would be in the next few minutes. Well. A man did what he had to do and fuck the rest of it. At least he was armed now, and if he went down, he would go down fighting. There were worse ways to die if you were a marine. And being eaten from the inside out by an alien baby was as bad as anything he could imagine.

Two troopers using hoop-lifts were busy loading the aliens into the ship. The name stenciled on the side was CMC MACARTHUR.

"Pull around beyond the other truck," Wilks said. "Park it and step off on the opposite side, away from the loaders. There's a service bay forward, amidships, right?"

"Right."

"What do we do if somebody recognizes us?" Billie asked.

"Put them down. This ship is leaving. If we have to fight our way onto it, that's what we do. We can slag the hatch controls and lift right through the roof panel if we have to. Major? You got a problem with that?"

Powell shook his head but did not speak.

Wilks wasn't sure about Powell, but he didn't have a lot of choice about his allies at the moment. Billie, yeah. Bueller, if he showed up. Powell, well, he guessed he'd see.

The truck carrying its cargo of potential death rolled forward on its fat silicone tires.

Spears saw the last truck go past as he approached the ship. Another fifteen minutes and he'd be loaded and ready to leave. The first step toward his ultimate goal, the retaking of Earth.

The lieutenant he'd left in charge came up at a quick step. "Sir, the final transporter has just arrived."

"Load time?"

"Ten minutes, sir."

"Good, good. Once the ship is packed, you are to assemble the men at the *Grant*. The course has been logged in, you'll follow the *MacArthur* and the *Jackson* into orbit and we'll make the shift to E-space. Any questions?"

"No, sir."

"Good. Carry on."

Spears looked at the men loading the *MacArthur*. Nodded at one of them who glanced over at him. Strode away, toward the command ship *Jackson*.

●   ●   ●

Wilks and Billie were almost at the service hatch when somebody behind them called out.

"Hey, you three! What are you doing there? This area is off-limits!"

Wilks turned, ready to pull his carbine up and start shooting. But Powell moved into the line of fire between Wilks and the trooper behind them.

"At ease, trooper," Powell said.

"Major Powell?"

"That's right."

For a moment the young marine looked confused. It had been drilled into him from his first day in the Corps: If an officer says jump, you're in the air before you ask how high he wants it. But this was one of Spears's troops, and the major was no longer in command. The trooper's intellectual waters might be muddy but one thing was clear: A general outranked a major and the general was giving the orders.

"Keep moving, Billie," Wilks said softly. Since Powell blocked the marine guard's view, he slowly shifted his weapon, swung the barrel around carefully.

"You'd better come with me, sir," the trooper said.

"I don't have time for this, marine," Powell said. "General Spears and I have settled our differences and I've got business that cannot wait. Call him, if you like, but hurry it up."

From his angle, Wilks could see the trooper reaching for the bonefone control over his right ear. In another second he would be online with whoever was running the operations channel and the game would be over. Wilks now had his carbine aimed right at the trooper—only Powell stood right under the sights. Now or never.

"Powell, get down!" Wilks yelled.

The major was pretty quick. He dived to his right, hit flat on the deck, giving Wilks a clear line of fire.

The young marine was confused again. He didn't know whether to finish his opchan call or shoot. He tried to do both.

Wilks fired a single round, hit the man square in the middle of the chest. A clean heart shot. With the 10mm high-velocity slug, such a hit would usually put a man down pretty fast. The head and spine were better targets, but while a single shot might go unnoticed in all the mechanical noise and fuel venting in the hangar, a full burst would not.

The trooper went down, still looking confused. His carbine sagged. Went off. Half a dozen rounds blasted from the uncontrolled weapon, bullets *spanged* off the deck. Damn!

Powell, who was rolling, caught at least one of the slugs when he came up in the wrong place. Wilks saw the man's head explode.

When he'd been a boy, Wilks had once put a big firecracker into a watermelon. The effect of the bullet at this range was much the same as what had happened to the watermelon when the firecracker went off.

"Ah, shit!"

"Wilks?"

"Get in the ship, Billie. Fast!"

• • •

Seated in the control cabin of the *Jackson*, Spears got a call on the opchan.

"Sir, there has been some small-arms fire near the *MacArthur*."

Spears reached out and put the control computer online. "Cause?"

"Sir, we found Major Powell's body next to that of one of the sentries."

"I see. Any other activity?"

"No, sir. The *MacArthur* is loaded and sealed."

"Good. Let Powell's traitors bury him," Spears said. "I will be lifting off in three minutes. Clear the hangar and cut the gravity."

"Yes, sir."

Spears slaved the *MacArthur* to the *Jackson*, checked the codes to be sure the computer didn't have them wrong. Everything was green, all systems functioning properly. Overhead, the hatch covering the hangar began to slide back. He could feel the drone of the big pumps as they sucked the air inside the hangar into storage tanks. The gravity began to fade. A small tap on the repellors and the ship would rise. Once he was clear of the hangar, he would light the engines and boost into a slingshot orbit.

"Launch minus one minute," came the dry voice of the control comp.

The infocrawl on the screen sped by. The *Jackson* was clear to lift, the hatch over the *MacArthur* would be fully retracted in thirty-six seconds . . .

Spears nodded to himself. Perfect.

• • • •

Inside the ship, Billie and Wilks looked at rows of aliens in their containers, stacked on their sides in bins, three high.

"Christ," Billie said.

"Yeah. Come on, let's find the control room."

They'd taken half a dozen steps when the gravity faded considerably.

"Wilks? What is it?"

"I don't know. Maybe a malfunction in the station. Or maybe . . ." he trailed off.

"Maybe what?"

"Nothing."

"Come on, Wilks. Don't start holding out on me now."

"Could be we're about to lift. Inside a hangar they'll shut down the faux grav and use the repellors to boost, that's SOP so they don't fry the hangar with the engines' exhaust."

"We can't leave. Mitch—"

"I know, I know. Let's see if we can find the control room and do something."

With the gravity reduced to that of the planetoid, normal walking was impossible, they'd bound to the ceiling with every step. Wilks moved using a kind of swimming hop. He'd take a short, tiny step, grab something anchored, and pull himself along as if they were underwater. Billie figured it out pretty quick and it seemed to work.

They hurried toward the control room.

"Lift-off commencing," the computer said.

Spears felt a slight tug as the repellors kicked on, shoving the ship straight up. After a moment the repellors cut off and the massive ship drifted upward like a hot-air balloon on a cool and crisp morning. Spears touched a control. The external hardskin armor retracted and the inner polarized plate in the control cabin cleared. The blackness of space lay over the ship and planet like a shroud pierced with laser points.

He liked space travel, the sense of going vast distances to do great things. Made a man feel powerful, knowing he could conquer the galaxy that way, secure in his machine from the killer vacuum that would steal your air.

Can't touch me, he thought. He grinned at the vac for its impotency.

He switched another control on and got external cameras going. Put the rear viewer onscreen. Saw the *MacArthur* begin to rise from the base.

When the second ship was clear, Spears found another control, one that had not been installed when this ship had been built, a jury-rigged button atop a powerful transmitter. He had put that one in himself. He shoved the button down with his thumb.

Below, the engines of the remaining starships would begin converting themselves to molten waste. In less than a minute, what had been the acme of man's technology would be no more than a white-hot soup of swirling metal and plastic and electroviral matrices, all cooked beyond repair by anyone less than a god. And if God could fix them, he was one hell of an engineer.

Carefully, Spears opened the plastic box containing his cigars. He picked one from the middle of the box, pulled the tube out, twisted the airtight cap free. A tiny *whoosh* as the inert gas escaped, bringing with it the smell of a fresh cigar. He tilted the tube, removed the dark Jamaican Lonsdale, and looked at it with reverence. Worth a fortune, the dark-leafed beauty was about to go up in smoke. He smiled. Wasn't that the way of things? Even a great cigar would be nothing but ash after it was smoked. Things didn't endure. Only deeds lasted. And nobody had ever done a greater deed than to reclaim an entire planet from an enemy, and the motherworld of humans to boot.

He clipped the end of the Lonsdale with his cutter, wet the fragrant leaf with his lips, sucking on it lightly, then reached for his lighter.

The first puff filled his nostrils and sinuses and he blew it gently into the control cabin's cool air, watched the blue smoke pulled into the cleaners.

It didn't get much better than this, thought the savior of mankind. No, sir.

23

"**W**ilks!" Billie yelled. "Stop the ship!"

The gravity was gone, the ship was lifting, and Wilks knew there was no help for either from where he sat. The control board for the vessel was locked; nothing he tried got any response. Still, he tried.

"Wilks, goddammit, you promised—!"

"So fucking sue me! I can't do shit here! We're on automatic!"

Billie stared at him as if he had suddenly sprouted horns and a forked tail.

"This ship is probably slaved to Spears's," he said. "We go where he's going. I'm sorry."

She stared, not speaking.

Wilks sighed, leaned back, and pulled his safety straps tight. Okay, it was too bad about Bueller, but it wasn't his fault. He would have held the ship down for the android if he could have, but there was no help for it. It galled him to leave a marine from his unit behind, but he'd done it before. A lot of his comrades had died along the way. When your number was up, it was up. What the hell. Billie would probably come around to that view, and if she didn't, too fucking bad. Life was hard. She should know that by now.

Spears had his com on and it was only a matter of a couple of minutes before the frantic calls began to come through.

"General Spears! This is Pockler, on the *Grant*! There's been an engine malfunction! The ship is nonoperational, sir! We can't lift!"

Spears looked at the com. The transmission was no-pix, so he couldn't see the man's face, but he could tell well enough from the tone of voice how rattled the trooper must appear.

"General Spears? We're getting reports from the other ships, somebody has sabotaged their engines, too! Sir! Please answer!"

Spears took another puff of the cigar. God, this was a great smoke! He'd have to toke it all, of course, you couldn't smoke half and save it for later, it wouldn't store even in dead gas, not and be fresh like before.

"General Spears! Sir, we are trapped here! You'll have to bring the *MacArthur* back down!"

The ventilators sucked the used smoke away. He thought about shutting the things off and blowing a few smoke rings—they'd hang there for a long time in the greatly reduced gravity—but no.

"Sir, the alien drones have all gone crazy! They're hammering at the ship, they're everywhere, it's like they've lost their minds!"

Spears observed the glowing end of the cigar, held the thing up so the nearest intake vent could draw the ash away. Wouldn't do to foul the cabin with the residue, no matter how valuable it had been before. So, the aliens could tell that the queen was off-planet. Interesting. He wondered if the empathic connection was shut off by distance. Must be something like that. Mama had left and the children were upset. Most interesting.

"General—!"

But a good cigar, ah, now that was *really* interesting.

The ship's controls were locked but the com was operational. Wilks wasn't gonna be making any outgoing calls; he didn't want to take the chance somebody might overhear them—so far, he didn't think anybody knew they were here. And not that he had anybody to call, anyhow.

But somebody knew they were here. The board cheeped with an incoming, complete with visual.

Bueller.

Damn.

"Mitch!"

He didn't look any the worse for wear on the holoproj. Billie couldn't tell where he was, there was some bland officelike background behind where he sat behind a desk. His new legs weren't visible and if she hadn't known better, she would have thought he was as whole as when they'd met. So long ago. So far away.

"Hello, Billie. I've got this channel in a security pipe, computer-guided, nobody can overhear us if you want to talk. If you don't, I understand."

Billie looked at Wilks.

The marine shrugged. "Go ahead. Anybody figures out we're here, fuck it. I just realized this boat is like a pay ship, we're carrying the cargo Spears wants." He touched a control.

"Mitch, I'm here."

"I'm so glad to see you're okay," he said. "I was worried you'd been hit when the shooting started."

"You saw it?"

"I was across the way from you, yeah."

"Mitch, I'm sorry—"

"Not your fault," he cut in. "Spears has your ship slaved to his; you couldn't have stopped it without wrecking it."

"Can you get on another ship?"

He grinned, a small and tight expression. "Probably, though it wouldn't do much good. The troops all piled into one and the motor wouldn't start. My guess is that Spears slagged the engines. He doesn't want anybody following him."

There was a muted explosion in the background.

"What was that?"

"Grenade, probably. The alien drones left here are running amuck. Spears took the queen. I think they can sense that, somehow."

"Oh, God—"

"There's nothing to be done about it, Billie. I'm here and you're there. If there is a God, he or she or it has a warped sense of humor, from what I have seen."

"Mitch, I—I—"

"Don't, Billie. I have had some time to think about things and you're right. We're too different for it to have worked long-term. We'd have tried and probably beaten whatever we felt for each other to death sooner or later. It isn't just that I was made one way and you another. Our frames of reference are different. Even if we could have worked out all the stuff that went before, the ride wouldn't have lasted much longer."

"We could have made it last, if I hadn't been so afraid," she said.

He shook his head. Another explosion drifted up along the radio and television channels to where she sat watching him.

"No. The newer model androids, the really slick APs, maybe they've made the crossover into full-fledged humanity. Until I was torn apart by the alien, I could fool somebody's eye, that's all. I could even fool myself for a little while. In the end, I'm not really human, not in the same way you are."

Billie couldn't speak.

Wilks butted in. "You're better than we are, Bueller. That's your problem. Tougher, smarter, faster, and when it gets right down to it, more humane and more forgiving. If I were in your boots—if you still had any—I'd be royally pissed at what had been done to me. You're letting us off the hook too easy, man. Mitch."

Billie blinked and stared at Wilks. It was the first time she'd ever heard Wilks use his first name.

Mitch got it, too. "Thanks, Wilks," he said. His

voice quavered, he was barely able to choke the words out. Oh, God!

"You take good care of Billie."

"I will."

"Mitch."

"I've got to go, Billie," he said. "There are people out there dying and even though I've learned that not all people are worth saving, I still can't break that little built-in ethical rule. Take care of yourself, Billie. I love you. I realize now I always did. And for whatever time I have left, I always will. Good-bye."

The picture vanished before she could say it.

"Mitch!"

"Carrier's down," Wilks said. He stared at the blank spot where the projection had been. He wouldn't look at her.

If she'd been him, she wouldn't have looked at her, either. She felt like shit. Mitch was an android, but Wilks was right. He was a better person than she was. Much better.

She cried for what seemed like a long time.

"We've broken orbit and are moving at a pretty good clip," Wilks said.

Billie nodded dully but didn't speak.

"Probably we'll shift into Einstein space pretty soon. There are half a dozen sleep chambers in the forward crew section. The others have been torn out to make room for the aliens but those still seem to be in working condition."

Billie didn't speak to that, either.

"We should go down and check them out. No telling how long we'll be in transit once we shift. Could be months, years, maybe."

She looked at him. Her silence was getting on his nerves.

"Look, I already checked for a lifeboat. They took it out for cargo space. If they'd left it, we could have gone back. There are a few deep-space and C-suits, but they wouldn't do us any good. Even if we survived the trip down—and that's real iffy—we couldn't lift again. The aliens will eventually take over the base, you know that. Going back without a way to lift would be suicide. We couldn't help anybody."

"I understand," she said. Her voice was dead calm, flat, unemotional.

Jesus.

"Maybe when we get wherever we're going, we can make Spears pay for this," he tried.

She looked at him. "Whatever it costs him won't be enough," she said. Same tone.

"Maybe not. But it'll make me feel better."

After that, neither of them had anything to say for a long time.

In his bunk, tucked in with nothing more than accel-gee and a few bungies, General Thomas A.W. Spears slept, the peaceful sleep of a man without worry, a man without shame, a man without guilt. His rest was only a little disturbed by a pleasant, slightly sexual dream of war. He was riding with Stonewall Jackson, it was early in the Battle of Chancellorsville, before Jackson received the wounds that would take his arm, then later his life. "The Lord has given us this day in victory," Jackson said. Spears, who had nothing but contempt for any kind of religion, smiled and nodded. The Lord helped those who had the troops and the best strategy and tactics. But then again, victory was the key word, wasn't it?

Always. Always.

24

Wilks sat in what passed for a rec room on this tub, staring at the view of the *MacArthur* provided by the nose cam he'd managed to program to track Spears's vessel. The other ship was maybe half a klick ahead and slightly offset, relative to their ship. They could have been directly astern of the *Mac*, given that gee drives didn't spew dangerous flux, but the maneuver was an old one, adopted when such things had still been a problem.

Against the backdrop of blackness and pinpoints of unblinking stars, the other ship appeared frozen. There was no sense of movement, Spears's ship just seemed to hang there. Even the drone of their own engines was merely background sound, like being inside some big factory that throbbed but certainly wasn't going anywhere.

As in all military ships designed to be sailed or flown by men, the *Jackson* had certain supplies carefully stored away. Ship's rations weren't ever going to top anybody's culinary lists but you could survive eating them. There was enough food stashed to keep Wilks and Billie alive and even healthy for years, all the proper vitamins and minerals carefully included. That was assuming they stayed in normal space, droning along under the gravity drives.

Billie didn't talk much these days, but Wilks understood that. She was grieving, and the way he saw it, rightly so. He'd tried to warn her, back when he'd first seen it coming, but she hadn't listened. It didn't make him feel smug to think that he'd told her so. That was the problem with being older and maybe a little wiser in the ways of the galaxy. You thought you had something to offer, only thing was, almost nobody ever wanted to hear it. Billie was a kid, he was old enough to be her father. Not that he'd ever thought of himself as the fatherly type, but he had seen the grief between her and Bueller coming a long way off. He'd tried to tell her, to spare her, but she was like the new Colonial Marine recruits he'd seen over the years. Fresh, convinced that nobody had ever done anything except them, reinventing the wheel for themselves. They seldom said it but Wilks had learned to hear it in their unspoken thoughts: Old fart like you? What can you know, gramps? You were never young, or if you were, it was so long ago you've forgotten what it was like. Save your breath, old man, you'll need it to totter off to your grave. Fucking kids.

They were right about one thing, it was hard to remember when he'd been that stupid. He could recall it, but it made him want to shake his head. If he got stuck in a lift with the topectomy he'd been at nineteen, he probably would throttle the self-righteous little bastard after five minutes. Three minutes.

"Wilks?"

"Huh?"

"What are we going to do?"

He shrugged. He could have taken her question to mean a whole bunch of things but he knew what she meant: What are we going to do about *Spears*? The man was long past sanity, he'd left his troops to die, had killed many of them himself, and was now on a fool's errand that would certainly be the end of them all.

"Wilks?"

"Right now, nothing. We don't have any armament, nothing to shoot with except the hand weapons, which don't do us any good against a ship like that, even if we could figure out a way to hit it from here. Oh, yeah, we could go EVA, we got a few suits, but we're accelerating and there's no way we can make up the relative speed. The squirt guns in the suits won't push us hard enough.

"That's not to mention what would happen if Spears decided it was time to make the leap into Einstein while we were outside dicking around."

Billie blinked. He couldn't tell if she was really interested in this or not, but he pretended she was. "See, the drive fields pretty much follow the contours of the ship generating 'em. If we were hugging the hull, maybe we'd go along for the ride. But anything that stuck out, an arm or leg or a head, maybe, would be left behind."

Billie blinked again, didn't speak.

"The field is better than any armor we've ever devised, you know, nothing gets through it, so we couldn't get back inside. So, even if we didn't get razored in half, there we'd be, outside the ship for however long we were in the warp. Months, a year, maybe longer."

"Maybe that wouldn't be so bad," Billie said.

"Maybe, if you don't mind running out of oxy and choking to death on your own CO_2. Then when the ship did drop back into n-space and eventually started to decelerate, our bodies would zip on ahead and probably spend eternity tumbling through space. There are better ways to shuffle off."

"And worse," Billie said.

"Yeah. There are worse."

"So where does that leave us?"

"Waiting. We can wreck this ship. Spears doesn't want that, not with his little army of monsters onboard. Maybe we can threaten him. Tear out the computers, get control somehow, ram the son of a bitch. Or maybe once we come out of the warp and start to slow down, we get a chance at something."

"Such as . . . ?"

"Hell, I don't know, Billie. I don't have all the answers. You got here at the same time I did. Maybe if you weren't feeling so fucking sorry for yourself you might come up with something!"

She stared at him. "You knew Mitch was an android. Before I ever met him, you knew. You didn't tell me."

Wilks glared back at her. "Yeah, and I tried to tell you to stay away from him, didn't I? You weren't having any of it. You can't blame this on me, kid. I did everything but lock you in your quarters to keep you away from Bueller. It never occurred to you I might know what the hell I was talking about, did it? Old chem-head twenty-year grunt, what the fuck could I know about anything, right?"

Billie looked down, said, "You're right. It wasn't your fault. I'm sorry."

He felt his anger evaporate. Jesus. Big tough marine, beating up on the little girl. "It's okay. I'm sorry, too."

That was all either of them had to say for the moment.

Before they could pick up the thread of the conversation again, the ship's warning buzzers sounded.

"Shit. That's the ten-minute signal. We're going into warp," he said. "Better get to the sleep chambers."

"What's the hurry?"

"Warp space does ugly things to your mind if you stay awake. I did half an hour once, part of a test group. It makes your worst nightmare seem tame."

She shuddered and he knew how she felt. They had both dreamed about the aliens too many times and those visions were horrible enough.

They hurried toward the sleep chambers.

Spears had three chambers from which to choose, all of which were functioning perfectly. He was normally not a triple-redundancy man when it came to his personal safety, but this mission was much bigger than a single human. Nothing must be left to chance at this stage.

He climbed into the center chamber. All three of

the hypersleep tubes had been rigged with special
alarm systems. If any of the bioelectronics in his
life-support system should malfunction, he would
be awakened and given the command to transfer to
another chamber by a recording of himself. Even if
he were half-asleep he would understand the order
well enough to make the change.

Not that he thought any such malfunction would
happen, but if it did, he was prepared. In due
course he would arrive in the vicinity of Earth. In
due course he would choose the spot where the retaking of Terra would begin. He intended that it be
some historical battlefield: Gettysburg, the Alamo,
Waterloo, perhaps the Plain of Jars or the ruins of
El Salvador. Somewhere symbolic, to rally men behind him and his new army. He had considered a
new place, somewhere untouched before by the
mighty engines of war, but no. Standing on the
shoulders of some historical giant would only add
to his own stature. Besides, there were so few spots
on Earth that had never seen any war. Offhand, he
couldn't even think of one. Might as well choose a
site with well-known glory.

As the lid of the chamber clamshelled down and
the medical machineries hummed to life and connected themselves to him, Spears considered his
choices. Iwo Jima. Hiroshima. Normandy. Cape-
town. Bunker Hill. The Rio de Morte. Pearl Harbor.
The Golan Heights. Baghdad. The 38th Parallel.
Sparta. Rome . . .

So many places from which to select. What a
wonderful thing war was . . .

25

Sleep:

The software of three human minds chemically shunted and spun Zen-like through the wet hardware of their brains with liquid neuronic flows, dendritic capacitors zapping, the subconsciousnesses singing hormonally to themselves.

Alone in a million-kilometer emptiness save for each other and things not human, they dreamed.

One mind was filled with joy. Two minds were caught in the clawed grips of horror. Of this latter pair, one faced certain death but fought valiantly, knowing Death would win. The other discovered she would live forever—but with the monster she faced as an eternal companion.

There was really no question as to which was the more terrifying dream. No question at all.

26

Billie awoke and for a moment didn't know where she was or how she had come to be there. Her back ached, her arms and legs were sore, her mouth was gummy. Puzzling, but in its own way, it was one of the happiest moments of her life: she had no baggage.

Then she remembered.

The lid of the chamber fanned up, the circulators kicked on, and a breeze of stale ship air wafted over her. She heard the *click* of Wilks's sleep chamber as the lid yawned like a hydraulic clamshell, saw him wince and turn his head as he came awake.

Wilks sat up, rubbed at his eyes, stuck his tongue out. He looked over at Billie and nodded. "Time to rise and shine," he said. His voice was a hoarse croak. "Another glorious day in the Corps."

Billie stared at him.

"That's what my old platoon sarge used to say every time we finished a session in one of these suckers," Wilks said.

"What happened to him?"

"Something he disagreed with ate him."

The two of them padded to the showers and cranked the sprayers on. Billie stripped unselfconsciously and stepped under the water. The spray was more of a drizzle but the water was hot and she felt some of the soreness from the months of sleep ebb under the warmth.

Wilks looked at her, taking in her nakedness, then turned back to let the water soak his hair and run down his face and body. Billie saw the scars on his body, some worse than the one on his face, marks of combat she supposed, either in wars or pubs or on some street somewhere. She wondered why he hadn't had the scars resected and wiped. Even with the marks on his body, he was in pretty good shape for somebody old enough to be her father. Nice ass.

Funny, she'd never really thought of Wilks that way, except in her nightmares. But that was more or less a standard feature of her dreams, had been since she was a kid. A monster tearing itself out of somebody she knew. All the more horrible because it had actually happened to some of the people she had known. Her parents. Her brother.

Wilks turned around to let the water play on his neck and back and Billie glanced down. If he thought of her in a sexual manner, it sure didn't show. It was kind of difficult for a man to hide that kind of reaction. Not that she had all that much experience with men, there had been a few, but one didn't grow up in a hospital without learning a little anatomy. She knew what went where, and what it had to look like before it could get there. There was no salute from Wilks to show any interest in her as a woman.

"How long were we asleep?"

Wilks, eyes closed against the stream of hot water, shrugged. "I dunno. I didn't check the meter. But if the ship woke us up, we must be close to where we're going."

"What now?"

"We finish our showers, get something to eat. Figure out our next move after that. One thing at a time."

Billie nodded, leaned forward a little so the water could trickle down her spine. Maybe that was the only way to get through life without going crazy. Take it one thing at a time, little bites you could chew without choking.

Spears made the discovery almost by accident. He'd been awake for six hours, had cleaned up and eaten a meal, dressed in ship fatigues and run a few system checks. This latter was more for his peace of mind than anything else, the ship's operational computer being sufficient to handle virtually all the chores without regulation from him. But being a careful man, he occasionally checked to be certain things were running as they should.

In this case, things were not running as they should. A tracking system on the cargo ship floating there a couple of klicks behind the *Jackson* said that two of the sleep chambers had been activated and utilized during the trip through hyperspace. Water had been drained from the storage tanks and then fed back into the recycler. Power consumption was up slightly from that necessary to maintain the troops in their suspension tanks. Oxygen consumption was also higher than it should be.

On the face of it, there were two scenarios that came to mind: one, a malfunction either in his computer or the internal systems on the *MacArthur*; or, two—

Somebody unauthorized was on that ship. They'd slept in the chambers, and were now breathing the air, drinking the water, and using the lights. There would be food stores being eaten, too.

Other than the drive, Spears had not thought to slave the ship's internal controls to his board, it hadn't seemed necessary. He had no eyes on the cargo ship, no way to shut down the air or power. True, he did have some weaponry on the *Jackson* capable of disabling or even destroying his companion vessel, but the last thing he wanted was for anything to happen to his precious cargo.

He leaned back in the form-chair and looked at the computer-generated infocrawl. All right. So there were a couple of stowaways on the ship behind him. No big deal. They didn't know he knew they were there. When he put down on Earth, he would take care of the problem before they knew what hit them. A pair of deserters, of frightened *human* troopers, wouldn't give him any trouble. A concussion grenade through the hatch and anybody standing around would be out of it. The tactical advantage was his. They were still a couple of weeks away from landing; he had plenty of time to plan the best way to take care of sniveling ship rats.

Meanwhile, there were other things to do. He had to get himself prepared for the coming battle. War was imminent. And about damned time, too.

Wilks exercised, using parts of the ship not designed for such activity but things that could be made to work. A thick pipe for chins. A pair of stools for dips and push-ups. Anything he could hook his feet under for crunches. He worked hard at it, harder than he would have had he been alone on the ship. That episode with Billie in the shower had called up a bunch of mixed emotions. On the one hand, he remembered her as a ten-year-old child, crying in fear as he saved her from the death her parents had suffered. On the other hand, standing naked next to her in the shower, he saw that she was a grown woman, attractive, and it had been too long since he had been with somebody that way. Billie had done it with Bueller, Wilks knew that.

But—Jesus. He was old enough to be her father. And for a brief time had more or less functioned in that role. True, he hadn't seen her for a decade or so after he rescued her, and that child and this woman hardly seemed related. Still, it wouldn't be good to let these thoughts continue. Not at all.

He finished his third set of fifty crunches. His belly burned, the muscles dancing on the edge of cramps. He lay on the deck, sweat beaded all over him. He'd been working out for about an hour, he was done. He'd run the water cold in the shower this time.

• • • •

Billie opened a meal packet. The reconstituted and heated food in the plastic container smelled like meat and gravy, with vegetables on the side, though it was all soypro.

Wilks entered the galley and nodded at her. She opened a second packet for him.

They ate in silence for a minute. It had been three days since they'd dropped out of warp. Wilks had spent much of the time exercising.

"Are you avoiding me?" she said.

He looked up from his food. "No. Why do you ask?"

"You seem distracted."

He stared at the brown goop in his container.

"No, I was just working on a plan, that's all. Thinking."

"Yeah?"

"Yeah."

"You want to let me in on it?"

"Well. It's a little rough."

"I'm not going anywhere."

"Okay. I'm pretty sure we're in the Solar System. I can't do shit with the instruments, they're all locked out, but it makes sense. With the gee drive it won't take long for us to get to Earth. Couple weeks, tops. We'll be moving along at a good piece of light-speed, and the last few days we'll be coasting, then using retro drive to slow down."

"All right, I follow that."

"So once Spears puts it into reverse, we're decelerating at the same rate. The ships, him, us. If we suit up and go EVA, we can use the suits' squirters to accelerate. We're all moving faster than a speeding bullet, but it's relative."

"So we suit up, jump off, and catch up to Spears. Then what?"

"Well, since he doesn't know we're here, maybe we surprise him long enough to make it there."

"Maybe?"

"Uh, yeah, he'll have proximity mass detectors. Plus radar and Doppler and luxflect. If he happens to be sitting in front of a sensor screen, he'll see us coming. Or probably there's an alarm rigged to tell him something is coming if he happens to be on the crapper."

"Then he shoots us to pieces, right?"

"Maybe not. Maybe he just cuts the retros and leaves us hanging in vac with no place to go. Assuming our ship doesn't splatter us like bugs on a flitter's windscreen when it 'speeds up' and zips on by."

"Why does this not sound like a good idea to me?"

"Or we could wait until we get where we're going and clonk him over the head when he opens the door to our ship to let his tame monsters out to pee."

"That's Earth, right, where there are a few million more monsters, none of them tame? No, thanks."

"All right. His detectors are likely set to pick up ship-size masses or stuff approaching at high speed, asteroids, space crap, like that."

"So?"

"If we catch up real slowly, maybe the system doesn't kick in until we're right on top of him."

"Sounds kind of iffy."

"I could go down into the engine room and take a hammer to the drive. If it didn't go spastic and warp us into a supercompacted ball, which it could, maybe we could disable it and make him come to see what's wrong. He doesn't want to lose this cargo."

"I don't like that plan much at all."

"Me, neither. So unless you got something better, I say we wait until he hits the brakes and then we go to him."

Billie sighed. "It's always something, isn't it, Wilks? Never boring, being around you."

"That's me. Life of the party."

In his cabin, Spears laid out his uniform for the initial upcoming battle on Earth. He'd saved one dress uniform, the billed cap with the gold braid and his star, the regulation black silks with his ribbons and medals, the evershine orthoplast over-the-calf boots. He'd wear a belt with his two antique revolvers, and the uniform's dress sword. Strictly speaking, of course, it wasn't SOP to wear dress blacks and ceremonial weaponry into a combatsit, but while he was going to be on-scene, he wasn't going to lead the new troops into battle. No, he would command from the rear this first time, he was too valuable to risk himself in this foray. Too bad. He'd never considered himself a REMF—a rear echelon motherfucker—no armchair commander. But in this case, he would have to forgo the pleasure of standing shoulder-to-shoulder with his men when the guns began to speak. He would be the most valuable man on the field not simply because he was the *only* man on the field, but because if something happened to him the war was over. Only he and the queen could command these soldiers and he could hardly trust her to continue the fight if he were gone.

No, he would stand back, this once, until he had more troops, more humans to help him. He was, after all, the commanding general of the Colonial Marines now, indeed, commander-in-chief of all military forces. And why not? Once he brought back records of his success, once he showed whoever was left how the job had to be done, who would dare to deny him the rank? And if anybody could be that stupid, a wave of his hand would remove the obstacle. Sic 'em, boys.

Spears smiled. It was all going so well. Aside from a couple of minor glitches back at Third Base, nothing the historians would linger over unduly, everything had run as smoothly as lube on glass. It was only a matter of days now. All the years of preparation were about to pay off.

He rehung the uniform, put the sword and boots away.

He had decided to land in South Africa; a northeastern section of which was once called the Natal province. In the late 1800s, the area had been ruled by a native named Cetshwayo, who commanded a large army of warriors known as the Zulu. They were fierce fighters, the Zulu, and there had been a lot of them, but even so, they'd been no match for the technologically advanced British when it came to war. In one famous battle, a small unit of British soldiers withstood an assault against a vastly superior number of Zulu for some days, due to their better weapons, tactics, and training.

Spears related to that. A tiny force, well directed and focused stopped an entire army. All things being equal, it was the commanders who decided battles. The aliens were fierce, savage, hard as iron, but they fought like ants. They had not learned the arts of war as had men, and few if any men knew those arts as well as Spears did.

Give me a lever and a place to stand and I will move the galaxy, Spears thought. He had his place. His lever flew in the ship behind him. He was so full of anticipation he could hardly breathe.

27

"**Y**ou awake?"

Billie rolled over on the pad and looked up. She was in her underwear, the room was warm enough so she didn't need any covers. Wilks stood there, dressed in a spacesuit liner, white stretch that fit him like paint.

"I am now."

"We're decelerating," he said.

"Oh, shit."

"Yeah. Time to get dressed for the party, kid."

Only a week away now, Earth loomed large ahead of Spears. He tried to settle down with a history of the Gladitorial War, but the text did not hold his interest. Over the years he'd forced himself to learn patience, to wait, but it was hard now that he saw the goal so tantalizingly close. Here was the light at

242

the end of the tunnel, the finish line for a race run long and hard. He found himself staring at the image on the viewer and when that wasn't enough, lifting the outer armor and looking directly at the distant planet through the thick, hardened glass.

Don't worry, I'm coming to save you. I'll be there soon. A few more days and your liberation will begin.

Wilks knew he couldn't think of everything that might go wrong. And even if he *could* he didn't really want to anyhow. If he knew all the pitfalls, he probably wouldn't go. But hey, fuck it. If you sat around worrying all the time, you'd never get anything done. Get a plan and move on it, that was the way.

The two of them stood in the lock, mostly suited, carrying what they thought they would need. Strapped to them with cro-tape were extra oxy bottles, their carbines and ammo, all the squirters they could find. They were joined to each other by a three-meter length of cable, connected to lock rings on the hips, his on the right, hers on the left. There wasn't really any way to judge their relative speed once they left the ship, hell, even while they were on the ship, but Wilks was hoping to move slowly, to make up the two klicks or so in an hour, no faster. They had enough air for three hours and if they hadn't managed to get inside Spears's ship by then, well, too bad. Wilks had rigged both suits with grenades from the carbine's launcher. If he ran out of air, he wasn't going to choke to death slowly out there. Move a protective cover and a sharp rap with the suit's pliers and boom, end of story.

"Billie?"

She was fiddling with her crotch plate, still unsealed.

"I can't get this damned plug in right. Do I have to use it?"

"Unless you want yellow globules floating up in front of your eyes if you have to pee, yeah."

"Doesn't seem fair to me," she said. "This operation must have been designed by a man."

"Nature of the plumbing, sorry. You need a hand?"

There was a moment of silence.

"Maybe not," she said. "If you do that, maybe we won't get out of here for a while."

Well, there it was. Wilks nodded, managed a smile behind his faceplate. So the thought had crossed her mind, too. Made him feel a little better, for some reason he couldn't quite figure out. Kind of like, well, if they both saw it, they didn't have to follow up on it.

Billie returned his smile, and Wilks felt as if she understood what he was thinking.

"I've got it," she said. "Yee, it's a cold little devil."

"It'll warm up. You ready?"

"As I'm going to get, yeah."

"Okay. Seal it up and start your air flow. Might as well get this show on the road."

Billie smiled at Wilks's back as he moved to the outer door to open the lock. So that's what all those push-ups were all about. He'd thought about sex, too.

Maybe in this case the thought was better than the act. Not *doing* it, but afterward. Somehow the idea of waking up next to Wilks the morning after seemed utterly strange. And maybe what she had felt had something to do with putting her life on the line again. That urge to reproduce yourself when you thought you weren't going to be around much longer. She'd learned about that in a class at the hospital. It was, so they had said, a common reaction to near-death experiences, especially in sudden and violent confrontations with the grim reaper. Something about releasing stress.

The hatch slid open. A little flurry of air blew out and turned into white crystalline swirls. Wilks stepped out, used his magnetic boots, and stood on the side of the ship, sticking out like a thorn on a stem. Billie followed him.

When they were both outside, free of the ship's faux grav, Wilks turned so that his back faced the distant dot of the other ship. "You okay? Don't speak, just nod or shake your head."

Billie nodded. He'd told her they'd be using line-of-sight laserlight coms, short range and focused in the same direction that the speaker was looking. That was so Spears couldn't overhear them. If you can see Spears's ship, Wilks had said, don't open your mouth, don't say a word. The coms were supposed to be good for a couple hundred meters, no more, but you never knew. If he knew they were out here, it could get real tricky real fast. If she wanted to speak to him, they had to take turns looking away from the *Jackson* when they did it.

Wilks clumped along the side of the ship. Without anything to relate to, up and down didn't have
much meaning, and Billie quickly adjusted her
mind-set so it seemed she wasn't walking on the
side of the vessel but on top of it.

It took a couple of minutes to get to the front of
the *MacArthur*. When they were perched on the
nose like flies on the end of a banana, Wilks turned
around to look at her. "Okay, you remember the
drill?"

Billie nodded.

"All right. Cut the power to your boots and use
the squirter, on three. One . . . two . . . three!"

Billie shut off her magnetics and triggered the
squirter. It looked like nothing so much as an in-
door plant sprayer; there was a narrow neck with a
lever, a kind of handguard loop over that, and underneath, a small thick plastic tank with the compressed gas in it.

The squirter tried to pull itself out of her hand,
but she tightened her grip and stiffened her arm
and was lifted clear of the ship. She twisted slightly,
saw Wilks pointing behind them, and aimed her
squirter that way and depressed the control again.

The gas made faint sparkles as it spewed and
froze.

It took a little adjustment but after a couple of
minutes she and Wilks evened out and flew side by
side, the thin coil of line connecting them left a bit
slack. He faced forward more than Billie did, but
she could shift her head enough inside the suit to
peripherally see the ship ahead of them. All too
quickly their own ship seemed to drop into the dis-

tance behind them, dwindling to the size of a toy model.

Wilks puffed out a couple of short bursts on the squirter and turned himself so he could speak.

"Might as well relax and enjoy the ride," he said.

Billie nodded. She realized she was breathing too quickly and made an effort to slow that down. It really was something, to be floating along in the middle of nowhere like this, soaring like some magical bird across the bleakness. Whatever else happened, this was truly something.

Unable to sleep and knowing he could not allow himself to become exhausted at this stage of the invasion, Spears used a soporific popper. The medicine felt cold as it blasted through the skin over the crook of his elbow. Within a minute he was feeling drowsy. He decided to fall asleep watching the approaching Earth, now a small half ball lighted on the "top." That meant the sun was "above" it, relatively speaking, and bright enough even at this distance to cause the polarizers to darken the glass.

The drug washed over him and he drifted on chemical tides into the doldrums of Morpheus.

Wilks could make out details on the ship; he guessed they were maybe six or seven hundred meters away. He'd already slowed them down twice, and it seemed they were still moving too fast, but now he figured they were either going to make it or they weren't and fuck it.

He'd laid it out for Billie that they were going to try for one of the aft locks. His reasoning was that if Spears was forward in the control area, where he ought to be, checking his damned sensors if he heard them coming, then it would take him a minute or two to get from the front of the vessel to the rear. It wasn't a huge ship, but there wasn't any reason for him to go aft unless he thought somebody was knocking on the door there and maybe that would buy them enough time. More iffy shit, but hey, there it was.

Once they got into the ship, if they did, they'd shuck the suits, grab their carbines, and take Spears out.

That was pretty much as far as Wilks had gotten with his plan. He assumed that Spears was alone, Bueller had seemed to confirm that, but maybe he had company. A bedmate or somebody. They'd look real carefully, if they got that far.

Still, Wilks was optimistic. They'd gotten *this* far, hadn't they? With some pretty good odds against them, they were still alive. Maybe they had a patron god with nothing better to do than watch out for them. Or maybe all the good luck was about to go sour. No way to know, nothing to do but keep on going.

Billie realized as they neared the ship through the void that she wasn't ever going to get used to this. She had avoided death for what seemed like dozens of times in her life, from Rim until now. Somehow, she expected that she would become acclimated to it, like getting into a soak tub that was a bit too hot. Once you settled in and got still, your body adjusted itself.

That wasn't happening here. The rush of adrenaline through her, her rapid heartbeat and too quick breathing, those were the same. Her bowels twisted, her mouth was dry. And it was a good thing Wilks made her put that urinary plug in. It was as if fear had her in its grip and was squeezing her tightly. The closer they got to the ship, the more Billie wanted to turn and run away. Her conscious mind knew they had to do this, but some deep part of her, way beyond the Billie who was usually in control, that part wanted her to find a deep hole and crawl into it. *Leave*, it said. *Flee! Hurry, before it's too late!*

On the one hand she was more fatalistic about survival; on the other hand she was just as scared of dying. Not the dying itself so much as the way of it. Going to sleep at a hundred ten or twenty, surrounded by your family who loved you, grandchildren, great-grandchildren, that was not so bad. Being eaten by a mindless alien monster or running out of air in space were not such pleasant ways to end one's short life.

But there was nothing to be done for it. It was take the risk now and maybe die or for certain die later.

Wait until later! her inner voice screamed. *It's always better to wait until later!*

Spears stood near the new road built by the Royal Engineers at Laswari, the dark earth packed and rutted by the passage of horse-drawn cannon. Sir Arthur turned to him and said, "Well, old man, what do you think? Can we stop the bloody buggers?"

Spears nodded. Sir Arthur wasn't yet the Duke of Wellington—how Spears knew he would be wasn't quite clear—but in the matter of the fight against the Sindhia and Bhonsle families of the Marantha, he knew the Indians would lose.

"We'll stop them."

"Then let's have at them, shall we?"

Sir Arthur waved at his officers, who had been watching him carefully for the signal.

The cannons opened up, the muskets began to speak.

God, Spears loved the smell of black powder in the morning.

The wails of the dying Indians began to float over the battle scene. The screams of one poor soul in particular rose louder, a rapid series of yells, as though the man were screeching, pausing for breath, then repeating the same monotonic noise with machinelike regularity. Aaahh! Aaahh! Aaahh . . .

Spears awoke to the sound of the proximity alarm's intermittent and nerve-jangling wail. In his drugged sleep fog, the sound made no sense to him. He reached out and slapped the shut-off control. Closed his eyes. He had incorporated the sound into his dream . . .

Spears struggled against the grip of the chemical urging him back to slumber. The proximity alarm.

There was nothing threatening through the glass in front of him. Despite all the high-tech gear, that was the first place Spears looked, through the window. Then he began operating the sensor board.

Nothing showed on the radar or the Doppler screens when he brought them up. But it didn't take long to get the log showing what the problem was. Two man-sized objects had come to rest aft on the *Jackson*. A quick extrapolation determined that they had come from the *MacArthur*.

As if there were anywhere else they could have come from.

Well, well. His ship rats had decided to pay him a call. Obviously they were braver than he had figured. Odd, he hadn't thought any of his troops would have been so—

Spears grinned. Of course. He knew who they were. That damned sergeant! And since Powell was dead, it had to be the woman with him. Amazing. If in fact this was them again, they had more lives than a cat.

Spears was glad they were here. This way he could eliminate them without any risk to his cargo.

Quickly he stood, grabbed the belt with his sidearm, and started aft. He didn't know how long he'd slept after the proximity alarm had started blaring, but it was long enough for them to arrive on the ship's hull. Since the locks weren't coded to keep people out—who would expect visitors in deep space?—then they'd get onboard. He had to kill them before they did any damage—

He slowed his pace. Hold on a moment. He had to figure they'd be armed, that they knew who was in command of this vessel. If he went barreling in, he might well be shot. That wouldn't do. He stopped. No, cowboy heroics were not the way to go here. They were pests, he would treat them as such.

Spears turned around and went back to the operations board. Unlike the *MacArthur*, he *did* have control of everything on this vessel. Air, power, even gravity. The rats had walked into a trap, only they didn't know it yet. Time to roll the recorders again. The military historians of the future would love this.

28

"**N**ow what?" Billie said. "Can we get out of these suits?" She had her faceplate open, as did Wilks, so they could talk, but it would only be the work of a second to slap it shut and seal it.

"No. Because Spears hasn't come blasting through the door doesn't mean he doesn't know we're here. You can shuck the extra gear but keep your weapon ready."

Wilks was already checking his own carbine. The dry lube used in the mechanical part of the weapon was supposed to be more or less impervious to high or low temperatures but he cycled the action and ejected a couple of live rounds to be sure. It wouldn't do to have the damned thing frozen solid by the cold vac if Spears did show up waving a gun of his own.

"Okay, mine works," Billie said.

"Good."

"What now?"

"Now we wait a little while and see what he does. If he knows we're here, he'll do something."

"Or maybe he'll rig another concussion grenade like he did back on the base and wait for us to walk through and trigger it," she said.

"That's possible. That's another reason for us to stay here and wait. Nothing happens for the next hour or so, we'll work our way forward. Carefully."

Billie nodded. "You're in charge."

Wilks nodded back at her. Yeah. He wished he felt as good about it as he tried to sound.

Spears finished his preparations. He had to assume that the sergeant—what was his name? Watts? Jenks? something—was a good enough soldier to do a basic recon before embarking on anything precipitous. If he were him, he'd assume he'd been spotted on arrival and suspect that his enemy was prepared for him. Which was true. In the sergeant's boots, Spears would dig in, find a defensible position, and wait for his opportunity to take the opposition out. A single well-placed shot would do it. The sergeant must be hoping Spears would make a foolish misstep and give him the chance.

Sorry, marine, not this time.

Too bad he was no longer interested in leading human troops. This sergeant would make a good officer, he was brave, smart, willing to take chances. In another lifetime, Spears would have bumped him up in rank and been glad to have him in his service. And he was certain, even though he had not seen him, that one of the two hiding down in the aft cargo area was ... Wilks, that was his name. Wilks.

Spears offered the unseen enemy a sketchy salute. Better luck next incarnation, son.

He moved to the attack.

Billie hunched down across from Wilks, trying to hide behind a modular cargo container, empty, it seemed, and to get comfortable in the spacesuit. She didn't think she managed to do either very well. The suit hadn't been designed for such contortions and the joints didn't bend easily.

They were in a place where they could watch the hatch leading into the bay from the rest of the ship. The only other ways in or out were through external hatches, and while he didn't think Spears would try that, Wilks had fixed those portals so they couldn't be opened from either side anymore. Nobody was going to sneak up behind them, he'd said. And nobody was going to be leaving that way, either. Not without a lot of work first.

Waiting for something to happen was driving Billie closer to the edge every minute. She hated this.

Suddenly it got dark. And when she jerked around to look for Wilks, Billie floated up into the air. Shit—!

"Billie, close your faceplate! Now!"

Wilks reached up and slapped his own plate shut, then reached for his oxy feed. He heard the door to the corridor slide open on its track, and he tried to bring his carbine to bear that way. It was

hard to do in zero gee. Spears had cut the lights
and gravity, probably the air, too, and Wilks guessed
he would either shove a gun through the door—bet
your ass *he* was braced when the faux grav shut
down—and hose the room, or maybe toss a grenade inside. It wouldn't be anything big, nothing
that might hole the ship.

Concussion bomb, maybe a little fragger.

The suits wouldn't even slow down the shards of
a fragger, much less a 10mm caseless. Damn,
damn, *damn!*

When the timer shut off the power and air and
faux grav on the *Jackson*, Spears was in position.
Even if they were braced for an assault the cessation of weight ought to throw them for a moment.
Long enough to lob a concussion grenade into the
hold. Once they were out, it would be the work of
a moment to finish them.

The door slid open. Spears, braced and holding
himself down, tossed the grenade through, then
pulled himself out of the doorway and flat against
the wall. Some of the blast would enfilade back
through the opening, of course, but he wouldn't be
in its path. Without gravity to slow it, the grenade
would sail a long ways before it hit a wall and
bounced back, it was possible it could come
straight back out the door, he supposed, but that
wasn't going to happen, because the grenade's fuse
was a short timer and in about a second . . .

The gravity came back on. Spears was prepared
for it. The thumps inside the hold told him his enemy had not been. He grinned—

•   •   •

The emergency lighting had been suppressed, of course, but the tiny red and green power diodes mounted next to the door's control panel were battery-powered. They didn't put out much light, but there was enough of a glow for Wilks to see something moving fast in the doorway.

He was still half a meter above the floor and twisting and to shoot the carbine would produce enough recoil to move him like a small rocket would; still, he had to do something.

Wilks shoved the carbine toward the door. He squeezed the grip and thus lit the laser sight. The tiny red dot danced crazily across the doorway. When it disappeared, he figured he was as lined up as he was going to get. He fired.

The recoil spun him through the air, like a wobbly planet on its axis—

Billie saw the muzzle flash from Wilks's gun, a spearhead shape of red and orange. The light from the blast showed her where he was, but he vanished in the dark immediately after the flash died. Her helmet muted the sound somewhat. She heard the bullet *spang* against something past the door. She thought. It was so dark—

A brilliant light splashed her, strobing the hold, then something heavy thumped against her, knocking her backward. She flew like a bird with an injured wing, tumbling.

The gravity came back and she fell to the deck, slid a little, stopped—

Jesus—!

·   ·   ·

Spears knew carbine fire when he heard it, and the bullet punched through the wall behind him and to his left as he shifted his regained weight to a careful stance. The shot and the grenade's blast came almost together. He'd wait a second and see what happened—

Wilks hit the deck hard, landed on one shoulder. He rolled to a prone firing position, thrust the carbine out, and found the laser's dot against the far wall next to the door. On the chance that Spears might be flattened against the wall there, Wilks opened up and drew a dotted line from the wall across the doorway to the opposite flanking wall. He fired on semi-auto, for control. He hoped Billie had enough sense to stay down, wherever she was—

A round burst through the wall between Spears's body and his arm. A few centimeters either way and it would have hit him. Damn! The grenade had missed them!

The bullets chewed fist-sized holes, moving away from Spears, spraying insulation and bits of wall plastic as they mushroomed and tumbled.

Time to regroup, he thought. His initial attack had been thwarted. He knew when to cut his losses.

Spears slapped the door control. The door slid shut. He moved away quickly, toward the blast door a few meters up the corridor. Once on the other side of that, he stopped. He lowered the door. This hatch had been designed as a pressure safety device. It was airtight, constructed of duralloy, and capable of stopping something as puny as assault rifle fire.

From his belt, Spears pulled a spot welder. He lit the arc and braze-feed, and ran a bead along the base of the door. To be sure, he added a half meter on each side. Then he opened the control box and slagged the electronics. Finally, he lifted the manual safety hatch and welded the crank handle to the steel safety cage. This door wasn't going to be opened from the other side unless somebody had a cutting torch and he didn't think Wilks was that prepared. But just in case, he set two fragmentation grenades on stik blobs to the wall at eye level and ran a trip wire. If by some miracle they managed to raise the door, a careless step would get them. And he rigged the trip so it was three meters away from the doorway itself. They'd maybe look for a wire on the way through, but probably not so far away.

Not, he thought, that they would ever get through in the first place.

He couldn't micromanage the gravity on a ship this size, but he could keep them cold and in the dark, without air. Even if they had their own air supply, they couldn't last more than a day or two.

Ah, well. Better shut down the recorders. This hadn't come off quite as neatly as he had hoped. No problem. A win was a win. It might not be pretty, but they were bottled up back there and that was the end of it. He gave them credit for trying, but close wasn't good enough for a cigar.

Spears laughed softly at his own joke and went forward.

• • • •

Wilks and Billie had the suit lamps lit, so they could see each other okay. It was dark and it seemed to Wilks already getting cold and stuffy.

"Might as well breathe his air for as long as we can," he said. "When whatever is already in here is gone, that'll be it. We're back to the tanks. Shit."

"Wilks? Are we screwed?"

"Yeah. He's dropped the pressure door down the hall. Fucked the controls up. He must have known we were coming all along. We're lucky the concussion bomb didn't get us, but yeah, we're screwed. We ain't going anywhere now."

"Can't we get outside the ship?"

"Maybe. I could probably manage to unseal the hatch we came in if I tried hard enough, but the minute we step outside he'll shake us off like fleas from a steel dog. We'd never find another way in in time."

"Can we blow the ship up?"

He looked at her. He understood the thought. If they were gonna die anyhow, might as well take the bastard with them.

"I don't think so. This is a military-grade vessel. I could set off what grenades we have but it wouldn't do much more than ruin the aft section, if that. These ships are built in segments, airtight compartments. We could take out some inner walls, but segments are armored like the hull. The drives are amidships and out of reach. Even if we did cripple it we'd die as a result, and he could probably just transfer to the *MacArthur* at this point."

"So that's it?"

"Well, we might get to the oxy stores buried in

the walls here and bypass his control. We might get enough air to last a couple more days."

"But not to get to Earth."

"That would be my guess."

"Damn."

"Sorry, kid. We tried. We lost. That's the way it goes sometimes."

"Nothing we can do?"

"Not unless we can convince Spears to turn over the keys to the escape pod."

"Maybe if we said 'please'?"

Wilks thought about that for a second. "Hmm. I got a better idea. Maybe if we said 'or else.'"

"Hello, General Spears," said the voice from the com. It was on the suit radio opchan, right where he thought it would be. Spears leaned back in his form-chair and nodded at the com. "I was expecting you to call, son. Nice try but you lose."

"Maybe, maybe not. Billie and I, we were hoping you could see your way through to cutting us loose."

"What would be the point, marine? It's a long walk home. You'd never make it."

"We could if we had one of the two escape pods."

Spears grinned. "That you might. But I'd have to give you one and I don't really see that as a possibility. Nothing for me to gain."

"We'll trade you for it."

"Son, you don't *have* anything to trade."

"How about nine linked M-40 grenades, all set to go off at once?"

"So you blow out the ass of the vessel and kill

yourselves, it won't even dent the armor amidships.
Nice try, but you ought to know better."

"Oh, I didn't mean I had the grenades *here*, General."

Spears leaned forward. "What are you talking about?"

"Well, Billie and I, we figured you were pretty good when we flew up here. Given our experiences so far, we had to bet there was a good chance you'd take us out."

"Good bet."

"Yeah, well, you're a general and I'm a sergeant. But we figured, what the hell, if we died, we could have the last laugh."

"Keep talking." He had a feeling he knew where this was going and it sent a chill through him.

"So before we left, I rigged a little explosive in the *MacArthur*. Kind of a going away gift, you know? With a timer. We gave ourselves plenty of time to get here and beat you, plenty of time. Got an hour or so left."

"You're bluffing."

"I can see how you might think so. But we aren't. And can you take the chance? If we *did* wire the ship, your tame monsters get an E-ticket ride to nowhere in about fifty-eight minutes. Your command, General, adios forever."

Spears stared at the com. Wilks was bluffing, he was pretty sure. But if he *wasn't* ...

Damn. Could he take the chance?

"Now if you want to trade, here's the deal. You cut one of the pods loose, within the next two minutes. That way you don't have time to go and play with it. Billie and I, we leave the ship, rendezvous with the pod, and radio you the location of the bombs. You can get to the ship and deactivate them in the other pod easy enough, with twenty minutes to spare."

"Assuming I believe you and do this," Spears said. "What's to stop me from blasting you and the pod into atomic dust with my ship's guns the second you radio me the location?"

"Your word that you won't."

Spears grinned wider. "My word?"

"You're a man of honor, aren't you, General?"

"Of course, son."

Spears chewed at his thumbnail. He couldn't take the chance that Wilks was telling the truth. Not with his army at risk. Besides, once they were outside the ship and in the pod, he could pot them easy enough. As long as they were in the aft cargo bay, they might figure out some way to get out and into the rest of the ship. Damned fucker was resourceful.

"All right, marine. You have a deal."

Billie grinned at Wilks. "He bought it!"

"We ain't home free yet," he said, but he grinned back at her. "He'll probably plan on taking us out with the ship's guns as soon as we're in the pod."

"What about his 'honor'?"

"Are you kidding? He's a sociopath, he's got as much honor as a spider."

"So how do we stop him from shooting us?"

"I have an idea. If we're fast and lucky, it'll work. If not, we're no worse off than we were before."

"I'm with you all the way," she said. "It's not like I've got another engagement or anything."

• • •

Once they were inside the escape pod, a small ship capable of a couple of weeks of cramped flight, it wasn't twenty seconds until the com lit with the incoming call.

"All right. Where are the bombs?"

Wilks was busy putting the drive system online. He powered up the small engines, activated life support. "Strap in," he ordered Billie.

She obeyed. "Where are we going? There's nowhere to hide out here."

"Yes, there is. Watch."

He tapped a control and the little ship moved forward.

"Wilks, I want the location of the bombs now or I will cancel our agreement and blast you."

"Too late," Wilks said as the pod moved almost back to where it had been launched from the ship.

"What good does this—?"

"His guns are on top, the sides, and under the nose," Wilks said. "His field of fire covers a full sphere, but there aren't any guns directly under the pod launch bay and he can't elevate or depress any of them enough so he can accidentally shoot himself. Or, in this case, us."

The tiny ship rode a few meters away from the larger vessel.

"Can we stay here?"

"Not for long, he'll start playing with the drives and we'll lose contact. But he can't wait, the clock is running. Hold on."

Wilks touched the com. "General, you want to go to the power control box for the aliens' tanks, the main cable from the generator to the control cabin where it leaves the forward circuit breaker and the gee drive housing next to the gyroswitch complex."

"Damn, I thought you were bluffing."

"No, but I lied. You've got about ten minutes to pull the charges, not twenty. If you dick around trying to shake us so you can chew us up with the *Jackson*'s guns, you might not have time to save the *MacArthur*."

There was a moment of silence.

Then, "You would have made a good line officer, son. You got more guts than a slaughterhouse."

"Thank you, General."

"All right. You can tell your grandchildren you went up against me and survived. That'll mean something someday."

To Billie, Wilks said, "Hang on."

With that, he turned the pod so it faced the ship two klicks behind them and hit the thrusters full power. The little ship shot out from under the *Jackson*'s belly like a minnow darting from under a shark.

The gee force was strong enough to press them back into their seats. "I don't think he'll shoot in this direction," Wilks managed to say through stretched lips. "He won't want to hit the *MacArthur*. I hope."

"I . . . hope . . . you're . . . right," Billie said.

This time, Wilks was.

The escape pod shot past the following ship so fast it was only a blur on their scopes.

29

Spears shook his head as he raised from his squat next to the drive housing. There weren't any bombs connected to the gyro-switch complex. Nor had there been any in the other locations. The son of a bitch had bluffed him. He felt a moment of irritation, an urge to wrap his hands around the man's throat and throttle him, but it passed. It didn't matter. So one marine and one civilian had saved their skins by lying to him. So what? After he demonstrated how he would liberate Earth, who would believe such a story, assuming that tricky bastard sergeant and his woman were foolish enough to try to spread it around? The guy was career marine, he knew what pissing off a general was worth in the long run. No, chances were they'd dig in somewhere and pretend to be invisible. If they kept quiet, there was a chance he wouldn't find them later; if they shot their mouths off, they'd leave a trail. No. It wasn't going to happen.

Of course there might be bombs hidden somewhere here on the *MacArthur* but Spears didn't believe it for a second. No, he'd been foxed. Once more, he offered a two-fingered salute to Wilks. Good marine, that one.

"Did we make it?"

In the tiny cabin of the pod, Wilks blew out a big breath. "Yeah. We did. He's outside our radar range, but he must have gone back to the cargo ship to check it out. I'd love to see his face when he realizes there weren't any explosives rigged."

"I'll pass on seeing his face again, thank you."

Wilks laughed. Then frowned. "He got away, though. He beat us and got away. I wanted to get him in my sights."

"You ought to be glad he didn't get us in his sights. Where are we, by the way? And where are we going?"

"We'll be inside Luna's orbit in another couple of days, if the guidance computer on this piece of junk can be trusted. I'm getting some signals from the region, too faint to hear much. Could be automatic from Earth. Or something from the colony on the moon, if it's still there. Gateway Station in L-5 orbit, maybe. I've got the scanner set to pick up the strongest input and home in on it. You can shuck the suit if you want. There's a chemical toilet in the back, behind the blue partition. We'll have to sleep in our seats and our diet will be a bit limited, but we should make it okay."

"You did real good back there, Wilks. You're a lot smarter than you let on."

"You think so?"

"Yeah, and a *whole* lot smarter than you look." She smiled and he returned it. He fucking hated losing Spears, but she was right. It was better to be alive to fight another day and at least they had that much.

Spears brought the queen out of deep sleep first, still securely in her cage, of course. She could see him through the clear walls, and he flicked the cigar lighter over and over, watching the little flame reflect off the heavy kleersteel plastic.

"Oh, yes, I know you remember me. The time has come for your children to go forth and do battle. You can lay a million eggs if you do as you're told, if my soldiers obey me as they should. Do you understand?"

He put his hand on the plastic.

The queen turned her head slightly, but did not move.

She understood, he was sure of it. Not the words, maybe, but she was smart enough, he knew that. The drones weren't too swift, their wattage was real dim, but the queen wasn't stupid. She knew him, and she remembered him and he was certain he'd put the fear of God in the form of Spears into her. It would all go the way it was supposed to go. And soon, the moment would be upon them.

"Approaching vessel identify yourself," the call came. "This is Gateway Station calling."

Wilks smiled at Billie. "This is the escape pod

from the Colonial Marine vessel *Jackson*," he said. "Two passengers aboard, uncontaminated, repeat, no alien contamination of this ship."

"Escape pod *Jackson*, open your control modem for grid computer override."

They were still far enough away so the transmission turnaround time took a few seconds. Wilks gave control of the pod's engines to the grid computer.

"Pod *Jackson*, you are in the grid. We'll fly you in lazy eights until the decontamination team can rendezvous your vessel. Estimate arrival time nine hours."

"Copy, Gateway. We'll be here."

Billie lifted an eyebrow.

"They have to check us out to make sure we aren't carrying any little toothy surprises," he said. "That means the station is clean. Gateway is pretty big, half the size of the old Luna One colony. Twelve, fifteen thousand people before the trouble on Earth. Probably built a few more modules since then to make room for escapees. We'll be quarantined until they are damned sure we're not infected, that'd be my guess. Run us through a CAT scanner or a fluorproj and then we're home free."

"I can't believe it," she said. "We're finally going to get somewhere safe."

Maybe, he thought. But looking at her face, he didn't say it. He only nodded.

It would take most of his remaining fuel to land the carrier, but he had the APC for his own return to orbit. The reason he had brought the *MacArthur* was that it could stand a dunking in atmosphere and normal gravity. He expected to take heavy casualties, despite the training and arms his men had, but that was to be expected, and the ship would have to stay behind. It was unimportant.

As the ship spiraled down toward its landing in South Africa, Spears showered, shaved, and put on his dress blacks. He strapped the revolvers on, the sword in its sheath, his boots. Looked at himself on the monitor. Sharp. The way a commanding general should look. Fit, ready, imperial, almost.

He took one of the remaining cigars and tucked it into his belt, to open and light when the ship achieved a landing. The troops were already being decanted, although the queen was still safely in her cage. By the time they reached the ground, they would be ready. There would certainly be a hive nearby, he had his computer searching for one, and they would put down close to it. When the wild aliens streamed out to attack the ship, they would get a big surprise.

The cameras were on, the automatic director picking the most dramatic shots according to the program Spears had installed. Low angles on him, mostly, with plenty of background stuff he could cut together later.

Fully dressed, Spears moved to the staging area where the troops, numbers glowing dimly on their heads, stood quietly, awaiting their orders. Slime dripped from their mouths and there was a slight clatter of hard chitin when they moved or touched each other.

"Stand by, men," Spears said.

He went to strap in for the final approach.

Weather radar said there was a storm front mov-

ing across the landing area. Damn. He had hoped
for a sunny afternoon. Well. The cameras could adjust for the lighting; he could clean it up when he
edited it. Besides, a little lightning and rain would
only add to the drama. This was all background
stuff anyway. Once they were down, he would have
his computers send out a live broadcast of the battle. The fortunate watchers could say they had
seen it as it actually happened.

On Gateway Station, Billie and Wilks cleaned up
and went to make their report to the powers-that-
were. A lot had happened since they'd left Earth,
nearly all of it bad. So the medic leading them to
the debriefing station said.

"Yeah," the man continued, "nobody knows how
many people are still alive downlevels. Those who
are are pretty tough and good at hiding."

Billie thought about the little girl she had seen
on the 'casts back at the military base. Was she still
alive?

"Hey, Henry, check this out."

The medic leading them slowed as a woman
nearby waved at them. "Whatcha got, Brucie?"

"Live 'cast from Earth. Look."

Billie and Wilks moved with the medic.

"Jesus," Billie said. "Spears!"

Henry and the woman Brucie turned to look at
her. "You know this nut?"

Billie and Wilks looked at each other. "Yeah,"
Wilks said. "We're old friends."

The ramp lowered and Spears walked out into
the rain. His hat brim offered enough protection so

the cigar stayed lit, though it was getting pretty damp. He sucked on it hard to keep it going.

In the rainy distance Spears saw shadowy forms approaching. He drew his sword and pointed at them. "First squad, front and center. Second squad, fan out and cover the flanks."

He had decided to hold off on giving his men weapons until he saw how his close combat tactics worked.

Number 15 moved close to Spears. Turned its head and looked at him.

"Go get them, trooper," Spears said. He waved the shining stainless-steel blade.

Number 15 stood motionless. Then its mouth gaped and jellylike drool dripped from its open jaws.

"I gave you a direct order!" Spears said.

Number 15's inner jaw oozed past the outer teeth.

"I'll not have disobedience!"

Spears swung the sword. It was heavy, made of good surgical stainless, with an edge sharp enough to shave with. The blade caught the alien's thin neck. The strike was perfect, slicing between the vertebrae into the thinner and more flexible material over the spine.

Number 15's head toppled off and fell.

Enough acid clung to Spear's sword blade so that it immediately began to smoke. The metal dissolved and ran under the pattering of the rain.

Spears stared at the ruined blade. "Goddammit!" He dropped the sword and pulled both of his S&W revolvers. He fired at the corpse of Number 15.

•   •   •

"Holy shit," Brucie said.

Wilks and Billie stared. Wilks looked down and realized that Billie was holding his hand.

Half a dozen of the troops came out of the ship behind Spears. They were carrying the queen in her cage. She made a gesture at one of them and it fumbled with the locking mechanism.

"Get away from that!" Spears yelled. He emptied the remaining rounds from his revolvers at the drone—Number 9 he saw—to no effect. The soft lead bullets flattened against the recruit's armor.

The cage door opened.

Spears dug for his cigar lighter. Held it up so the emerging queen could see it. Flicked the lighter on. Despite the wind and rain, the lighter's flame sprang up and danced in the storm.

"Fire, see! I'll burn every fucking egg you ever laid! Fire!"

"Oh, man," somebody said. Billie wasn't sure who. She was squeezing Wilks's hand hard. And he was squeezing back.

The queen paused in front of Spears, looking down from her four-meter height.

"That's right, bitch! I'm the man with the fire! I cook the babies! Fuck with me and we'll scramble some eggs, you bet!"

Like dogs, the aliens could not really smile. But the queen seemed to, the way her jaws moved. She flicked out one of her smaller arms and slapped the lighter away.

"Fuck—!"

Then she grabbed Spears and lifted him, using her larger arms. He struggled, cursed, pulled the cigar from his mouth, and tried to poke her with the glowing end. It was all going wrong! It wasn't supposed to be like this! He was supposed to be in control!

The queen reached up and caught Spears around the throat with one mighty claw.

"Don't do it, men!" he screamed. "Don't listen to her! *I* am your commander now! Obey me! Stop her! Stop her!"

Those were his last words. His last thought was that somebody had made a mistake. He had time to realize that it was him, that the queen had merely been biding her time and that her time was now—

With a quick move, the queen pulled Spears's head off. She did it as easily as a man might pull the head off a flower. She dropped the body into the mud below the ramp. Held the head for a moment longer, then tossed it aside.

As luck had it, the head hit right in front of one of the cameras, and rolled to a stop facing the lens.

The expression on the dead man's face was one of absolute horror.

"So much for the revolution," Wilks said, staring at the picture.

The onrushing aliens stopped and looked at the newcomers. After a moment the would-be attackers turned and moved off through the storm.

The newly arrived queen led her children away.

The glowing numbers on their heads were visible for quite a distance before they faded into the rain.

Quite a distance.

"Fuck," Henry said.

Oh, yeah.

30

After debriefing, Billie met Wilks in a conference room nobody seemed to be using. There were viewscreens on the wall, but Billie didn't feel much like looking at anything.

"He deserved it," Wilks said. "I only wish it could have been us who did it. We've been blowing around in circles for a while, kid. Haven't been much a part of the solution."

"I know."

"Then again, Spears wasn't much help, either."

Billie shook her head. "You know, crazy as he was, I was almost hoping maybe he could pull it off. I mean, I hated him, for what he was, what he did, but in a strange kind of way, I kind of wanted him to make it. Maybe I'm as crazy as he was."

"Not quite."

"Big deal. Now we're back where we were before.

The monsters rule Earth, billions of people are dead, the rest are all waiting for their turns. And there's not a goddamn thing we can do about it."

"That's a bad attitude," somebody said from the doorway.

Billie turned and looked. A woman stood there. Tall, thin, hair chopped short, wearing shipper's coveralls.

"Do we know you?" Wilks said.

"I don't think we've met before," the woman said.

But Billie recognized the face. It took a few seconds to remember where she'd seen her before. It had been back on the station, in the communications room. She'd been on one of the old 'casts.

"Ripley," Billie said. "You're Ripley."

The woman gave them a brief, small smile. "That's right."

"You're supposed to be dead," Billie said.

"From what I hear, so are you two. The universe is just full of surprises, isn't it?" She grinned again, a little larger.

"Damned if that ain't so," Wilks said.

"I think we have a few things in common," Ripley said. "Maybe we ought to sit down and talk."

It was Billie's turn to smile now. "I think maybe you're right," she said. Ripley was right, after all:

The universe was just full of surprises.

ABOUT THE AUTHOR

STEVE PERRY was born and raised in the Deep South and has lived in Louisiana, California, Washington and Oregon. He began writing full-time in 1978. He is the author of a number of science fiction and fantasy novels, most recently *Brother Death, Black Steel*, and the nationally bestselling *Aliens ™: Book 1: Earth Hive*, as well as works for young adults and several Conan novels. He has written a number of teleplays, including those for *The Real Ghostbusters* and the new animated *Batman* television series. His short fiction has been published in magazines ranging from *Omni* to *Pulphouse*, as well as various anthologies. He has also taught classes in writing in the Portland and Washington Country public school systems, and adult writing classes at the University of Washington in Seattle. He has just finished, in collaboration with his daughter, Stephani Perry, the third novel in the *Aliens ™* series, *The Female War*. Perry now lives near Portland, Oregon with his wife, who edits and publishes a small newspaper.